TRIP

A Psychological Horror Novel

AJ Humphreys

DARK JOURNEYS PRESS

DARK JOURNEYS PRESS
L.L.C.

Dark Journeys Press, L.L.C.

Paperback First Edition / ISBN 979-8-9923303-0-4 / April 4, 2025

Hardback First Edition / ISBN 979-8-9923303-1-1 / April 4, 2025

E-Pub First Edition / ISBN 979-8-9867050-9-5 / April 4, 2025

Cover Design: Paramita Bhattacharji

Edited by: Stephanie Huddle

V. 04.04.2025

For Those Who Feel Lost

Contents

Mature Content Ahead

Mature themes, language, and scenes await those ready to take this *TRIP*. Below is a list of potential triggers that readers may find throughout this novel.

- Anxiety
- Blood
- Death
- Depression
- Gun Violence
- Intrusive Thoughts
- Invasive Thoughts
- Loss of A Parent
- Murder
- Negative Self Talk
- Substance Abuse
- Suicidal Ideation
- Suicide

If you or a loved one need help, please seek the care you need. Resources are listed on the next page. The book can wait.

<u>RESOURCES</u>

- CALL or TEXT 988 for the Suicide & Crisis Lifeline
- VISIT chat.988lifeline.org to access their online chat feature
- VISIT loveyourmindtoday.org for resources from the Huntsman Mental Health Institute
- VISIT the Substance Abuse and Mental Health Services Administration {samhsa.gov} for Governmental Resources & Assistance
- VISIT the National Alliance on Mental Illness {nami.org} for Personal, Caregiver, and Educational Resources

TRIP

PROLOGUE

"Thanatopsis"

So shalt thou rest, and what if thou withdraw
    In silence from the living, and no friend
    Take note of thy departure? All that breathe
    Will share thy destiny. The gay will laugh
    When thou art gone, the solemn brood of care
    Plod on, and each one as before will chase
    His favorite phantom; yet all these shall leave
    Their mirth and their employments, and shall come
    And make their bed with thee. As the long train
    Of ages glide away, the sons of men,
    The youth in life's green spring, and he who goes
    In the full strength of years, matron and maid,
    The speechless babe, and the gray-headed man—
    Shall one by one be gathered to thy side,
    By those, who in their turn shall follow them.
    . . . .

— William Cullen Bryant

SUNDAY

April 21st

EVANSTON, ILLINOIS
"The Gardens" Apartment Complex

1:55 PM

As she returned to her apartment complex for the last time, Gabriella Laska took in the grey cinder block masonry surrounding her.

For the first time, she wondered if the compounding of Chicago's grey, cold, and dreary days, alongside the constant drab architecture, had gotten to her. Had pushed her in this direction.

Could the vibrant greenery of the Pacific Northwest, or the sun-soaked beaches of the Gulf, have offered her a new lease on life?

She doubts it.

And unfortunately, clung to the momentum of her conviction, there was no stopping what she'd set in motion.

Then the mist slowly morphed into a drizzle.

It was fitting. She had no more tears left to cry herself, so the world wept for her.

Missed it by that much.

The refrain from a childhood movie with her father brought a nasally cackle from her diaphragm. It wasn't humorous.

Far from it.

But it was infectious. It spread through her without resistance, and when that fading voice of anxiety tried to stop her, she thought, why bother?

After she'd pilfered her deadly dosage of sleeping pills from the university pharmacy, she'd had a similar reaction. Her heart had raced like a stampede of innumerable beasts, cinching a brace around her lungs near tight enough to induce a full-blown panic attack.

What if I get caught? she'd thought.

What's it matter? It'll probably be too late by then.

The truth made her slap happy. Well, not happy. But it sure slapped her and made it easier to keep going. That and the wine she'd excommunicated from the church having fully saturated her veins.

She'd already amputated every limb; every last person who would give her reason to keep going was now shed from her life.

The pills and her farewells to the House of God, she'd saved for last.

It was His forgiveness that she would need most in the end. Though she figured herself unlikely to receive it.

But who knows?

Maybe it wasn't that bad of a sin?

Hell, she figured if bacon and premarital sex were on the list, then really, what was one more demerit to tack on?

The rain suddenly began cascading in sheets and Gabriella nearly stumbled on wobbly legs as she sprinted for the entry doors.

She'd been adamant during her ideations that she wouldn't be one of those women they found wet and naked in a bath.

Let them see she passed peacefully. Whoever finally found her.

She would put on a movie from her childhood. A happy one. Something fantastical. And the stranger who discovered her would see that her soul had found peace as it slid off to wherever happened to be its next destination.

MONDAY

April 22nd

CHICAGO, ILLINOIS
Office Of Glen Coppersmith, Literary Agent

DROPOUTS

BY

R. NOLD

Chapter 1

—

Before

—

A GUNSHOT. YEAH, WE'VE ALL HEARD THAT. THE LOUD BANG AND CRACK LIKE A FIREWORK. Movies and shit got that part right.

But there's something they can't and probably don't want to get right. The lifeless sound a body makes when it falls to the earth. It's shockingly quiet how it falls. There's no dramatic flair to it. Just like flipping a switch, it happens.

When I stole Ethan's phone and set up the meeting with his sister, I still dithered with the resolve to pull the trigger. However, her arrival, and threats to our operation, instilled a burning conviction within me. It spread from my mind to my hand in an electric wave of excitement.

I expected more drama. Sadly, the moment lacked any flair or spectacle, despite every nerve inside me building into a raucous chorus as the trigger passed its threshold and the tension released in a kick.

Then her body thudded to the floor. I can honestly say it was a let-down. There was no slow motion, no regret, just *click,* *boom,* *thump.* Time to move on.

When we started this journey, we were nothing more than a bunch of nerds who enjoyed drugs and making money. But, following this moment, the picture developed so clearly.

We had muscle now.

PROLOGUE

I have always possessed an innate sense of conviction. Once my mind set on something that I desired, nothing would get in my way. Even fear burned to ash beneath the conviction that steadied my trigger finger each time.

I was as sober as ever when I made that irrevocable decision. And yet, afterward, euphoria flooded through me, unlike anything a drug ever offered.

I took a step forward and saw an entire world at my feet.

I knew then that nothing could stop us. Not even the old lady sheriff, who was too good at her job and liked to stick her nose where it didn't belong.

She'd be next.

Before that, Ethan would need to be dealt with. Not that I worried about him. He was a coward. A follower. And so easily manipulated through his neediness.

Not to mention, his attraction to yours truly.

2:45 PM

The intercom buzzed, and Glen Coppersmith set down his client's debut novel.

His assistant's voice squeaked through the speakers. "R. Nold is here. I've buzzed him up."

Glen sighed and tucked the copy back into the box with all its siblings.

As he passed the last seconds before R. Nold's arrival, Glen basked in the view of his forty-third-floor corner office. From this vantage, he took in the patchwork of color, finally returning to the bustling grey Chicago streets.

Better late than never.

He'd still worn a jacket into work this morning, but now the sun shone brilliantly through his windows, sheathing the office in a golden glow.

The warmth compiled visions of summer.

Camping trips. Weekends spent on the beach. The occasional yacht on Lake Michigan. He felt like a kid, counting down the days till summer vacation.

The door swung open, only avoiding a fierce rebound thanks to his experienced secretary, who clenched the door with wide eyes and a grimace.

Glen's least favorite client bulled past. A distinct saunter in his step.

There was something about *R. Nold...*

Putting a finger on it remained difficult.

PROLOGUE

Like many authors, R. *Nold* was just another pseudonym. However, Glen hardly trusted the government name penned across all the man's documents. *Arturo Sobriquet.*

Glen was pragmatic, though. So, he fittingly went with the *nom de plume,* "Arnie."

Regardless of what the guy called himself, Glen had never been a fan of the person setting foot in his office. Each breath from his popsicle-red lips dirtied the air.

Not that the guy was dirty himself. He was always well kept—mostly— save the greasy hair pulled tightly into an oily ponytail.

Something about his visitor was naturally off-putting. A smugness.

But his natural talent for storytelling would sell.

Villainous exploits of unlikeable protagonists passively rehashed and actively reported through the vile voice of their sadist leader.

It unsettled Glen from the first pages.

But he loved that feeling. He chased it. Any author who could birth such cardinal emotions, Glen Coppersmith swore to nurture.

After a decade in the publishing business, Glen sought to provide a higher quality product to the world's readers.

An idealistic bit of nonsense that went back to his youth.

Which is why Glen took the initiative with Arnie. There was no way he would let something this good slip through his grasp. Though he almost changed his mind after meeting the man. The similarities between Arnie and his main character were unsettlingly clear from their first conversation.

At the very least, Glen believed the guy possessed similar dark urges.

In reality, he was hardly more than your quintessential recluse. Not exactly a personality that others flocked to. So, Glen hazarded a guess that the stroke of the keys offered Arnie an outlet. Which was certainly better than if the man acted on those same notions.

Not to mention, Arnie hardly shared so much as a PO Box with Glen. The man owned a cell phone, an old red flip phone at that. He seemed tied to anonymity. To this day, Glen was not sure if Arnie was local. He could have driven from Canada or the West Coast for all he knew.

Regardless, he kept all interactions between them as brief as possible.

"Here you are, Arn. Fresh off the press. Flawless covers. Binding looks good. We double-checked this morning."

The words didn't seem to register with his guest, who pried a copy from the box without so much as a word.

His dark blue eyes reminded Glen of an overturned iceberg. They were uncommonly dim, and their cold, unflinching presence often provoked a preternatural shiver within him. As if they held the same dark secrets as the world lurking beneath the arctic surface.

"Looks good, Glenny Boy."

Those eyes scanned the book hungrily, only lingering on the author bio, which featured a black-and-white picture of R. Nold donning a short and moppy blonde wig, a clean-shaven face, and thick horn-rimmed glasses.

Glen's authors always seemed to come from a most curious breed.

"Great. So, uh, any plans now that you've got those?"

The man's head cocked. A wary look slit his eyes into tenebrous apertures devoid of color beyond shadow. It nearly made Glen squirm.

Surprisingly enough, a response came from those fleshy worms he called lips.

"Yes."

That ever-present leer relaxed.

He added, "Seeing friends in Wisconsin."

The man's eyes dropped with a scowl.

"Oh, where? Love Wisconsin."

Arnie flashed a nod steeped in frustration and regret.

But Glen ignored it, giving way to his inner gregarious nature.

"Personally, I know a great little spot up in Dairyland. You'd probably like it. Would love to go there again myself. Get a little camping in, time at the lake, fresh air. There was even this one time—but never mind. That's a story for another day. Anyhow, sounds like a great getaway Arn. Enjoy—"

Arnie's hardened, mineral-like eyes pinned down a new subject. Tracing the gaze over his shoulder, Glen found it settled on a double inlay frame to his back.

On one side, a classically stylized first edition cover for the supernatural historical fiction novel, *Out West, Nobody Knows*. Opposite, was a blown-up picture of Glen and the book's author, R.C. Gaelic.

Glen's first client with any genuine success.

2:49 PM

Foremost, R.C. Gaelic was the pseudonym for Galen Ramsey-Cantrip.

More than that, he was one of Glen's best friends.

However, Galen had unfortunately disappeared into that world where, he too, qualified as a recluse. But Glen couldn't blame him.

The guy was knee-deep in a relationship with a Northwestern University cheerleader—or former cheerleader turned nursing student.

Can't be mad at that.

"Ya know, I read that book. Kind of disappointing. Pretty predictable ending. I did enjoy his use of hiding meaning in the character's names, though. I'll give him that. Very...*deceptive.*"

A cheeky grin puts a full stop behind the remark.

"Though, that *is* what got him in trouble with that next book, *isn't* it? Writing *outside his lane? Appropriation...*"

Taken aback, Glen sputtered out, "Oh. Well, everyone's entitled to their opinions. But I really felt it was natural for the story to focus on indigenous myths and legends. It worked well for most of the critics. After all, he's a huge history and mythology buff, so there's a lot of subversive meaning within his stories.

"To be fair, R.C. knows more about those subjects than most of the keyboard warriors who can hardly differentiate between representation and appropriation." Glen hated having this conversation.

So, he changed the subject.

"Doesn't matter anyway, because that was years ago and he's since moved on. He's supposed to have something new to me any day now. Already has a publishing advance. Speaking of which, I almost forgot."

Glen reached into his desk, and with a flourish, removed the first royalty check for *DROPOUTS*. The book was doing well on pre-sale. It had already cleared the meager advance that Arnie had strangely negotiated *down* toward.

"Fan-fricken-tastic." He eyed the check with hunger before tearing open the unsealed envelope. "You should tell little ole RC Cola to do some psyche-delics. Maybe that'll inspire him to avoid being so predictable with his disap-pointing endings."

Glen couldn't restrain the laugh that overpowered his anger and echoed throughout the spacious office.

"How funny would that be! Get him on some mushrooms—or hell, even acid! God, that would be hysterical. Ga—"

He had to stop himself from letting his friend's Christian name slip.

"R.C. would probably go for it too! Then again, there is the gal pal. You see—"

2:50 PM

R. Nold had lost interest.

He did not have the patience for Glenny Boy's little drug rant. So, his attention wandered.

From the height of Glen's office, everything below looked tiny and insignificant. Scurrying specks of humans were hardly more than insects that R. Nold would never bother identifying. Although, he did find the flowing waves of organization enrapturing. Channels of mindless bodies, cars, and bikes bustled between the glass and stone of the city.

He wondered about his own distribution channels.

Maybe there was an untapped market in this room. Every author since Moses had taken a liking to something hallucinogenic...

He nearly interrupted whatever unimportant subject Glen meandered on about, but decided against sharing the thought at the forefront of his mind.

Being overly brazen was not smart. In fact, it was outright foolish.

He snatched the books from the polished desktop and began sauntering from the office with as much disregard as when he'd entered.

But an idea struck him just as he passed through the open door.

Looking back, R. Nold saw Glen's attention twisted back towards the framed cover, offering R. Nold the exact opportunity he sought.

With seasoned fingers, he slid one of his 'business cards' into the hip pocket of the jacket slung overtop the coat rack opposite the door.

"Good luck with the disappointment."

WISCONSIN
Undisclosed Location

6:39 PM

THE DRIVE TOOK NEARLY FOUR HOURS, THANKS TO CITY TRAFFIC AND the thunderstorm that rolled in off the lake. But Arnie knew better than to speed or mess with back roads. It was always best to blend in. Just slip into the throngs of those insignificant insects.

As always, a quiet sigh of ecstasy escaped his throat when the Jeep's tires crested the roadway and tilted down the hillside, quickly building speed. He enjoyed the feeling of gravity taking him down the trail. The off-road tires and suspension doing their thing, careening him over nooks and crannies without ever rolling.

A fireworks display of lightning flashed, shunning darkness from the sky for an instant. A resounding *BOOM* followed shortly thereafter, signaling darkness's reclamation of the land.

The percussive symphony of the storm was a fair exchange for the blinding rattle of the clouds' incessant downpour.

Coasting off the descent, he pulled up to the cabin and carried his box of goodies inside.

The victor with his spoils.

The ground was muddy beneath his boots, but not even that could frustrate him, thanks to the good news tucked under his arm.

Another flash of lightning, closer than before. Thunder followed instantaneously, as if attempting to crack the sky open.

A bird shrieked in the distance. Its cry rode the night air. He'd never been sure which feathery nuisance made the sound. But once again, he could hardly care less.

Let it shriek, he thought.

"Fresh off the press lady and germs!"

He let the books slam on the wooden countertop of their kitchen island.

"And to top it off, my first royalty check! Ole Glenny Boy's actually got some skills. Basically said this is going to be a chart-topper. So, I've got our safety net and a brand-new laundry machine!"

"Hot damn! Let's go!" T shouted from behind the fridge door. The crack of a new can hissed before the man holding it appeared. Based on the lateness of the hour, Arnie figured T was well into double digits for the day.

He could sense Hill approaching him from behind. She slunk closer until she could wrap her arms around his chest. Her head then slid to a rest atop his own.

"We've also got good news. Win's downstairs working out the finer points on the formula, but T may have figured out all the math to make it happen."

"You mean?"

"Yup," she said, snaking her head down and over his shoulder. Her devilish green eyes evoked something primitive in him. "Lolly."

Part One
Memento Vivere

"Thanatopsis"

To him who in the love of Nature holds
  Communion with her visible forms, she speaks
  A various language; for his gayer hours
  She has a voice of gladness, and a smile
  And eloquence of beauty, and she glides
  Into his darker musings, with a mild
  And healing sympathy, that steals away
  Their sharpness, ere he is aware. When thoughts
  Of the last bitter hour come like a blight
  Over thy spirit, and sad images
  Of the stern agony, and shroud, and pall,
  And breathless darkness, and the narrow house,
  Make thee to shudder, and grow sick at heart;—
  Go forth, under the open sky, and list
  To Nature's teachings,
  . . . .

— William Cullen Bryant

WEDNESDAY
August 28th

CHICAGO, ILLINOIS
Office Of Glen Coppersmith, Literary Agent

1:13 PM

"Galen," Glen sighs.

I hate my life.

"What happened, mate? There's no way we can move forward with... *this*." The manuscript's collision atop the immaculate oaken desk delivers an audible *THWAP* that echoes throughout the private office.

Probably reverberates through the entire building.

Informing every occupant just how disappointing this manuscript is.

Terrorizing thoughts pierce my mind with an angered rasp. Each one hits like a bullet from a gun.

Independent and consecutive.

Just let me die.

Kill me.

I wish Glen's reliable and frank criticism pulled the trigger. But the assailing thoughts began long before this meeting.

And they have only gotten worse of late.

I am the trigger man. I am responsible. I am weak.

That dark rasp enunciates far worse things than anything Glen has ever said to me.

Thankfully, these current echoes are far more tame than what I've grown accustomed to.

You're not even paying attention. You're worthless.

Slink into a hole and die.

No one loves you. No one wants you.

I just want to die.

How long has this dark variant fed on pieces of me that I willingly sacrificed day in and day out? Payments in a transaction that hardly satiate the gluttonous hunger for my psyche.

And yet I pay the toll to remain above ground.

I have yet to submit. To give in. To quit.

What does that make me?

The victim resigned to live with an internal abuser that craves nothing more than my demise?

But if I did...quit, that is...wouldn't that spell its end as well?

What piece of me wants to—

What's it matter?

Just do it.

Quit.

Kill yo—

Galen. Stop. Just stop.

...

You can do this.

I can do this.

...

My trusty literary agent is saying something. But his lips move without sound as far as I'm concerned.

There's that framed photo of us nestled next to my first cover. Right there, in the bookcase's heart now filling the once idle space behind Glen's desk.

The photo ensnares my attention. It's the same one they used the first time I heard my name on national television.

'A young talent to be on the lookout for.'

That's how they introduced me. Just after my twenty-first birthday. Nothing to my name, outside a lone self-published title.

I hate myself.

I wanna die.

I was supposed to be a rising star.

A blonde news anchor, since moved to the set of a rival outlet, had said my success came *"by sheer will and determination."*

Partly true, I guess. But it was more so my mother's. She helped me see everything through. Ever since I was little.

Her, I didn't let them ask questions about though.

Mom was my biggest fan and guiding light. A professor of literature who bounced around the Chicagoland colleges and universities.

She edited all my stories. Right down to those final days when she was confined to a hospital bed. After her passing, the staff loved to tell me that when she couldn't sleep, she'd have a nurse bring her a pen, and she'd edit until finally succumbing to fitful slumber.

If only she could edit the whispers I tell myself.

Thankfully, Glen had seen that interview while getting a haircut. Young and hungry, he sniffed out opportunity and tracked me down.

Together, we sold book two to a Big 5, which re-released that first work in hardcover and marketed it internationally. It did really well and outsold the generous advance they had given me.

How far I've fallen.

More than anything, I wanted to live up to a single goal. I'd told Mom when I was little that I'd be a *New York Times Best Seller,* just like all her favorite authors whose works lined the shelves of every room in our house.

But that still hasn't happened.

That first book sold just enough for the dream of being a writer to remain an attainable career path. It was close to being more. So close to actual success that someone could be proud of.

However, close, *only counts with hand grenades and thermonuclear weaponry.*

Mom was in the hospital regularly throughout that second book.

The awareness of her mortality lit a small but significant fuse.

Unfortunately, fuses can create panic. And panic drove through the third act of that manuscript.

And what does panic lead to?

Fight or flight.

There was a time when I fought. That second novel, God, I fought to get it there. I toiled for hours on end.

I hardly slept.

I tended bar and waited tables.

I edited that 97,000-word manuscript a half-dozen times before I let my Mom see it.

I waited too long.

She never finished it.

In fact, she passed with it lying across her sunken chest.

That second manuscript was going to be my dedication to her.

I marketed it on socials. I did readings and book tours.

Not that any of it mattered.

Critics were quick to describe it as *"creative"* and *"original."* In the end, those monickers backfired.

Glen explained there would not be mainstream success.

Then why the fuck was a Big 5 publisher willing to print it?

Then came the social justice warriors. Spiteful criticism that the myths and folklore I'd studied religiously to incorporate in the narrative were— *cultural appropriation.*

That hurt.

Not the failure. Well, that too. But more so that they missed the message.

What if the old world was right? What if our ancestors' tales of things from beyond our understanding of the natural order were not a device, but a warning?

Despite my self-loathing and self-destructive habits, I received a contract for more novels. That had to mean something.

With only one book left on the deal, what I turned in to Glen needed to be remarkable. Otherwise, there wouldn't be another contract.

If I even want one?

I had. At one point.

However, with the deal's penultimate novel came the review that slashed through any self-confidence I had left.

"R.C. Gaelic's recent novels are unfortunately proof that he relies too heavily on the same formula. The answer is always the same. It seems Gaelic is committed to predictable endings for characters deserving so much more."

Predictable. Fucking predictable. I just—

God, that one word hurt more than my favorite professor being quoted as saying, *"Ramsey was a fine student. But as a writer, it seems he is destined to produce enough mediocrity to earn a local news segment following his death."*

1:16 PM

Sitting here, on this plush and enveloping chair, I nearly resign myself to fate.

I can tell from Glen's features that his words are sharp and critical. I should be listening.

Time has all but blended into suffering. All that I've accomplished proved hardly more than an underwhelming score in a direct-to-TV movie.

An inconsequential blade of grass in a sea of lawns.

The dream's been withering for years. That beautiful one. Where I move out to the country-side or maybe the mountains. Some degree of both? A quaint place where nature and silence meld into the soundtrack of a full-time writing career.

If I could just get that *New York Times Best Seller* banner slapped on a cover.

Then I would have proof.

Proof that I belonged. That I'm not crazy. That I have worth.

Instead, the only evidence I possess points to failure.

Deep in the depths of my body—or soul, or consciousness—looms this incessant reminder that if I can't make this work, my useless Fine Arts degree will fail me in the '*real*' world.

TRIP

Every single one of my eggs is in the author's basket. And not a single one has hatched into something viable. Nothing to save me from that looming threat of a tormenting livelihood wearing a monkey suit alongside all the other nine-to-fivers everywhere.

1:23 PM

I don't recall picking up the manuscript, but I can feel how cheap it is. Hardly of comparable value to the paper it's printed on or the ink bled to birth it. Every fiber of my being scolds me for having spent irredeemable time on this pile of crap.

I know that as well as anyone.

Whipped together in just over six weeks, it hardly balanced against the time given over to self-deprecation.

The only reason for the story's existence was Mrs. Financial Advisor's constant pestering.

I'm going to end up dead on the fucking streets.

Wouldn't you rather it just ended? Before that.

Where had the manic joy of crafting and creating characters gone? Delving deep within their minds to comprehend motives and motivations.

I remember sitting down with my mom, spending hours and hours alongside her, plotting the path that would connect all the dots. Refining the narrative so everything would weave into an ideal spider's web.

Those neat little bows of closure were the nails in my coffin. They were— *predictable.*

Now thirty was approaching, and Mrs. Advisor needled me with fearful vernacular like IRAs, 401Ks, Credit Scores, and all these vague financial infrastructures that the world dictates I take part in.

Or otherwise, succumb to failure.

I can go back to waiting tables and pouring beers for drunken blue-collar workers.

Or get a job behind a desk.

Fuck that.

If those are the only cards left on the table, I think I'll fold.

I mean, if Gabi couldn't survive this looming darkness, how could I possibly expect to have the strength to go on?

I'm not even sure who I am without that identity...

Author.

Filling the void with work suits, polos, and those itchy-looking forty-hour work-week cubicles, adorned with their knick-knacks, and a kitty telling me to *"Hang in There,"* would surely spell my end.

I'd let them find me hanging there by a necktie next to the damn cat.

The image startles a snicker from my throat.

1:37 PM

"GALEN, BUDDY, DID YOU ACTUALLY RETAIN A WORD I JUST SAID?"

I stammer out, "Er, uh, sorry. Lost in thought."

Where did the time go?

"Hey man, I'm sorry to be the bearer of bad news, but I know you're capable of so much more than *this*. What happened to the idea about the guy on death row who becomes trapped in a frozen moment in time just before his execution in old Salem? Or the nurse who talks with ghosts to solve the mystery of her missing family? Even that one about the eldritch god-turned-serial killer. All those had more legs."

My forehead creases as I try recalling any such ideas. Unfortunately, all that comes to mind are fugue-like memories of fervently spewing dribble onto the page. Anything to get Mrs. Advisor from breathing down my neck.

Though she is hardly my only problem.

'Past Due' has become synonymous with white noise.

That and *'Final Notice.'*

Even though it is never *The* final notice.

"Honestly..."

Honestly, what?

I'm scared? Depressed? A piece of shit? A waste of oxygen?

"I don't know. I'm so...Just, *bleh*, right now. I don't even remember pitching those, to be honest. When did I send them?"

Glen fixates on his laptop without responding.

An answer in itself.

1:40 PM

As is my trusty agent's style, Glen acts without communicating. An irritating habit for those in his orbit.

Thankfully, he finds what he's looking for rather quickly.

No surprise there. While Glen loves working with fiction authors, he is an avid reader of books on '*personal growth.*'

A menagerie of self-help titles line the office's entry wall, so only Glen can see them when a visitor sits across from him.

The man is a practitioner of meditation, mindfulness, stress-free productivity, and all that other mumbo-jumbo.

It's a wonder we're even friends.

I'm a slob. Point blank.

Glen, on the other hand, bestows upon all his possessions a '*proper place.*'

The upside, he always knows where to find something.

Exempli gratia, an email that would prove a handy trap for someone who can't recall their past words.

A small desk printer whirrs to life at Glen's back, and with a snap of his wrist, my agent flamboyantly flourishes the warm sheet of copy paper, spinning it across the desk toward me with a gentle flutter.

It's dated almost a year ago. Right at the top.

Below are two numbered bullets. Two ideas. A poorly formatted postscript offers a loose concept of the "eldritch gods are mortal serial killers" notion.

I hardly recognize the voice of this author's words. It's fervent and incessant. Not the way I would write today. Not since...

I can't go there.

I force myself into a reverie of sitting at my cramped clear-top desk, hammering the keys, unable to stop because the ideas are birthing themselves faster than my fingers can mash away.

The pretentiousness of youth would claim it wasn't so much the putting of words on digital paper as it was drafting a melody. Permitting the clacking of keystrokes to cajole tales from the void like a snake charmer waving his flute before a deadly cobra.

But in the memory, there is hardly a trace of such mania left to be coaxed.

How long has it been since I could drift into these flow-like states with ease?

Maybe, I have it backward.

After all, a nature documentary bender recently taught me that a cobra doesn't follow the charmer's tune. It sees the flute as an adversarial threat, and rather, mimics the movements of the instrument, like a boxer sizing up their opponent. Instead of being lulled into a state of melancholy or hypnosis, they are sentinels standing tall in the face of immediate danger.

1:43 PM

A cloud moves outside the window, allowing the room to fill with a bright and warming glow. The sun casts a ray upon my long-lost pitches.

There may still be legs here, after all.

A switch is thrown, and sparks begin to light inside me. Fed by the sun washing over the pit of darkness that I find myself rooted to, I know the infinite emptiness above is no more than an illusion.

Monsters and demons, however, don't feed on the light.

"It looked like I had you there for a second."

"Huh. Yeah." I catch myself stammering once more. "I just can't see the path. They're fine premises on paper. I think, for me, they're nothing more than epitaphs to lifeless ideas."

"Did you..."

"No."

It's rude to cut Glen off, I know that. But, I also know what he's going to ask. *Did you write it down anywhere else?*

Stories, for me, often only need two things: a beginning and an end. Like a coast-to-coast road trip, the journey in between remains unpredictable.

Life's too chaotic for anything else.

TRIP

Trying to plot out every inch would drive me mad at the first hiccup, or in this case, plot hole.

I've always had a fundamental belief that the best stories play out organically. There is no such thing as predetermined fate in real life, so why should I curse my characters with such impossibility? Only the choices they make in the moment make their world real.

"Well let's try and jump-start some ideas then!" Glen's face is vibrant and enthusiastic.

I hate to poo-poo his excitement, but he should know better than to suggest such things—to me, at least.

"I'm good, man. You know the brainstorm sesh isn't my scene."

"Oh, I know you too well by now my friend. *Your* scene is going home, smoking a bowl, and throwing on some stupid cartoon show while eating too much cereal."

I force out a half-assed chuckle. It's an acceptable fact, after all.

"Ouch. Be more honest, why don't you?"

I mean, it's not as if we're real friends, so what's he care about hurting my feelings?

Maybe we *had* been. At one point...

But now—I had allowed the friendship to devolve into hardly more than '*work friends.*' Happy to see each other in the office, but never going out of the way to hang out with one another.

Fucking liar. STOP!

There is still a haggard breath of fight left in me. It wants to shatter the chrysalis of melancholy entombing it.

But memories of weekend shenanigans seem like they belong to someone else.

We are hardly '*thick as thieves*' anymore.

But had we been? At one point?

Maybe... But...

STOP IT ALREADY!

I practically have to scream my thoughts aloud to fend off the dark and malicious doubts wriggling around my skull. Pulling me down into that pit of self-loathing.

"Listen. Galen, buddy. I'm going to be blunt with you. You're in a bad way. You gotta let me or *someone* help. I can see you fighting the voices inside

56

your head. It's okay. We all get them. But *YOU*," he points a well-manicured finger at me. "You need to talk them through, get out from under them. Get some fresh air. Open yourself up."

He's right.

That doesn't make it any easier. I'd rather do the opposite and retreat into myself, further than before.

1:47 PM

THE SILENCE BETWEEN US SHOULD SIGNAL THE END OF OUR MEETING.

I'm pretty sure we're done when Glen turns his back to me, his eyes drifting out to the mass of black and grey skyscrapers filling the horizon.

"So, you know with all of the travel restrictions out west, my camping trip got canceled?" He doesn't look at me.

For some reason, that makes it easier. "Oh, yeah. Your high school friends or whatever, right?"

In profile, I catch Glen's gaze drifting into the past with nostalgic joy.

"Yeah, the old-school crew. Anyway, we always do something really special for the trip, but this year, I was going to make it *extra*."

He reaches into his desk's center drawer and pulls out a key, which unlocks a separate compartment in his desk.

Glen has always been the epitome of *extra*. At times, this has made for great excitement, but now it's a bit of a histrionic display.

He pulls out a small fire safe, no bigger than that copy of *Infinite Jest,* perfectly aligned with the corner of his desk.

Inside, is what I would call, a *'dime bag.'* Its contents, a square inch of aluminum foil.

He rests the bag gently on the table as if it contained polished silver.

I am pretty sure I know what occupies the little pouch, but it's been a while since I've encountered psychedelics.

"Is that what I think it is?" I ask.

"What do you *think* it is?" Glen smirks back.

EVANSTON, ILLINOIS
Apartment of Galen Ramsey-Cantrip

4:24 PM

WHAT DOES ONE EVEN PACK TO DO ACID IN THE WOODS?

Supposedly, summer will offer us a reprieve from the triple digits. The '*experts*' predict temperatures will cool to a magical 70 degrees after thunderstorms roll off the lake this evening.

I figure for most people, that's probably great camping weather. However, my body, uninitiated to the world of bugs, trees, and sleeping on the ground, already seems vexed with the drastic temperature swings.

For the life of me, I can't decide.

Is it bundle up and bring extra blankets weather, or will I be fine in shorts and a t-shirt?

Just that good ole friendly neighborhood anxiety swinging in. That internal disquieting static that I've lived with for years, but has been buzzing away inside since I answered Glen with those three letters.

L-S-D...

Spoken as if we stood in the halls of a high school, rather than a corner office on the forty-third floor of a private building.

Glen filled the room with his signature boisterous laugh. Normally, I'd describe it as infectious—albeit surprising for the slimly built, clean-shaven, eighty-dollar haircut-having agent—but this afternoon, it proved torturous.

"We're not in school, mate," he'd said, still chuckling. "We're grown adults and this stuff right here, well, it'll be legal soon enough. It's only a matter of time."

That seems like a stretch, but what argument do I have?

It's not like I have anything better to do.

Or anything in general.

"I've got a car filled with camping gear, and enough acid to find, befriend, and potentially kill Bigfoot. So, we *are* going. I know of a great campground up in Wisconsin. We'll get your mind working right as rain in ways you never thought possible."

Somehow, I doubt that.

Despite the naysaying, I recall feeling this light wash over me. Pouring down into my pit, and with it, a glimpse of joy. An emotion I'd honestly forgotten.

As if it were a contraband item I was no longer permitted to hold.

And yet, I'd miraculously glimpsed that sparse happiness inside me.

Chained deep down in my core and forgotten like the Count of Monte Cristo, my happiness, so too, planned its escape from shadowy restraints.

Reluctantly, I said, "Yes."

That was before he mentioned the name of the place.

Devil's Lake.

The urban legends of acid trips gone wrong marched from their filed-away schemas. Panic engulfed my consciousness as thoughts of losing my mind in a place named for Beelzebub began tormenting me.

They still are.

If I'm going to avoid a panic attack, I know what I need to do next.

4:32 PM

EVERYONE'S GOTTA HAVE A 'PEDIA' THESE DAYS...

Excerpt on Devil's Lake State Park | Location: Sauk County Wisconsin, U.S.A | 43°25' 05" —

Yeah, that's enough of that.

I scan the sepia-toned page quickly, nibbling on the loose cuticle around my pointer finger.

The history of this place is *littered* with folklore and indigenous mythology. Exactly the type of thing I could use for a historical fiction piece.

I feel the itch in my hindbrain that wants to dive down into the depths of history. Maybe this could actually turn out to be a good experience, I try to tell myself while reading through a small section on the lake's history.

..."Devil's Lake" is an unfortunate misinterpretation of the Ho-Chunk (Hočągara) Nation's original name, Te Wákącąk. Though lacking a proper English translation, the name loosely translates to

"Sacred Lake" or "Spirit Lake."[1] According to the local orated history, the name originated from the Waterspirit or Wakjexi that carved the body of water into the Earth.[2]

The itch is there. I want to know more.

I can't say any ideas are flowing, but there's this flutter of hope.

So I keep reading. Doing my best to acquaint myself with the story of this land.

Despite the positive nomenclature, numerous tales from settlers moving west and north warn of spirits both good and evil inhabiting the area. Yet, to this day, no tribe holds any outward negative associations with the lake. [3] In fact, many members of the Ho-Chunk and other nearby tribes actively hold celebrations and ceremonies to honor the spirits. Few, if any, say that these are negative experiences. [4]

I'm gnawing at my knuckle. I will not say I believe in ghosts, but I'm also not about to poke the bear.

That familiar and uncomfortable tickle of anxiety creeps back.

But I can't stop reading.

During the naming selection, many of the local townspeople had indeed voted for "Spirit Lake," but all fell short of the anonymously proposed, "Devil's Lake." [5]

I hate that.

I hate it so much.

What do they mean, anonymously?

Some secret clandestine warning—or *worship*—of demons?

Or just a harmless, albeit possibly xenophobic prank?

I'm now feeling less and less like this is a place I want to visit, but there's a word in the next sentence that catches my eye—"*misguided.*"

```
Historians often agree that "Devil's Lake" won out
as a misguided attempt to stir up disillusionment
between settlers and native tribes. [5] However, one
well-known tale, if it indeed refers to this lake,
warns of a spirit festering with malevolent
intent, deep beneath the surface.
```

You've got to be kidding me.

Either a bunch of racist pricks named this place or the name's a warning for some ancient spirit or demon dwelling at the bottom like a sinister Nessie.

What am I getting myself into?

A foreboding sense needles my skin, warning that Devil's Lake, Wisconsin, is an unfit location for a weekend of hallucinogenic self-discovery.

Ghosts aren't real. Spirits, hauntings, poltergeists, ghouls, whatever, none of that is real.

You're just psyching yourself out.

No matter what I tell myself, I find no conviction, let alone comfort, in my words.

11:44 PM

THIS IS A BAD IDEA. WHY DID I AGREE TO THIS?

Because I'm a big stupid idiot.

Stop.

I'm not sure why I thought going to bed early would do me any good. It's been an hour—over an hour—and I'm still riding everyone's least favorite amusement ride.

The rumination wheel!

I just want to die.

Just die.

Kill yo—

Stop.

...

...

...

This is going to be so bad. I don't want to go.

Why do I have to go?

Not like it matters.

The epitome of inconsequential.

Fuck you, Galen.

Why don't you—

Please stop. let me sleep.
—just kill y—
STOP!

.

.

.

SUNDAY
August 30th

EVANSTON, ILLINOIS
Apartment of Galen Ramsey-Cantrip

11:02 AM

Another morning, jolted awake by the lamest nightmare imaginable.

Gotta be that over-the-counter sleep syrup stuff.

At the very least, I stopped brooding long enough to sleep a few hours.

Hardly restful, though.

Just like all the other times, this stupid night terror leaves me flushed and drenched in my still-pouring sweat.

It takes time to recover from the sickening visions of my head resting on a cold keyboard. The scratchy grey fabric of a lifeless cubicle that most drones call a workspace, forms an inescapable cage all around me.

Slowly, the cheap cloth of an overly bulbous double Windsor knot cinches tighter and tighter around my windpipe.

Then, those walls forming my cage collapse inward, scratching their shedding fabric along the floor until reaching me, where they slowly grind against my exposed flesh like sandpaper, scraping away the skin little by little.

Outside the bleak cell, an analog clock from the eighties laughs like the Cheshire Cat. Toying with me. Telling me to hang in there. All while it twitches its spindly arms as if standing on the precipice of moving but refusing to stray from the perch marking 4:59 pm.

11:14 AM

Be ready *precisely* at 4 this afternoon.

He hasn't allowed me an out from this little excursion.

I'd told him we could just meet at the campground.

He called me on my shit. So, 4:00 pm it is. On a Sunday. Apparently, that's when most weekend campers leave, so we should have the place to ourselves. Which I prefer, considering our itinerary.

And whether dream or reality, time never seems to fly for me.

Yet here I am. Essentially five days to prepare, and somehow every minute of that time slid through my grasp.

But there are a few hours left to get ready for my vacation from this monotonous hell of an existence.

I need to pack.

Except, I haven't done any laundry in who knows how long.

The dresser fails to contain a single pair of underwear.

You sad, sad man.

I've got no laundry unit in the apartment or the building.

So, there are options.

Go commando? No thanks.
Wear dirty underwear? Hard pass.
Laundromat? Can't be bothered.
So, it's settled. I just have to find my keys. They're somewhere.
Pocket.
Idiot.

12:59 PM

A SUCCESSFUL RUN TO THE STORE, AND I'VE GOT A FEW BAGS PACKED
with snacks, and I have freshly purchased clean underwear.

Now, what to do for the next three hours?

I give into the guilt hunkering down on my conscience.

"Alexa, play my writing playlist."

She's acquiescent to the request, and the bland eggshell walls reverberate
instrumental rock music.

Upbeat and motivating.

I can feel a sense of excitement.

That sensation bordering on hope might be brewing once more.

2:37 PM

Shameful.

Almost two hours wasted. The highlight being the time spent twiddling my thumbs while the cursor flicked at the back end of two bullet points.

So much for hope.

I should know better by now. Hope is as dangerous as any razor's edge. Though purposeful in its existence, its mere presence can spell disaster, even if only through happenstance.

I need to hear a movie narrator speak in some sort of omniscient, sultry, Morgan Freeman-esque voice of insight, *"And that was the moment that Galen understood the importance of getting his shit together."*

Instead, I allow the leather beneath me to become a glue trap and let my mousey attention span run manic in every which way except the one that matters most.

The nearby rolling tray of weed looks as inviting an oasis as any desert mirage.

Maybe if I fry my brain, Glen'll just leave my ass here.

3:24 PM

I FEEL LIKE THE PIECE OF SHIT THAT I SO REGULARLY TELL MYSELF I AM.

I shut off the TV and toss aside the remote in disgust.

Before long, I catch myself zoned out on the glossy cover of a brand-new hardback adorning my coffee table. The sheen insinuates its newness.

Like writing, reading has grown into a chore. An activity that I can't be bothered to exert the most minute level of effort toward.

Both had once been my escape from reality long before weed and screens ever were.

If I think hard enough, I can weirdly recall the scent of many books. There's the strength of heavy pages on my thumb. That crisp weight that comes with a hardback, my preference. But I even recall the delicate strength of mass-market paperbacks. Their soft pages gently rolling between pinched fingers.

Nothing else to do.

I slide my fingers across the dust jacket, which is a mixture of smooth gloss and grainy text.

Glen handed it to me just before leaving the other day.

I think he thought it would motivate me. And to some degree, it did.

It pissed me off.

It pisses me off now.

Still, I swipe it from the table and watch as a speck of ash floats from the dust cover to the rug.

I do my best to avoid spiraling down the chasm of negativity, but the fresh, bold cover and the disingenuous smirk of the author's headshot crawl under my skin.

I can't stand any of it.

We don't write the same genre, we're not competing for the same audience, but still, I find myself—*jealous.*

Can't believe I admitted that.

I'd gone into fucking debt to master my dream.

And here was this schmuck rolling off the street like—*Here ya go, make the check out to—R. Nold.*

His pen name is hardly more than a mononym, like Cher.

I really hate this guy.

He's making a mockery of all I went through.

One hundred rejections, self-publishing, marketing, editing, all of it.

Eventually, I had Glen and the Big Bird publishing house, but I was so... tired. And here's this mother-loving—

One, single video. It hardly seems fair.

Just one stupid social media video blew up for him, and the internet went wild. Like it was King, Koontz, or Coben announcing their next big release.

He was doing meet and greets at events before the book was even out.

Wearing his stupid wig. And his stupid raspberry-colored lips.

Glen had us do one circuit together. I tried to be nice.

We maybe exchanged ten words.

And he talked down to me with each fucking syllable.

I just need to unwind.

There's time to roll another joint.

R. Nold's debut makes for a surprisingly good rolling tray.

3:39 PM

STEWING IN THE HAZE OF POT SMOKE, ONE QUESTION CONTINUES TO torment me.

Where had I gone wrong?

Honestly?

Everywhere.

I am the epitome of a self-saboteur.

I sabotage everything. Relationships, friendships, health, career. All of it.

I try to ignore the anxious whispers whistling between my ears. But I know they're there. Always asking the same thing. Asking for death.

Each minute closer to the top of the hour multiplies my anxiety.

I feel fidgety when I shouldn't.

I'm high enough to play duck, duck, goose with the game's namesakes.

Maybe a little television will settle the nerves.

Despite being the introvert who won't leave the house unless they're dragged out, I feel some sort of necessity to watch every TV show in the zeitgeist. I have this irrational worry that without TV, I would be incapable of holding a conversation in public.

Should I ever find myself there again...

The irony is, I don't watch most popular programs.

Just trashy adult cartoons and nature documentaries.

4:01 PM

A flurry of knocks assaults my door, stirring me from the cozy confines of my hazy mental recluse.

"Hurry up, mate! I need to hit the head before we go!"

Glen's use of the word *mate* never gets old.

If asked, he'll drone on and on about making himself stand out.

However, his favorite line is, *'Plus it sounds better than dude or bro,'* which I believe is his strongest argument. That doesn't make it any less pretentious, though.

This is Glen to a T.

A peacock amidst a gaggle of geese.

Before the door is half open, Glen books it past me, taking a straight shot to the bathroom.

The echoes of splashing within a toilet bowl leech into the living room.

I've still got *The Book of R. Nold* in my hand. I couldn't toss it aside any quicker if it had been a thick, writhing millipede coiling around my hand.

4:03 PM

"Inspection time," calls out good, ole, type-A Glen, as he drags the palms of his hands against his designer, polyester hiking joggers, leaving dark streaks in their wake.

Guy really trusts me.

Properly chagrined, I direct him to my things, which he proceeds to tear apart and put back together with a quick visit to my closet included.

The first time we'd met, I'd watched Glen sitting in the lobby of a much smaller building, bouncing his leg, anxiously waiting.

For me.

When he finally noticed me approaching, he sprang to his feet like a dog for its master. He shook my hand and dispelled the nerves that nearly convinced me to turn heel.

Sometimes I think of Glen as an emotional support dog.

While I was content at home, alone, amidst clutter and chaos—I would say *organized* chaos—Glen offered a lifeline. Not only for my career but for civilized society.

I remember how impressed I was with his pristine, windowless office. Despite the cramped cube, lit only beneath the buzz of outdated florescent tubes, I felt at ease.

I still recall sitting down in his immaculate leather guest chair for the first time. It's all the same furniture he keeps to this day.

Glen is definitely a romantic in that way.

Maybe that's why he has an innate knack for knowing a good story when he hears it. It's certainly why he can spin, sell, and gaslight with the best of them. Yet, his greatest talent is on display when sniffing out pandering bull-shit and plagiarism.

There, he's an ace canine officer.

I had somehow neglected that fact about my agent, and it was now coming back to bite me in the ass.

Irrespective, he's one of the few people who understands what writing means to me.

At this point, he may be the ONLY person left who understands.

So, even when I fall down to the darkest of places, he's never once hesitated to go in after me.

SOMEWHERE IN ILLINOIS
Along Interstate 294/90 Interchange

4:47 PM

THANKFULLY, WE ARE NOT OF THE GENERATION THAT NEEDS AN ATLAS to cross state lines. Which makes my role simple.

Passenger.

Straight forward enough, considering the last few months seemed to whir past me with eerie similarity to the motorists whizzing all around us now.

But having Glen—*my emotional support dog*—centers me, prevents me from sinking into an isolating and dissociative quagmire. Though, it'd be difficult to slip down into that bog with Glen racing around like it's the Indy 500. His little red sedan weaves along the currents of the mechanized stream known as the 294 Interchange.

Without warning, a semi merges into our lane and the little hatchback directly ahead of us slams on its brakes.

Glen veers hard, and my body rides the g-force into the passenger door. The seatbelt's tightening mechanism does its best to restrain me.

The constriction creeps up my neck and disrupts something inside me.

Like an AM/FM radio losing signal. The tuning dial spun just enough to receive interference from another station.

My throat drops into my chest as I try to dispel the anxiety, but focusing on it only makes things worse. My diaphragm heaves, tugging harder against my windpipe, when I see that we almost took out some kid on a Moped.

Thankfully, the teen maneuvered quickly enough. But the sight of a sharp middle finger pointed skyward does little to hush the thrum of anxiety swirling inside me.

I hate my life.

It's only getting worse.

The fear in my throat cinches its grip tighter, dragging me down, and the static amplifies.

I'm afraid. Panic attack?

Unlikely. But—

No. No. No. No. No. No.

Dread leeches down into my stomach.

Familiar tendrils threaten to yank me toward a dark place I've been circling for a while now. This darkness is foreboding and unknown. Like the depths of the Mariana Trench.

Honestly, a fairly rational fear, if you ask me. There's no telling what lurks in those depths.

The unknown is objectively frightening. It doesn't have to be all supernatural monsters and creatures of the night. It can be as simple as failing to understand the sensations battering one's own body.

Before it can engulf me further, I expect the first wave of monstrous voices burrowed deep inside me will appear. I never know when they're going to speak. However, I can often predict what they'll say.

Inside, I chuckle at the irony.

Just when I think I've maintained some level of fortitude, they like to catch me off guard.

What if this trip only feeds them? Makes them stronger?

5:15 PM

Over these last few months, something sad and *angry* has germinated inside my mind.

It calls the deepest and darkest nooks and crannies home. When it's hungry, it fuels my worst emotions, in turn feeding off them.

It grows strongest when I am at my weakest.

The silence consuming our near miss on the highway feeds my fears while tuning the radio dial of my inner monologue to a channel I have no desire to listen to.

I almost pray for the static.

The anxiety is much more palatable than the turbulent buffeting of anger. And whatever else creeps around the ancient recesses of my reptilian brain.

Maybe I'm melodramatic, possibly a tad histrionic. But I almost feel— *cursed.*

Forced to live through a revolving door of dark, self-deprecating, and malicious thoughts.

Sisyphus ain't got nothing on me.

A slap-happy chortle nearly forces itself free.

I'm growing too accustomed to the process. How the ruminating fixations bury themselves deep. Devouring every other thought along the way until they've grown fat and wedge themselves tightly into the folds of my brain.

TRIP

Like a parasitic tapeworm, it's their offspring, the secondary thoughts that threaten my existence.

I once heard someone say, '*Your first thought is what society conditions you to think. Your second thought is the product of you.*'

But if the refrain is negative every time, what does that say?

That I am broken, diseased, simply contemptible in my truest nature?

That's the upside to the static. It's hard to focus on even the darkest of thoughts. That is its purpose, after all. To inhibit the radio from tuning into a very *specific* channel.

The last channel.

5:21 PM

"Hey mate, you good?"

I am not in this world. But Glen's words pull me back.

I'm inside the car.

Where had I slipped off to?

"Yo, Galen you there, mate?"

"Yeah, sorry. Just lost in thought."

"Not tweaking out on me, are you?"

Part of me is screaming.

Yes, yes I am TWEAKING out!

But I can't bring myself to share that.

What are the consequences of that truth?

The truth...

A concept I have always struggled with and have actively dedicated time toward with several therapists—all of whom, I tell myself I can no longer afford.

The truth scares me.

No. It *petrifies* me.

It freezes me in time, preserving me in a stasis that renders me incapable of moving forward. More than anything, offering honesty and hearing what people may respond with terrifies me.

'*Social anxiety*,' the therapists called it.

Which is why I write fiction. Writing's just lying with additional steps. There's no scarlet letter that comes with doing so, either.

Instead, they call our kind a *creator*.

"No man, I'm not *tweaking*. Just thinking about leaving the city."

Maybe it was time for a smidge of the truth.

"I haven't left since the last book tour."

Here comes the shame.

"Holy...You mean the state, right?"

Glen gets two truths in a row as I say, "Unfortunately, no."

Glen's laughter bursts from his gut with the strength of a parasitic alien.

"C'mon mate, you *can't* be serious? That's why you're in a funk!" His head shakes as his eyes dart back and forth from me to the road.

Me to the road.

Each glance fuels his laughter.

Fuck honesty.

Whoever said it was important to be vulnerable and honest clearly had better mental health than I do. Probably better friends too.

In hindsight, this is preferable to the other response—*pity.*

5:27 PM

"So...uh, Devil's Lake. That's a hell of a name for a place to take hallucinogenics, huh?"

Glen chuckles out an exaggerated, "Yeahhhh."

The lone syllable hangs there between us.

"It really is an awesome spot though. You'll appreciate the beauty, I promise. Don't let the name get to you."

It's my turn to laugh. "I did do some research on the place."

"Of course you did! My best Googling guy."

The warmth of the genuine grin curling the corners of my lips is nice.

I tell him about the Ho-Chunk spirits and the naming, and everything else I read.

Glen says exactly what I need to hear. "Sounds to me like I was right! It's just a name. We're going to have a grand ole time. But *you gotta stay positive.* The trip is only as good as the vehicle." He taps on my temple, taking his eyes off the road to meet my gaze. "And this is your only vehicle."

Cheesy.

Glen really is like two separate people.

Sometimes he's your standard Bradley Chadson frat boy type, with embroidered clothing and an obtuse personality to match.

But he's got *these* moments. The ones where he imparts an amalgamation of wisdom.

"Whatever you say, *Dahli Glen.*"

The car fills with laughter, and I kind of feel like a kid.

The skyline is barely visible to the south, as the automotive ants surrounding us form their neat, little lines making their way toward the chambers beyond.

Maybe some of my negativity will follow them.

Or maybe, I can leave it behind.

For the first time in a long time, I honestly feel—*kinda good?*

5:46 PM

"So, you wanna talk about the cheerleader? I haven't seen you post anything about her, let alone heard from you since..."

Gabi. You know her name's Gabi. And you know what happened. You just want me to fucking say it. Way to tip-toe around the situation, dick.

So much for leaving negativity behind.

Some days I think I miss Cobalt, the silver-eyed husky, more than I miss her.

But it's close.

"I..."

I can't finish that statement.

Gabi *was* amazing.

Ever since my mom died, she was the only person who ever brought the best out of me.

Glen could do a lot to motivate me, but Gabi made me into a better version of myself.

Watching her study had been my favorite thing to do. She would take notes with old-school golden number two pencils. All of which wore scars from her teeth.

She was a nervous chewer.

But her work ethic was second to none, and it motivated me to pull out the laptop and write.

Her desire to push through her own neuroses and frustrations was what I found sexiest. That desire to better herself fueled me, too.

And for a while, it worked. Sometimes, too well. I'd all too often find her tapping on my shoulder to get my attention because she had gotten her work done and was waiting on me for who knows how long.

Though, like most good things in my life, these times didn't last.

How could it, when an incessant chorus of dark voices chided me?

How had I landed this girl? It must be a fluke. I'm going to mess this up.

Some of the more popular tracks that compose the soundtrack to my life.

Then she'd go to the hospital for her twelve hours, and I'd hear her co-workers in my head.

Gabi, he's so dull. Why him?

Oh, Gabi, you're so much better than him.

You should break things off and find a handsome doctor.

Those dark thoughts froze the bridge between her and me, leaving behind a treacherous path that one of us needed to cross to reach the other. Simultaneously fulfilling a prophecy that I had placed on myself.

"There you go again, man. Off in your own little world."

He's right, but I don't need the scolding.

"I wish I could do that."

Well, you weren't expecting that, were ya?

"That's what makes you such a brilliant writer, Gale. You've got this spark in you, man. It just erupts at the drop of a hat, and you latch onto these ideas —it's honestly a pleasure just to watch."

A hitch comes into his voice, and I can't ignore the compulsion to meet his gaze. Sure enough, I can see the tears he withholds on my account.

"You're one of the few people I know who can take something so simple and guide it to places no one else could. I'm honestly envious, and I hope you see that, cause you are capable of so much *my brother*, and I need you to know that."

I can feel my own eyes filling up. I have to look away. This was one thing no one could do better than Glen. He could break down my emotional walls with his sage wisdom.

One reason he IS your friend.

But, of course, somewhere else, hiding beneath the static of my stirring reptile brain, a voice screams—

Don't trust it! He's trying to manipulate you like a pig for slaughter!

Strangely, those tormented howls sound distant. For once, I think I can ignore them.

Grateful for that assurance, I hear the words forming around the sobs that want to escape my chest. Words that all too often refuse to adorn my lexicon.

"Thank you."

Why is that so hard?

BARABOO, WISCONSIN
Devil's Lake State Park

7:10 PM

The dichotomy of the landscape in comparison to the city is unsettling.

Maybe it's the long shadows, and the deep orange glow of the setting sun, but my mind wants to say that neglect tattoos this place.

Nature grows without restraint.

Tiny sprouts of green force their way through the unnaturally cemented rock, leaving the entrance blemished and forsaken. Green cobwebs of vines drape themselves across nearly every tree in sight.

In Chicago, everything is manicured and shaped to look exactly as it should. Discipline reigns over the city.

You don't see this kind of—*chaos.* Well, you could. It just means you're in a rough area where people disregard the upkeep of their surroundings. Those are the dangerous places. Neighborhoods and areas where people operate not by conventional laws, but by unwritten societal understandings.

An eerie shiver zaps its way down my spine. The urge to run fills my nervous system, marking a return of imperceptible static that violently careens in decibels.

Just being here plagues me with some sort of anxious internal interference.

This place is haunted.

"Isn't it breathtaking?" Glen says as he finishes winding down the entrance road.

What am I missing?

Glen is from the same city as I am. So, how can he see the same thing as me and claim it's '*breathtaking?*'

He must have a vantage point for something I can't see.

Although it might be, I'm doing it purposefully. Wouldn't be the first time I actively eschewed something.

With a deep breath, I tell myself to blink away prejudice.

Can I see some sort of deeper meaning that I hadn't known to look for?

Can I just not be a pessimist?

My gaze hones in on the sprouts, struggling through the cracks in the cement and gravel-coated earth.

There's a fight there. How hard had that little sprout worked to get that far?

The vines on the trees aren't dusty cobwebs. They're alive. Desperate to reach out for the sun's vital rays. A type of symbiotic relationship with the trees.

Or parasitic.

This is the natural state of an ecosystem. It's not unkempt, nor is it in worse days.

Here, life exists as it should.

Probably because no one comes here.

An ecosystem unfettered by man is not synonymous with dilapidation.

"Yeah, it's cool. And looks like we're the only ones here," I say.

As the sun continues its final descent toward the horizon, the yellows and oranges seep into the ground, adding a surreal warmth.

I ask, "Where's the lake?"

Glen drives us in further, and as the confining greenery abates, he points over to a shimmering expanse of glistening orange beyond a wide swathe of grass and haphazard picnic benches.

"Just past there."

A flicker of green infiltrates the burnt mirage of the sun spotlighting the lake's surface. As if glittering off scales.

But there's no sign of any such source as far as I can see. Probably just from the plants or a shack or something.

An inaudible whisper tickles the leaves of the trees, an attempt to tell me something. I strain to hear more. Confusion steeps my consciousness, but there is no repetition of this message.

There are no answers.

Typical.

Fuck. Am I already hearing things?

You'll be fine. Just ignore it.

If you can, you crazy piece of —

Ignore it, Galen.

Glen slows the car and his brakes loose a squeak as we approach a lone brown shack standing sentry over the large gravel lot used by day-trippers. All of whom either retired for the day or were never there to begin with.

The shack elicits images of an outhouse. Of grime and filthy human excrement.

The untreated wood needs an afternoon with a power washer and a fresh coat of stain. Behind, is a large, rundown, Lincoln Logs-style building. Actual cobwebs are visible in its overhangs. Holes big and small mar the roof like necrotic lesions.

Next to it, a faded sign reads:

N T RE
C NT R

7:12 PM

As we approach this myopic entrance to the vast and expanding park, an old cheery gentleman without a single hair on the crown of his head sticks his neck out of the window.

"Eve'nin' bays."

His southern Louisiana drawl is thick beneath the shimmying of one of the bushiest white mustaches I've ever lain eyes on.

"Y'all got all ya tags and geayuh?"

His smile is warm and infectious beneath the furry critter resting atop his upper lip.

Glen, ever prepared, has the printouts in a folder on his lap.

"Ahh, we got some bays from down city," he says, passing back the folder. "Now, what brings ya up heeyuh to this neck of d'woods?"

"My friend over here." Glen slaps me on the shoulder. "He's a writer, and lately, a lousy one at that."

Thanks, buddy.

"He's in need of a little inspiration. So, I figure, no place better than the woods and the water to get the mind right."

"Well, I'll be. Ain't that the truth? But aren't ya just a tad young to be an author, boy? Ya even old nuff to enjoy a fine scotch or a finah woman?"

Glen and the old man share an uproarious laugh.

Perfect. Now I have to be dragged into this conversation. And be the butt of their jokes.

I try to feign laughter. No easy feat.

Any positivity I had eked from the verdant scene before me—with its sprawling hillsides peeking out amidst the lush pillars growing in every direction—has pulled a vanishing act.

People suck. Shoulda stayed in Chicago.

No. Shoulda stayed in my apartment.

The man's 'Southern charm' isn't doing him any favors, either. I feel myself growing to detest him. A part of me almost craves a vow of pure loathing for the egregious act of disturbing my solitude.

Before I can sort through my thoughts, the man snaps at me.

Not figuratively, but literally. Three in quick succession. *Thwap, thwap, thwap.*

"Earth to planet writer. *Hello.* You don' talk much, do ya son?"

Every fiber of my being wants to *snap.* I am already sick of this old coot. Calling me son, and...

That stupid drawl.

What the fuck is he doing all the way up here in Wisconsin, anyway?

Shouldn't the job belong to some cheese-head obsessing over beers and brats?

"No, sorry. I just prefer writing my words, I guess." An ambivalent shrug serves to punctuate my meek reply.

A chasm begins opening between us. However, from where I sit, it's a gorge, safely separating me from him.

Unfortunately, I get the sense that Glen may be on the opposite side as well. The look on his face says, *'What are you doing?'*

What AM I doing?

A part of me knows the old guy's probably lonely out here, and he's likely a genuinely nice person.

The thought brings my mother to mind. She would have scolded me for taking someone's kindness out on them.

She knew I hated small talk, but she also knew how to unleash waves of guilt with a single look. Releasing an unseen vapor to surround me with a fog of shame and disappointment.

'Stop it with the mental pity party.'

107

Even after all these years, she can still make me squirm with embarrassment.

She raised me better than this. So, I recall the question the old man asked.

I try to play it off with a chuckle and a long drawn-out, "Yeahhhh." The word dangles an extra second. "Sorry. I got sidetracked, thinking about something."

I add a meek head scratch and as genuine a laugh as I can muster for character effect.

"He does. *Literally, all. The. Time.*"

Thanks, Glen.

"The curse of youth. You even outta high school, yet?"

A resounding chuckle works its way through our trio, and with Mom's voice ringing between my ears, I make a sincere effort to keep the conversation going.

"Yeah, I get the, *I look too young,* all the time. But, if I don't screw things up any worse this would actually be my *fifth* book."

Don't let contempt seep into your tone.

I respond as if writing dialogue for some unknown character yet to exist. "Who knows, maybe I can find a place in it for a genuine southern park ranger."

It doesn't quite come out right. It sounds backhanded. At least, to me it does.

Maybe his hearing isn't great, and he thinks it's funny. Or at the very least, he's good at ignoring the condescending shot my subconscious lobbed at him.

He doesn't seem offended. In fact, his jaw is bouncing up and down with an amused grin as he adds, "Well the name's Troy. Yer welcome t'it. All I ask is that you don't leave out the mustache."

He adds a guttural, disarming laugh.

How dare he try to placate me! I have my barriers up for a reason.

Some weak barriers to be taken down by an old man's laugh.

Like a pyromaniac, my mind revels in spraying gasoline across the fire of my anger.

My mind is so fucked.

"I'm not much of a reader, so I wouldn't even know if you were Harry Potter, but I hope ya find what yer looking fer out theyuh. You wouldn't be the first and certainly won't be the last."

I thank him as politely as I can, and fortunately, Glen's picking up on my frustrations with good ole Troy.

Offering one last grin and a wiggle of his mustache, the old coot says the park is mostly empty until the weekend, and we can set up camp at any site we want in the Quartzite Campground.

"Otherwise, you bays are going to end up addin' an extra mile or two to any hiking, being settled back as far as ya are. I'd recommend site forty-five or forty-six. That's gonna give ya the most privacy, they're not *as* private as some, but I only got one other group, and they're in a big, ole RV on the other side of the grounds."

He also mentions a path that runs right along our site, making it easy for hikers to get to the lake and trails without having to traverse the roadways.

Not that the roads should be busy.

Better for us, anyway.

As we pull away from the little wooden shack, a wave of excitement runs headlong into my frustrations.

The cogs shift once more, and I know that I'm moving into a familiar higher gear that has failed to operate for some time.

Energy, much different from the interfering static of anxiety, surges through me. It feels good.

7:28 PM

If you asked me before Wednesday to do some acid, I like to think I'd have said I was getting too old for drugs.

Well, *illicit* drugs.

I don't exactly see acid as being on par with my favorite—and I might add *legal*—recreational activity of smoking the Devil's Lettuce.

There He is again.

However, let's be honest, it's not PCP or meth. Not even close.

Rationalization at its finest.

Glen parks the car and is out the door with the hastiness of anyone trapped atop four wheels too long.

The way he moves and dips into deep stretches is like an athlete. Though Glen's not a big guy, the man's built like someone who played a lot of sports growing up.

For me, getting on my feet doesn't seem so imperative.

I take in the scenery from the passenger seat, having yet to unfasten my seatbelt.

The sky casts a waning, burnt shade of orange. Nightfall is circling overhead.

The campsite itself is interesting.

There's a dusty little fire ring, and a patchwork of brittle, straw-colored grass. Otherwise, it's mostly gravel and dirt.

I can't help but wonder what kind of sleep that's going to provide.

Like the old man said, the privacy isn't great either. Across from our slip lies a vast forlorn field of empty sites peering into ours.

To our backside, there's some overgrowth of prairie grasses, tall and flowering, but also thick and ensnaring. Mixed throughout are big oak and hickory trees that offer a sort of private semicircle.

There are only two ways out. Through the opening driveway space where Glen parked the car, and a trail that disappears into the woods and brush of the semicircle.

Most every site, except the ones forming columns up the center of the field, has a similar design. But none seem to offer the seclusion that the trees provide this space specifically.

Glen takes initiative, first directing me from the car before explaining the need for laying a tarp down prior to raising the tent. Which is a chore in and of itself because Glen has to demonstrate what it is I'm supposed to be doing with these infernal threaded poles for said tent.

It's an uneventful process. No major hiccups or funny business.

Glen's a good instructor.

"Hey, I'm going to put in these stakes."

He holds up some tiny metallic rods shaped like the letter J.

"You pop the cooler out and get me a beer," he says, laughing.

With a grey rubber mallet, he sets to work on the first J.

Glen works quickly.

I do my part and get the cooler out. I haven't been doing much happy drinking as of late, so having a cold one with Glen has a novel quality about it.

"*OW! Fuckin. Sonofabeestingingassmotherfuhhhh!*"

Whatever comes out of Glen's mouth after is a guttural mishmash of syllables.

"What the hell was—" My words cut out at the sight of Glen bunched up, rocking back and forth on the ground, his hands clasped to his crown.

A burst of laughter hurls out from my chest.

"Fucking acorns," he grumbles.

I look around and sure enough, the damn things litter the ground.

TRIP

Above, the movement of a squirrel shakes a cluster of dense nuts. I hear another one fall. It ricochets off the gravel just to my right.

"Guess we've got to stay on our toes," I say, snickering.

Glen reaches out a hand from his scalp and beckons for a beer.

Can in hand, relief tattooing his face, he happily clutches the perspiring aluminum to his scalp.

7:49 PM

Apathy. Complacency. Hate.

All, alongside their kin, flutter about my insides like despondent insects.

Yet, that despondency makes them easier to ignore.

It helps that I'm not alone. As if Glen's mere presence disrupts the whispers of noxious enchantments between my ears.

I've taken up refuge on a log next to the fire pit. Glen has opted for the ground next to me. Neither of us cares to set up the folding chairs, it seems.

He groans and his face twists to reflect the epitome of the noise. "Ah fuck. You don't know how to start a campfire do you?"

I don't.

Glen instructs me to gather sticks for kindling while he unpacks a bushel of firewood from his car.

In no time, he's done it all. The fire crackles as it swims skyward.

This time, I join Glen on the ground. With new beers in hand, we let the score of nature surround us.

Content, we sip and stare as the current of fire spits out its tiny fireflies to flutter upward before disappearing into the slowly illuminating stars above.

The settling darkness confines us to the orange glow and its furtive inhabitants.

Nature cultivates an entirely different city.

Cicadas simulate the thrumming of traffic. Actual fireflies flicker their taillights before dematerializing into the blackness. All while mosquitos whizz about our ears and crickets chirp before bounding around our feet. Grasshoppers the size of cockroaches add to the cacophony with their snare-like clicking.

Until now, I don't think I knew they had wings. Wings that go *clickity-clickity-clickity* like an old baseball card against the spokes of a 1940s bicycle belonging to some good ole boy.

Bug spray keeps the annoying pests from nibbling—*mostly*—but I can't help wondering what's out there, moving about this forest metropolis in the impending darkness, unseen.

"You know, it *was* R. Nold who reminded me of this place. It was a few months back, but I'm glad he did."

R. Nold.

I hate the name.

I hate that I know Glen's about to bring up his book.

But most of all, I hate that I know his book just cracked the *New York Times Bestseller* list.

Same shit, different toilet.

Glen beams while discussing his newest writer and his manuscript.

Had I ever written anything that made Glen this excited?

No. Probably not.

My historical cosmic horrors could hardly even compare to a wild premise like a quartet of evil genius college kids. Focused on contemporary violence, drug use, and anti-hero themes, the story is hardly something I would ever consider authoring.

So different from my formulaic writings.

Which is what they are.

Happy endings, heroes' journeys, and incessant hope.

Hardly original.

Sure, my characters possessed a level of originality, and their tales had never taken place before in the scene and time in which I had written them. But ultimately, I just plugged in new numbers to an old formula.

Predictable.

How long did it take readers to guess the ending?

The first chapter?

I can wind the roadway with twists and turns all I want, but does the journey mean anything if the destination is obvious?

After all, endings are what separate a good book from a great book.

People always talk about the journey.

Life is about the journey. Yet we all know where the road leads.

Death.

Except, there are good deaths and bad deaths. There are comfortable graves, and devastating mutilations never to be discovered.

Does it really matter if your journey was great if its conclusion is sad, lonely, depressing, and predictable?

"How's the ending?" I ask, twiddling the tab of my current beer can.

"Oh, the ending! It's fucking wild. Originally, he said he just had an idea, and it would be a stand-alone, but I'll get him to do a series. This puppy is selling like wildfire already, and I know the money'll be too good to neglect a sequel. Not to mention, the sly devil turned down an advance that I'd worked my ass off to get him. But I'll give credit where credit is due, the ending just leaves you craving more."

This time Glen isn't picking up on my bubbling resentment and depression, to which the cans of Busch Light dancing in my liver amplify.

He dithers on, but I'm not listening anymore. Something about a revelation that their leader/narrator kills a member of their gang's older sister to prevent her from ratting them out...

BUT THE MEMBER FINDS OUT AND IS OKAY WITH IT!

Would I be able to rationalize Glen murdering—I don't know—

Who is even left for me to care?

"So they all have to work together to get out from under not one but two murder investigations and deliver on the drugs they've promised to some mafioso-type that they've gotten themselves mixed up with."

Glen takes a long sip, getting his wind back.

"Ugh, and then there's the epilogue! I don't think I should spoil any more than I already have. But he's going to be big, R. Nold is."

Glen beams at this. I know that as much as Glen has invested in me, I have hardly returned the investment of late. The twinkle in his eyes tells me that my time of value is nearing an end. If I can't produce success, Glen won't need me anymore.

Because he has R. Nold.

Maybe it's the mosquito that just bit my hand.

Maybe it's the fire burning at my feet.

Maybe it's the way Glen's big brown eyes glisten with child-like joy.

Or a combination of it all.

But devastation reaps through my chest.

There is something else, though. As if that anxious static has compacted into a wadded ball between my lungs. It's grown heavy and—*and alive*—alive with contempt and anger.

I need to redirect. I have this beer in my hand.

Pound it.

Why not? I'll take anything if it calms the internal dissonance of my emotions.

"To the success of all Glen's writers!" I bellow, simultaneously cracking open another cold one.

We toast, drink, and prepare our hot dogs for the campfire.

However, the pokers one would use for hotdogs, or marshmallows, or whatever, aren't so easily accessible to the inebriated. So, we impale our cheap wieners across sticks too large for kindling and grill them over the roaring flames.

My dog slips off into the inferno.

Reach in and grab it. Do it.

9:55 PM

IN THE FLICKERING DARKNESS OF OUR RECLUSIVE CUBBYHOLE, GORGED on hotdogs, and squashed into a child-sized folding chair, I try to direct my thoughts toward writing.

How many stories need to be told? Countless.

So why have I pigeonholed myself into a single style? To one journey? To one destination?

And why happy endings? My life has hardly ever been happy.

I have never thought to write about villains. Not in the sense of them being the protagonists.

However, society has changed. People almost seem to prefer anti-heroes these days. Maybe that's because no one is as good as the pure and righteous heroes of the golden age.

Burdened with globalization and incessant media, it's apparent to many of us just how flawed we are as a species. Makes sense why these broken and fallible characters are so attractive. Their struggles are our own.

The good guy doesn't always win.

And yet heroic tales span every age, every gender, every color, every nation, and they all inevitably overcome some sort of failure at one point or another.

After all, absolutely no one makes all the right decisions. Sometimes good guys make bad choices, while "bad guys" do things to help others, or their plots and schemes simply go un-foiled.

There is no formula for the perfect hero. Not anymore. Which is why anyone can be the hero nowadays. Perfection is no longer a prerequisite for the title.

I need to abandon the pattern that seeds my vision for each narrative I've told so far. I need characters on a journey I have yet to travel. Where their journey ends is something we can discover together.

Like I thought Gabi and I would?

I really fucking hate myself sometimes.

10:01 PM

GLEN'S SILENCE STRIKES ME AS ODD. HE HAS SAID NOTHING FOR...WHO knows how long?

Not one to shatter silence, I rest my head back and allow my attention to stray toward the dark void beyond the canopy above.

The twinkle of the galaxies overhead and the insect consortium below lure me back toward introspection.

Because in that endless void, I can see her dark black hair dangling above me, framing her piercing, near-purple eyes and her gentle smile. The thin-lipped grin she flashed when bashfulness set in.

There's nothing wrong with them in my eyes. But she was often coy about her teeth because one incisor had nestled against its neighbor like a lover.

The crying starts.

Well, weeping.

Such a baby.

I drop my gaze to wipe my tears and notice Glen staring curiously as a dog does.

Though Glen is "woke," his innate response is unsure and awkward. He moves from the log and sits in the chair next to mine. With a firm grip on my back, he hands me a cold, sweat-dripping beer.

The night seems to take on an unnatural silence.

Where are the mosquitos and cicadas? Where is the life hidden in the shadows?

If I weren't such a self-absorbed wimp, I'd be able to hear.

"You've got to move on man."

Why does everyone always say that?

Because I'm pathetic, that's why.

People talk about loss and grieving like they're just a stop on the light rail that you can freely pass on from. Simplifying grief as if you could just walk from one platform to the next.

I feel like Glen doesn't understand. I feel like I'm on an island, and no one can communicate with me, no one can see me.

The real me.

I need to change the subject. "Yeah man, sure." I try to drink my beer and soak up my tears. "So, what's the plan for tomorrow?"

"I'm glad you're trying to change the subject, mate, but honestly, you need to reach acceptance with your grief."

Despite Glen's preceding statement, it seems he won't permit me to heed said advice so easily.

"Yes, it's over. There's no going back. Yeah, she hurt you in more ways than one, but you've got to move on. She made her choice. There's unfortunately no changing that." He pops up to his feet and finishes his beer. Then pulls out another from his back pocket.

"For fuck sake, I've known a lot of relationships in my thirty-ish years, but seldom love. However, when I did find those rare encounters—and *clearly*— none worked out for me, either," he says, pointing to himself.

"But, you know that. I've never developed a full partnership. One where we took care of one another during the darkest times. *But*—ah fuck, where was I? Hold on."

He's looking penitent. His beer a holy artifact handled with delicate fingers, as if it contained the answer to his question. He gulps down an uncomfortable swig.

"Right. *Love.* Love allows us to put up with a lot, and love also allows us to be vulnerable with our partner and work through the darkest issues. We have to share those things with each other. We have to ask for help from those we trust most," he says with a triumphant toss of his can, hands held high, framing the belch that lurches into the night air.

Glen has so much passion and his heart's in the right place, but I can't help but remember that he doesn't know everything.

He doesn't know how I pushed her...

Why Gabi had no reason to confide in me.

"Well, let's talk tomorrow. No sense dwelling; I don't think it'll get us anywhere. So, once we get through this inevitable hangover with a rousing breakfast of beans, hot dogs, and eggs, we'll drop and head up toward the hills overlooking the lake. Hopefully timing the two perfectly."

Quite the empath, he's definitely realized his little speech wasn't helping, and he's hypocritically changing the subject.

With a cheeky grin, he produces another beer as if from the ether.

I'm not sure what number either of us is on, but I feel flushed and loose.

Aware that a depressive weight is likely lurking nearby, I force myself to stand tall and join Glen for a toast over the fire.

MONDAY
August 31st

BARABOO, WISCONSIN

Devil's Lake State Park

7:03 AM

GLEN ENDS UP BEING RIGHT ABOUT THE HANGOVER.

We had gotten after it, climbed the proverbial mountain as my estranged father put it on those mornings that I actually spent with him.

As were many of those mornings for Dad, this one was fuzzy.

The night's events trickle back, but it's a struggle to uproot much from my subconscious.

I have zero memory of going to bed. But waking up inside the tent is a win. Even if I didn't get my shoes off or use my comforter as anything more than a pillow.

It was one of those sleeps where I know I woke up a handful of times, hoping it was later than it was.

By this point, I can no longer justify, let alone stomach, trying.

A death metal orgy of bird songs does their best to cleave my head in two.

Glen, however, silently snores away somewhere beyond the canvas walls, held steadfast in dreamland.

Jealous, I lay there wondering what can be done about the meddlesome jackhammer rampaging across the front of my skull.

All I want is about 100 ounces of water, a greasy bag of drive-thru breakfast, and a nap...

Is that too much to ask?

7:13 AM

I make one last attempt at sleep since water and fast food aren't readily available.

It does not go well.

Outside the tent, the air is hardly fresh. The coagulating scents of stale beer, smoldering embers, and what could only be vomit, beckon up last night's meal.

I need water. I need the cooler.

Thankfully, Glen only purchased the best. Because it certainly looks like the local wildlife had attempted to reach the contents of the heavy-duty name-brand cooler.

After turning it off its side and undoing the latches, I greedily steal the first bottle I can lash my fingers around.

A sports drink... At least it's blue.

The ground doesn't seem as enticing as the night before. There are sticks and acorns everywhere. Our chairs lay toppled beside the fire pit's still smoking ash.

There's also the litany of beer cans. Each crushed into a unique Picasso.

I'm betting there were more before the critters came through.

I flip a chair and don't bother swiping off the detritus clinging to the seat.

Happy as a pig in shit, I let the chair support me as I guzzle down the blue drink.

Could be the hangover. Could be the fact that I never *really* wanted to come on this trip.

Who knows?

But in the daylight, this place gives me a vibe.

I don't feel welcome here.

More than that, I feel this sense of shame weighing down my shoulders.

Is this really what I should be doing?

Is this headache worth it?

Isn't being here just running away from my problems?

And there's vomit on my chair.

Avoiding the cool globs of last night's meal, and regretting the accompanying overconsumption of light beer, I climb to my feet.

I know sleep won't come, but I am also well aware that this is not the place to nurse my ailing body and mind.

The only other place I think I can reach without getting lost is the water.

So, with my bottle of sugary electrolytes and my pack filled with whatever munchies Glen hadn't left behind in my apartment, I set out for the lake. At the very least, maybe I'll walk a bit and then be tired enough to go back to bed.

7:17 AM

THE JOURNEY DOWN THE NARROW TRAIL AT THE BACK OF OUR CAMPSITE is uneventful. It's just a dirt path winding through thick greenery on all sides.

That is until I reach the trailhead. Here, there are options, but I am pulled toward a set of old railroad tracks that look to run out alongside the water.

I can't imagine they're in use.

The ties look as if they're splitting and worn. Weeds blemish the surrounding hunks of loose white stone.

Further along to the right, there's parking, a beach, and boat launches.

The tracks lead away parallel to the lake, and though I'm disheartened to see another parking lot along their route, I continue following them.

This next lot, like its predecessor, is barren.

It's nice knowing we've got the place to ourselves.

A sigh of positivity leaves my lungs.

A spot where the plants briefly yield has caught my eye. A snug, person-sized alcove invites me to the shoreline. The gravel slopes downward amidst larger stones, terminating at the water's edge.

The clarity jars my expectations. I did not anticipate the lake to be so clear.

The sun's morning stretch casts its reach into shimmering ripples atop the water. Beneath the surface, veins of sunlight traverse the shallow depths along the shore.

Just shy of the waterline are these flat stones that practically call my name. As if they're a seat nature carved out just for me.

There's something about this spot that tickles my brain.

It's difficult to put words to it, but it feels oddly significant, almost as if fate and I finally synchronized after all these years.

7:35 AM

From my odd, stone La-Z-Boy, I listen to this itch that can only be scratched if I remove my shoes and let my feet take in the cool current beneath the water's surface.

They barely reach. Seems the water level is low.

The cold is gentle, yet a stark dichotomy to the warm fever of morning rays swimming down my back and neck.

The lake is larger than the internet led me to believe.

With the naked eye, it's easy to view the opposite shore. It's littered with giant stones—boulders, I guess—that from this distance appear plum purple. Like a purplish-red. I can't quite make out the color exactly, but it sure is distinct. Not exactly a color I'd call natural.

The further shore—the south shore—is impossible to see. The surrounding hills and trees that line it are apparent, but the actual shoreline must be a mile or more around the bend from where I sit now.

Take this moment in.

The water almost appears to shimmer with a green hue from the surrounding hills. It doesn't belong. As if it were a trick of the light, I blink and the verdant flicker vanishes.

The humidity is low, and the wind whispers across the water, bringing forth the all-too-familiar scent of the elements coming together where water dominates.

I can see how this place, maybe even this spot, would have been *sacred*.

Not just during the day, but at night.

It must be beautiful at night.

To have been a young Ho-Chunk sitting at the water's edge five-, six-, seven-hundred years ago, there would be no avoiding the mysticism of this place.

The way the wind's secrets sigh atop the water is evidence enough to radiate a spiritual aura.

7:37 AM

In a moment of self-reflection and honesty, I admit to myself how afraid I am that this upcoming trip will be the end of my career. Confirming all the suspicions I hold about myself.

That I am a bad person.

That I am broken.

That there's something...Wrong with me.

There's more than one thing.

It'll be me who ruins it all.

We won't go on a happy-go-lucky romp through the woods.

There won't be a fantastical Hunter S. Thompson adventure providing the impetus for the next great American novel.

We won't have some heart-warming revelation that the veritable treasure was inside me all along.

This could prove to be the destruction of my psyche and validation of all my fears.

7:55 AM

IT TAKES A WHILE BEFORE FINALLY BREAKING FREE OF THE LAKE'S trance.

My head is still pounding, but the toiling waves twisting my stomach have receded somewhat. Though it aches intensely.

I need a snack.

My bag's heavier than I think it should be. I hadn't cared before, but curiosity steers my fingers around the contents. Rooting through, my hand finds the source of the heft.

A hardcover.

I don't have to remove it to know what it is.

Yet some form of masochism compels me to withdraw it. A pressurizing anger claws its way from its cave in my reptile brain.

DROPOUTS.

Fucking R. Nold's bestseller.

On his first try, too. Don't forget.

Thanks, brain.

A pristine cover. Fresh and somehow untainted through its travels along the bed of my bag. The front image is an illustration comprising a cluttered chalkboard with chemical equations, most noticeably MDMA and LSD—of course, labeled—set before a classroom table adorned with a bloody sheriff's badge, a pile of what looks like cocaine, and some sort of pistol.

The smooth semi-gloss-and-matte finish of the dust jacket shifts in my hand as I flip the book over, revealing a slick black-and-white photo of the author. Big enough to suggest he is overcompensating for something.

He looks younger than me, not older. That smug smile and a baby face airbrushed free of any stubble.

His eyes track the way the Mona Lisa is supposed to. They're deep-set, almost a raccoon mask. The eyes of a writer. Rimmed with the exhaustion of Red Bull-fueled late nights and excessive screen time.

There was something about him. Hidden behind a large pair of glasses that looked like they belonged on the face of a serial killer from the 80s or 90s are a set of predatory eyes.

There's also his hair. Even in grayscale, it's a disorienting contrast to his caterpillar-like black eyebrows.

The eyes are the worst, though. There's a dark voice behind those orbs. The kind capable of creating the novel held in my hand. Kin to the voice cursing my own thoughts.

Fed up, I flip the book onto a nearby rock.

Gently, of course. It is still a book, after all. And I'm no savage.

8:01 AM

A SECOND SURPRISE AWAITS ME IN THE FRONT POUCH OF MY BAG. My little stoner kit.

This will be the highlight of the morning.

I make quick work of rolling a joint and inhaling it down to its last dregs.

From that first exhale, I can feel my headache evaporating into the water lapping at my feet.

Sacred Lake.

A warmth spreads across my chest, and I recognize the unfamiliar sensation of my lips slipping upward into a gentle smile.

The world is silent. No mosquitos. No cicadas. No cars or people.

It's just me, and I think about that Wisco-Pedia entry.

Sacred Lake.

Now I can see it.

I can see the world removed from technology.

To be a young Ho-Chunk man starting his morning here in worship.

Paying reverence to the spirits of ancestors and nature.

Of *this* nature.

The serenity of the moment envelops me.

Where to go from here?

Can I possibly capture this surrealism in the story that I need to tell?

I hardly feel myself.

I'm a stranger in my own body, but it's not uncomfortable.

I decide the only fitting thing to do is make a silent prayer, asking for The Lake's guiding assistance.

The cloudless sky allows its bright blue reflection to meet the shimmering clearness of the water in a way that nearly reaches out to me in an audible hush.

The conversation is private and intimate.

My vulnerability in this moment of isolation feels quite the opposite, as Nature enjoys the serenity at my side. Quietly whispering words meant only to be shared between the two of us.

I slide down out of my stone recliner along the gravel, allowing the pebbles to roll beneath my feet like a conveyor belt.

Perched like a catcher hovering over the water's surface, I cup the cool liquid and take a mouthful in.

It seems—I don't know—*silly*.

But, in order to match the reality of my desperate needs, being silly is something I don't mind.

Our privacy permits a visceral knitting of my being with that of the water.

The invisible burden clinging to my back begins losing purchase as if sloughing off. Maybe the combination of marijuana and lake water has tranquilized the weighty beast.

Unsure how much time passed, I carefully maneuver back to my La-Z-Boy.

But something is watching me. I say that like I possess a supernatural awareness.

Which I don't.

However, instinctually, the culprit is easy to locate.

DROPOUTS.

Or more aptly, R. Nold's matte mug.

Those predacious eyes challenge me.

And I accept.

The book feels lighter in my hands as I peel off the dust jacket and crack the spine.

I'll read this novel and in doing so, channel what I hope is the Lake's... *guidance?* I guess.

8:04 AM

Jealousy and loathing writhe away, coiling around my innards.

Obviously, this is far from objective, but there's no way this violent attention grabber and its accompanying B.S. en medias res opening, deserves a *Bestseller* banner.

I recognize my own flawed logic. I've hardly read one hundred words.

A sense of self-awareness looms at my proverbial fingertips.

The chasm of negativity boring at my insides doesn't surrender entirely to the ether. Its growth, more impeded than ceased.

The high must be dealing with more than the now absent queasiness in my gut.

Drawing the crisp morning air through my nostrils lets me relish in the serenity of this gorgeous morning.

The air dances around me. The water shimmers despite being as smooth as glass. And the sentinel protection of the verdant hills all combine to soothe me into a broader appreciation than I've ever held for nature.

Exhaling, I relent.

The time has come to push through my detestation and read on.

In fact, a mild curiosity paws at my consciousness regarding the rhetorical question the narrator poses in the very first line.

What was the *'lifeless sound a body made when it fell to the earth'*?

8:07 AM

WELL, THAT WAS ANTICLIMACTIC.

I don't see the fuss from the jump.

So what? A body is quiet when it falls?

Is that surprising?

No, not really.

However, it has a visceral sort of flair, I guess.

But then it looks like there's a time skip.

The narrator said their little gang had been "floundering."

He refers to the act of taking a life as him being "tested."

That feels like an overly dark summation.

I skim the next paragraph, chuckling at R. Nold's pretentiousness.

I have always possessed an innate sense of conviction. Once my mind set on something that I desired, nothing would get in my way. Even fear burned to ash beneath the conviction that steadied my trigger finger each time.

I can hear the tool on the back cover's stupid fucking voice spewing some nonsense about how, when the annoyingly terse author R. Nold writes, he makes the tough decisions others wouldn't.

If he's "muscle," then I'm mentally stable.

I mean, I am. I just—

My feet are back in the water.

Had my stone throne slid down under my weight? Could the water level have risen somehow?

I'm pretty sure there's no tide...Pretty sure.

Hardly making the case for myself in the mentally stable category.

Why worry about such matters?

Fair.

I spin my feet, climb back to my throne, and go back to the book.

It's still early, maybe I can find something redeeming.

8:13 AM

Now I don't normally do this, but I skimmed the next few paragraphs into the second chapter.

It reads like a manifesto.

Mostly ranting and raving about the similarities between the drug trade and Silicon Valley. And how the narrator and his cronies offered a boutique drug shop experience with Wall Street-level savvy and a Mafia-esque flair.

Another deep breath.

The water plays with my toes.

What would my MFA professors say?

What would your mother say?

She wouldn't say a thing this early. She'd chide me for even suggesting it.

But she would have humored my enmity with a discussion.

The narrative problem is apparent. It stares the reader in the face. There's a megalomaniac fancying themselves some sort of drug racket kingpin, and he had finally run across a threshold that was long overdue.

What else would she want you to see?

I catch my gaze lost across the water.

A light breeze picks up. Its warm breath dances lightly like a ballerina atop the water's surface.

There's this sense of discovery that I need to explore. The academic in me senses a challenge.

She'd say, "What can you learn from this?"

Or re-learn?

I peek ahead.

There are only a few pages left in the chapter.

Screw it.

8:16 AM

He writes exactly how I thought he would. Arrogant and abrasive. But it can definitely elicit gasps and shock value from readers.

So fuck it, I guess that's how I should write too. I'll just invent a story about some fucking criminals and write it with a bunch of swear words and overconfident d-bags.

Even the thought of doing so makes me sad.

That's not me. That's not what my mom would have enjoyed reading.

I feel genuine disgust at the thought of writing like this prick. And yet, I still finish the chapter.

Two chapters down, and from where I'm sitting, the only way this novel gains notoriety is from readers powering through to see the protagonist's head get blown off.

Never have I read a more detestable character, and in first person, too. Made me even more angry to be in the sociopath's head.

I almost put the book down.

But I don't.

I will say, I'd hate to be this guy's friends.

I feel better about having Glen as a friend.

This narrator is an absolute piece of shit.

I can't imagine the people he based these characters on being too thrilled with the comparison. But maybe he thought them up entirely.

I want to doubt that.

I want to hate every part of this book with every part of me.

Yet, for some ungodly reason, I go back to reading.

8:32 AM

THE FUCK.

I can't read a single line more.

My dumb self never noticed the "BEFORE" and "AFTER" format.

In my opinion—I know what that's worth—this is a shambly collection of literary clichés stacked atop one another like a house of matches.

Was that the point?

Stupid people will eat it up.

I know that's jealousy. Yet, a fragment of me possesses a burning urge to turn the page. With so much exposition in just a handful of pages, I doubt the narrative has yet to take its stride.

Where would this story head?

There's a lot going on. And I, for the life of me, can't remember the damn synopsis Glen droned on about just last night.

Still, the itch to turn the page persists. Normally a dopamine rush that has morphed into a loathing and irritating sensation.

The sun rests its caressing glow atop my shoulders like a gentle lover.

I can be done with the book for now.

8:42 AM

Watching the last of the smoke billow from my mouth—a second, smaller joint having felt necessary—I let the tranquility of the scenery embrace me one more time.

Seconds run like minutes, watching the grey clouds linger in front of the glowing orange orb overhead.

It's a hypnotizing effect. The kind that stalls time only for those bearing witness. Just long enough to savor some peace, quiet, and solitude.

I could stay here forever, but my gut tells me it's time to return to camp.

However, I decisively opt for the long route. The park's empty, after all.

8:49 AM

THE TREK'S ABUNDANT SIGNS OF LIFE BELONG EXCLUSIVELY TO THE natural ecosystem around me.

The parking lot is the exception.

Poking out from the entry to the welcome shack, like rejected fingerling potatoes, is a set of old gnarled toes. Thick yellowing nails offer the appearance of odd growths on swollen spuds.

A small projectile arcs over what I presume are feet belonging to the same old man from last night.

The miniature bolides are difficult to discern. Part of me figures sunflower seeds, but from a closer distance, the accumulating mass is actually a collection of wood shavings.

How stereotypical.

The only things missing are a linen pantsuit and a corncob pipe.

Maybe he's carving one.

A wet *thwwtt* echoes out of the shack as a brown glob of spit finds its way to the asphalt. There it settles to petrify in the sun alongside other thick stains. Chew or dip, whichever, proves an apt substitute for the pipe.

The first prickling static of anxiety tells me I've gotten too close.

Taking a wide arc, I catch his reflection in one of those huge rounded mirrors that let you see around corners. Which means he could probably see me, too.

"Mornin' Cityboy! How's ya evenin'? Get aftuh it a bit? Y'all cityboys tend to." He laughs to himself. A sound nearly slow enough to match his cadence.

No one else to laugh with around here.

"*Morning.*" It's not my most friendly greeting.

But maybe if a stereotype like this exists in real life, then I might just be able to caricature him into a story. At the very least, capture a snippet or two of dialogue.

Plus, I'm higher than those horn things on a giraffe...

So, what else can I do?

I certainly don't want to read any more of *DROPOUTS*.

Waiting for Glen to revive could take a while.

Begrudgingly, I admit to myself that the conversational effort is the most valuable course of action.

"You the only one who works out here?"

"These days I am. Grandson used ta. But he's off at school now. Up at the Big W. Proud'a that boy. He's in a doctoral program now. Gonna be the first of us to make somethin'a themselves. Unlike his no-good pappie. And unfortunate mother. Rest their souls. But school's been good for the boy. Though, I do miss havin' him round the summers. Practically raised him on my lonesome. Always used to help me with the kayaks and canoes. Now, I gotta ask folks ta do it 'emselves. On accounta this old back-uh-mine not being what it once was."

This guy has fallen right out of the encyclopedia of stereotypes for the southern gentlemen. The soft and drawn-out twang of each syllable feels oddly formal, yet humbling.

"You boys got any plans for the day other than toking down by the lake and getting mad at a book?"

Time slows.

My features gradually morph into those of a deer in headlights.

It's legal in Illinois! Is it legal in Wisconsin?

The old man laughs the same way a parent might when their toddler asks why the old balding man is missing hair.

"Pull them britches outta yah crack boy. I ain't the police. Hell, ya want to enjoy a morning spliff?"

How high am I?

The answer, pretty. But I can't be *that* high.

The coot already has a damn joint in his mouth.

As he lights it, I can smell the aroma pulling me in like an old cartoon character to a pie on the windowsill.

"I don't much care round these parts. DNR officers're mostly family. And they're the only enforcement round here, so ya ain't gotta worry bout bunny cops nor the real ones for that matter."

He hands me the spliff.

Still a bit dumbfounded, I take a nice, long drag.

The guy has good weed.

"Not bad old man." I let loose a long exhale that muffles the words. "This was not how I expected my morning to start."

A chuckle escapes my chest as we exchange the miniature prize.

The nicotine buzz is a welcome surprise. The sensation floods through my body like a waterfall of bliss spreading into each extremity. Muscles, veins, cells, they all get a taste of the euphoria.

"Ya know son, you don't go through Korea, Nam, Woodstock, and legal weed without picking up a thing or two. Grow this stuff myself. Pretty proud-uh-her too. Call her Devil's Lettuce."

His laugh is infectious this time. I feel uplifted by it.

"It was actually my boy, or my grand-boy I should say, that come up with it. Not the best parentin', but can't have done him in any worse than that dead-beat son-uh-mine. Rest his soul. His mamma and grannie would've killed me but seein' as they'd already departed, I weren't too scared." He lets out a haggard sigh and performs the sign of the cross.

He's led a real life.

A thought hits me like a freight truck, and I almost lose my balance, succumbing to spinning thoughts and swirling nicotine.

Is he my protagonist? This old coot? There aren't stories about him. All journeys are about the young hero who meets the old sage.

The old ones are wise.

No one wants to read another story about some little twerp needing an aging mentor to guide them through trial after trial!

Let wisdom guide your story.

Would I read a story about a geriatric stoner who goes through a ridiculous trial unheard of before?

My head swims with possibility. Amidst the haze of nicotine and pot, an idea fights to claw free of its cement-like cage.

"Hey, I gotta go write. Thank you for this though."

Without thinking, I just run.

Then I smell it, and dig my heels into the gravel, sliding to a stop that nearly sends me face-first into the jagged collection beneath me.

The old man's spliff is still between my fingers.

Embarrassed, I jog it back to its rightful owner, only realizing as I glimpse his reflection once more that I'd forgotten something else.

What is his damn name?!

I give up and ask, passing him his spliff. "Sorry about that, and thanks again Old Man. Or what would you prefer I call you?"

Deadpan, he responds, "Skeeter."

"You fucking with me?" This couldn't get any more ridiculous.

"Course, I am! What kinda stupid name is *Skeeter?* Appreciate ya not thinking my mama'd be so callous as to bestow such a damn ridiculous name. That said, name's Troy. Troy Witherspoon. Friends call me Clint though. Long story. Speakin'a which—"

He rummages around for something. I can't see what he's doing, but I've got to wait for him, despite the burning itch barreling through my fingers, desperate for a pen and paper in hand.

"Ah, here it is!"

He comes back to the window a bit flushed in the cheeks. The remnants of his hair billow wildly on the sides of his head. "This here book's been floatin' round our family for generations. One of the few I ever read."

It's a wafer-thin paperback.

In the sun's light, the pages are a deep dijon pocked with stains of what's likely coffee or dip. Frayed edges announce where dog ears were torn out. There's a vascularity to the spine that webs its way to the covers. It's certainly seen better days. It's a wonder the thing could still hold itself together.

Written across the sickly yellow cover are the words:

151

Devil's Lake
Original Tales of the Hočągara

The confusion breeding from that sentence seems to force my brain into a stutter.

I can't process how I know that word.

Hočągara.

"I don't know what your goal is for the day, but something tells me you might appreciate some-uh these tales. 'Specially the one bout the Seven Headed Green Water Panther Spirit thing-a-ma-bop. Hopefully'll give ya some inspiration this afternoon."

Focusing doesn't seem to be in the cards, and I think Clint's got a sense of that.

"Well come on now *Thoreau*, you've got work ta do. Don't stand round gawkin' about."

Snapping back to reality, I laugh and offer my gratitude. "Thanks, *Clint*. I appreciate *this*."

"My pleasure young man, and you keep it. Just come back and visit sometime. Oh, and tell me what you think bout the story of them purple rocks too."

I wave and take off for the campground, doing my best to hold on to those ideas that have been metastasizing throughout my mind.

"Oh and don't go using my name in yer book now. Old man needs some privacy!"

"You got it, *Skeeter!*"

8:58 AM

I'm out of breath and desperate for something to drink to combat the horrible affliction that is cotton mouth when I reach the tent.

Inside our cooler, the first thing I get a hand on, amidst the icy slosh, is good-ole light beer.

Fine by me. It's hardly more than water, anyway.

Prepped, I grab a notepad from my pack and begin brainstorming. The cicadas lurking throughout the treetops serenade this process.

Swiftly, the page turns into a spiderweb of thoughts and narratives.

I refuse to curb any of them.

For the first time in what seems an eternity, adrenaline pulses through me.

Sensations of past joy play beneath my skin, catalyzing into a shot of dopamine.

The tattooing of ink on the page would never make sense to any other person.

But to me, they're a woven tapestry of interconnecting threads. Aimlessly pulling at one creates a reverberating pathway through another.

Some of these strands need a little love and flushing out—but I know that's not a bad thing.

"If your first draft isn't shitty, then you spent too much time on it."

Wise words from my high school English teacher.

9:12 AM

For the first time in God knows how long, I've tapped into that youthful obsession I once held for the craft.

'*All or nothing mentality*' a therapist had called it.

Fairly apt terminology, if I do say so.

Because I *need* to let these ideas flow through me. I can't just hit pause.

Like a junkie, I chase the high from reveries of late nights and early mornings obsessively scribbling out the plot lines that gripped me.

About fifteen or twenty minutes pass and it's damn near overwhelming, this urge to write and write until my mind is empty.

But I sputter at a fork in the road of this prepubescent narrative.

Galen, the writer of twenty-four hours ago, would choose to have my old man protagonist make the noble, heroic decision.

The antithesis is then to write the villain's journey. An alluring option thanks to fucking *DROPOUTS*.

But screw heroes, and screw villains altogether. Heroes and villains aren't real. Only those with flaws that they can overcome and those that they can't.

Ultimately, it's up to the character. They have to make this choice.

Not you?

I've got the nicotine itch thanks to Skeeter's spliff.

Fortunately, Glen is always quitting and un-quitting. In fact, he is the guy who tells everyone he meets that he's quitting, despite always having a cheat pack hidden somewhere nearby.

With as much stealth as I can manage—which isn't much—I somehow snake Glen's bags from the tent without waking him in his nearby hammock.

Sure enough, a partially obscured side pocket contains a sealed pack of cancer sticks.

Predictable.

However, there's something else in his bag, and curiosity urges my rifling fingers to continue their way through my friend's belongings.

The mystery item has a weight to it. The kind that sags the bottom of the bag down like a drip of ooze.

As if a gravitational pull exists around the object, my fingers stumble through Glen's possessions without shame.

Until they trot across a cool and metallic surface. The iciness of it extends to my nervous system.

I don't want to pull it out, but in order to appease some baser instinct, my fingers wrap around the cold stock.

A fucking pistol.

Why the hell does he have a pistol? God damnit.

Maybe you should hang on to it?

Didn't Glen know the laws of storytelling?!

A gun shown in the first act will inevitably fire by the last.

And I would really appreciate it if the third act, where I planned to be tripping balls, did not contain gunfire.

Personally, I don't know guns. So I can't say it's anything other than a pistol. Yet, I can't bring myself to remove it from the bag.

I hope to push its existence from my mind.

The weight is intoxicating, though. The heft of it. It almost emanates a sense of comfort.

I feel stronger with it in my hand. There's something here that feels *right*.

You could kill with this.

I try to shake the thought free like a wet dog, but there's still that violent refrain ringing between my ears.

KILL. KILL. Kill. Kill. Kill. kill. kill. kill. kill...

TRIP

I should get rid of it. Or hide it.
But what if we need it?
When have I ever needed a gun?
That settles it. I'll put it back and forget this ever happened.
Why surrender such power when you are, in fact, so weak?

9:23 AM

A muffled "*fuck*" breaks the weapon's trance, and my fingers fly to the bag's zipper.

Another swear, more indistinct this time, fades into the sounds of fabric on fabric. My eyes draw toward Glen's hammock, where an awkward, writhing, tumor-like bulge struggles for release from its nylon tomb.

I make sure the bag looks untouched and sit down with my notepad and the pack of cigarettes. Quickly, I light one to hide the panic on my face.

Nestled into the undersized folding chair, a rush of nicotine soothes my frazzled nerves. It makes focusing on anything but the gun whispering its icy presence in my ear a tad easier.

Glen continues to groan and move throughout the parachute hammock, before eventually mumbling something audible. "You out there, mate? I think I'm dying. Will you please shut those damn birds up?"

A genuine chuckle explodes from my gut. I know all too well how he's feeling. The chirps and chatter seem quieter now, melting into the ambiance of cicada warbles.

"Get on out here man. A little hair of the dog and some food'll get ya going."

Glen emerges from the hammock first on his hands, then falling to all fours, limping out like a wounded dog.

"Toss me one of those squares," he says as he props himself against the stripped-down log at my side. "How can two people drink so much in one night? Fuck, my brain hurts."

He lays his head back against the log, lights his cigarette, and quickly exhales a bulbous cloud of smoke.

"This used to be so much easier when we were younger." He takes another long drag.

I don't think he's done much quitting as of late.

"You make breakfast yet?" he bellows out behind a noxious cloud.

I shake my head and decide to tell him about the morning I've had.

Staring at the hungover and disheveled Glen, I see a character in him, too.

That odd mixture of wisdom and, well, fuckboy-ness, reminds me that no person is perfect. We're all just an amalgamation of imperfect tropes.

That's what I want for my characters.

To exist as genuine people that readers could empathize with. Not necessarily every character, but their emotions, dreams, and personalities would create a different level of investment.

In the past, my goal had always revolved around creating unique worlds that were aberrations of our past. However, I understand at this moment how that level of divergence alienates readers.

So, I needed characters. The kinds that an audience will connect with at the pathos level, and for me, that means a contemporary setting will likely benefit my characters and my focus.

Glen's staring. He looks like he's waiting for a reply.

The panic must be showing on my face as he asks what I have to think is the same question for a second time. "Why is my bag out here? I don't remember that."

What do I say?

Duh. There's a simple answer. It's staring me right in the face.

The pistol still freaks me out, but I know to play it cool—cool as a cucumber.

You sound like the old man.

"I can't remember a thing after, fuck, I don't know. We were up all night."

Hopefully, I don't sound too obvious.

Glen groans.

"Typical. Well, today's gonna be a different animal," he says, cracking open a light beer. "Give me till," he points about a third of the way down the can, "and I'll make some food. A little grease in our veins, a dip in the lake, and we'll be good to go this afternoon."

10:01 AM

Glen does all the cooking in a cast-iron skillet. Bacon, eggs, and beans with sliced-up hot dogs. The open fire seasons it all in rich smoke. The taste does the aromas justice.

With plates cleared and cleaned, we are new men.

The only problem. I'm coming down.

Too much food and the world encourages me to lie down for a nap.

Thankfully, Glen is on the same page.

I crawl into the tent and Glen clambers back into his parachute hammock, which he had hastily set up at some point during the night.

That I truly do not remember.

12:46 PM

My wake-up call comes as Glen's ass thumps to the ground.

Realizing what has happened outside my tiny nylon bedroom, another laugh just escapes. Unforced and authentic. If only I could start more days this way.

Positivity? What is this?

It's just shy of one in the afternoon. Plenty of daylight left.

So, we march down to the lake to take a little dip, wash up, and give the old nervous system a pleasant jolt.

Feeling revitalized, I think about smoking again, but ultimately decide that entering this looming psychedelic experience with a clear head is for the best.

Galen, you are not the same man as yesterday.

We begin our walk back, and as we traverse the road, Clint's shed gets close enough to make out a wad of dip spit arcing through the tiny window, where his elderly feet have found new purchase all these hours later.

"Hey there Skeeter! Good shot!"

His infectious laugh echoes inside the tiny shack. "Thanks Thoreau! Y'all fully recovered from that late night?"

Despite being unable to see him, I can picture the old coot grinning like a fool behind his bushy mustache, and it just fills me with—*joy*.

TRIP

For the first time in a long while, I think it's safe to say I'm living in the moment.

"Couldn't be better! How long you going to be in the shack today?"

"Depends. May need a nap, not s'posed to have any more visitors the rest of the day, but I'll be around. We'll catch up after yer day's adventures." As an afterthought, he hollers out, "Make sure to read a tale or two from that book I gave ya!"

"You've got it!"

There's this little voice inside me. It's more muffled than normal. Quieter too.

Still, I hear it.

Who's this old fuck think he is that we'll want to hang out later?

Despite the thought, I sort of hope we do.

1:27 PM

MAYBE IT WAS BECAUSE GLEN HAD GONE ABOUT RE-PACKING MY BAG, but I cannot help being amused as he emerges from the tent dressed nearly identical to me.

Only, I'm the dollar store version of his department store attire. Everything from my shorts and boots to my flannel, which I forgot I owned, was cheap and worn.

Glen, on the other hand, probably just bought this new wardrobe.

However, I have something Glen doesn't. A bandana. Black.

As I knot it at the base of my skull, the tiny bit of cloth makes me feel like Rambo going off into the jungle.

Just as I think we're about to set off, Glen wordlessly pulls the pack from my back and discards its contents into an empty grocery bag.

A childish sadness wells up in my throat, watching all my remaining candy and sweets being replaced with granola bars and tiny oranges.

The perfect soccer mom.

He checks to make sure that I have multiple notebooks and pens before returning my backpack.

Though, if he could stop testing the pens and just let us go, we'd already be on our journey.

With a sudden alarming panic, Glen's hands fly into his duffel.

I know it in my soul.

He's going for the gun.

A torrent of anxiety crashes into me. I can literally feel my feet growing unsteady as I stand motionless.

His hand returns, fingers gripped tightly around a bottle of allergy meds, which he offers.

I hastily decline, still reeling at the thought of the hidden firearm.

"One last thing." He gestures to the cooler. From its depths, my friend pulls out an empty peanut container, which holds the infamous Ziplock bag. Glen nestles the baggie as gently as a mother does her young into one of his breast pockets.

With that, Glen conducts us from the camp.

1:33 PM

Our walk is silent.

My heart has yet to stop racing from the memory of that deathly cold metal clenched in my palm.

Does he have it on him?

I need some water or something to calm my nerves. The clunky wide-mouth bottle sloshes recklessly as I try to sip and walk at the same time.

"You've got to upgrade from that old Nalgene, G. These Hydro Flasks are the new wave man."

A little late on the suggestion.

Glen laughs as I wipe the water escaping down my cheeks. "At least get yourself a splash guard. I think you'll enjoy hiking more if you don't end up wearing as much of your water."

I can laugh with him. It seems my unwelcome friend, Anxiety, is ebbing back out to sea. The day is too nice not to let the incident drip off me.

The sky is a picturesque blue. Not a single cloud blemishes the azure dome.

Meanwhile, the unfettered sunlight blankets a temperate warmth across the landscape. It is *literally* the perfect day.

"So, you really come out here all the time?"

"Not all the time," Glen says. "We pick different campsites, and it's been a few years since we came up here. In fact, this may only be the second time I've been to Devil's Lake. The first being not long after I moved to Chi."

"So, you're really no more an expert on this place than I am!" I laugh.

Glen does too.

Once our decrescendo of chuckles is complete, Glen shares the plan of attack.

He wants to take a long walk around the lake. Only once we've reached the other side will we take the acid. Afterward, the plan is to head into the hills toward the *East Bluffs*, where he says we'll see something called *Balanced Rock*.

It's more of a plan than I have.

1:42 PM

GLEN'S LAUGHTER RIPS ME FROM A POOL OF SWIRLING, HARDLY intelligible thoughts, and I shoot him a glare as if to say, *the fuck you laughing at?*

"Sorry, mate. I just...Jeez...I can't believe we're doing this. I can't believe *you're* doing this." He laughs his infectious laugh, and I can't resist its orbit.

After all, I hardly believe it either.

It's almost like a dream. Something doesn't seem quite real about it.

I'm not sure what happens if I can't flush out this story today, but my guess is it'll look a lot like the last few months, only worse.

The sun beating down a gentle glow encourages optimism.

Maybe, I like nature.

"Enjoy the hike boys!" The bayou drawl echoes out from the park's ramshackle vestibule.

"Thanks, *Skeeter!*"

"Mate, I still can't believe you smoked a joint with that old guy."

I shrug. "Stoners recognize stoners."

Our laughter echoes across the nearby lake as we span the space between the beach and parking lot.

"Seriously, the guy's alright. Not at all what I expected. I still don't quite get why he continues to work here by himself. Apparently, his grandson used to help him, but now it's just him."

"Oh shit. Did the kid die?"

"Fuck–No–*What?* Man, he went off to school or something. Shit, did I make it sound like he died?"

"Yeah, a little. Sounded really morbid."

"Shit. My bad. Definitely not dead. Well, I guess he could be. But, *as far as I know,* the kid's alive. *Supposedly,* off getting his doctorate."

We have a chuckle at that. I think our minds are on the same track.

Looking back over my shoulder, I consider the drafted character I'd been working on that morning.

A dead grandson might make for a nice touch? Elicit some sympathy for an old man who struggles with getting his life on track.

"Hold up!"

My pack is on my chest before Glen can stop walking. I quickly mull over the idea of grabbing a picnic table on the shoreline. But I know we both want to keep moving, so I walk and write.

At least, I try.

1:48 PM

Trying to write and walk is hardly an effortless task. Thankfully, I'm just capturing a few big-picture ideas.

As we leave the shade of the western hillside's overgrowth, I note the path changing. Becoming more precarious. I shove my notes back into my pack.

The trail running alongside the lake quickly morphs from dirt and brush into a rocky passage interlaid with patches of cement.

For the first time, I take in our surroundings. Giant boulders litter the trail sides that run up the hill and down to the water. Which, despite being clear enough to see the bottom in the shallower sections, looks to have a tinge of green to it.

That's not the only odd coloration, though.

A purply wine color tinges most of these craggy behemoths. I want to call it mauve, but I have no clue if that's correct.

I've never seen rocks like this before, and it's not just the stones near the lake. The strange-colored boulders cascade all the way down from the bluff overhead.

Swathes of forest form a dense perimeter around the lake, but the shroud of giant mauve stones besmirch the otherwise sea of green for hundreds of feet up.

I had to have been oblivious to not notice this morning.

TRIP

The pitted trail winds through spaces where lesser stones once rested, while a collection of more mammoth boulders sits like halves of an eggshell, framing the passage.

The rocky coastline is dubious to navigate, yet it's exhilarating. Childhood reveries of carefree wandering envelop my senses until I spy the perfect rock. Flat and smoothed atop into a plateau.

Sit there.

It's a compulsion. Adolescent in its demand for immediate gratification.

So, with some far-from-nimble moves, I navigate toward the water and this natural perch overlooking the lake. The moment my boots grip the tabletop stone, a surge of inspiration urges me to expand on the ideas I had just been drafting a few minutes earlier.

Glen looks at me curiously, and I wave for him to keep going, but that I need to stop. He appears flustered at first. Then he sees me pull the scrawls of my notepad out, and his features soften.

As I sit down, I consider how I'm likely looking toward the spot I'd sat this morning.

Nearby, Glen skips stones while hopping from boulder to boulder with a cigarette hanging loosely across his lips.

My focus contracts to the blossoming web of words in front of me.

1:55 PM

As I finish with my crazy scribbles, Glen tightropes across a chain of boulders tracing the trail.

"You know what," he looks forward, and although we are certainly shy of halfway around the lake, he says with Christmas morning excitement, "let's drop now!" Glen accents the statement with a dramatic hop and spins back onto the path.

He sticks the landing.

"We'll still have a good thirty to forty minutes before the trip hits. Should give us plenty of time to reach the trailhead and crest the hills to one of the overlooks."

My heart skips a beat.

We're actually doing this.

Before now we were just having a guys' weekend. Getting me out of my shell. But now—

Your purpose for being here has arrived.

I already have some story ideas in conception thanks to my newly redis-covered passionate urge to write.

Do I really need ten hours of drug-induced shenanigans to fill the story out?

A hand infiltrates my vision of the calm water.

"Don't think about it, mate."

The fingers unfurl, revealing a patch of tin foil. Just askew of center rests two tiny squares of blotting paper. Each printed with odd, yet familiar chemical symbols along their surfaces.

"Channel those happy thoughts, pop this bad boy under your tongue, and keep it there until it's gone. All that's left is to have ourselves one hell of a fucking day!"

1:58 PM

The paper is slightly bitter as it dissolves under my tongue.

We turn a corner and my heart skips a beat as I narrowly miss bumping into a young mother and her two sons in full hiking gear. They've got fancy walking sticks, camelbacks, and all the name-brand attire necessary for hiking.

That was close.

I thought we had the whole place to ourselves.

A silly thought. Even if the place is run down a bit, it's not like there'd be no one at a state park during the Summer. Even if it was a weekday.

Yet, one look at the happy family, and I feel horribly ill-prepared.

I have no walking stick.

You can make one.

I only have a little bit of water. No camelback.

You'll be fine. You already drank from this water right here.

My clothes are aged, pathetic rags in comparison.

Those who once called this place home lived with less and did more.

I'm fighting the spiral.

Fighting myself?

2:01 PM

Once the woman and her kids are out of sight, Glen pulls a Bluetooth speaker that hooks onto his bag and syncs it to some upbeat folk music.

Can't say I know the band, but the combination of the music and Glen intentionally dancing around the trail like a court jester pulls me back to the moment.

I must've let it show.

"There you go! Can't have you going all negative on me from the get-go. We're the *G-squad*. Glen and Galen. The good guys. So, let's act like it and enjoy this beautiful day in this beautiful place!"

I nod in affirmation. "Thanks, man."

"Any time, mate. Now *onward!*" He dances to the beat emanating from his pack.

As we near the south shore of the lake, we turn inland.

The trail navigates through the woods, sputtering between cemented rock and dirt.

Leaving behind the sun-glistening water, I find the woods and stony hillside almost claustrophobic.

Just up ahead, the foliage parts enough to reveal three run-down cabins.

I can only imagine when these were luxurious vacation rentals where good ole midwestern families cultivated generational memories.

Kids jumping off docks into the water. Barbecue fragrances filling the canopy, while stacks of board games lingered nearby for when the weather turned sour.

It takes a few more minutes before we are spit out onto a dirt trail that widens enough for any sort of vehicle to navigate.

The dusty road leads into a large parking area under another canopy of trees, and just beyond, I catch the shimmer of hot blacktop.

A worn sign directs us to the shoulder.

Thankfully, no cars whizz through.

That is until we reach actual sidewalk.

A harsh grumble fills my ears, radiating from the tunnel of trees feeding the road into the woods.

Before I can register the sound, a giant semi barrels through the hidden turn as if to answer my question.

My heart leaps into my throat as the mass of steel takes the bend a bit too confidently for my comfort.

It departs just as swiftly, blowing the stink of diesel exhaust in its wake.

2:16 PM

THE SOUTH SHORE OF THE PARK IS DEPRESSING.

There is more parking here, but the lot's cracked pavement fills me with an odd sadness.

Broken picnic benches line grassy knolls preceding the beach and the waterline.

There's a rental building with faded signage. Still, it's easy to discern that travelers could rent a canoe or kayak here.

On the far side, there appears to be a drive-thru type window. Except it's cracked and stained a dijon yellow.

Greenery scales the sides, dangling from the roof to reclaim the wooded structure.

Nature has a way of making chaos look beautiful.

Faded wood signage directs us toward the lush green woods of the eastern shore. The concrete sidewalk switches back to dirt-laden trail beneath wide cavernous tree coverage.

The open-air scent of water and soil gives way to an immersive fragrance of pine and pollen. The trees grow thick as boulders litter the floor like a smattering of Legos.

These, however, don't possess that odd mauve color. They're tinged blue and black. Some huge and monolithic, others torn into a myriad of lesser slabs.

Large craggy rock faces extend high above the treetops, standing silent watch over the leaf-covered earth, as if in steward to fallen brethren. Until one day, they too, descend downward to join erosion's unrelenting melody.

2:20 pM

FURTHER DOWN THE TRAIL, THERE'S A SMALL COLLECTION OF YOUNG kids, hipster millennials, and lean shirtless men free-climbing a trio of fallen boulders.

Their slow and deliberate movements leave behind dusty white swathes of chalk. The old men, in particular, conjure images of hairless sloths. The way their long digits feel up the sides of the giant stones with purposeful intention.

It's almost like watching a nature documentary.

The woods buzz with life's soundtrack. Mammals. Birds. Insects. Leaves and plants. The steady thud of acorns crashing into soil.

And the voice of the Lake. That quiet rustle of wind whisking the water's score from a distance.

I chuckle.

Something feels—*different.*

Is it my head? Is it lighter?

I can't place it. A breeze tickles the back of my neck, and the sensation softly reverberates throughout my entire body. Subtly euphoric, like a partner toying with the hairs at the base of my neck.

Suddenly, there's a shift.

How deep into the forest have we gone?

Leaves and pine needles...I don't know...they begin to *breathe*. They move and twirl, contorted by an invisible breeze. A breath that ebbs and pulses *through* my body.

Yet, the air is still.

A wave of ecstasy explodes in my chest, bursting like a water balloon. Slowly, seeping into each extremity.

I think I feel my own soul.

Our pace slows, and I realize our communication has regressed into subtle sounds. Mostly chuckles and pointing at things we think are...*interesting*.

We both offer each other only the most minimal affirmation. But it's enough.

Inundated with new stimuli, language is a passing fancy.

A fork in the trail doesn't even inspire conversation.

Glen and I lock eyes. He nods, and I follow him up a steep route that traverses a hillside of mauve stone, which seemingly returned from nowhere.

Between each giant boulder are steps, carved into the rock and held in place with more concrete.

It continues like this until we reach the top.

Here, the trees guard more of the view than they did on the steps. I regret not taking in the scene as we'd climbed.

Occasionally, patches open up for us, ushering us toward the destination Glen has in mind.

Without exchange, I know we've arrived at "Balanced Rock". A giant stone sat perfectly before a steep edge where we sit down in synchronized silence. The water and valley beneath our precariously dangling feet draw our gazes.

Yet, I have this odd sense of safety. Something in the ethos of the woods has found me, and seen me. I know in every fiber of my being that the forest's heart lies below at the center of this lake. This beautifully green-tinted lake with burgundy stones lining its shores.

The Sacred Lake.

The Spirit Lake.

I can feel it in the air.

I tell myself the spirit wraps me in its warm embrace, and I feel it. The sun's doppelgänger performs a dance upon the still stage of the lake far below us.

TRIP

Thank you.

In this blissful moment, something so beautiful and new, a tear works its way from my eye.

Once again, I'm smiling.

Through it all, I hear a voice. One I associate with the Lake. It fills me with optimism and hope.

For the first time in forever, I picture the future. A few more tears fall in congress.

7:33 Pm

It's a strange thing, *TRIPPING*.

Trying to translate the experience that an individual undergoes is probably more difficult than translating dead languages.

Thoughts, emotions, feelings, and perceptions bleed into one ubiquitous experience.

A language of exposure, of exploits.

All five—or even six, for the believers out there—senses roll into one, coalescing into an almost inescapable understanding of the human condition.

Yet it's not that uncommon.

Both mankind and even some animals have been altering their own consciousness for millennia.

It's possible that a young Ho-Chunk member, maybe an outcast like myself, once sat on this very ledge contemplating *their* place in this world. Maybe while on some rite of passage. A fast? A hallucinogen? Both?

I don't know, but it was oddly—what's the word—*satisfying?*

Maybe.

Who knows?

My fingers dig into the tiniest patch of soil exposed beneath the limestone.

What if the world's innate euphoria can seep in through my pores?

My body quivers in response to a gentle breeze riding through the air. It permeates through my chest, a spirit of nature passing through me.

With it, Nature's breath surgically removes every last ounce of negativity from my being. Offering a sanctuary in which to heal.

I can't say how long I've been smiling, but I am vaguely aware of a soreness in my cheeks at the renewed taxing of my atrophied smile muscles.

The trees in the valley and the water held within the lake breathe as I breathe.

Everything in this moment must be a part of one great organism. Functioning together to enjoy the pure ecstasy of conscious life.

I must sound like a complete nutter to the uninitiated, but I believe those who know would understand.

It's a euphoria beyond anything I've experienced.

I stifle a hereto subconscious impulse to check the time on my phone.

There's no time for time.

A *'Eureka!'* moment as crucial as when Pythagoras suggested his understanding of triangles.

Each moment is most important on its own.

It's the childlike wonderment of only concerning oneself with the present. Searching each instant for greater gratification.

And just like the restlessness of a child, there grows a point where the soul yearns for something new.

I see Glen has wandered off. I turn around to find him perched on a small boulder.

Concentrating on the valley below no longer holds the same degree of reverence.

This may be a moment for a little more inspiration.

I needn't be told more.

Instinctively, my hands work Ole Skeeter's paperback from my thigh pocket.

My fingers slide across the bound pages until something tells me to stop. Here, I flip open the text to a title that I can hardly pronounce, but I let intrigue spur me onward.

7:37 p M

P.14
THE WAKČÉXI OF TE WÁKĄČĄK

THE CREATOR NEVER BESTOWED A NAME UPON THE WAKČÉXI OR
WATER SPIRIT. SO, THE SPIRIT LIVED IN ANONYMITY UNTIL IT TOOK
RESIDENCE UPON THE HOLY LAKE [TE WÁKĄČĄK]. IRREVOCABLY, THE
NAMELESS SPIRIT BEGAN TO TAINT THE HOLY WATERS. FOR THE WATER
SPIRIT WAS A DIFFICULT SPIRIT, AS ARE THEY ALL, BUT THIS ONE,
INSULTED BY ITS NAMELESS EXISTENCE AND PLACING GRIEVANCE FOR ITS
CONCEPTION UPON THE CREATOR, SOUGHT REVENGE. UNTIL OUR TRIBE
SETTLED THIS RANGE, IT HAD NO OUTLET. ITS FESTERING WRATH FOUND
THE HOČĄGARA'S MERE PRESENCE A BLIGHT ON ITS HOME.

THE ANCESTORS SPOKE AND TOLD TALES OF A CREATURE THEY
CLAIMED POSSESSED A BRAIN NO BIGGER THAN A PEBBLE. YET THE
WATER SPIRIT WAS NOT DIM IN ITS INTELLECT. FOR THE BRAIN WAS ITS
SEAT OF LIFE, IT TOOK SPECIAL CONSIDERATION TO BIND THE SOURCE OF
ITS BEING SAFELY WITHIN THE INTERIOR OF A PEBBLE. THIS CORE
PELLET, THE SPIRIT HID DEEP WITHIN ITS MASSIVE SKULL. THOUGH
THAT WAS NOT ENOUGH FOR THE WAKČÉXI. THE BESTIAL SPIRIT'S
CUNNING INEVITABLY SPAWNED ANOTHER SIX HEADS MORE, CONCEALING

THE SEAT OF ITS EXISTENCE WITH THE CARE OF A STREET URCHIN HUSTLING ITS WAY THROUGH THREE-CARD MONTE.

AS OUR PEOPLE EXCHANGED SIGHTINGS OF THE SPIRIT, THOSE WHO BEHELD THE SWIMMING AMALGAMATION OF HEADS BELOW THE SURFACE WOULD NOTE THE SHIMMERING BRIGHT GREEN COLORING, INEVITABLY LEADING THE CHOSEN PEOPLE TO BESTOW A NAME FITTING OF THE VERDANT HUES UPON WHICH THE SPIRIT WAS KNOWN. HENCE, IT BECAME KNOWN TO THE HOČĄGARA AS "ČO."

KNOWING THE POWER OF A NAME, ČO SPOKE. AT FIRST, ONLY TO A MEDICINE MAN TO WHOM ČO OFFERED A PIECE OF ITSELF FOR THE MAN TO CURE HIS AILING DAUGHTER. GRATEFUL, THE MAN WOULD RETURN REGULARLY TO SPEAK WITH THE SPIRIT. BUT WHEN HE SOUGHT TO ASK FOR ANOTHER PIECE OF THE SPIRIT, ČO REFUSED. FOR IT WAS TOO WEAK TO PART WITH MORE OF ITSELF. IN TURN, THE MEDICINE MAN OFFERED RESTORATIVE ELIXIRS. BUT ČO REBUFFED THE MAN'S OFFERINGS WITH CLAIMS THAT THEY WOULD NOT DO TO RESTORE THE SPIRIT'S STRENGTH.

KNOWLEDGEABLE OF THE WATER SPIRIT'S POWER, THE MEDICINE MAN SOUGHT FRIENDSHIP WITH ČO THROUGH A SERIES OF OFFERINGS. SEEING AS ČO WAS GRACIOUS, IT LEARNED THE MAN IN ALL THAT COULD BE ACCOMPLISHED WITH THE POWER OF ČO'S BODY. FOR THE SPIRIT COULD REGENERATE ITS STRENGTH. HOWEVER, IT SOUGHT SOMETHING MORE FROM THE MEDICINE MAN. ONLY FLESH WOULD HEAL FLESH, AND THE FLESH OF SOME WAS PREFERABLE TO THAT OF OTHERS. SO, ČO PETITIONED TO SPEAK WITH THE CHIEF IN EXCHANGE FOR ANOTHER OFFERING TO THE MEDICINE MAN.

WITH SILVER WORDS, THE MEDICINE MAN CONVINCED THE CHIEF TO GRANT AN AUDIENCE WITH THE WATER SPIRIT. UPON THE WATER'S EDGE, HE LISTENED AS THE SPIRIT PROMISED A YEAR'S WORTH OF MEDICINE FOR THE TRIBE. IN RETURN, ČO WOULD REQUIRE A SACRIFICE TO RESTORE ITS FLESH. THE ONLY FITTING OFFERING, IT CLAIMED, WOULD BE THAT OF THE TRIBE'S MOST BEAUTIFUL MAIDEN. SPURRED BY THE GREED OF MAN, FOR THE CHIEF HAD NEVER KNOWN THE PRIVILEGE OF RAISING A DAUGHTER, HE ACCEPTED THE BARGAIN.

A CENTURY PASSED UNTIL THE GREAT RIVER CHILD WAS BORN AND MATURED. OUR PEOPLE'S HERO. RAISED UNDER THE WATCHFUL GAZE OF

PROPHECY FROM THE STURGEON WHICH SACRIFICED ITS OWN BONES TO BIRTH RIVER CHILD.

"THE RIVER SHALL SWALLOW THE LAKE."

THEN CAME THE NIGHT WHEN RIVER CHILD'S LOVE WAS TO BE THE SPIRIT'S NEXT OFFERING. WITHOUT HESITATION, RIVER CHILD TORE THROUGH THE WATERS, HIS TRUSTY NET IN HAND. HE TORMENTED THE BEAST INTO A GREAT AND POWERFUL STRUGGLE. FOR THE SAKE OF HIS LOVE, RIVER CHILD PLUNGED HIS GREAT KNIFE INTO WHERE ČO SEQUESTERED ITS MIND, DESECRATING THE SPIRIT'S BODY IN AN INSTANT.

THOUGH IT NO LONGER POSSESSED CORPOREAL FORM, IT IS SAID THAT ČO'S SPIRIT REMAINS TRAPPED IN A PRISON BELOW THE SURFACE OF THE LAKE. SOME SAY THEY STILL HEAR ITS HORRID SHRIEKS WHENEVER A THUNDERSTORM SHOULD ROLL IN ON THE WINGS OF THE BEAST'S MORTAL ENEMIES, THE *THUNDERBIRDS*.

7:50 pm

THE NUMBERS ON MY PHONE SCREEN LOOK STRANGE WHEN I CHECK.

"Something new, mate?" Glen's hand rests on my shoulder. I can't say how long it's been there.

"Yeah." I slide the device back into my pocket, along with the paperback.

Looking down at the water, and its green tint, I think about čo. About its manipulation. Why would a great spirit live to torment?

Though, I do understand the whole, 'insulted by its own existence' thing.

Yes. Existence without purpose is torment.

There's an idea there. It feels pre-ordained, divine even.

It's becoming increasingly difficult to communicate the multitude of swimming thoughts dancing like dolphins at play through my mind.

Everything that needs comprehending courses throughout my brain as if the thing weren't a segmented processing machine. Instead, operating as a giant interconnected pool. Overflowing the assembly line, until the workers fail to keep up.

Too many metaphors. Or were they similes?

Focus.

As we walk, my fixation turns toward the world around me.

How did people create language?

What if I were dropped into a universe of...*things*? Stuff I'd never seen before? Mind erased and incapable of acknowledging any foundational memory? How would I name a tree, a leaf, water, or rock?

I see myself pick up a palm-sized stone, knowing I need some sort of redirection, but I want to *name* it.

What if all rocks were teds? Leaves were...fluusseses.

So stupid.

Easing away from the cliffs into the woods, Glen motions me off the trail.

It feels like the right move as my feet forgo the path's structure. We create and explore our own paths—like creating our own language.

I think how exciting this is. Exploring the uncharted.

I have no fear either.

We have cell phones, food, and water. Glen has a compass and a map in his bag, maybe even a gun. I can't be sure he's brought it. Regardless, even in the worst-case scenarios, it's calming to know we should be prepared for whatever comes our way.

We are on an actual adventure.

My feet navigate it all on their own.

There are downed logs, boulders, and the occasional ominously bulbous pile of leaves that requires every fiber of restraint to resist leaping into.

Along the way, we stop here and there to observe our surroundings. We stare at singular leaves and trees. We become infatuated with life above, as birds and squirrels traverse about.

There's one squirrel in particular that we watch race up and down trees, wild and spastic.

"Okay, so he's like the secret agent squirrel." I follow Glen's train of thought perfectly. "And he's scurrying around trying to catch a terrorist. A bird that just flew off after assassinating the—the squirrel ambassador to *Birddom.*"

Through laughter, I add, "Agent *McNutt.*"

Pride swells as the story unfurls from my lips.

"He knew that time was of the essence. He threw his body from tree limb to tree limb, his safety never guaranteed. But, at this point, his entire race was far from safe. If the squirrels took the fall during this unprecedented time of peace, it would ruin all he had worked so hard for."

"I hear Agent McNutt is only a few days from retirement as well."

"He had already purchased his retirement cabin on the lake! But that won't stop him from getting the bastard who assassinated the Ambassador. Because, now, this was personal."

"So the truth comes out? The Ambassador was McNutt's—younger, half-brother, *Oakley*?"

"*Unfortunately*. Which is why Forrest McNutt Jr. is putting everything on the line now. He knows his wife and kids would understand his inability to rest if this monster got away. There would be no retirement until this crisis was averted. He has the little ones' futures in mind. A consummate forward thinker, there was no way he could allow his sons to be dragged into a war that he knew he could prevent. The thought of generational war is not something he wants for his future grandchildren."

"What a squirrel. Just like his father, am I right?"

"Too true Glen, too true. Forrest Sr. had been a squirrel amongst squirrels..."

Suddenly, Agent McNutt leaps through the air.

As his four limbs spread out in shadow against the peaking sky above, Glen and I simultaneously hold our collective breath. There's this palpable silence in the air as Glen takes my arm in a death grip of apprehension. Anxiety courses from him to me as fear grips us in the wait for what will happen to our protagonist.

The distance is too far!

His tiny paws flail as he comes up shy of the branch he was aiming for. The gesture sends him tumbling end over end through the air.

Glen's gripping my arm even tighter.

Agent McNutt somehow manages to snag the sapling end of another branch extending several feet below his target. His tiny paw clings to the limb for dear life, suspending him in mid-air.

Glen and I watch on and cheer.

But Agent McNutt can't get another paw up.

As he dangles from just the one, visible panic courses through the critter. Each time he sways, it looks like he'll fall and he aborts the awkward motion. He's shaking harder and harder, trying to reach one more paw, any paw, to purchase and steady himself along the branch. The entire limb sways with his overwrought movements.

He's not going to be able to hold.

Suddenly, Agent McNutt loses his grip.

Once more, the squirrel tumbles through empty space.

Both Glen and I cry out a synchronized, *"No!"*

The sound of his body hitting the ground beneath a pile of leaves that swallows him whole zaps my heart with a jolt of pain.

The air is still, and we can't believe what we've just witnessed.

Suddenly, our hero rockets outward with an explosion of dried leaves. Unscathed, he darts across the forest floor like nothing happened.

Before long, he's scurrying up another tree, off to save the squirrel world.

We share a laugh before continuing our journey deeper into the woods.

3:11 PM

HUNGER IS NOT A SENSATION PLAGUING ME WHEN GLEN TAKES A SNACK break.

"We need to eat," he says, jogging over to a craggy boulder covered with drips of moss.

It is a good-looking boulder, though. The urge to climb it is there, so I follow him regardless of hunger or not.

"Need" feels like a strong word, anyway.

I can't say I'm much of anything, let alone hungry.

I'm basically Nothing, and Nothing doesn't *need* anything.

However, if I *am* anything, I'm something *simple*. Maybe a thing so simple that consciousness is new to it. The fledgling mind to which thoughts consume. But it's encased in this body. So, it's more like I'm this conscious meat husk wandering around the woods on autopilot.

Glen sits cross-legged atop the flat of the jagged boulder.

I'm not quite sure when he made it up there, but it should be simple enough to navigate.

I place a hand on the blue-ish-grey stone and in an instant it ripples beneath my touch. The leaves in its shadow begin breathing at my feet, and I can feel their exhalations in my chest. It's a moment bordering on *too vivid*. The grooves and edges of the boulder's face swim and swirl. A wave of euphoric ecstasy cascades through my entire body from head to toe. It's rooting me to where I stand.

If I let go...If I try to move...

You will fall.

Simple breathing exercises. That's all I need. Not necessarily something done for its calming effects, but to orient me.

I'm spinning, flooding. Panic wants to envelop me before joy can jostle it away.

I haven't felt this good in so long.

Not since...Gabi?

Now why would I go and think that?

The tears start without warning. It's not a sob. My tear ducts simply open wide. Undeterred, the salty liquid travels down my cheeks.

Happy tears?

When was the last time I cried out of happiness?

The tears become a gentle brook, reminding me that life gets better. That my happiness didn't end with Gabi's end.

That it was never my fault...

That there is plenty in life to live for.

It all seems so profound. Like discovering the meaning of life, or a lost civilization, or how many licks it takes to get to the center of a Tootsie-Pop.

Above me, Glen appears fixated on his own reverie. The serenity of his features births another wave of joy.

We have both found these solitary pockets of time for ourselves amidst everything else in the world. Here, in these fractal moments, the only thing that matters is embracing the present and everything that comes with it.

I look to the sky and notice the bright light of the sun tiptoeing across the treetops. Leaves flutter in the breeze, and so too does the sun. Its warm corona picturesquely framed beyond the canopy.

Lolling my head side to side, I bask in the glow, allowing it all to seep through me.

The idea that humans are independent of one another envelops me. As much as each and every one of us relies on one another for love, food, and shelter, our experiences are entirely our own. We all see and perceive the world through a distinct set of eyes, living experiences we take for granted as being universal.

However, under the right circumstances, we can share. We can communicate, but to do so—we need language.

And we've gone full circle.

The face of the boulder suddenly becomes easy to navigate.

Making quick work of the lips and crevices, I reach the top. There, Glen remains stoic.

Though I want to disturb him, I don't want to rob him of these precious moments. There is plenty of space for the two of us to enjoy the plateau.

There's an instant. It's brief but permanent. I have my character's name.

Cliff.

It felt maternal, no, paternal.

No, neither is right. It's as if he's introduced himself to me.

But I love it. The name feels right coming off the connection between teeth and lips.

Cliff.

Simultaneously, it doesn't. Maybe it's a nickname.

Like Clint.

Irrespective, I see Cliff and all his fundamental failings. I allow my pen to trace these running thoughts to my notepad.

Things like smoking and drinking are gaping character flaws to some, but not others. He will enjoy both to the brink of moderation and like most flawed humans, occasionally in excess. A coping mechanism for the trials of a life lived. Shortcomings that will set others off, while keeping him relatable and human.

I feel like a man with this nature needs religion as well. Not church every Sunday religion, but a cross on his neck and a prayer most days, kind of guy.

I think about Cliff's relationship with religion, and I find it difficult to follow this thread. My lack of religious beliefs doesn't give me much to go on. However, I 'm certain he must have some tie to the grand mythos of the universe.

I attended church as a kid, but it was never a priority, and when my parents split and stopped forcing me, I stopped going.

But this worm of a memory works its way into the present.

Tammy Shupe. She was the girl whose sister died in that house fire.

Why am I thinking of Tammy Shupe?

Then it all clicks into place.

Tammy started coming to church after her sister died in that fire. She was always late and seemed like the first to leave. She just needed that hit of religion to connect her to the sister she'd lost.

That's what Cliff needed. It was the tie that bound him to a lost brother or son.

Maybe grandson...

We are all independent creatures, needing to design our own reality. Our way of coping with the personal traumas of our existence.

A book or a sermon can't dictate those strategies, the person themselves has to assimilate them. But there are those occasional nuggets of wisdom and advice from those who lived before us.

That's what Tammy, and now Cliff, held out for.

If nothing more, what they have in common is the fact that they somehow found sanctuary and comfort in turning to a higher power in times of need. A despondent man raised in that realm might cling to those things during dark times.

"How you doing, G?"

The words rock me from the reality I had been working in.

Down on the page in my hand, the letters wave back and forth, uprooting the lines they are written atop as if signaling a farewell from whatever world I'd just left.

What world will you enter next?

3:45 pm

THERE'S THIS SENSE OF PASSING THROUGH CHECKPOINTS.

It's like being on a cross-country road trip and not remembering the entire drive. Instead, only recalling the change from rural highway to interstate. Or the stops made along the way to take in the world's biggest thimble, or whatever.

Or that time you saw that car wreck. With the overturned mint-colored station wagon.

There was so much blood. I wasn't supposed to look. Mom told me not to look.

So, don't look.

For the hallucinogenic trip, that's almost as effective as the switch of an optometrist's lens.

"You still good?" Glen stares like he's already asked this question.

"Really good man. This stuff is great."

"I know it, mate. I'm having one of the best trips of my life. How's the writing?"

"I think I've got my protagonist."

"That's wonderful, mate."

A slurring lull drags between us.

It's both peaceful and enjoyable. There isn't the awkwardness that Silence occasionally allows to accompany it.

The wind sweeps through the forest in melodic whispers, finding a chorus among the leaves.

"So, what does the writer do next?"

"I don't know man. I've never been here. I could go to the water. The water might feel really good."

Glen says nothing.

Not that he needs to. His face is littered with tells that he's itching to say something.

"Glen, you okay man?"

He slowly comes back. A resolute line forms across the eyebrows hovering above eyes teeming with conviction. "Can I tell you something?"

"Sure man, anything."

A deep breath draws into his billowing cheeks and chest. Then he exhales.

"I can't swim."

My brain wants to reject the idea.

Flabbergasted is a word that comes to mind.

Glen practically lives on the largest lake in the entire country. His social media is jam-packed with photos at the beach.

Something clicks...

Vacant are the slots where memories of him getting into the water should be. At least not past his ankles.

I recall this afternoon jumping into the water to give myself a shock.

Glen stood there cupping his hands.

A weird feeling washes over me.

It reminds me of the lake washing over me this morning. It entered my pores. It filled me.

But Glen.

Glen.

I can't betray Glen.

I cannot betray my friend's vulnerability. I can't allow him to have a bad trip. You should worry about yourself.

You, Galen. Could have a bad trip. For you. It'd be so easy.

Fuck you, Galen.

"That's okay man. We don't have to go down to the lake. Once is enough for the day. Let's do the opposite then." My eyes scan the scenery, trying to discover our next attraction.

About five hundred yards away stands a cliff face that must lead to one of the highest points in the park. I imagine how, from that vantage, we'll be able to see beyond just the lake valley.

It'll be inspiring.

"Let's go up. That looks cool." My finger points to the top of the rock face, and Glen smiles with an affirmative nod. It seems as if he might be on the verge of tears and that talking will be difficult.

It doesn't feel any easier for me.

So, I lead our descent from the boulder in deferential silence.

3:5⧈ pM

Navigating the trail-less woods would be difficult under normal circumstances, yet somehow, everything seems to go our way.

The cliff face, with its moss and colorful crags, lures us closer and closer.

Glen points out a few trodden-through areas that he calls "game trails." The padded down treks lead one way before veering off in others. They make for convenient paths until they twist and turn away from our destination.

It isn't a sheer drop, but the gradient is steep. Yet, as long as everything is solid, I'm not sensing any apprehension from Glen.

Or myself, for that matter.

He calls our upcoming adventure '*mountaineering*' as we reach the base of the stone wall. I guess that makes me feel better. Knowing it's a thing enough people do that it has a name.

Except we're in Wisconsin, and this is hardly a mountain.

Wrapping my fingers around a comforting bit of rock feels right in my hand. A coursing sensation fills my breast as I pull and step upward to the next hold.

The lizard brain takes control as all four limbs crawl up the side of this hill.

I feel like a predator moving in silence. Cautiously stalking its next meal.

We traverse horizontally as much as we do vertically to keep going. Occasionally, I have to stop Glen from climbing up into me.

Nearing the top, Glen catches my boot to point out stunning little bits of nature.

Like a large tree growing perpendicular out of the stone wall's face. It's almost like watching a petulant child defy the world as it stretches for the sun.

Suddenly, a large red-tailed hawk swoops down and perches itself on one of the thick branches we are admiring. It is a deadly majestic creature, and it's *so* damn close.

My eyes draw first to the bright black talons curving out of stunningly yellow feet.

Then to the creature's eyes, almost just as yellow, wrapped around drops of black ink.

It's watching us.

The curve of its beak is a lethal angle. Perfect for piercing and tearing.

The evolution of nature, ensuring that the strong are rewarded.

I'm fixated on it, and it's fixated on me. It's studying me. Part of me wants it to come at me.

Challenge me. Test my metal.

I dare you.

This stare-down seems to last an eternity.

Until the winged raptor scoffs with a disapproving squawk.

It unfolds giant wings before gliding down toward an opening in the tree-tops. It dives with ferocity, breaking through the canopy, and I can't help but wonder what it could have possibly seen from all the way up here.

The remainder of the climb is uneventful.

At the top, I pull myself over the edge and roll across the choppy outcrop of limestone.

Resting on my back, I realize how sopping wet I am.

The giggles hit.

How had I not realized that I sweat so much?

A hit of euphoria carries me away on its giggling wings. So, there I lay, while Glen clambers over the edge.

I close my eyes to calm myself, and it works gradually.

I'm surprised to hear Glen's footsteps muffle off behind me.

He's continuing on his own journey, which means it's a-okay for me to stay on mine.

My head swims with ideas about Cliff.

Like poor ole Alice, I find myself falling further and further toward Euphoria's burrow. Ideas are slipping through my grasp. Any concerted attempts to focus prove futile.

It's as if they're not my own.

No, they all belong to you, Galen.

They're moving too fast through my head, sifting through my proverbial fingertips.

I need to capture some buzzwords or something. So at the very least sober-me has a chance of interpreting the flood of thoughts later on.

Unfortunately, he'll have a hell of a time just trying to decode my handwriting.

I'm not sure if this is a hallucination or not, but through the waves and curls of the psychedelic visions, I get the sense that my handwriting has taken on a peculiar style.

Is your hand unsteady?

Or am I too high?

You need a diversion.

You should probably open your eyes...

Ц: ⊐ ☺ þ℔

My hands tear at my hair, any grip I can get on reality to stop the flooding of my brain.

I feel like this is what it'd be like to be caught in a whirlpool. Gasping for breath as I fight the gripping waves pulling me down.

The world around seems to constrict, swallowing me within my mind.

Nothing makes sense.

Then I start rolling across the detritus of the forest floor.

I feel the need to throw a temper tantrum. To scream.

But the rolling, it's just made me aware of something. I stab my hand into my thigh pocket, ravenous for stimuli, my fingertips tear Skeeter's book from its seclusion, and I thank my stars for something to fixate on.

P. 3
Who Are the Hočągara

The Sacred Voice People, The People of the Big Voice, and The Sacred Voice People of the Pines are all loose translations of the Hočąk language for the name that the Hočągara were given by Earthmaker, the creator of all things.

4:2夕Pm

No.

　Too much.

　My phone is in hand.

　How quickly we fall into our worst habits. I don't need a history lesson. But I don't need to be on my phone either.

　I need a story.

4:30 pm

P. 37
WAKJĄKAGA & WAŠJĮKEGA

SHIT. I KNOW IT'S NOT GIBBERISH, BUT HELL IF I CAN PRONOUNCE IT.

Walk-jun-kaw-guh & Wash-jean-kay-guh.

The unfamiliar tones of confident whispers assure me that's the correct pronunciation. There's no way the psychedelic isn't playing a part.

The euphoria of this trip hales from an entirely different cosmos from which—

There I go, getting all Lovecraftian.

If not for the paperback in my lap, I would like to explore the existential repercussions of my soul forming a consciousness of its own within the shell of my body.

This makes for a daunting endeavor, reading, but I pick through passages that stand out to me, often needing to reread the different sections with intentional focus.

I've gathered that Walker Texas Ranger is the patron Trickster of the Ho-Chunk, and Wash Jeans is his little brother, also known as Hare.

Walk-jun-kaw-guh & Wash-jean-kay-guh.
I KNOW.

...

Both brothers were supposed to serve as protectors of the Ho-Chunk tribe and all mankind.

Amongst the "Earthmaker's" children, these were two of the few spirits created in the likeness of man. But both could alter their appearance on a whim.

Reminds me of Loki.

Reading on, I learn poor old Trickster winds up relegated from his post as guardian over the "People of The Big Voice" because he enjoyed deceiving and subsequently playing tricks on humans. A bit too much.

But he was the Earthmaker's firstborn, so big EM took pity on the Trickster, and bestowed on his son a station in the heavens.

If I understand correctly, he essentially became a St. Peter-type figure, ushering the souls of the deceased to their next destination.

Unlike the man watching the pearly gates, Trickster, on occasion, circumvents the laws that bind him to his station and sneaks down to Earth, where he can spread mischief among mankind and spirits alike.

Hare, on the other hand, was the baby of the deity spirit family.

Like most last-born children, he had a rebellious streak but cared dearly for mankind and tried to give them immortality.

An idiotic gift.
I sure as hell don't want to live forever.

...

stop.

I know this may not be the most enthralling read of all time, but there is something here. Almost as if it wants me to discover it. Something about myths, legends, and lore always grips my attention tightly.

But the next passages give me pause, sending an electric chill down my spine.

HARE LONGED TO JOIN HIS ELDEST BROTHER, TRICKSTER. HOWEVER, ONLY MANKIND JOINED THE PROTECTOR OF PARADISE ABOVE. AS HE SOUGHT A WAY TO JOIN THE RANKS OF MAN, THE DARK VOICE BENEATH THE SURFACE OF SPIRIT LAKE TANTALIZED HARE, CONVINCING THE

YOUNG SPIRIT TO SEEK OUT THE CHIEF'S DAUGHTER. THE VOICE WITHIN THE WATER SPOKE OF HARE GIVING HIS FLESH TO THE WOMAN, AND IN RETURN, SHE WOULD USHER HIM INTO THE HALLS OF MAN.

UNFORTUNATELY FOR MAN, HARE'S ACTIONS HAD CONSEQUENCES. DEATH CAME INTO OUR WORLD AS HARE NO LONGER RETAINED THE POWER TO STOP THE MALEVOLENT FORCE OF THE COSMOS. WITH DEATH'S ULTIMATE FOE HAVING GROWN MORTAL, HUMAN MORTALITY BECAME PERMANENT. DEATH DREW STRENGTH FROM HARE'S BITTER-NESS AND SADNESS UNTIL DEATH BECAME ROOTED TO THE MORTAL WORLD. HARE WAS FORCED TO WATCH AS THOSE AROUND HIM WERE CONSUMED BY PLAGUE, FAMINE, WAR, AND ALL THE PERVERSE ACTIONS OF MANKIND.

Images swirl in my head of a Jester God and a man with bunny ears. Both clad in Indigenous garb, yet separated from one another across planes of existence.

Sympathy for the Jester roars through me. Practically shackled to his station as that green demon—

čo

—lurks down in the lake below. Playing devilish games that permitted Death to infest the world, tormenting The Trickster's younger brother.

It also reminds me of Tammy Shupe.

That helplessness. That despair.

What do I have to be depressed about?

Nothing. Yet, here you are.

Here I am.

Ⴑl:Ⴑl8 ꝑηη

"Hey mate, I found a trail back here. I think it's a people trail."

⎿|:⎿|ꞯ ℘ηη

GLEN HEADS OUR TWO-MAN CARAVAN, WHILE I DRIFT INTO SILENT consort with myself.

The "vibe."

What about it?

I don't know, it's just like. Ugh, how do I say this? It's in control.

Expound.

*It's the—**author** of this experience. It sets the mood, the tone, and it knows the destination. So if I listen, I'll find my way.*

Listening. That's something you're good at...

Shut it.

I know it's a subconscious tick, but I shake my head as if in an attempt to fling the thought away like a spider.

Euphoria once more swells in my breast like a deep, aching familial love.

This trip feels like it will last forever.

But it won't.

I know. It's just—What am I trying to say? I want to enjoy this as long as I can. I know there will be a point where what we're doing won't feel "right."

...

It just feels like a bigger, more existential decision.

What's your point?

Isn't there a strange philosophy in that?

...

It's like—see, every decision we make is a decision we—like have to live with and should be a decision we are comfortable with. Even though decisions may seem small, they can have an exponential impact on our lives, far beyond the moment we are in.

The Butterfly Effect.

Yeah. Exactly. Like, I think how Dr. Malcolm explains chaos theory with a droplet of water on the hand in Jurassic Park. You never know where it's going to fall.

4:56 Pm

I LOVE SEEING NUMBERS IN A ROW LIKE THAT.

The odd satisfaction calms the ping-ponging of my thoughts. The world around me shifts and breathes a sigh of relief in unison with my phone returning to its pocket.

The sun is in the lower third of the sky. We still have plenty of daylight left to explore and appreciate, but it seems so abjectly clear that we have transitioned into a different act of the day.

The trail seems to agree. Through my inebriated eyes, I see the path slither as if beckoning us to follow.

Regardless of hallucinations, I'm fairly certain this is not a manicured path like most trails.

But it's not a game trail either.

Something tells me there has been human influence.

There are no consistent boundaries. It widens, then narrows with overgrowth. Yet, trees have been removed. Thick and thin trunks alike display saw-blade scars.

Except it's inconsistent. Several monstrous oaks grow diagonally through the trail unscathed.

Ahead, Glen treats the course as a game. He's ducking and weaving around limbs and vines. It looks fun.

Might as well join.

I feel like a kid again. Playing pretend diamond heist, dipping beneath lasers, contorting through obstacles in search of the golden Fabergé egg.

Enjoy the journey.

A wave of optimism tells me that even if I don't have a flushed-out story come tomorrow, I may have my smile back. Maybe it's the vibe taking control, but I have this overwhelming sense that the payoff from today will be monumental.

Glen has soldiered on ahead of me. Thankfully, he's stopped up ahead.

Bathed in an orange glow from above, I can't help but think how he once again reminds me of a curious puppy. His head cocked to the side. His eyes wide and joyful. I feel bad for ever writing him off.

Glen truly is my best friend.

But are you his?

I run up and notice the wide clearing in the canopy overhead.

We have this little pocket of space, all to ourselves, and without a word, we seem to agree it's as good a place as any for another break.

Glen encourages me to have some water and a snack.

I oblige. Slowly.

There's something gnawing at me, and I'm trying to figure out what it is while enjoying a granola bar.

Taking a seat on a short stunted log, something—Clint's book—slaps the back of my thigh from inside its pocketed home.

"Hey, Glen?"

"Yeah, mate?"

"What is it that you like about the new guy's book?"

"What new guy?"

"You know, the one that writes about making the drugs?"

"Oh, Arnie?"

"No, uh...R. Nold, or whoever wrote *DROPOUTS*?"

Glen seems lost, as if he doesn't know who or where he is.

"Oh fuck, that's right, Arnie's just what I call him. Yeah, R. Nold."

He's just staring back at me. Well, more through me. His puppy dog face turns to confusion rather than curiosity this time.

"Uh, sorry, what was the question again?"

Hahahaha. Shit.

I must be returning an equally confused gaze because lucidity is escaping me. I cannot for the life of me remember what I had asked.

"Right!" he blurts out. "What's it that I like about that book? Well, it's just like...You know how you like writing the hero's journey? Well, for him it's the villain's. It's sort of, well, this evolution, you know?"

A deafening roar of cicadas fills the silence.

"He's, er, the protagonist's just some college kid, who, well—well, he becomes a straight-up villain. But the enticing part of the character's development is that he doesn't see himself that way. Despite all the horrible things he does, he continues leading the reader astray. It's just a twisted tale, mate. I mean, the protagonist thinks he's a good guy. Never realizing he's the villain of the story. So, you begrudgingly root for him for a bit, and well, you *will* feel bad doing it. But still, you *will* root for him. Despite all those horrible things. It really just kinda fucked with me as I read it. It was one of those stories you read, and know you gotta offer representation quickly."

I thought on that.

"People are complicated."

Real esoteric thinking there.

I don't know why I said that, or even what it meant in context. Was I referring to Glen, R. Nold the author, the character in *DROPOUTS*, or maybe myself?

5:07 PM

THE IMPETUS FOR AN IDEA SLAPS ME ACROSS THE FACE AS IF IT'S BEEN staring at me, waiting patiently to be noticed. Until it could no longer put up with my pea-brained attention span.

"Can I share the idea I'm working with?"

"Of course, mate! Why else we here?"

He has a point. A poorly worded point.

I chuckle. "Okay, so, you kind of just gave me the idea to finish it out. But, so, I want the protagonist to be an older guy who goes by Cliff, who's like Clint. So, his real name is..." I check my notes, and it's written there.

But I don't remember writing it.

"Harlow Fogarty?" I'm not quite sure why it came out as a question, but Glen notices it too, and just laughs.

Don't dwell on it. Move on.

"Anyway, he's this old dude who seems stereotypical, but like, you find out quickly he doesn't make great decisions. He's guided by beliefs of doing things that bring him satisfaction and align with like, I don't know, his innate sense of religious obligation and moral foundation. A classic loose cannon who plays by their own set of rules. But for him life changes after his brother dies, and he'd, like—go down some rabbit hole, becoming some sort of disgraced cop or PI. Or a PI who is a disgraced cop. I don't know which. Still working things out here."

"You just want to call him a 'Dic' don't you?"

I hadn't thought about that part, but it could make for some slightly irreverent humor. "That's just an added bonus." I chuckle and jot a note down.

I feel good. I feel strong. I feel—

Healed.

"Anyway, he'd, like, somehow, come across this kid, like late teens, sixteen to nineteen, somewhere in there. But the kid is a straight-up sociopath. Cliff makes poor decisions, sure, but he's a flawed human, and like, he knows that. This kid, *'Trip—'"*

"Oh yeah, I like that keep going." Genuine intrigue tints his eyes.

It nourishes the euphoria. One which blossomed the moment the name *'Trip'* left my lips. Maybe it was the fact that I am absolutely, intensely, no-holds-bar tripping, but the name feels—*predestined?*

No, that's not the right word.

It feels like—*something.*

I don't know what, though.

Maybe *obvious* was the right word. It's like I've known the name my whole life, only to have lost it on the tip of my tongue all these years.

A vignette of hyper-fixation settles over my mind. Permitting only a single track for my attention span.

Glen's childlike wonderment feeds the fixation.

"Okay, so Trip is like, um, she's just like this sociopath of a kid."

"*She?*"

I look down at my notes.

Yep, it says *she.* Not to mention, I have a name written.

Mara L. Cantrip.

Weird, why would I use that name?

I don't remember writing this either, but I don't remember writing a lot of this.

Trip *is* right there in the name. Seems fitting that I'd go to a name I know first. But I should probably change it. After all, I don't want people thinking—

Glen clears his throat as he sits waiting patiently.

My best buddy.

My emotional support dog.

"Sorry. Okay—"

"No worries, mate, go on."

I don't mind him cutting me off. There's this grin plastered on my face. I can feel the soreness of it in my cheeks.

"So, yeah, *she's* often very glib but can be charismatic and charming when she needs to be. She's manipulative to a point that most people would pass off any peculiarities about her character, attitude, and habits as just another teenage phase. Slowly, the reader learns the kid's fucked up back story of, like, abuse and whatnot. Just adding to the passable peculiarities because people would say, '*Oh, she's so well adjusted, despite...*' But, you learn all of this through Cliff's detective work, which he is not being paid to do. There's something that has propelled him to look into her—

"*Oh shit!* I got it." My hand scribbles fervently.

"Cliff's world collides with Trip's during a straightforward, mundane case that he had been hired to do. Something like having to track down a lost, no wait, *stolen* puppy. The book then becomes this, like, chess match between Cliff and Trip. Cliff's unorthodox methods, which had normally been his biggest asset, become his glaring weaknesses, ya know?

"Cuz, Trip, she can, like, manipulate things to make it look like Cliff is responsible for her wrongdoings, which are escalating. And to most, ya know, Trip, she's just this kid. Maybe shy and awkward, but she can't be this horrific sociopath that Cliff is trying to paint her as. Ultimately coming to a climax in a head-to-head match of sorts during the third act.

"I can see it playing out where Trip will have to die at Cliff's hands. She'll use some belief that Cliff would never do it because she's just this kid. But Cliff's going to be the, ya know, um, martyr. Yeah, he's the martyr. Because he just knows, or it's revealed, I guess, that by killing Trip, there will be no evidence, or like, *anything*, to implicate her. We'll end on Cliff going to prison not only for all of *her* crimes but as a child murderer, not the protector that he and the reader know him to be."

A natural pause allows for the ignition of one final thought.

"Or maybe we don't say he *knows*, but hopes. Maybe details aren't always clear? Maybe the tale is a limited third-person narrative where the reader has to decide for themselves? Was our protagonist right in what he did, or did he make a huge *mistake*?"

That last word, *mistake*, hangs in the air before me like a spirit. Haunting and irrevocable.

"Fuck."

Oh no.

He hates it.

It could have been a good fuck...

Or a bad one...

The quiet of our little sunny bubble goes from peaceful to unsettling.

How long has the music been gone? When was the last time I heard it?

Anxiously awaiting what *'fuck'* means in this context, my hands busy themselves. I scribble what I can grasp of new and fleeting ideas. If only the lines on the page would sit still. But they refuse.

I abandon the current page for a blank one, and scribble with reckless abandon. All the while, I can feel this lone thought eating away at my mind.

Had Glen uttered the curse because he was realizing this was a waste of time?

Or a holy shit, that's great, 'fuck?'

Glen looks like he's settling on the words to use. I am absolutely terrified of what they'll be.

All excitement and euphoria drain from my pores. A light sweat coats my entire body. There's a primal need to steel myself against the rejection I am near certain is about to come.

Glen sucks in a breath of air.

"Okay, mate. I'm certain that the fact my mind is swimming in itself right now is a large part of this, but I think if you can pull that story off, anti-hero versus villain, and nobody really wins, well that's the kind of shit people are scared to write. It's not going to be fuckin' easy but nothing worth doing is.

"Everything's gotta have a fuckin' happy ending these days. Even these stories of villains tend to have happy fuckin' endings in a sense. The villain just rides off into the sunset or is defeated by the antagonist good guy."

The cicadas chirp louder.

"But, *fuck*. Mate, this shit's different. I can't say I know this story. I can't say I've read it in a different medium either. I mean, there's always been tales of the anti-hero, but they're not usually older. I don't know. Fuck, this is like..."

A groan whistles through his lips.

"I don't know, I'm too fucking high. And making the villain a teenage girl. Fuckin' *brilliant*, mate." He punctuates a groan with an endearing grin before adding, "I need a smoke."

ちゎヨ දက

WE SIT THERE PEACEFULLY SMOKING.

The soundtrack of the forest plays its melody all around us. The sensations of the nicotine and LSD collide in an electrifying euphoria.

I think back to this morning and how this moment now is a dramatically better experience.

"Glen, one more question?"

"Sure mate, anything?"

"Why'd you bring a gun?"

There's the uncomfortable silence.

The vibe has changed.

This is all I can feel. The unsettling atmosphere of looming change. Frozen on its precipice.

Bet you regret asking now.

You're such an idiot.

Why don't I just ki—

Stop.

My heart races as Glen's soft eyes scan me up and down.

I don't know why, but something ancient is clawing with unrestrained frenzy at my innards.

Fear.

With a deep inhale, he says quite calmly, "So, you saw that, eh?"

I nod. My teeth are ground so tightly together, it's as if my jaw is wired shut.

He exhales, and time seems to restart. As if the entire world had held its collective breath in anticipation of what was coming.

"I didn't want to make you nervous and potentially cause a bad trip if you knew I had it, but there's a potential that we could see some sort of wolf, big cat, or even bear out here. And I wanted to have protection. But my dumb ass left it in the bag at camp, so I don't even have it with me."

Something dawns on him. "That's why my bag was out this morning," he says, looking back to the fraction of a cigarette nestled between his forefingers. "You knew I'd have smokes, you wanted the smokes, and saw the gun. Shit, probably felt the damn thing, since it's just so fuckin' heavy. Am I right?"

I can't help but laugh. Relief consumes the vibe.

Of course, it's probably not great that there's a loose firearm at our campsite, but that's someone else's problem.

"You seem relieved?"

"Hell yeah, I'm relieved. Animals don't scare me. Guns do. Don't you know about Chekhov's Gun?"

"Gun in the first act, fires in the next? Yeah."

He laughs with that uproarious chortle of his.

"You writers, always a flare for the dramatic, allowing it to breathe into your everyday lives. Though we've already left the first act, wouldn't you say? So, unless you've seen some predator that I missed, then yeah, you're probably right. We've got more to fear from the gun, Ole Man Clint, or hell, even Agent McNutt."

We both reel over, laughing uncontrollably.

The thought of tiny squirrel guns in tiny squirrel paws sends me into a fit that I know will make my abs sore in the morning.

I can't say how long this goes on, but my sides already ache when it's all said and done.

Seeing that it has gone out, I go to flick my cigarette into the woods, only for Glen to reject it with a swat like that of a seven-foot NBA center.

"Hey, mate, don't ditch that. They're not good for nature. Toss it in this empty water bottle."

I laugh. Here we are being environmentally conscious on acid.

Hippies.

"Can I get another?"

"Here, mate, just have the pack. I've got a second one. I knew we'd probably need it."

He tosses me the gold package. Its remaining contents rattle inside.

"So much for quitting, right?" Glen stands up to stretch his appendages, which appear odd and gangly. "How do you feel about navigating down this trail a bit further?"

I think about writing or reading and light another cigarette.

Yes. You should explore.

"Lead the way cap'n."

I, too, require a deep stretch once I'm back on my feet.

The crackling of my spine releases another flood of the trip's juicy euphoria. The rollercoaster continues. Sometimes, it feels like chugging up the hill, until suddenly hitting the crest, and the actual ride begins.

And, right now, we are definitely on one of those descending sections. Building momentum for an upcoming loop-de-loop.

ᔅ:ᒪᕁ ᒣᐤ

ALONG THE TRAIL, WE HOP AND SKIP ABOUT, SWINGING AROUND TREES and jumping from rock to rock, giggling like schoolgirls.

"Where do you think this leads?" I ask, more to the void than Glen in particular.

"My guess, it's a shortcut. Probably created by some regulars who wanted a faster way down the hill."

Makes sense to me.

We trudge forward, continuing with our little games and exploring our own minds.

I'm not sure when it started, but now I'm looking down at Glen's head rather than the back of it.

He must have been right, we're starting to go downhill.

A wave of euphoria wells up and over me.

The color spectrum shifts before my very eyes. Greens seem greener. Browns browner. The bits of blue through the treetops are a special hue that I've never noticed before. There are these oranges and reds and yellows, flecked throughout nature. Despite standing out, they seem...*commonplace.*

My footfalls slow gradually, and I stop after narrowly avoiding a collision with a gargantuan spruce growing in the middle of our trail.

We seem to have reached a plateau, and I have this burning desire to take in this hidden world of color that I have been missing all my life.

Everything pulses and breathes alongside me. The entire world perceptively flows back and forth like the ripples of a pond.

With every breath, the trees breathe, too. Not to mention the sticks, the ground, the sky. It all pulses in a way that has escaped my perception until this moment.

I am one with it and it is one with me.

Birds seem to sing louder and more beautiful than ever. The wind adds a chorus through the rustle of leaves, and my heartbeat sets the bass line for it all.

I finally calm down enough to discover Glen's put some distance between us. Though, it's impossible to be concerned.

Even if he'd gotten as much as 100 yards ahead of me, I know he's still on the plateau. His head, level with mine.

Oddly enough, he hops off the trail.

Curious, I watch as he seems to track something across the ground.

A flash of red pulls at the corner of my periphery, and it's the brightest cardinal I have ever seen. It lands on a branch right above me.

I can't believe it. He's so close.

Those tiny ink drops for eyes shine brilliantly as they peer into me. He perches himself on a low-hanging branch before fluttering to the next tree over. This one is lower.

He's still staring at me. Only now, he's at about chest level. I wouldn't even need to extend my arm fully to touch him.

I can't say I've ever been this close to a bird. I can't imagine why he won't fly away. Does he understand I am appreciating his beauty? And I have absolutely zero intentions of causing him harm? I am not a predator, but an audience.

For the first time ever, I get a good look at the creature up close.

I'd always thought cardinals had pure black oil spots for eyes. At least, that's how they looked from a distance.

This guy in front of me has an iris. It's dark, maybe a deep brown, but I can see it circling the large black pupil. Like the falcon, its eye sits in an orangish-yellow eyelid, but the cardinal's is more round. Despite the perfectness of each circle, it makes the bird seem as if it's, I don't know, *conscious*.

I think back to an old wive's tale about cardinals and the spirits of the deceased.

My thoughts on the spiritual and paranormal shatter at the sound of a thundering *craaackkk,* almost immediately pursued by a man's scream.

Glen.

My feet are cold, frozen to the ground, and all the warmth seeps from my body as the bright red beacon of the bird's mohawk soars away in slow motion.

Are you going to investigate?

I can't.

Coward!

I know!

FUCKING GO!

My feet break free from the slog of twigs and decaying leaves.

Gradually, my pace gears up to a full sprint. A track runner's stride that I haven't known in years.

I can't see Glen anywhere.

I've got to be close.

Terror's icy clutches grip at my insides in a manner that violates my core.

It's all so sobering. The world seems to stop moving as I come across Glen's bag.

It lay in an impossible melancholy for an inanimate object.

Looking around, there is an oddly curved tree to my right. The trunk bent away as if avoiding its neighbors.

I take my steps carefully.

Something is wrong.

Very wrong.

As my perspective shifts, I observe something more odd about this tree. It looks as if a branch has just broken off. It was a big sucker too. One nearly the diameter of my thigh. A fresh, jagged stump protrudes violently.

Be careful!

I don't need the echo of caution, but I step gingerly in my approach. It's maybe ten feet away when my eyes glimpse the tree's roots. Thick and unwieldy, they sprout from the edge of an unseen slope. The ground is peculiar as well. It appears to be eroding away.

A web of wispy tendrils shows where the tree is coming free from its perch.

TRIP

Instinctually, I inch down to my stomach and army crawl with care to what I assume is a ledge, hoping against all hope that the ground is sturdy here.

I hardly pay any mind to the twigs and leaves stabbing at my underbelly.

It's a steep, jagged, and angular drop-off. Totally capable of being mountaineered with little risk. But, going down…Well, that looks a bit trickier.

That's when I see him.

ζ:3o Þm

I thought the trip was the start of our second act. Clearly, I was wrong.

Fuck. He's just lying there.

...

Oh, fuck. His leg.

There's no way I can stop the retch fighting its way up my esophagus.

The sight of his leg is torture on the eyes. A kneecap is not supposed to bend that way. Thinking about it knocks the acidic contents of my stomach loose, and my insides paint the ridge below in a painful coating of orange, acrid bile.

This can't be real.

I beg the universe to unravel a hallucination that I'll never fully comprehend.

Is he even alive?

I have no clue.

From all the signs, it appears Glen rolled down the entire hillside, which means there's a chance. If it had been a sheer drop...It wasn't a survivable distance.

Fuck. Fuck. Fuck.

You're way too fucked up for this.

Yes! I know! Leave me alone. FUCK!

Some people say they sober up in moments of crisis.

I think I'm experiencing the opposite. The surrounding scene begins to whirlpool again.

Worse, I want to call it a black hole. I can almost feel something dragging me toward depths of myself that I am too terrified to explore.

I'm drowning in something.

Maybe if you just give in, it'll all be over in a second.

That's nonsense. You need to focus up. Take control.

Okay. Okay. Okay. Let's say there's a hundred yards to get to Glen. What's the best way to cover that ground?

Then what do you do?

Oh shit!

Yes. How do you move Glen somewhere that an ambulance can reach him?

Stop talking to yourself. Deep breaths.

That's all I want. At least one sobering gust of oxygen, and I can re-evaluate the scene.

From this high up, I can't see blood. I can't trust my vision, though.

The sun's getting lower, the shadows are stretching, he's so far away, and the acid *isn't* helping.

Then it dawns on me.

My cellphone!

5:35 pm

It feels stupid doing it, but I can't possibly think of other options.

It takes a second for the call to connect, and the ringtone in my ear startles me once it finally initiates.

At first it's nothing more than a twitch, but then Glen's moving his hand.

He's stirring!

I can even hear a groan!

The call switches over to his voicemail. But I'm too excited.

He's alive! Holy shit! Yes! He's alive!

Elation and heightened euphoria convince me to leave an excitable voicemail.

What the fuck are you doing?

Embarrassed, I quickly hang up and redial.

He picks up after only two rings this time.

"Glen! Glen, are you okay man?"

There's a long groan and an icy silence before his voice creaks out through the speaker, "Mate. My leg fucking *hurts*."

No shit dumbass.

Don't panic.

What do I tell him? Everything's going to be okay? Do I call the police?

Of course, you call the police, idiot. Why didn't you do that in the first place?

"Alright man, I'm gonna call the police and we'll get ya some help."

I hang up.

He calls me back almost instantly. "G?"

"Hey man, what's up?" As if this is some run-of-the-mill how-do-ya-do conversation and not, *'Holy fucking shit man you just fell down a cliff tripping on acid, and your leg is bent in a direction that shouldn't even be physically possible for the world's greatest Yugoslavian contortionist.'*

"Don't call the cops," he says, hardly more than a whisper.

I am so fucked up, but the rational neurons of the frontal lobe are active enough to be taken aback by the stupidity of that statement.

Don't listen to him!

I know!

It will not matter.

Stop!

"Seriously man. Don't do it. I don't want to go to jail."

Fuck. Would we go to jail for this?

Not if you save him.

You won't—

Shut up! SHUT UP! SHUT! UP!

I am too far gone for this. I know I have to get him some medical attention. There should be no second thoughts about this.

Yet—

This is a Stage-5 emergency. I have to sober up and think clearly at this point.

Right. So, let's think. If there's no blood. If he's able to think clearly enough to call and recognize that he doesn't need immediate medical attention, that means—

That means things may not be too bad.

So, keep calm?

Exactly, keep calm, and think about what real-life trials and tribulations you might glean from tripping balls, mountaineering down a cliff to help save and carry your equally fucked up friend back to camp?

I can't believe I'm even considering this.

Not only would you have ammo for a book, but you'd also be a hero.

That's not—

I am hooked on one word. It echoes over all other thoughts fighting through my mind.

Hero.

That's exactly what I want to do. Play hero. Cliff might have to do something like this during his battle with Trip. It's fucking perfect!

Why would he—

"Okay, man. I'm gonna save you. I got you!"

"Thanks, mate. I may just take a quick nap, while I wait for you."

"That's fi—wait! No! No naps! You've probably got like, um, a concussion or something."

Rational frontal lobe back at it.

I spin my head around. It's too fast and half-hearted to see anything other than setting-sun-shadowed woods for as far as the eye can see.

Thankfully, on the second pass, nature's magnetic magic halts my search at the familiar sight of the trail. It's not far off.

The 'people trail.'

It should continue heading downhill.

But how sure of that can you be?

"Um, man are you bleeding?" I drop to my stomach, lying prone once more.

"Uh, hold on." He leans toward his busted leg. He surveys the appendage with muffled pain.

Time stills. I cannot feel the psychedelic, but I know it's there. Fighting the sense of sobriety attempting to assume control.

I realize I have been holding my breath. I try to release a gentle exhale, but the trip floods back in as soon as I do.

The ENTIRE hillside takes a deep breath in unison with me. My chest heaves with the pulsating earth beneath me.

Glen says something.

"Sorry man, what?"

"No, mate. I'm not bleeding. Leg's just, ya know. Like, bent the wrong way. There's like, a lot of pain. But then it kinda just goes away. The acid takes over, and it's like, *woah*, I'm not aware of the pain, but then I'm just like SO aware of the pain. Does that make sense?"

"Not at all, bud. Not at all. Just sit tight. I'm going to head this way." I point toward the haphazard trail, unsure if he can even see me. "Hopefully, I'll be able to take a shorter, less steep route down to you."

"Alright, mate, I'll make myself comfortable. No naps."

"No naps."

I hang up and push myself up from the edge. But my phone's still against my palm, and I need to avoid pushing my weight into it. Now is not the time for a cracked screen. My weight shifts to the heel of my palm and I push up with as little pressure as I can manage on the phone's edge. The case should hold against the brief force.

Then I feel it before I see it.

The phone rockets out from the stress applied to the lip of the case.

Reality slows, and the phone soars, tumbling and dancing through the air.

Then, it stalls and takes a nosedive toward the forest floor below, ultimately crashing into the brush a small distance from Glen.

I can feel it coming on. Like the undercurrent of the ocean before a wave towers overhead. The phone is gone, and there's nothing left to do but suffer.

Defeat ices over my veins.

5:39 pm

I KNOW I HAVE TO MAKE MY WAY TO GLEN STILL, BUT FEAR BORES itself into my chest.

I might be having a panic attack, and I need something to settle me.

Before I even realize it, there's a cigarette on my lips. The nicotine's wave deters the panic beating behind my breast. It balances the flood of euphoria and dulls my sorrow.

Quick smoke break, then save your friend and deal with your phone.
Idiot.

Once more, I hear the unmistakable pop tones signaling an incoming call.
Hope?

Looking down, my eyes adjust through the billowing visions of settling worldly hallucinations.

Glen's managed to crawl the entire distance and waves the illuminating face of my phone like he's at a concert. I can barely make out what he's saying, but it sounds like he's leaving a voicemail.

This should register much higher on the 'we're so fucked' scale.

I try to finish my cigarette and avoid a strange urge to cry when a grotesque sob rattles down below. *"BLEEDING!"*

Mr. Frontal Lobe attempts to pry through the blanket of fogginess that envelops him.

I have to get over that edge, and now. There's no time to waste. I can't trust myself on the trail, anyway. I know I'll get distracted if I take that route.

Sobriety is a fleeting fancy.

At least I still have enough presence of mind to know that, which has to count for something.

With no time left to reconsider, I wiggle over the edge and slowly climb, slip, slide, and tumble my way along the steep drop-off.

It's an eternity.

Glen is getting closer and closer, yet I'm never there. A few, foot-wide plateaus allow me to gather my balance and watch some moss breathe—

Stop petting the fucking moss!

This stuff is way too strong.

Glen needs a hero.

Instead, he's stuck with me. A drugged-up lunatic story writer.

So, I do the only thing I can. I embrace it. I treat the remainder of the journey as nothing more than a story.

Where I am the hero.

The hero doesn't sit around petting fucking moss. I guarantee that.

The forest floor rushes upward as my mind narrates the private heroic journey.

I move faster, spurned on with the thought of dodging a hail of unseen bullets.

The slips and slides become an invisible avalanche that I must outrun, and a final dance to the bottom is a tip of the hat to a femme fatale.

It all culminates in reaching Glen's side unscathed.

My friend, despite his injury, looks quite comfortable. He's watching something on his phone, while mine rests at his side. The screen is cracked to hell. Finessing the thing from the ground slices open my finger. There's no way I can unlock the screen without doing more damage.

I have to take in Glen's condition, though. He's watching old concert videos. Some jam band.

What does a hero do here, dumbass?

He slaps the damn thing out of his friend's hand and says:

"It's time to focus up man. It's hero time, and we're going to get you to safety. Are you with me?"

A look of awe brightens his features. His dark hair is a matted mess of dirt, sweat, and blood. "Oh shit, mate. You're like a *genuine* hero." He looks as dumb as he sounds, but the word 'hero' is intoxicating to my ears.

"Let's do this. Let's *fucking* go!" I start to help him up.

"Wait! Wait! Wait! We can't forget it."

"Forget what?"

"My head. My head, and uh, my leg. We need, um, *fuck*. A switch for my leg and a turncoat for my head."

I know what he said is wrong. Thankfully, my brain translates it.

Glen tells me it was only after he moved to my phone that he realized there must have been a hairline fracture at the back of his skull, leaving behind a tiny crimson puddle where he'd been lying.

So, we have that to deal with on top of his mangled leg.

Luckily, Glen brought a pretty sturdy knife, which I somehow manage to use without further injuring either of us.

In a few swift motions, I've sliced off the sleeves of my flannel and wrapped up his head wound. It's smaller than I expected, and therefore, seems less concerning.

The rest of my flannel aids in splinting some branches to his leg. Glen roars in pain as we do it. He tries to bite down on a stick as I work, but it only serves to muffle his agony. Each time, his cries pierce my heart.

But it's finally my turn. My turn to help Glen out of the darkness he's fallen into.

I owe him that much.

BARABOO, WISCONSIN (?)
???????

5:55 ƒ∧∧

EVENTUALLY, HIS SCREAMS AND CRIES DIE OUT. THERE'S NO WAY WE'VE properly splinted the injury. If we can hold out long enough to get medical attention, I'm sure Glen will pull through just fine.

In the meantime, it's up to me, hippie John Rambo, to escort Davey Jones' fucked up nephew.

We must be a sight to behold for sure.

To be a fly on the wall—

A bird in the trees would probably be more apt.

As we wander in no particular direction, I have doubts we're doing the right thing. My shoulders are already feeling the burn of supporting Glen as he limps and hops at my side. But we both agree, getting far away from that hill is our best course of action.

See, it had, well—*bad vibes.*

Still, I can't shake the pounding of rationality, demanding I call for help.

Even if you did that, how would anyone know where to find you?

We're not that lost...Are we?

My mind drifts. Traversing the forest is slow going.

I think about time and how we must be roughly halfway through the trip, yet the visuals don't seem to be letting up.

The tangerine glow of the sun leaks through the canopy with the last rays of the afternoon fading fast. The area is bathed in the warm hue, and it creates this strange sort of dissonance.

The beauty of nature, apparent now more than ever, contrasts the physical acts of the present—literally dragging around a friend as he bleeds out in mortal danger.

A part of me wishes, above all else, for a guardian angel.

Except it's a selfish wish. If someone can swoop in and save Glen, I don't have to let go of the trip. It's been too special.

I can feel it nudging me in this direction. That I need more time with it.

Even Glen seems to enjoy himself. To a degree.

"Have ya ever seen something so beautiful, mate?"

"The sun?"

"Yeah, mate," he says dreamily. Or maybe it was drowsiness, or fatigue. "But, also the way that *that* smoke just like, I don't know pulses in front of it, like it was coming from the sun, ya know."

"Yeah, man."

Wait! Smart brain.

"Holy shit, Glen! There's smoke!"

"Yeah, mate, fats wha' I jus' said, i'nnit?" His pronunciation was slack and slurred beneath a Londoner delivery.

"Are you trying to do an accent?"

"Yeah, brov. What you fink?" he asks in his pronounced South London cadence.

"Honestly, not bad. I totally bet you could trick some people with that."

Wait! Dumb brain! The smoke!

"Fuck!"

Deep breath. Sobering breath.

We stop walking. "Hold up. Glen let me get my brain right. There's smoke, yeah?" He nods in reply. "Which means that there's fire, and if there's fire, then there's probably people!"

"Or iss a foress fie'uh." His dry Londoner accent is in full force.

"Could be. But we gotta check it out. I can't keep carrying you for hours. If we can find help, we should take it."

"But what about your story?"

"Fuck the story man, I've got my ideas, I've got my notes. We need to make sure you don't die out here."

"I'm not gonna die out here. If anything gets me it'll be a mountain lion or some *Children of the Corn* shit. But, as long as I got you, I'm aces, mate." He finishes that last bit with the accent again, and he laughs.

I can't help but get caught up in the laughter myself. It seems to escort some of the stress out of the situation.

It's a chore and a half to maintain any semblance of a grip on reality, but auto-pilot kicks in occasionally, and I steer us toward the smoke, rejecting the flood of stimuli around me.

Glen needs to be priority number one.

Meanwhile, he's not exactly making it easy.

Glen's as light-hearted as a child on their birthday. He wants to stop and stare at random bullshit. Thankfully, he's easily coaxed away.

The shadows are disappearing into the darkness of evening when I hear noise from the smoke.

Okay, not *from* the smoke, but we're close, and there is no doubt about it...

We're not alone.

৩?:ৰয ৬ত

THERE'S A RHYTHM IN THE AIR.

It's definitely music.

As we get closer, I can feel the bass in my chest. It reminds me of how strong the trip is.

The beat's invisible hands caress my face like the hands of a lover. Rubbing my cheeks and whispering into my ear an audible salve to soothe my fears, doubts, and worries.

Thankfully, some part of me knows the goal, and somehow, I maintain enough self-control to not dance alongside Glen, who hops and sways his weight across my shoulders in a poor excuse for dancing.

A noticeable ache spreads through my upper back from bearing Glen's weight. He's not a big guy, but we've been walking for what feels like ages. It's near sunset and very possible we've been at this over an hour.

I need a quick second to shift Glen's weight around when I recognize a familiar bass-line pickup.

They're listening to hip-hop.

That has to mean they're younger. Which means cell phones.

Which means we're saved!

Glen's nodding along with the beat when a bonfire comes into view through the trees. It's a big one. Larger than any I've ever seen.

A chill shoots up my spine, the kind that convulses the entire body in a small, yet rapid, involuntary spasm. My dad used to call it a *'piss shiver.'* Regardless of whatever it's called, I don't like *the vibe.*

Trust the vibes.

We're here, at supposed safety, but something doesn't feel right.

The slow, intentional crawl of gooseflesh up my arms highlights that fact. Each minuscule bump ignites the next to spring forth bit by bit as they consume the entire surface of my body. It's the most uncomfortable I've felt all day.

With darkness seeping in, I feel better knowing they're not likely to see us coming. I know we need help, but I'm wary of this fire.

"Glen, I'm going to perch you behind this tree, while I go and investigate. Something just doesn't feel right, ya know?"

It's a large oak that easily conceals Glen.

"Honestly man, well, I just..."

He pants as I slide him down the trunk of the tree, and I can see he's growing pale.

"I just, *do* want some help. But it's like, *yeahhh,* the vibe's weird, right?" His words melt into one another. Unfortunately, there's no accent to blame this time.

I nod and hand him the water from my pack, worried about how much time we have.

I have to investigate.

So, I inch my way toward the inferno. There's this gleam of fire on metal as I get closer.

Further in, from a different vantage point, I spot two parked vehicles. Just beyond is a structure.

No, two structures.

I feel ridiculous, crouched low, sneaking from tree to tree like some sort of army grunt. Except it's more like this innate childish mindset of *playing* soldier.

I don't actually feel brave.

I stumble and roll across the sticks and leaves dressing the forest floor. The picture I have of myself is cartoonish.

A snicker escapes.

I brace behind a tree and quickly ball myself up, bury my face in my thighs, and clasp a hand to my mouth. Hoping I haven't revealed my location, I sit and compose myself, listening.

As the jittering nerves calm, I realize just how close I've gotten. I can make out the shadows of at least two people.

I also have a better vantage of the vehicles.

Pristine Jeep Wranglers. Nice ones too. The model with the bright red tow clips and all black tires. One was a metallic grey, and the other a bright blue.

I'm taking it all in, but something's wrong.

The music's gone.

"I heard something." It's a woman's voice. Soft, but deep and venomous.

"Is that why you paused the music? There's nothing out there, we took care of all the bears and mountain lions last year," came a man's reply. His voice possessed an oddly comforting bass to it.

"No. I think some–*one*–is out there. I swear I heard *giggling*." She speaks cooly with a malice that I can only describe as serpent-like.

Fuck.

The fear amplifies my anxiety, which roots deeper into my chest.

"Then just go inside and check the deer cams, you'll know instantly, but I mean wouldn't T have noticed and let us know?"

"Yeah T's going to be fucking *useless* to us tonight. Did you not see? He brought that pint of *Everclear* in his back pocket. He's on that shit again, I bet he's already in full code mode until he passes out."

The man chuckles to himself. "Ah shit, you're right. Amazes me every time though. If I had half his talent and all it cost me was to be a complete lush, I'd do it too." He chuckles again, the bass in his throat still oddly soothing. "I guess it's up to us...or we go get Artie."

"No. He's cooking. Unless *you're* going to go interrupt him?"

"Yeah, *fuck that.* I'm not making that mistake again."

There's a long pause. I want to poke my head out from my hiding spot, but I don't dare.

"Alright, I'll go walk the perimeter. You seen my gun?" the man asks, a hint of humor in his voice.

Oh. No.

There's no point in getting shot.

I run out from behind the trees. It's a movement of pure instinct.

"No guns. Please, no guns!" I scream, running towards the fire. My hands are as high in the air as I can stretch them, fighting the strenuous ache in my shoulders to keep them skyward.

"The fuck's this? You know him, Tay?" The man asks, turning to the woman.

They both look utterly bewildered.

Both are younger than I expected. They could be anywhere from their mid-twenties-to-thirties.

The woman has that look of maturity about her. She's tall and slender. There's no way she stands any less than six feet. Atop her tall frame sits a strong yet pale face emphasized by a square jaw and a sharp nose bookended by two dark, deep-set eyes. A long ponytail wraps down from neck to chest like a chestnut serpent.

'Tay' had been what the man called her.

He's of Asian descent, but I can't say what nationality. He has high cheek-bones with soft features and medium-length shaggy hair that extends just below his eyebrows. His face is clean-shaven and gives the appearance that he's even younger than his counterpart.

"Why the fuck you saying my name, dingus?"

"Sorry, *Hill*," he retorts with a wry smirk.

"Fuck you. And no, I don't fucking know him. Who the fuck are you, guy?"

I'm frozen.

I had been unsettled listening to 'Hill' from the shadows, but seeing her now—instills fear.

My gut tells me she was the sort of girl—*woman*—who grew up around boys. She doesn't have a drop of make-up on, and she doesn't need to. There's a strange beauty about her.

More so, she exudes strength.

My primitive brain forewarns me to beware both her physical *and* mental strength.

She seems like she's in charge.

"I'm, uh...I'm ahh..." *Should I tell them my real name?*

"Spit it the fuck out guy." Her voice zaps my spine with fear.

I vomit out a nerve-wracked response. "My name's Cliff, and my friend and I were hiking. He fell down the slope back there. About a hundred-yard fall, maybe more, and he's hurt pretty bad. Please, can you guys help him? Please. I can't let him die."

The two strangers exchange a glance, holding a silent conversation before turning back to me.

As they do, I take in our full surroundings.

Behind the fire is a large wooden cabin, but it looks new. It has to have been built just these past few years. Beyond it and off to the side, there's this barn or shed thing. All the trees in the area have been cleared, but the canopy still grows haphazardly to fill in the gap left overhead.

The Asian guy turns on his heel and strolls back toward the cabin. Leaving Hill, whose dark eyes pierce and pin me in place like a frog for dissection.

Her long legs move at a methodical pace. It's like watching a predator. A sort of lioness advancing toward the kill.

I can't look away. The soles of my feet are incapable of tearing free from the earth. Invisible, impaling instruments bolt them in place.

The woman's grace is frightening as she maneuvers around the fire and a litany of stumps blemishing the ground.

The static returns.

Oh, God. It's so much worse.

The anxiety spins into an icy-hot fear that spreads like poison, and seers nerve endings.

I hate this. Why'd I do this to myself? I should have just stayed home.

Closer still, I ballpark her height. At least six-three, probably taller.

No.

The sight grows more intimidating as she strides between me and the fire. The blaze casts a mutating, demonic glow around her darkening silhouette.

The flames flicker and continue transforming her visage into something towering, slender, and malevolent that prowls through shadows in pursuit of me.

Run!

Why aren't you running?!

...

Worthless.

ꩭ꩞ꩪꩩꫵꩠꩡ ꩡ ꩜

I don't recall hitting the ground.

I am, however, well aware of being cold-cocked between the eyes.

The spot still aches, and I've got a splitting headache that worsens with the assault of ammonia rushing up my nostrils.

Vivid memories of a time spent in a surgical suite bloom. Though, it becomes clear this isn't an O.R.

My vision focuses on the unfamiliar hand holding out a smelling salt.

As my eyes adjust to the dimly lit room, I can see there's a new character in this story. Before I can take stock of the newcomer, he's firmly patting my cheek in a way that feels belittling.

Strangely, he then takes the smelling salt to his own nose for an overzealous whiff.

"Wahhh! You got all the good smell! But, that'll still sober a guy up a bit." He's short, broad-shouldered, and has one of the darkest complexions I've ever seen. I can't place his nationality, not that it matters, as he speaks with an ambiguous midwestern accent.

"T, will you calm down? I need you focused before Artie gets up here," the tall woman from earlier, *Hill,* says.

"I thought you said *I* was the dingus for saying your name earlier," blurts the sturdy Asian man.

"Well, thanks to you, *dingus,* they already heard my name. And the other one looks to be knocking at death's door, so I doubt there's anything to worry about there." She walks over to me.

I flinch at the thought of her striking me again, except I can't move. They've restrained me to a chair. My hands are duct-taped behind the low back of the seat.

The room we're in is large and dark. Maybe the barn-shed-thing. I can't say for sure.

Terror eats at my insides, and I honestly feel the urge to piss myself.

With the same frightening grace as before, Hill crouches her long frame in front of me, her eyes even with mine. They're a piercing green. The idea of a serpent sits with me.

"What're you boys fucking on?"

I laugh.

The fear has me so uncomfortable that I have literally just laughed in the face of danger. It was the way she structured her sentence.

A large backhand zips across my face. "Listen here, fuck face. Tell me what you're on and where you got it."

Her green eyes transfix my gaze. They're hypnotic. Whatever she was saying went in one ear and out the other.

A sense of dread sweeps through me as I realize the trip isn't over. In fact, it feels like things are about to ramp up.

Focus.

But her eyes pull at my consciousness. Shiny verdant pools shimmering beneath florescent lights. They're intoxicating.

Smack!

Another backhand.

C'mon Galen, get your shit together!

"Sorry, what did you want? Can I talk to someone else? Your eyes are too trippy."

Why would you say that?

Idiot.

She cackles a skin-crawling chord of malice. Gliding upward to her full height, she looms over me. A towering and shadowy figure.

"How about we try *this?*"

The sucker punch to my gut keels me over, but my hands catch the back of the chair, and I feel like I'm teetering over the edge of a cliff as the seat's back legs come off the floor. The only thing preventing me from toppling over the precipice of the seat is my straining tiptoes.

I can't say I've ever been hit that hard.

Each gasp hurts, but panic urges air back to my lungs.

"Now, while you're looking at the floor, how's about we try this again? You tell me what you're on. And where you got it."

No matter how desperately I try to heave the words out, I can't get them past my need for oxygen. All I can manage is a series of painful grunts that amplify the static anxiety of what's coming.

Don't interrogators ever think this through? How is someone supposed to talk if they have the wind knocked out of them?

The sensation of her fingernails digging in hard against my scalp is enough to force my gaze into her shadowy silhouette. It still doesn't stop her from yanking.

"I'm waiting."

"Where's my friend? Where's Glen?" I gasp the words out.

The roots of my hair steer my gaze to the right, and sure enough, there he is, bound and gagged next to me. He's conscious, but he looks pale. The bright flannel still wrapped around his head and legs contrasts how much color he's lost.

"Start. Talking," she hisses.

All that's left are my lizard brain instincts. Heart racing, anxiety through the roof, gooseflesh metastasizing, and it's only getting worse.

I've got to say something.

Anything.

"Okay, yeah. Um, Glen. Him over there. He got it. I don't know from who or when, but we planned it all this week, and I think he'd already gotten it by that point. Wait, yeah, he totally had it because he did, like, this extra thing where he had a key to open the drawer with more keys, then those keys were to open another drawer, which had the safe, then he had even more keys to open a safe, and he did this whole, like, flourish routine and whipped out the aluminum foil. I asked him something like is that *Lucy*. And he's all, *'We're not kids just call it acid.'* Sorry, I don't know why I'm talking so much. I'm just really nervous, and this acid trip is like, super, ya know, *acid-ey*. But also, I'm kind of freaking out right now, and—"

OW!

Did she really just tape your mouth shut?

"Jesus. Fucking. Christ. Remind me to never let *you* write a book."

The dig aside, there's legitimate relief in knowing I don't need to speak anymore. I can feel the stress dissipate slowly from my pores.

"Oh. *Fuck!*"

"What is it T?"

"Hill, I know this guy! The pale, fucked up one."

He's high-fiving himself and laughing his ass off.

Composing himself enough, he adds, "Yo, this that publishing agent dude." There might have been a slight slur to his words.

He takes a swig from a pint of clear liquor before returning it to his back pocket.

I get a chance to study T for the first time.

He's in jeans, flip-flops, and a dark hoodie. His sleeves are rolled up, exposing veiny forearms. His shoulders are noticeably broad, while his hair is neatly cropped and lined at the temples.

Although, the most striking thing is the animation of his gestures. While he speaks, there are lots of hand and arm movements that don't quite line up with what he's saying. At the very least, they're distracting to those of us presently tripping our faces off.

"*Yeah*, he's the fucking guy. The one who got Artie the book deal. *Fuck.*"

"You may be a drunk, but damnit, I think you're right on this one T." With her frightening grace, Hill saunters to Glen and peels the tape from his mouth. It leaves a cherry-red rectangle against his fading complexion.

He's slumped forward.

He, too, would topple if not for his restraints.

His leg is without a doubt incorrectly splinted, and the flannel tourniquet around his head leaks crimson from the back and has turned spine-shivering purple.

"Hey guy, focus up!" She pats his cheek aggressively. Glen tilts his chin forward to meet her gaze.

"You're kind of pretty. I like your eyes. We should get dinner sometime soon." His voice is soft and heart-wrenching.

Both Hill's counterparts laugh hysterically. They quickly turn away from the scene to quiet themselves as they pat each other, whispering like kinder-gartners.

"The fuck you say to me, you fucking creep?" She still looks caught off guard despite her fury.

"Oh, sorry, I was just saying I know this great sushi pla—"

"Shut the fuck up. I was being rhetorical."

She bores into her counterparts until they turn to meet her eyes, as if they'd felt her monstrous leer.

"There's no way this guy is a publishing agent, he's a fucking moron."

Okay, okay, okay. Think. Is it good or bad if Glen is who they think he is? Would we live if he is? Is there a chance we won't if he's not?

We're probably destined for a short life regardless.

What is life? What does it mean to die?

Stop! Focus you idiot!

"Okay, let's try this again. Hit on me one more time, and I *hit* you. Capeesh?" Her tone is eerily calm now.

Glen nods. He is even more pale than a moment ago.

"Are you that publishing guy that Artie's working with?"

His voice is softer than before. The faint rasp sinks my stomach. "Um, I don't know. Artie? *Artie? Artie...*" Glen's gaze is lost.

He's dying.

And he's feeling ALL THIS too.

Poor bastard.

"Sorry, spaced out, I don't feel so good. What'd you ask?"

The silence of the room cracks as T takes another swig. "I don't think this guy's doing so well. Can you imagine tripping face, while hallucinating from blood loss? Probably concussed too. Not to mention that fucking leg. *Tsk, tsk, tsk,* poor bastard."

That's what I said.

Hill shakes him off. A stern shot from the corner of her eyes clearly says, '*Shut the fuck up.*'

She must be the leader and brute here. She's bigger in stature than the other two. However, neither of the men looks like a slouch.

Sliding back to her full height, she reaches for her chin, and the iconic image of *The Thinker* comes to mind.

"Get Artie."

"You sure? I think he may be in the heart of something."

"Well, *Win*, it sounds like you'll have to take over for him, *doesn't it?*"

The tall Asian man rolls his eyes and leaves the barn, shed, whatever building we're in.

Hill pulls T aside for a hushed exchange after turning their backs to us.

I have to get Glen's attention.

He's still free to speak. But those eyes of his are dulling with each second. He looks lost. Fallen into some part of the psychedelic, and I don't even have a way to communicate with him.

Could I tap Morse code to him?

You'd have to know Morse code, idiot. And that's clearly not up here.

The wind deflates from my sails. I can almost see myself from above.

I'm pathetic in every sense. It'd be better for everyone if they just killed me.

...

All that's left to do is resign myself to the trip.

¿ ?:¿? ₽ⅿ⁲

THE ANXIETY AND THE DANGER OF THE SITUATION SEEM TO DRAIN OUT my feet, leaving me free to bask in euphoria.

It cascades, allowing each strained breath through my nostrils to shepherd forth a revitalizing sensation of life.

Clarity wants to return. Not a sobering clarity, more of a—*every other concern in the world fades into the void*—sort of clarity.

Why worry about past, present, or future? Just exist.

There's a revelation here. It feels so exceedingly clear.

Existence is pleasureful.

You want to exist.

And you desire to exist.

So, exist.

Hope births a renewed vigor. I must formulate a strategy to escape this predicament.

Making peace with this newfound desire to not quit on life, the door jolts open with a ferocity that unleashes a sobering shiver in me.

Lucidity drapes itself over this moment where palpable malice has entered the room.

I thought I had felt fear before. I thought I had felt terror.

But those times pale in comparison to what I now know to be true horror.

Most any seventh-grader could talk about the human flight, fight, or freeze response through the sympathetic nervous system.

A system not aptly named for this experience.

There isn't an ounce of sympathy in this room. My insides turn to ice, shattering any peace and serenity I'd known a moment before.

It'd be impossible to avoid describing his eyes as anything other than *dark*. I think there is a hint of blue, but it reminds me of eldritch creatures from the darkest reaches of the cosmos. Or possibly the extensive carvings of trenches beneath the ocean.

Deep-set in their own shadows of exhaustion, there's this illusion—maybe it's the acid—but they seem to take up his entire face.

His dark hair brings new meaning to the word oily, as it runs in thin waves to his shoulders. A quintessential Bond-villain goatee frames his jawline.

I might have a subconscious fixation on the idea of malevolent spirits thanks to my light reading earlier, but I can't help but ruminate on one central question.

Am I in the presence of something demonic?

I want to belittle the thought.

It's just the acid.

Only, I can't bring myself to do it.

The demon sizes me up. I can't meet his gaze as my skin crawls at the thought of those sunken eyes, seeing things that I could never.

The sight of his lips may be worse. They're too red for his face. Like he's been sucking on a scarlet popsicle with fellatio-esque exuberance. I don't think even scarlet rivulets of blood would be more unsettling.

With deliberate slowness, he seats himself on the front of an ATV covered in dust. The precision and pace of his movements are methodical. But I know every story's demon will trick you into meeting their gaze.

Before I can give any further thought to such craziness, I notice his attention loll toward Glen. It's like watching a wolf when he cocks his head to the side. He's perplexed. Something unexpected has happened.

"Well, well, well, if the rumors ain't true. My amazing agent, Glen Coppersmith, has graced us with his presence. How are you Glenny, ole boy, Glenny, ole pal o' mine?"

The voice that unfurls from his lips is unexpected. It's softer and about an octave higher than I expect. Then again, my expectations had been brimstone and thunder.

So what do I know?

Glen's head lay still. Thankfully, his gaze tilts ever so slightly.

Then it hits me.

What the demon said. What his cronies said.

Glen doesn't appear to be in shock or thrown off in the least.

"Not so good, mate. My head hurts." There's hardly any life in my friend's voice.

"Well, *mate*, that's because, by the looks of ya, you fell down a fucking cliff." He doesn't wait for a response. "So that must make this the disappointment author. How are ya, *Disappointment?*"

I lock eyes with those hollow orbs, and I fear our story has become one of horror.

"Looks like you're doing better than ole Glen here." He performs that stupid behind-the-hand exaggerated whisper, "*I don't think he's going to make it.*"

Without warning, the demon launches forward and becomes frighteningly animated. "But, I'm not a doctor, so who am I to say? T, well he could have been a doctor, if it weren't for well, *probably me*, but most likely the *glug glug glug.*" His performance now includes alcoholism mimicry.

Looks like we have an entertainer.

"You see, I'll let him cook fucked up. To an extent of course. Can't have him ruining my product. Sorry, sorry, sorry, *our* product." He winks and waves toward his posse, "But ain't nobody letting *him* cut people open while plastered. *Can you imagine?*"

He once again becomes a mime. This time an imaginary scalpel slices the air, while he sways back and forth.

"I like this better anyway, less debt," T adds from behind, sharing in the chuckle.

"So, anywho, *Disappointment*, how's the trip going? You like the stuff? I made that batch special, just for ole Glenny boy. Though, never did I think I'd run into y'all *here*. Guess, he took my advice all the way to the bank. Didn't you, Glenny?" He pats Glen hard across the cheek several times.

Ice-cold claws wrap around my heart and lungs. Each breath feels like it offers less oxygen than the last.

Something is fighting a war to escape from my chest. Like my sternum needs to burst open at any second, expelling an amorphous sci-fi creature.

"I'm glad you like it. How's the book coming? Still haven't heard anything..."

He stares at me, and I can't look away. Those dark pools sunken into his head possess a gravity well. One I'm not strong enough to escape.

He slides into a crouch at my feet, never breaking eye contact.

The demonic newcomer hovers there for an eternity.

Just when I can't seem to stand it, he slaps me with enough brutality that my chair's legs pop off the ground for an instant, before crashing back to the concrete floor with a rocking thud.

My skull rings.

An anger I hadn't thought I possessed pulsates between my temples.

No, it's beyond that.

It's a white-hot rage.

"Ohhhhhhh, somebody looks mad now." He rips the tape from my lips. "I'll ask you again. How's the writing going *confrère*?"

He seems to wait for my reply in earnest.

"I don't know," is all I can muster.

Coward. Coward. Coward. Coward. Coward. Coward. Cow—

"You don't know? C'mon, my guy. We both know that's a crock of shit. You either do or you don't."

Somehow, this demonic piece of shit has me feeling shameful.

There's a hunger in his eyes. A familiar sneer across his face, and in the strangest of understandings, realization falls into my lap.

DROPOUTS.

He's in disguise on the back cover.

He's R. Nold.

Everything clicks into place now.

"I have this idea." The words are out before I fully grasp what I'm doing. "But I just don't know if I've found the spark for it. Ya know?"

It's honest and contains more vulnerability than I've felt throughout this ordeal.

Are you actually anxious for his response?

The demon chuckles. It's high-pitched and self-serving. "Ahhh is that all? Now c'mon, that's an easy thing to sort out."

He chuckles again.

"Sparks aren't found. They're created. Created through work and friction." He's conversing with me as if he were a mentor addressing a pupil, not captor to hostage. There's a sincerity to his voice.

He reaches behind, and I can see Hill place *something* in his hand.

Being the performer that I am understanding him to be, R. Nold reveals a dark black pistol. My eyes fixate on the barrel waving in front of Glen's forehead.

There's no fear in Glen's eyes. Blood's starting to pool and drip down all parts of his head. It looks so dark and malevolent in contrast to the translucent hue of his skin. "You see here, *Galen*, yes I know your name, don't look so shocked, friend. Or is it R.C.? Maybe *Cliff?*"

He and his compatriots have a laugh at this.

"Actually, ya know what? I think I'll just stick with *Disappointment*, that's how Glenny-boy and I refer to ya."

He laughs again. I know it's not true, but it doesn't sting any less.

I am a disappointment. A failure.

"Anyhow, see this here hammer on the back of this here pistol? It generates a spark when it knocks against the firing pin. But, only by putting in that effort to pull the hammer back will the spark stand a chance at creation."

He cocks the hammer back.

"Then we must apply force to the trigger. That action sends the hammer forward with great speed. Only then will you have the spark that ignites the propellent, and," my ears ring with the high-pitched echo of the pistol's *crack*, "the projectile flows like the ink of a pen. Thus, your spark is both *createe* and *creator*."

He grabs my jaw and pinches it tightly, smashing my lips inward. He forces my gaze to his, while my skin crawls with not just the sight of him, but his touch.

Over the deafening ring in my ears, he whispers to me.

"So, you see, your writing can only project forward if you've created the friction, and the easiest way to do that is just put pen to paper."

Part Two
Memento Mori

"Thanatopsis"

So live, that when thy summons comes to join
    The innumerable caravan, which moves
    To that mysterious realm, where each shall take
    His chamber in the silent halls of death,
    Thou go not, like the quarry-slave at night,
    Scourged to his dungeon, but, sustained and soothed
    By an unfaltering trust, approach thy grave,
    Like one who wraps the drapery of his couch
    About him, and lies down to pleasant dreams.

— William Cullen Bryant

##:#1

AN UNRELENTING TORRENT RINGS THROUGH MY INNER EAR. No matter how far I stretch my jaw or how many yawns I force out, there's no escaping the shrill pest.

My eyes water from overstimulation. Fervent blinks do little to upend this blurred and buzzing reality.

Gradually, the world *does* ease back into focus. Starting with where the slug found home.

Right between Glen's eyes.

The Demon must see that I've finally noticed.

His dark presence rotates down to squat at my side, a maneuver that places him between Glen and me, obscuring the sight of my friend slumped against the side of his chair.

But I've already taken it all in.

The chair's back keeps his bound hands in place, prohibiting him from sliding off. Leavin//g a corpse dangling limply over the ground.

A deafening *plop* collides with the cement beneath.

Anxious static consumes every synapse across my flesh.

Can I taste iron in the air? No. No way, there's no way any got on me. Right?

My therapists have always preached the importance of identifying emotions, and in this moment, there's almost too many to count.

There's fear.

There's sadness.

There's anxiety.

But there are also tears and snot. Lots of snot.

Except, I'm not sure any of it is for Glen.

Is it all selfish and self-serving?

I am afraid for *me*.

Sad for *me*.

Anxious for *me*.

Desperate for *me* to find a way out of this alive.

I can't stop the tiny whimper that escapes my chest, though I wish I could have.

"No, Mr. Demon. Please? No." I beg like a coward.

Inside me, there's a wild animal flailing about its cage. Desperate to survive, to live. It would not, could not, die here and now.

The Demon laughs. I think he can see through me. The way those eyes remind me of the unimaginable horrors of the ocean's depths...

"Stop freaking out, buddy. Is that how you want to die? Sniveling like a toddler? But I guess it's a pretty good trip, eh? Calling me a *demon*."

He laughs again.

"I don't want a man's last image of me to be demonic, though. That's just. I don't know, what's the word. *Sardonic*."

His smile epitomizes the word.

"The name's Arthur Witherspoon, but my friends call me Artie."

Yup. I'm going to die. One-hundred-and-fifty-thousand percent going to die here and now, covered in snot and my only friend's blood and brain matter.

Artie puts metal to my forehead. It's warm, maybe even burning, but there are too many other senses competing for control for it to hurt.

Like an impossibly pink slug, his tongue slithers along those unnervingly red lips.

The heat of panic burns through me.

The trapped creature inside frantically claws for survival. But the body knows defeat, and that truth cements itself as I hear the cock of the pistol's hammer.

I'll never get the chance to redeem myself as an author.

The Demon's words mock me.

Just put pen to paper.

As if it were that easy.

Cl'k.

Nothing happens.

Cl'k.

Cl'k, cl'k, cl'k.

Lady Luck is a sadistic bitch, and she apparently isn't through with you, after all.

"The fuck?" Artie drops the magazine to the ground. It rattles, another monstrous echo filling the room with its hollow metallic ting. *"Who the fuck just leaves one round in the chamber?* You people have to be fucking kidding me!"

The room is silent. Each of his goons appears unsure of how to respond.

I'm quite convinced that The Demon is the leader of this crew.

If he's not, he is, without a doubt, the most terrifying.

And I don't think it's just me who feels this way.

T looks chilled to the bone. The woman, Hill, still possesses a violent flicker in her eye. But she's distanced herself from the rage.

I had once read that all demons have a name and an aura. This one is Artie and his aura is ice-cold.

A long deep breath, and an even longer exhale, precede poisonous words. "T, where the fuck are the rest of the bullets?"

T takes a swig from his pint. But before it's off his lips, the bottle tips again, and its contents renew their meeting with the man's gullet. Conviction drives the liquor past his bobbing Adam's apple.

He tosses the bottle into the shadows of the shed without so much as a face or a cough, wipes at his chin, and utters a watery, "No idea man. Win's been on the ammo, and he's cooking now, so..." A shrug punctuates the sentence.

Fear is written on T's face. There's a rattle in his voice that hadn't been there previously. It could be from the massive amount of grain alcohol he's just ingested.

However, I would not bet on that.

As The Demon navigates his fury, Hill eases behind him until her long arms slither around his waist. She's got a handful of inches on him, so she has to crouch to whisper something in his ear. A sinister grin creeps from her face to his, and without another word, she snakes her fingers between his and starts leading him from the shed.

I find it odd that he allows this.

"Keep an eye on things, T. We'll be back in thirty minutes...*or so,*" Hill says commandingly as the door ricochets shut behind her and The Demon.

##:#2

Now it's only T and I.

His eyes have grown glossy, with thick webs of blood vessels crawling out from their corners.

Despite the liquor catching up with him, he pays a visit to a retro mint-green fridge that predates everyone who'd been in the room by several decades and comes out with a beer.

Then he looks at me. He's reaching back for something else.

It's a second can.

Damn. It's almost impressive.

He lobs the second can in my direction, but there's no way to dodge it. I quickly brace for it to thud against my chest. Not well enough though, as the can knocks the air from my lungs.

As I gasp, a serene sense of lucidity creeps back in, along with the scents of death.

Piss, shit, and stale, coppery viscera.

"My bad. Forgot the whole hands thing. Sorry bout your bud too. Hate the sight of blood personally, but hey, some things come with the territory, right?"

Another swig.

"Like those two fucking weirdos. Bro, I swear. She gets turned on by the violence. She's always wanting to fuck after shit like that. Honestly, creeps me the fuck out." He's less animated than he'd been before, but still, a plethora of gestures and movements accompany his speech.

"Yeah," I mutter.

They hadn't remembered to tape my mouth.

But what can I even say?

I feel like I've forgotten how to communicate. How do I even speak to creatures so utterly separated from humanity?

"So, you can't have beer?" It sounds like a question, but one he's posited to himself.

With a snap of his fingers, my host goes to the freezer and announces, "I've got it."

There's something small hidden in his hand.

Until he is close enough, there's no telling what it is.

Only when T is directly in front of me can I see he's holding an eyedropper vial, frosted with little crystals. His hands move gingerly like that of a surgeon.

While he goes about this process, I can only imagine how much of a professional this man is. Despite the pint of Everclear, T speaks without a slur and his movements are meticulous.

He staggers briefly, composes himself, then grabs my face, forcing my mouth open. His grip is powerful and calloused. Each finger capped with broken nails and torn cuticles.

There's no fighting it.

A single bitter *plop* splashes across my tongue, and immediately he's clamping down on my jaws like I'm a dog he's forcing to take a pill.

"At least you won't die sober." He laughs, pulling his hands away.

The taste is chemical and radiates.

"Oh fuck. What'd you just give me? Did you just give me *more* acid?"

He continues to chuckle. "Kinda."

"What the fuck does *kinda* mean?"

"I gave you the newest product, MDMA-cid or Lolly, as we're calling it. Ya know, like LSD and Molly. You get it. We were going to try it tonight until you and..."

There's a pause as his gaze falls on Glen's slumped form. His bloodshot stare then drops to the dark, shimmering pool of blood beneath Glen.

"Yeah, like I said, not my favorite part of the job. But, hey ya gotta tell me how that Lolly is. Super stoked on that shit."

It's sudden, but I can feel my lips purse and my face contort backward to stave off the onslaught of tears that decided now is the appropriate time to make an entrance.

That's a battle I won't win.

So, I submit.

It feels good to let the warm salty streams cascade down the sides of my face. As if they allow every ounce of fear and stress an escape route along the creeks trickling toward my jaw.

T's laughing and playing some game on his phone. Already back to drinking.

I fucking hate him.

Well, we'll have to do something about that then.

As time continues to pass, my composure returns.

Relieved of pent-up emotions that made a mass exodus through my tear ducts, I feel as if I've run through all the stages of grief in an instant.

I understand mortality, knowing that this will probably be the day I die, and I've got some regrets.

Thankfully, acceptance overwhelms me with a calming embrace.

##:#3

THE WAVES OF THE PSYCHEDELIC CREST, AND I ACCEPT THEIR PRESENCE.

Might as well enjoy what time I have left on this Earth.

With all deliberate speed, the trip creeps back in. Refreshed and reinvigorated for another round.

I'm feeling a bit chatty. "It's *T*, right?"

He looks up from his phone.

"Why are you guys doing this?"

Looking confused at first, he pulls an old metallic barstool from the nearby workbench and sits down across from me. The overwhelming stench of stale beer emanates from his breath in an inescapable fog.

A slur finally leaks into his words, "Did ya not read the book?"

"What book?"

"You's fucking dense bro."

He taps a large, rough, sausage finger against my forehead.

"Artie's book. Ahh fuck, what's it called? Ya know, *Dropouts* or whatev."

"*Right.*"

I'd almost forgotten about that revelation.

"None too bright are ya?"

He lets out a long, echoing belch.

"That's a bit better."

"Wait. *Does that mean the book is true?*"

A drunken smile creeps along T's face.

Damn, his teeth are immaculate.

The pristine white choppers contrast his flawless dark chocolate skin.

With a shrug, he says, "Ish. Gotta be switched up a bit to protect the operation. It helps with the uh, um—above board cash flow, ya know?"

"How long have you guys been at this?"

I feel like I'm riding a rollercoaster of exhaustion, while a creeping sense of adrenaline snakes its shadowy presence up my backbone.

"Shit man. Who knows? Few years."

He counts on his fingers.

"So, we were freshmen when it started, and now, *one, two, three...*" He trails off. "Prob'ly like seven now. Maybe more. I don't do the counting, just the math."

It's hard to believe this guy is their savant. He certainly can't be their historian. But I think there's something he'll definitely know the answer to.

My eyes shift to the corpse formerly known as Glen, dangling at my side.

The occasional *plop* rings out below him as gravity carries another spot of blood into the pool spreading atop the dusty concrete.

"How many people have you all killed?"

Surprisingly, T's reaction portrays confusion, as if a game show host had just stumped him.

"I d'know. Kinda lost track over the years. Artie does it all. None of us has the stomach. Hill may seem like it, but she's really a softy. Well, softy that'll fucking kick yo ass," he says with an almost infectious laugh.

Lost fucking track!

Remember, the lush isn't counting.

The fear storms in. A full-blown panic attack seems inevitable.

I think my pecs are about to shred through my shirt. Uncomfortable patches of sweat gather at my nape and in my palms. The magnitude of the situation grips me, amplifying the physical euphoric sensations of the Lolly.

I need something to focus on.

Don't think about dying.

I also don't want to think about the overwhelming experimental hallucinogen coursing through my veins that may be as likely to kill me as any fucking bullet.

Panic slows things down. Everything that billowed with breath, stills, and I know what this is.

The sympathetic nervous system.

The damn thing is doing its best to kick in.

Last time, I froze.

This time, I won't.

Take inventory

My hands are behind the back of the chair.

I flex my shoulder blades, and I can tell the back isn't very tall. It's definitely possible to get my hands over if I just—

Stand up?

The idea seems too idiotic.

Yet—

They never bound your legs.

It could be that simple.

T looks like he is in great shape, but he is clearly drunk off his rocker with no intention of stopping.

Hell, the degenerate mess just cracked another beer.

Panic continues building behind my rib cage. I know I need to decide now.

Otherwise, I *will* freeze.

It's fairly clear I'm not the center of T's attention. His eyes seem glossy and unfocused.

His phone beeps, and he starts texting. Or maybe he's playing that game. I can't be sure which, but whatever is going on in front of that vacant stare seems enthralling.

Luck has already been on my side one too many times tonight. Regardless, I am not about to start looking in the horse's mouth now.

Cautiously, I roll a shoulder forward over the low-backed chair, able to perch an elbow on top.

T remains engrossed in his phone, not noticing a thing.

I lean forward just slightly, enough to roll the other shoulder, this time getting the crook of my other elbow situated atop the chair.

T looks up from his phone.

Don't freeze.

268

I press off my elbows and stand straight up. He mirrors me, "The fuck you think—"

I can't give him the chance to finish that sentence. There's one escape plan that comes to mind, the only guaranteed way to ensure distance between the two of us.

I kick upward as hard as I can, nearly spinning myself off balance. Thankfully, my foot finds its target.

The result is dead nuts.

T crumples to the floor, clutching his manhood as I bolt for the door, which is lighter than I expect, and crashes open as I barrel through.

Outside, night has swallowed the sky, the sun's watch ended, and not a drop of it remains in the canopy-covered sky above.

Adrenaline pumps ferociously throughout my veins while my heartbeat rips through every inch of me.

The panic is still there.

I have no way of telling which way I need to go, and running is awkward with my hands bound behind my back, but I don't dare address that now. I know what stopping means, and at this point, I *fucking refuse* to let that happen.

Pick a direction.

And don't stop.

It's that simple. I take my best guess and run toward the backside of the bonfire, leaving the front of the buildings in my rearview.

Now, if I could just find the hill that Glen had fallen down. The one I'd somehow traversed to get to him. Then maybe, just maybe, I could get back on the trail toward camp, the car, and freedom.

One step at a time.

Move. Move. Move. Move.

I hear the echo with each and every step.

Move. Move. Move. Move.

A door slams open as my feet leave the sickly orange glow of the fire.

MOVE. MOVE. MOVE. MOVE.

Eyes strain forward into the darkness. I have to dissect the abyss. Any misstep might cause a stumble.

In the silence of the woods, I hear a faint, distressed wheeze chorusing behind me. I can't help myself. I steal a peek over my shoulder.

Just past the fire lurches a lumbering T.

I try to pick up the pace, but I'm about at my limit considering my hands. Each step seems like it'll be the one that sends me ass over tit.

"Get back here...you...son of a...bitch!"

A dark spectral shape is sprinting behind me.

My eyes have yet to finish adapting to the grim shadows of the wood.

"I'm gonna...get you...back, mother fucker!"

T does not sound good. His breathing labors with each shout.

Suddenly, the pursuing footfalls halt before a retching cough precedes the splashing of beer and Everclear off the forest floor's menagerie of detritus.

It's enough. Adrenaline's spurs dig deep.

Just a bit faster.

Ignore the sharp pain scorching through your side.

You can't stop.

I won't stop.

Turning back is no longer an option. If he gets me, he gets me. T's huffing and puffing resumes behind me. "You're...gonna...get it!" he cries out through gasps, and yet, I picture him closing that gap.

Why are there twigs and leaves snapping off to the left?

It was just a few quick sounds, but they came from the void.

Someone else from the cabin must have caught up. What else could it be?

The crunch of the brush sounds like something heavy. Too big for a squirrel or a bird. It can't be a vehicle either. Too inconsistent.

Plus, there'd be some sort of light, right?

Images of fangs and claws creep across the back of my imagination, but I am not about to play investigator. Whoever it is, *whatever* it is—they're moving alongside us. Following.

Tracking.

Stalking.

Until they make a move, the only pragmatic option is to keep going.

That's when I hear T trip and roll into the underbrush.

I so desperately want to look back...

Don't fucking do it!

All you need to know is that you need more distance between you two.

A crunch echoes from my left.

It's just the one sound.

270

It can't be T getting up.

It's too—*perfect*. A movie-esque, after-effects *crunch*.

This time, I dare to look back.

T's nothing more than a dark mass on the ground. I can't judge the distance, but it's significant. And it's growing. The mass isn't moving.

Without warning, the void of darkness births a large figure crouched on all fours. It growls. A full-body numbing sound that glues my feet to the forest.

It's instantaneous.

My heels dig into the loose earth, and I nearly tumble headfirst into the brush.

Somehow I maintain my footing, watching in horror as this...*thing* leaps toward the mass that I *know* is T.

His scream is instant. It comes out high and scratchy, and—*pure*.

Pure in the sense that it's—I don't know—*palpable*.

The echoing cries slice into me like that of the mountain lion's teeth and claws savaging their way through T.

I find enough inertia to dive behind a tree, where I can quickly maneuver my hands from behind my back.

Despite still being bound, I can make use of them for one reason, and one reason only. To cover one ear while burying the other into my shoulder with as much force as I can manage.

Here, I plan to wait for T's shrieking cries to vanish into the moonlight.

##:#4

How long's it been?

A paralyzing dissonance of euphoria and fear courses through every vein in my body.

They forced me to sit next to the corpse of my only friend, as his head dripped into a puddle of itself along a dusty floor.

Now this.

A man. A living person who I had spoken with only minutes prior. Not an actor or cartoon. A human being. Eviscerated between the jaws of a mountain lion.

The last few minutes of crunching meat and bone rings a haunting rhythm through the air.

The final relics persist after the screams have ended.

T's bones now serve as the mountain lion's chew toy.

I lost myself in those screams, but now I feel *transfixed*. The sounds are hypnotizing. Despite a singular inaudible scream deep within my being, urging me to keep moving from this place, I can't.

##:#5

Here you still are.

I begin to crawl. Testing the waters at first before slowly picking up the pace as the beast's snacking echoes behind me. The sounds numb me past caring about the sticks and stones impaling my forearms and knees.

I know to keep going.

Unsure if I'm heading in the right direction, I find solace in putting distance between the cabin, the predator, and myself.

It's hard to believe that the rest of their gang isn't right on my heels.

I guess good sex will even block out the sounds of your friend's dying screams. I chuckle at the thought, knowing all too well the laughter belongs to a madman.

Traumatized. PTSD. Anxiety.

All words a therapist will probably use to diagnose my mental state.

If I make it out of this night alive.

##:#6

IT'S NOT CLEAR HOW LONG I'VE BEEN OFF THE FOREST FLOOR, BUT THE indents along my arms and knees say it hasn't been long. A steady and unrelenting itch lingers along the trenches, serving as mementos from my four-legged ambling.

I need to get my hands free.

It doesn't take long before I stumble, almost literally, onto a rugged stone able to tear through the tape binding my wrists.

Invigorating freedom greets my arms as the bindings come off, but I'm well aware of what may lurk around any corner. I preach silence to myself and move with prey-like wariness to my feet.

The shadowy sounds of cracks and crunches haunt the air like black wings beneath a tenebrous canopy.

Whether they are remnants of reality or hallucination remains up for debate.

Above the treetops, the moon and stars have infiltrated the visible sky. Together, they cast an ethereal glow along the landscape that lengthens shadows and reveals no monsters.

However, in consort, they offer enough detail to lift the veil from an encroaching hillside.

I don't see any signs of Glen's fall. But there's no point in searching, either.

Giving into instinct, my hands traverse the rock face and dirt-laden incline. Quickly, they develop a melodic rhythm as they reach skyward.

Hand up. Foot up.

Other hand. Other foot.

First hand. First foot.

It's instinctual and calming.

The stars above epitomize freedom.

And they're so much closer than they could possibly be.

That is not a deterrent.

The pattern fuels me until neither rocks nor crevices remain beneath my fingers. Only level ground dressed in twigs and leaves.

That was too easy.

Worry seeps from my pores.

Have I somehow gotten myself up the side of a different hill?

The crisp night air fills my lungs, replenishing a calming euphoria. Something in my gut ekes out a whisper that this is indeed the hill that took Glen's life.

That I should have ascended it so easily, and without issue, elicits a twisted sense of accomplishment. With it, stirs a sense of pride.

A rewarding realization that I refuse to deny myself.

Not this time.

At pride's behest, I reject the weight of the world clinging to my back, and take the next step.

All hope flitters into the darkness of an abyss.

Which way do I go now?

You're all alone. No one to help you.

Alone. Alone. Alone.

The solitude takes on a frightening chorus. What had been a security blanket now petrifies me.

I yearn for some form, any form, of human contact. Someone capable of keeping me distracted; to dispel the loneliness of the foreboding nothingness.

In this light-deprived world, no bewitching colors dance their enticing steps around me. The pallet of night has consumed all their fervor with its arrival.

TRIP

I force out another step, and once again, the loneliness ushers in unintelligible terror.

So, I confide in the only comrade I have left.

Myself.

##:#7

WELL, NOT EXACTLY *MYSELF*.

The flooding presence of a memory returns.

A professor discusses a writing exercise.

The professor hands us a recorder. I press the red button. Chronicling dialogue with a character long since forgotten. An exercise in visualization and empathy I never enjoyed, and am hardly excited about now.

However, the shackles of loneliness are cold, and I need the comfort of another's presence.

The opportunity to channel solitary confinement into productivity.

An assaulting chorus of mosquitos buzz, and cicadas drone. An offering to consummate the conversation.

I set out in the direction that my gut's compass points.

"Cliff, I, uh..."

What am I supposed to ask the old, grizzled detective?

"I have to know."

I can't believe I'm doing this.

"Who's more evil, Trip or The Demon?"

The reply comes with ease, as if I have been waiting to answer the question.

"C'mon now son, ya can't actually be referrin' to this man as *The Demon*. He's a mortal being, call him by his God-given name."

A burst of hatred explodes outward. The fact he, or I—I don't know—that someone is right.

I'm higher than a—fuck knows.

I'm sick of metaphors and analogies.

I've frustrated myself, and all I want is to go *home*.

"Fine. Artie. Artie what's his dick."

His reply should come with a wry smile.

"Witherspoon."

The smirk creeps along my face.

This might be method acting, but the experience blurs boundaries I've been desperately clinging to.

"I don't know that you can compayuh evil. But any man who's capable of pulling tha' trigger without flinchin', is a man that's dangerous to your future. But he's no demon. Monsters are all too reeyuhl, but Artie, he's nothing more than any mortal." The drawling Louisiana accent is perfect.

That name, though.

Witherspoon.

Why can't I let it go? There's something familiar about it. "Cliff, do we—I —*fuck*, this is confusing. But, yeah Witherspoon. Do I know that name?"

"Son, I don't know why you're askin' me. I don' have a magical vault key to unlock all ya memories, those are yours and yours alone."

"Screw you, Cliff. You didn't even answer my question, who's worse?"

"If ya must force my hand on this matter, I'd say that girl, Trip, is by far and large worse. This Artie fellow's a wolf alright, but he's got his pack. He has people in his life, and he may even care for them in some perverse nature. That's yet to be seen. But, I will say, Trip, from everything I know, the girl's a shark. Sharks are not gregarious creatures by nature. Their antisocial lifestyle is a powerful asset when hunting. Cunning creatures, to be sure."

My eyes roll as his monologue ends. "Are you really a metaphor guy?"

"Boy, a metaphor's the only way to translate the knowledge of one world into that of anothuh, so don't ya dare go knockin' a good 'un."

"Fine, but I want to know from the horse's, or I guess, I should say the *shark's* mouth."

Going down this road? I have to admit that's a bit crazy. There may be no coming back.

It's one thing to talk to a single made-up character, but introducing a second personality, even I, in my present state, recognize how problematic that could be.

There's no choice, though.

I have to keep moving.

But the fixation of an idea is too powerful.

If a part of me can create a monster, and I can understand that monster, then maybe I can comprehend Artie...

##:#8

It's obvious I am not sober, but the visuals, euphoria, or any other sign of psychedelics, take a backseat to this conversation.

As if shackled, it lacks the freedom to run upon my psyche.

Steeling myself against this notion of slipping my feet into the shoes of a cold-blooded killer, I ask, "Trip, why are you like this? A shark that is, I guess?"

A nasally burst of mirth manifests itself without my consent. Maniacal malice surges along my back. Footfalls cease and her ominous joy coils around my innards.

Every word preparing to depart her mind comes from somewhere inside me, yet I don't expect to recognize them.

My skin crawls from my fingers to my shoulders, sending serpentine shivers through me, leaving an unnerving stream of goosebumps in its wake.

Deep inside, she grows from a place forgotten, or maybe just neglected. Somewhere old, and somehow familiar.

"What kind of question is that? Ya idiot. *Why am I like this?* I'm like this because I was raised free. No one forced me to adhere to your normal black-and-white, this or that, cookie-cutter standard of reality. You think that I'm bad. That that Arthur guy's The Demon? That's simply—"

"That may be the dumbest crock of shit I ever heard," the drawl rips out in protest. "There is no standard. Literally, considering yourself outside of it is to standardize yourself amongst those who think they do the same. Traits of a narcissist every damn time."

The scoff is alarmingly not my own. "Sure. You think every good man was a white knight, who led others to make the world a better place? No. Whoever changes the world says, '*Fuck you*' to the standard operating procedure because everyone else was afraid to break society's ethics and conduct."

"Okay, so the D—Artie is a gangster? Like Capone?"

"Fuck sakes. You're an idiot, guy. What did Capone do?"

"*Bootlegged alcohol?*" I ask, more than say.

Another snide laugh floats into the night. "You think Capone saw his *bootlegging* as bad? Nah, he simply provided people with what they desired. Something, it seems, everyone else was too cowardly to do—and hypocritically all too happy to indulge in the final product. It's all the same. So, whatever the fuck this Artie guy's doing, you can't deem it right or wrong, especially if all he's doing is protecting his assets and industry as he challenges the status quo.

"Me, on the other hand. I'm not like any of those losers. There is no one like me. And before you start talking about narcissism or pride or whatever the shrink tries to get you to believe, know it's bullshit. Because of the seven-point-five-billion people on this Earth, not one of them is out here doing what I'm doing. And that's simply proving that I am fit to survive."

This line of thinking is difficult to grapple with.

Trip knows to illuminate her line of thinking.

"You ever gone hunting?

I shake my head.

"Well, it's fucking boring. You hide and it's impersonal. Even hunting little rabbits and oversized birds—*dull*. Even with my own two hands...*Tell people about it?* And it'll scare the shit right outta them. So, I invented my own hunting. Taking down a prey that doesn't know it's prey, but can think and fight in a split second. That's exhilarating. That's living, kill, or be killed. *The Most Dangerous Game*. That's how it always used to be, and a return to that time will prove who truly deserves to fit into the coming world."

"*What?* That doesn't make any sense. Are you telling me *you eat people?*"

"Why is that where your mind goes? Do you believe I am a man-eater?"

I can feel her palpable silence.

I am in control...

Right?

Yet, I can feel her rejecting the thoughts I believe should be her response. I've truly birthed a disgruntled teenager.

When she finally responds, it's a reply only an adolescent could muster.

"I would never expect you to understand. You play by the rules. The formula. For fuck's sake you can't even write a damn story without an equation. Life's not always about heroes and villains. All too often it centers on those in the grey. The tales up here, in your head, are all a lie. The ones you've got there in your pocket, well, they're a little different aren't they?"

The mounting self-deprecation possesses a palpable weight. But it's far more pointed coming from Trip. As if she isn't me. Rather, someone I just met, who has already broken me down to my simplest self.

Where's Cliff to be the voice of reason when I need him?

"Now see, son, that is fuckin' evil." He returns. "This is someone who *literally* only feels when she can pierce flesh. She toys and torments and plays. It's all a game to her. This's why she's gotta be stopped. Regardless of whatever form she's in. It's her core that's vile. She'd need to be put down if she were a dog or a cat. 'Cause if she's not, things'll only progress toward her vision."

As we say this, I find myself overlooking the edge of a cliff face.

The moment offers a reprieve from my specters. Permitting the hallucinogens to ebb back once more.

##:#9

Hope carries my movements down the steep mountaineering trail with an inherent belief that I am heading back toward the lake.

That hope provides a sobering moment once more.

The night is silent, blissfully so, molding a momentary gap to escape from everything.

This is simply a task—crawl back down the earthen façade without thought. My feet root out for the next ledge instinctually.

It all feels so natural.

Yet, a worm of fear creeps its way alongside the cliff with me.

One false step, and I could end up just like Glen.

My focus falters. It could be the drugs, maybe it's just being extra careful on *this* descent, but my mind wanders, trying to steer clear of the fear accompanying me.

Eventually, a question stares me straight in the face. A reverie of the Red Tail's oil spot of an eye pulls me toward thoughts of the old man and the young sociopath.

Was this even a viable tale?

These are certainly not the characters of the hero's journey. They weren't even the antithesis of it. They're muddled.

Complex.

As if on cue, my heel rolls across a vine hidden beneath an outcrop and my stomach lurches with the sensation of the uncontrolled slide.

I've got to make it to my ass quickly, but I lose my balance and it feels like I might careen headfirst.

My hand extends towards something. I can barely make out its outline as it dangles in the moonlight.

Yet, as my fingers wrap around what must be a sturdy root, a heaving sigh of relief deflates my lungs.

Premature.

My shoulder's socket takes the brunt of the drop. Lost in space, panic assaults my insides before the rock face comes back to greet me with a crash.

Somehow, I'm safe. I'm alive.

That was real, right?

Catching my breath as doubt floods through me, my gaze tilts upward. There's no way to tell how far I slid. The moonlight is timid and cannot illuminate the tracks of my descent.

A slight thrum in my shoulder suggests it was all an exaggeration of the mind.

However, my heel still tingles with the phantom memory of that vine sickly spinning beneath me, stealing the traction that keeps me upright.

Panic returns, staking its territory within the empty cavity of my chest. There it winds and plops itself down like a wolf in its den.

I don't trust myself.

You shouldn't.

##:10

THE REMAINDER OF THE TREK TO THE FOREST FLOOR IS SHORT AND uneventful.

Urgency dissipates into the night air, and the ground becomes a seat upon which I can rest. The cliff offers a place to lay my weary form against.

The glow from the surging moonlight reveals jagged crevices that carve their way through the steep, angled path overhead.

Euphoria's pressure decides now is the time to weigh down my vision in a swirl of thoughts. I close my eyes and try to center myself, but it seems to exacerbate the sensation of spinning. A bent knee gets my foot flat against the dirt beneath, and I find this small anchoring point aids in slowing things down. With this comes an acute awareness of the sweat drenching my clothes.

My shirt feels cool as it clings to my chest and back. The craving for a drink envelops all my senses.

I wish I had grabbed something, anything, during my escape.

My pack, gone. Confiscated and left behind at the barn. If I'm lucky, my cargo shorts can deliver.

Both pockets still hold something weighty within. One burdened with the pack of cigarettes Glen had left to me.

The last thing he will have ever given me.

You're going to need a new agent.

That's the least of his worries.

Sadness wells up within me.

I need something to redirect my fraying thoughts.

A target.

Something to focus on other than that pit of loss and despair that I have grown familiar with.

My fingers find a lighter, as well. At the very least, I'm set for a nicotine buzz renewal.

What's in my other pocket feels foreign. It offers a weird sensation as my digits wrap around it—like it shouldn't be here.

Images skip through my head, and I know exactly what the object is.

In the night's darkness, I can't make out the faded yellow cover, but I can still read the title with the moon's help.

Devil's Lake

Original Tales of the Hočągara

It feels good to flip the crumpled pages between my fingers.

A few pictures jump out at me here and there. Although, trying to make heads or tails of most seems impossible.

Then there's one that clips my fingers to the page.

It takes up the entire spread. It is the precursor to a story titled "The Last War of the Wakąja and the Wakčéxi."

The picture digs its claws into my cheeks, forcing my gaze upon it.

The style is that of the old pre-industrial black-and-white sketch, with admirable detail emphasizing the indigenous artistry.

Humongous stones fall from the top of the page, implying a broad sky above.

While below, in the waters of a giant lake, a ferocious panther-dragon-serpent creature thrashes tidal waves upward at the falling boulders.

The grand depiction is that of a grueling battle between the first creature and a giant eagle-vulture hybrid donned in a jay-like crown of feathers and what appear to be eyes on its wings.

There are other creatures too.

Some are anthropomorphic beasts like a rabbit-man and a wolf-man. They look more like spectators of a gladiator match than they do participants.

There is a lone human. A goofy-looking fellow. He's wearing pants on his arms and a poncho-type thing over his legs while walking on his hands. He's off behind the rabbit-man and if I didn't know any better, was mocking him.

Studying the image, I fish out the contents of my other pocket and light a cigarette.

The nicotine showers me in its feathering high, leaving me to ponder the tale behind the photo.

Meanwhile, the fingers of my free hand traverse itself, detailing the cuts and nicks that accumulated along my slide down the cliff.

They don't hurt.

They're tantalizing.

It takes all the concentration I can muster to avoid descending the rabbit hole of 'the human condition.' Our ability to heal, regenerate, age, and all the lovely metaphysical concepts accompanying that.

Humans are complex.

Complex indeed.

Putting any one of us into a simple box just means that you'll be surprised. Always expect that it's near impossible to expect what a human might do next. We are a dangerous game.

I try to recall a story by this very name, read long, long ago through the eyes of a boy.

There was General Zarif, Zaroff, Zoriff, I can't be expected to remember. But he and his deaf-mute slave, Igor or Ivan, or whoever, hunt the hunter who washes ashore on their private island. At first, the hunter is all lulled in with General Z's hunting collection until he's forced to become the quarry. General Z gives the man a head start and tells him he has to survive for, like, a week or something to earn his freedom.

Why was this something to internalize to her character? Maybe it's the lulling aspect? Build trust and break it. It would be hard for a reader to know whether she's trustworthy if all the victims trust her, and deaths are always off-page...

The finality of the thought flitters through my mental grasp.

Ideas tumble through me with increasing velocity. Catching hold of any single one is likely impossible.

##:11

I AM UNCERTAIN WHEN, BUT AT SOME POINT, I'D SLID OFF THE HILLSIDE onto my back. It can't have been long, though.

Right?

My attention hardly belongs to me. As if it endeavors to explore my mind, while simultaneously noting every pressure point connecting with the forest floor beneath me. Euphoria leeches into each prod and stitch.

Through the patchwork awning of leaves, stars shimmer in morse code, a sweet soliloquy that wraps me in a comforting embrace.

Held to The Mother's bosom, an ethereal warmth washes away my fears and soothes my soul.

Receding is the static interference that somehow was an ever-present companion throughout this ordeal.

Within that moment of secession, movement in the distance stands the hair up on the back of my neck.

It's just from the corner of my eye.

I can't even be sure if it was really there.

My heart launches back into the rapid acceleration of a jet engine.

A foot steps out from behind a tree. Its master looms amidst the shadows. There's enough distance between the two of us for the moon's radiating light to reveal nothing beyond an approaching silhouette.

##:12

The mind doesn't often manifest something from nothing. That kind of breaks the laws of physics.

Matter can neither be created nor destroyed, or something like that.

And while remaining *well* aware that a hallucination is not itself matter, I can't shake the weight of the presence approaching. An animated being capable of thought, conversation, and movement.

But that's impossible.

Except he *is* standing right there.

Old and beaten down by life, an elder gentleman steps into the light of the moon. Instinctively, I know the man before he ever reveals himself. Albeit his physical appearance is hardly familiar.

Some traits are similar to that of old man Skeeter, but he lacks that plucky spark in his eye. These have sunken into a leathery face, cracked from years in the sun, and permanently darkened from too many caffeine-fueled late nights. Not to mention, the accompanying nightmares that withheld a restful night's sleep for more years than not.

His hair is wispy and unkempt. The man doesn't care to put effort into his appearance. The only part of him that seems regularly tended to is the bushy mustache perched between his nose and upper lip. Finely manicured, it contrasts the glimmering lackluster stubble lining his chin and cheeks.

He appears to suffer from the quintessential body of a bachelor in his late 50s, maybe early 60s. A physique devoid of exercise and predominately sculpted through a liquid diet.

His attire is hardly appropriate for the middle of the woods, but he looks the part of a gumshoe.

He's draped in a beige double-breasted trench coat that appears at least one size too small, and a wrinkled ebony button-down that tucks into his dark and worn bootcut blue jeans. A set of deep-soil-brown combat boots stands out as the most well-kept part of his ensemble.

When they say a man's old-souled, never let that be a comment on your boots.

A bland, grey tie, that complements his all-seeing eyes, hangs loose around his thin neck. The knot dangles just above his chest, while the tip terminates right over a simple, silver-set-on-black, Fleur de lis belt buckle.

I personally would never be caught dead with a belt buckle.

But on Cliff, it works.

He carries himself with a quiet strength. He's the type of man that I'd think little of, maybe even look down on, until shaking his hand, catching his glance, or becoming the subject of his questioning.

His strength lay in his character as an observer.

His soul has taken a battering like mine. But unlike me, Cliff wakes each day and gets out of bed. A humble strength.

An air of southern hospitality he'd picked up around the bayou emanates from him. Enough creole in his formative years to have taught him manners and respect, but also spice and fire. He'll pick his words carefully enough, but won't fuss with using a thesaurus to get his point across.

A point ain't worth making if yah audience needs a dictionary to hear it.

Old southern street wisdom.

"Son, what are you doin' down theyuh? Ya trying to get yuhself killed?" The southern drawl emphasizes his slow and deliberate cadence. The accent is thick but clear. Formality clings to it, commanding respectful attentiveness.

But his eyes—even in the darkness—shine with a spectral and haunting visage. A silver-ish hue that pierces the night with LED-like intensity.

"Sit round here waitin' any longer and you'll be finding yourself in a whole heap-a sorry."

That last bit doesn't sound right, but my conscious brain isn't in control...

Of course, that's not possible, either.

Unless...

It's a psychotic break. That's it. Dissociative Identity Syndrome or Disorder or whatever.

With my psyche shattered and inundated beneath the hallucinogenic cocktail flowing through my veins, maybe it's simply overdosing? And this is my mind's way of creating a coping mechanism?

Although, I've never heard of anyone going through a hallucinatory episode like this.

Then again, I don't know of a single soul who, while tripping, was forced to watch the murder of their friend and the vicious mauling of a grown man by a mountain lion.

Yeah, psychotic break sounds likely.

"I don't want to move. I'm just so comfortable."

My arms wrap tightly around my midsection as the grey gaze stares daggers in response. The embrace feels like it contains a collapsing star. Preventing the implosion of my body toward the eternal void of safety.

Inhibition gives way to animalistic urge.

Life, in this moment, centers on immediate gratification.

"Jesus son. You've chased tha' rabbit further down the hole than even poor ole Alice."

He's crouching down beside me. His piercing irises a sliver around dilated pupils.

"And I don't want ya to die, which means ya don't want to be dyin', which means get the lead out before that Mad Hatter of a man and his Queen of Hearts come snoopin' round for ya. Or worse, that goddamned Cheshire cat that done tore up that T fella."

A sense of control ekes back between my mind and body. "I can do without all the hokey metaphors. But point taken. Help me up and let's go exploring."

"Explahrin'! Son, this is life or death, and do I look like fuckin' Saca-jawea?" A hearty mirth trickles through his words. "We ain't got no Lewis *or* Clark to go frolickin' round the woods with. We get to camp and get that gun."

I'm helped to my feet as it all clicks.

"The gun. *Fuck.* Are we in the second act?"

"For once I agree with that old coot. Even if he is always prying into things where his fat nose doesn't belong." I don't recognize the voice. It's soft, young, and feminine, with a noticeable raspiness.

Intuition steers my gaze on an internal compass twisting toward a young woman sitting atop a rock, legs crossed.

Sleek midnight hair, braided into perfect little scales, slithers over the woman's shoulder. It's a plain face; nothing distinctive adorns it like a beauty mark or scar. Beneath a noticeably wide and flat nose are a pair of thin lips pressed into slits. A slightly pronounced, yet dimpled, chin tapers out her oval face.

She unfurls her long legs, clad in tight corduroys the color of ink. They stop just shy of a pair of dark canvas tennis shoes. Above the waist, she's wearing a cable-knit sweater vest the color of pine needles. The fabric hugs her form tightly, exposing smooth russet arms and a trim neckline, unaffected by life's culminating stressors.

She's alluring, but any thought tangential to that makes discomfort squirm through me.

After all, she is just a teenager.

Over the course of this night, I have felt a handful of emotions, but what engulfs me now is like bile fighting up the esophagus. It's acidic and vile. I want to scream.

She's just a figment of my imagination.

Except, I detest what my imagination is concocting.

"Awww," she says mockingly. "Are someone's hormones discombobulating their thinking? How disappointing. Sounds just like kids at school. But you're not in school, are you? *No.* You're a grown man."

She laughs, and my shame sinks deeper.

Trip taps a finger to her temple, lolling her head to the side just enough to be noticeable. Her eyes, though. Ringlets of a brilliant amber train on me like a predator.

The red-tail hawk revisits my imagination.

"But you're not an idiot like most of my peers. Those blissfully ignorant members of the low-IQ populace. See, the three of us..." She trails off, standing from her perch. Hands clasped, she stretches lanky spider-like appendages skyward, revealing a youthful, flat stomach.

"We've got sense enough to know. That gun needs to wind up in our hands. ASAP." Her voice stretches alongside her body.

"I hate to agree with the monster, but she did with me first."

The kid rolls her threatening eyes as her head comes to rest on her shoulder with the disrespectful glare of a teenager refusing to listen.

"Wait, I thought you said not to call my guy *The Demon*? How come you get to call your kid, *The Monster*?"

"Well, ain't that obvious son? Your guy's just a guy who likes drugs and writing books about drugs. My guy, or gal I should say, is a damned hell-spawn sent to troll the Earth with the bones of her victims for her own sweet enjoyment."

"Oh, come now sir, is that any way to speak about a lady?" She makes a *tsk-tsk-tsk* sound. "That's dark even for you, old timer."

Trip turns that vibrant gaze back on me, and I notice something. Her left eye possesses a tiny sliver of green blemishing the near-perfect, golden iris.

Mom had that. Except hers was blue.

"You remember well and good though—*it's not too dark for me.*"

She hops to the forest floor with a gentle thud.

"Now let's get going, I'm growing bored of sitting here. These legs need to be stretched."

She tucks her hands behind her head and strides off the way only a woman who knows you're watching will. Lanky steps deliberately shift her weight from one hip to the other. Back and forth. Hypnotically eliciting feelings that breed genuine disgust in my gut.

Hopefully, she's wandering off in the right direction.

"Now, what do you know about this kid?" Cliff asks as he pulls me in stride.

"What the fuck do you mean, *what do I know about this kid*? I just invented her, and for that matter, *you,* a couple hours ago!"

"Christ son. Can't ya see the forest through the trees?"

It's my turn to roll my eyes.

What the fuck am I doing?

Talking to myself? Two times over. Envisioning characters from a novel that I barely have a grasp on.

You have to pull the hammer back to even stand a chance of generating a spark.

If this was pulling the hammer back, did I want that spark?

What could it hurt?

##:13

Silence ensnares the area around our trio for...

How long's it been?

The quiet won't dispel my accomplices' existence.

I think it feeds them. Nourishing their corporeal forms.

I'm doing everything in my power not to think about either of them. To focus on the fireflies flickering in and out of existence. The woods' luminescent heartbeat.

Looking back offers the knowledge that those brief distractions held no weight on the specters' forms in the slightest.

Time disintegrates beneath the wash of warbling shouts from hidden cicadas. What I want to remain a soothing anchor, albeit oddly enough, lurches into an unnerving provocation from unseen spectators high overhead.

On Earth, the two figments of my imagination catch back up and fall in alongside me.

Following me.

Parasites?

Or symbiotes?

Well, if they're not leaving anytime soon, there's no reason *not* to get to know the creations that strolled right out of my imagination.

Trip's the kind to blaze her own trail. As she does now, moving to the front of our column.

She carries a laissez-faire demeanor.

From behind, there's a subtle twitching movement of her head. A sign that she endlessly analyzes her environment.

Objectively, I can see she might be likable to some, but only in the way the quiet kid can be. Because she does nothing to attract attention—unless she wants to. She exudes a mostly neutral presence. But I'm reminded of Cliff's words about her.

A shark.

The creature known to lurk in the shadows beneath a calm surface.

Cliff, on the other hand, oozes negativity.

He hangs back with me and moves deliberately beneath hunched shoulders as if his neck grew from the front of his chest rather than behind the collarbone.

But it's those haunting grey eyes that stand out. Fixated on his prey, conviction cements itself within those icy orbs.

"She's a beast, that girl. Can't ya sense it? She just swims along, but when she strikes, it's with fear and force."

I think about that. She may be nothing more than a wiry psychopath.

Or sociopath.

I know one is worse, but I can't keep them straight at the best of times. How am I expected to now?

Regardless, there's something to consider here.

What makes her that socio-psychopath?

Menace.

It lies beneath the surface. Even if you see a shark lazily swimming below the surface, you can't let your guard down. When it's least expected, they can leap with speed and force. I know force comes down to mass and acceleration.

Not sure why I remember high school physics amidst my drug safari, but I do and that's when I realize, *so would Trip.*

She's too smart for her own good, and *that* brain, *that's* what would make her scary. A massive brain that could accelerate across thoughts quickly and effectively. That was force. And force makes her a menace.

Mass times acceleration.

"Trip?"

She keeps walking but wheels her head back just enough to shoot a leer from those beady eyes. I can almost hear her voice in my head.

'What do you want? I'm in the middle of something.'

"If you were hunting us, me, I mean, what would you do?"

"Easy. Track yours or Glen's phone. But you took care of that already when you smacked Glen's out of his hand and *forgot to pick it back up.*"

Venom drips from her terse response. It's so egotistical; it reeks of a superiority complex.

"Even if they hadn't taken your phone..."

Damn.

I had forgotten about my phone. Or I guess I hadn't if Trip remembers.

"They'd have no way of tracking you without your number. So, then they just go and find you in the woods. Well, that is until they see their *mate*, dead and rotting, alongside mountain lion skat on the forest floor. So, then the only logical move is to go to your prey's den and wait for them to return."

"*The camp?*" I practically scream the question, knowing it's directed back at me.

Both travel companions nod their agreement.

Or approval?

There's a race that I've been neglecting to run and only now have I realized how far behind I might be.

At this point, escape may be a pipe dream. Yet, hope lives on within the confines of Glen's duffel bag.

But would it be enough?

It's not like I know what I'm going to do with it once it's in my hands.

I've seen it used on TV before, and Artie's words still reverberate through my memory.

Hammers and *sparks.*

But I'm unsure it will do me much good when the time comes.

Will it even be enough?

I have seen four members of this posse in total. Three were left.

But had I seen everyone?

"There aren't more." It's a snide remark.

Trip stops ahead of me, holding *DROPOUTS* with a smug look on her face.

Was I hallucinating the book too? Am I holding the book, and I don't realize it as my subconscious transcribes it to her?

I stare down into my own hands; *nothing*. Just the forest pulsing like a kaleidoscope beneath my outstretched fingers.

Yet there she is, backpedaling, unfaltering, twirling the book inhumanly atop a finger as if it were a basketball.

I nearly collapse to the floor in an existential breakdown.

I'm losing my grip.

But then I *feel*, yes *feel*, the large palm and thick fingers of Cliff's hand pat my back. He looks down at me and shakes his head dismissively.

"Son, we don't agree on much, but the girl's right. There're only three. You can trust that. It's a feelin' in yer gut, ain't it?"

My face is melting ever so slightly, warm and contorting with confusion.

"Alright Trip, how is it that *I* know there aren't more than four, er, uh three?"

The sound of crunching bone echoes between my ears, racking my whole body as surging adrenaline relives that moment.

"You started the book, didn't you?"

"Well, yeah, but that was only a single chapter or two. T said they'd been doing this for years, they could have plenty more people."

"*Well*, here's the beauty of you being me and me being you. I can assume because the only person who is getting an ass made of them is *you*."

Cliff chuckles, "What? She got ya there kid."

"*Fuck you, Cliff,*" I mutter under my breath.

"Anyhow. The man's a killer and he makes drugs. Do you think he's admitted many people within his inner sanctum? Probably not. The four we saw are the original four that were introduced to us in the novel. While it's possible that there are more goons on the payroll, if he's his own muscle, as the book, and T for that matter, stated, then he wouldn't want others to show him up on his home turf.

"We can surmise by the remoteness of the operation that only a minimal number of people likely know that place exists. I'd bet your life we've only got three baddies remaining, and once I get my hands on that pistol, it'll be zero, *real* quick."

She points a finger gun at three trees, rapidly firing off invisible rounds at the defenseless wardens of the forest.

"The fuck ya mean, get *yer* hand on the pistol, *Ms. Cantrip?*"

"*Don't* call me that old man." Trip stops dead in her tracks.

Cantrip.

"Oh, I'm sorry, would you prefer I call ya *Mara?* Maybe *Lilith?*" Cliff returns that smug, toying look I'd seen on Trip's face earlier.

Or maybe I do.

I don't know. I am as confused by this ridiculousness as anyone observing would be.

"Or better yet. How's about—"

Trip turns around. "*Watch it, old man.*" Her dark eyes are piercing. The green speck flickers like the shaking of a rattlesnake's tail. "I will *gut* you where you stand."

I see it now.

Cliff is not perfect, but this girl might be the exact monster he described her to be.

A shark.

Those amber eyes disappear into an oil spill of dilated pupils. Empty black voids that consume all the light around them.

It happens quickly, too.

She'd just been swimming along, then everything changed in a second.

With a scoff, she turns heel and marches off.

Cliff leans in close. I can imagine his breath on my ear.

"The kid's full name is Mara Lillith Cantrip. Her father was a complicated man. Abandoned the girl real young. Only came back when he needed something. Mother was never in the picture. Ms. Cantrip had siblings, but they're all gone now. Moved away or passed. Can't say for certain little Mara might not have had a hand in the passin' part, but she's a ward of the state now. Trapped and confined to the foster care system, which hardly ever does a child good. Certainly ain't doing the children around her any favors."

I hadn't thought up that backstory before all this. I know I hadn't.

Yet, here it is.

It feels new.

Well, to me.

To Cliff, it's old news.

Trip doesn't break stride, but adds without prompting, "Don't listen to the old Dic. He's about as big a fool as they come. Sure, people die, but to say that

I might have had a hand in it is just a sad accusation. Of course, pops had abandoned us all, why then should my siblings be any different? So, throw around your slanderous remarks *Sergeant,* oh wait no, *Mister* Fogarty. Or are we on a first-name basis, *Harlow?*"

The youth laughs to herself. A menacing and vengeful sound.

I can't remember writing that down either. But there's a familiarity to it.

I hear Cliff mutter under his breath, *"Insolent lil' shit. I can' wait till I get to shoot ya in the head."*

That's right.

The ending. A dark fate destined for these two.

From behind, Mara, Trip, whatever she's called, seems as ordinary a teenager as any.

Opposite her, Cliff carries himself like an old curmudgeon.

I feel bad for the kid. I feel bad that her creation serves only one purpose: to be slaughtered by this old man. But then I remember.

She's a sociopath.

Which births further contemplation.

Does that make me one too?

#:14

Our conversations wither. My subconscious abandons me to my own devices.

Until, without warning, or without my noticing, the trees unfurl their grip on the landscape.

Overhead, stars dazzle alongside their heavenly, spherical counterpart. It's enamoring, to say the least.

Beyond, the land dives downward.

Serenity envelopes all and the urgency of this godforsaken evening takes a back seat to the magical sight of the lake valley coming into view below.

To my left, strides Trip. Young, lanky, and looming with an unidentifiable emotion matting her features.

Reflections of cosmic life cast a whisper of their truths upon the lake's serene, glass-like surface. The stars' twinkling luminescence circles their lunar counterpart like a school of resplendent koi performing some archaic ritual within the depths.

To my right, the old detective hunches back. His gaze lingers on the sky. He looks younger. Almost like a different person.

Discerning what lies beyond each apparition's placid features proves an elusive task. Intuitively, I know meditations of the past and hopes for the future consume them both.

However, this is my story.

My own feelings become acutely present. Familiar, yet foreign. A surging happiness that is so out of place. For the first time since sunset, joy and giddiness well up within my stony heart.

Somehow, my sociopathic subconscious teenager has led us back here, to the lake, and now I have hope.

"Thanks, Trip," I say without realizing.

"Why are you thanking me? Aren't I just a *figment* of your drug-addled mind?"

I know that rhetorical tone.

"You wouldn't even hear me if it weren't for all the drug abuse plaguing your paltry brain. It's embarrassing. How are you even supposed to interpret and process worldly details if your mind is so clearly inebriated?"

She pauses. Her face offers no clues to the machinations my subconscious considers.

"That was rhetorical. Don't go answering it."

"Told ya she's a lil' prick."

"Alright, I'm getting tired of your bickering, or my bickering. Whoever's bickering." The train of thought tries to jump the rails. "*Fuck.* Let's just get down to the lake, and we'll figure out what's next. And maybe, *just maybe,* we'll make decent time if the two of you would just *shut the fuck up.*"

"As you command, master." Trip curtsies, and with a flamboyant flourish of her arm, directs me down the trail.

I give her a sharp middle finger as I stomp by, knowing only the shadows and trees are its recipients.

Maybe it's just my imagination, but the cascading stone steps seem steeper than before.

A creek trickles right alongside us.

Reassurance envelops the thinking processes as we carve our way down.

The other two members of my fellowship, while still visible, remain quiet. Though I enjoy the silence in earnest, I can't escape this mosquito-like nagging suspicion that they somehow confer in private.

Without me.

##:15

THE URGE TO MAKE IT TO THE LAKE, TO REACH SALVATION, ESCAPES ME.

A youthful wonderment pesters my consciousness in its place.

Explore.

This primal compulsion shepherds in conscious acknowledgment of the world. Of not needing to learn what ancestors learned the hard way. An appreciation for the mundane world that beckons me home.

After what feels like an odyssey into the abyss at the foundation of our reality—that tenebrous chasm where I lost so much—I should feel broken. Yet, here I am, whole and returning to familiar ground. Guided by these specters of my mind.

As if the full moon aids our journey, it bestows provisions of ample light across our path with sanctified glory.

The most peculiar sense of bliss saturates the deep recesses of my person with each footfall.

Off the path's edge, looms an old oak tree. Its gnarled trunk serves as a sturdy base for bulging appendages to spread skyward, groaning beneath an imperceptible weight.

It beckons me. Calls to me. And before I realize it, the giant looms directly overhead.

My hand reaches out for the jagged bark, which is soft underhand.

How long has it been here? What has it witnessed? What has it endured?

My mind constructs a vision from the Ho-Chunk book.

Phantom images of giant eagle spirits and water panthers fighting a desperate war throughout my imagination.

It all plays out from this tree's perspective. From a time when everything around it was much smaller. Still, it stood tall, undisturbed by the chaos of war raging around it.

An existential lesson skulks nearby. Something to discern from this tree's existence.

My mind twists in on itself, forming some sort of Mobius Strip.

The feeling is akin to standing at the ocean's shoreline.

The wet depths of the sand devour each foot as waves wash ashore and ebb back toward the vast, dark bowels of the sea. Those saturated granules of sand work in consort to grip each foot tighter and sink them down to whatever may lie beneath.

Here is my mind, experiencing the waves of this hallucinogenic trip flooding across it. Simultaneously, pulling it beneath the surface of consciousness. An unrelenting current slowly erodes the barriers of inhibition.

A compulsion strikes.

There's something that I *need* to see.

The spiderweb of branches invites me skyward.

The minuscule tactile sensations of the bark against my fingers ignite a reverie of Agent McNutt tight-roping atop the branches above.

Childhood memories climb up from my past.

A mother with thick, voluptuous hair and colorfully round cheeks looks on as I climb higher and higher.

A friend sits across from me, a large oaken desk between us. There's laughter and revelry at day's end.

There's a girl with a dog in the park. She throws me a frisbee, and I spin it back as the dog races between us, its tongue flapping between slobbery cheeks.

Then they're both gone. Sirens. Strobing lights. Hushed, sorrowful cries and a long, despondent howl.

"Sweet heavens above, do ya have *zero* sense of urgency?"

Below, the ground breathes and pulses. Euphoria smashes into me.

Rational thought threatens to drown.

I try to see myself, a drugged-up, lonely, adult man, climbing a tree.

Something beyond that lingers.

"I'm with the coot on this one. We've got a lot invested in you, and climbing trees isn't exactly conducive to escaping murderers. In *my* humble opinion."

Trip saunters off, and I'm left with Cliff's sharp, silver eyes relaying the disappointment of a grandfather I never really knew.

My vision of the world pulses and breathes faster. Yet, my two hallucinations seem as vivid and solid as ever.

##:16

Nestled in my tree, something changes.

Inside me.

Like a cracked wall finally burst. Except, this time, it isn't the wavelike sensations of euphoria.

It starts as a ship's hull springing a leak.

Instead of brackish water, something much darker floods in. A relative to that infernal demon of self-hatred that I've tiptoed around this entire day.

It moves with ferocity. Exponentially, it gushes inward. I can feel it in my body, but it hasn't reached my mind.

I fear what happens if it does.

Fight it.

Doing so means giving in to the trip, which terrifies me. Not because of what occurred this evening, but because I can't escape the idea that this will mean losing a piece of myself—forfeiting control to a part of me that enjoys the darkness.

I'm not ready.

But what options do you have?

Still hunkered amongst the branches, I recall the advice of a long-forgotten therapist.

TRIP

And inhale.
One, two, three, four.
Hold, two, three, four.
Exhale, two, three, four.

##:17

THE EXPERIENCE PEAKS WITH ROLLERCOASTER-LIKE INTENSITY.

Then it lulls, but I know in my gut this is the climb. All the previous speed expels from that last summit.

The trip offers a vibrant—*shine,* is the word I want to use—capable of expelling the inebriating shadows toward the most remote corners of consciousness.

Then comes the drop.

First, the clamber down to the forest floor.

My feet settle atop dirt and the psychedelic plummets into my chest.

Heaving waves of feelings amalgamate into an Akira-shaped monster that no one emotion dominates.

Forming words into sentences feels as impossible as being fearless in outer space.

Thoughts escape my mind with the haste of startled prey. Their rapid abandonment stirs up the lingering scraps of emotion.

The gravity of the world seems heavier, compressing me down towards the dirt and soil underfoot.

I'm losing it.

Just in the nick of time, the world brightens. Darkness peels away, leaving behind a shimmering reflection of the cosmos. Mystical. Otherworldly. Transcendent. All words that fail this moment's grandeur.

It's that point in the film where the archaeologist's heroic journey—navigating through wild, foreign, and overgrown jungles—culminates in a shot where they burst into a clearing. There, they finally bear witness to that light at the end of the tunnel, and something akin to hope spurs them over the wall.

The euphoria steers me from the woods to the water.

However, I feel more aware of it this time. More in control.

The faint memory of the lake's chill lapping against my feet beneath the morning sun invites me further.

But the refreshing reverie of the taste as it slithered down my throat ignites my lust.

The water holds answers.

I want it. I want that shock of submerging below the cool surface. Intrinsically, I crave it.

The lake has me in its gravity well, promising sobriety and control in beckoning whispers.

Near the edge, the lake's stillness is near crystalline. Not even the slightest ripple passes from the wind or against the shore of jagged, glistening rocks.

A mirror to the world.

A flicker of something below the surface catches my eye.

Something green?

Probably a patch of algae or whatever.

Before I locate the aquatic anomaly, I discover myself.

My eyes. Wide and flickering. They lock on mine. Or vice versa, and the world stills. A moment of privacy.

I watch as my twin removes everything from his pockets, tossing each item haphazardly aside.

Unburdened, he climbs atop a jagged stone barely larger than my foot. I do the same, as if I were the reflection, and we meet in a crouch at the water's edge.

He wants to tell me something. A wry smirk says as much.

It's an invitation.

I take a deep breath before turning to see Cliff cross-legged on a large flat stone covered in moss. He lights a cigarette from the pack, which ends up at his feet as if in offering. The slick tendrils of smoke mask his features and warp them into something otherworldly.

His head shakes in forlorn resignation as his features settle.

Is it working?

I turn back to the water but catch sight of Trip. Shoes removed and forgotten, pants rolled to her knees, she wades into the shallows. Almost in a sort of dance, her long, slender legs kick at the water, splashing droplets toward the heavens, warding off a coming threat.

I take in the view one last time.

Where to next?

A problem for future Galen.

For now, I listen to the impulsive whispers.

One last, deep breath, and off a bounding leap, I plunge into the water.

It—is—*cold*.

Every ounce of air rockets from my lungs, and a comforting coolness embraces me as my head dips below the surface.

A respite-filled sanctuary swirls around me, defensively denying me entrance. As if waiting for an answer to a question that I unknowingly missed. But desperation compels me to gain admission.

I'd give up anything right now, just to know what it is I'm chasing.

Gratification and fulfillment surge from the water flowing across my skin as it huddles me in an almost motherly embrace. It expels the dark doubt and fills me with a euphoric bliss that brings to mind the verdant hues of the healthy forest in the realm beyond.

Eventually, the need for air extends my legs downward, and my feet find purchase against the slimy algae-covered mass of gravel underfoot. With a grace beyond myself, I rise from the shallow depths.

The most satisfying breath of air I've ever known greets my lungs, and I resign to linger within the euphoric waters of Devil's Lake a tad longer.

Floating on my back, the pristine view of the stars overhead delivers a stint of awe as something accompanies it.

Something intrinsic.

Like the water has flushed something from my veins, and assumed residence in the vacated mortal highways traversing within.

Or maybe it's the other way around...

Maybe I've left something behind...

##:18

Rising from the water, I feel unburdened.

There's no sign of either Trip or Cliff, for that matter.

I think about calling out, but what's the point? If I want them to answer, they'll answer.

Still, I miss them. They were more real than a hallucination.

Cliff touched you.

There's no time for that.

I need to take my mind off the wet clothes clinging to my skin. It's a maddening sensation—nails on a chalkboard, grating. I want to rip everything off and give these threads back to the water, but that level of anger seems disingenuous to the surging sensations coursing through me.

Go.

Get. To. Camp.

Wet socks and boots squirm from the pressure of each step. It's an alien and distracting sensation, punctuated with unnerving squelches that fracture the night air.

Unfortunately, the acid trip isn't over.

However, it may have dulled.

Revive it...

It's a primitive craving to exit reality.

The night's stillness disorients.

Where is the camp?

I pick up my cigarettes, light one, and return them, along with the Ho-Chunk book, into my sopping wet thigh pockets.

The nicotine calms the nerves.

I'm on one of the lake's longer sides. Like a rectangle or an oval, the water has two long and two short sides. I need to get to a short side.

But which one?

Right?

Or left?

You don't know, do you?

What a surprise.

A twinge scuttles under my skin at that thought. The weight of everything settles before the gravity of the situation crashes down. Paralysis of analysis. There's just too much to consider.

Isolated, away from civilization, in a foreign place. Cold and wet. Running from people who want to kill me.

Quite the predicament you've found yourself in.

Fear grips and squeezes at my bladder. I sink to the Earth just in time to grip my knees tight and fold into a ball, preventing more than a minor accident. But there it is, a small patch of warmth spreading in my lap.

A grown-ass man, that's what I am.

Yet, I don't feel that way.

I thought I was regaining control. Instead, I'm reminded how lucidity has not been a regularity for me these last few months.

I can't do this. Why am I still trying? Should I have just let them kill me?

I wish I had anyone right now—mostly Gabi. Or my mom. Except that's impossible. At least, not without some sort of satanic necromancy.

If it were an option, I'd take it.

There isn't anything I wouldn't do to have my mom roll up in her old busted Trail Blazer, with its myriad bumper stickers, scoop me up, and take me to McDonald's before falling asleep on the car ride home.

The impossibility of that notion tightens me further into the fetal position.

My cigarette smolders on the rocks. A bright red eye staring into my soul.

##:19

I'M SITTING UP NOW.

The world around me sighs, and my own breath steadies. Relief accompanies each inhale.

Along with a fresh cigarette. Its palpitating cherry ember reflects along the unsettlingly calm surface of the lake.

No mention of a RED water spirit.

But nothing remotely panther or serpent-like slinks beneath this mirror to the heavens.

I hadn't heard the shriek of eldritch beings—or anything paranormal, for that matter—but there hasn't been a thunderstorm either. That was the prerequisite...

Wasn't it?

Was that today?

Feels like a lifetime ago.

Still, what creature spawned such a tale?

Or what MIND?

Seven-heads? Existing without corporeal form in this insignificant, land-locked lake?

Laughter shatters the night air, carrying across the water into the night.

Now, here I had been, throwing my body into its home with reckless abandon, something a Ho-Chunk man would have never done.

Unless it was a sacrifice. They had no problem with that.

River Child did.

STOP! GALEN, FOCUS!

I need a sense of urgency.

I've been here before, trying to will myself to do something, anything. But this time, the stakes are much higher. There are still people out there who want to kill me, and the longer I wait, the more I waste any head start I once had.

Focus.

There are two campgrounds. The Demon can't know which one Glen booked.

He and his cronies certainly could rationalize that I'd head to one.

But how would they respond?

Do they, 'A'—split up—creating a one-on-one, or possibly one-on-two scenario? Or, 'B'—move as a single unit from one site to the next?

B gives the prey too much freedom.

The moon, while full, does little to help me see in either direction. There's nothing identifiable on either horizon. One choice would put me where I need to be. The other, well, that'll place me as far opposite as possible.

It may sound immature, downright childish, but my decision comes down to a simple thought echoing like a whisper in my ear—*Right is right.*

Determination swells, adrenaline pumps, and euphoria amplifies with the first step.

It's like the excitement of competition. A bizarre, positive form of PTSD overwhelms the sympathetic nervous system, and for a moment, the trail becomes the path out to the old high school track on a bright and warm afternoon. I can feel the spikes of long discarded track shoes underneath each step. The rays of sunlight licking at exposed skin with the intense love of a rescue dog.

As if the world flips a switch, all that emotional memory vanishes.

The reality of this being a desolate trail around a dark and looming lake sets in. No sun to lap at my skin, just sopping wet clothes clinging uncomfortably to goosebumps.

A darker reverie enters my mind.

D.A.R.E. classes after school.

A runty Galen swears he'll never take drugs. He thinks they hamper intelligence and will prevent him from becoming the next great writer of his generation.

Remnants of a rainy day devoted to writing fantastical cosmic journeys, while parents argued in the background for the last time.

What happened to that kid?

Did I let you down?

No. NO. Of course not.

It was the father. My father. The one who'd burned that kid's stories in a drunken rage. The one who abandoned him. But there'd been a mom.

But what about after she got sick? What happened to that kid then?

He grew up and saw the real world.

Memories continue flooding in as my feet fly.

A more recent memory. Glen's gun. A cold metallic secret, hidden away. Now the symbol of violent hope.

My moment to be the hero and avenge Glen.

My moment to kill that fucker.

My moment to escape this miserable place for good.

"But what am I escaping to?"

No one answers. I wish they had. Abandonment isn't foreign.

Only the gravel rocks littering the path, bending and breathing under the hallucinogen's pressure, accompany me. An ethereal flow of psychedelic waves inspires another memory.

Not at the Sacred Lake. Instead, a lost evening on Lake Michigan—with Gabi.

Except, her hand isn't in mine. It never would be again. There's no pier where Glen is supposed to meet us.

It's just me now.

It can only ever be me now.

Still, there's that stupid song playing between my ears. A song she obsessed over. One about lovers on a summer night. My vision pulls back to this reality.

I want to sit. I want to think. I want to be sad.

I understand the irony of my skewing priorities.

There are literally murderers after you.

"Yes, there are," I laugh.

Considering the time spent remembering a dead ex-girlfriend and a depressing upbringing, it's almost as if this were my life flashing before my eyes.

Maybe I already died.

That'd be nice.

A lot less to worry about. No bills. No deadlines. No debt collectors. No more past-due notices. No more *final* notices.

There was already no Gabi—no Mom—no Glen.

Tears fly from my eyes, almost urging me to go faster. To escape their painful sting.

These moments are not my finest, but they lead to a vulnerability I can't say I know.

I've cried too many times in my life, but this is different. It's like the floodgates open, and I cry for all those dreams that little Galen never got to experience.

I cry for the memories that I smoked into an abyss.

I cry for reasons I can't possibly comprehend.

A weight dissolves next to my heart.

Suddenly, I can hardly breathe. A smoker's wheeze escapes into the air, and I halt. This heaving cry forces me to the ground.

I slap myself across the face, H A R D.

You are alive.

I have gone through hell before, and no one can torture me worse than I have tortured myself.

Hope, or something narrowly adjacent, ignites behind the tears.

Despite everything, I feel nearly invincible.

And I've got the runner's high to prove it.

##:20

DESPITE EVERY OUNCE OF FEAR AND LOATHING PLAGUING ME, I FIND the resiliency to plow on ahead.

Predominantly stemming from hope.

No hallucination can stop hope.

But they can wield it to your detriment.

The light at the end of the proverbial tunnel accelerates my pace. Terrains morph from woodsy trail to a littering of white rocks mimicking the heavenly radiance of the moon.

As if beckoning me back to this verisimilitude of reality, the train tracks gently guide my gaze to my stone throne from this morning.

Another lifetime.

The semi-paved and gravel-littered lot is silent, empty, abandoned. Yet, undisturbed in a way that sets that internal radio station off kilter.

Anxious static filters in.

Time to employ some stealth. For once, I can actually use anxiety the way nature intended. Staying alive.

There are a pair of cars in the next lot over, but I think nothing of them as I maneuver around.

On the balls of my feet, I tip and toe from vehicle to pole to tree, acting as if any of them might capably conceal my presence.

The movements become exaggerated. Caricature-esque.

There's a sizable gap of open space to traverse, and the only coverage available is a parked Jeep, lifted high enough to emphasize the petiteness of the owner's genitals.

A sound, muffled and unrecognizable, besets more anxiety. Without thinking, I slither beneath the vehicle.

I feel like a fucking *Scooby-Doo* character. There's no stealth in this behavior.

The image in my head expels a childish giggle. My hand slams against my mouth as another muffled sound reaches out from the distance.

This moment teeters along a line of reality and fantasy. I try to gather my frayed nerves under the spacious vehicle. But, as I lay atop the gravel digging into my chest, I notice something. A radiating heat at my back.

The car is still warm.

Fuck.

From the cooling undercarriage, there are no stars to triangulate locations. No sign of the moon to determine the current position of the night's timeline. And not a single speck of movement.

Fight or flight rages through me. Desperate for more stimuli to decide, the seldom discussed third option takes hold.

Freeze.

The air stills. The night quiets. No cicadas. No mosquitos. Silence.

Why not go drive directly to the campsites?

Maybe this wasn't The Demon's. It could be his lady friend's. Or maybe it belongs to a late arrival.

But WHY not park at the campsite?

Unflinching, ears straining, I fail to pinpoint any sort of presence out there.

No drunk campers chortling at the day's events.

No giggles from children accompanying the late-night roasting of marshmallows with their parents.

No lovers sneaking down to the water for some hanky-panky beneath the stars. Not even the Jeep rocks with the discretion of those same hyperbolic lovers.

Quiet.

The first ebbs of exhaustion seep in. This has to be how world-class athletes feel after giving everything they had, only to see the scoreboard tick away the final moments of the match. Their score significantly lower than their opponent's.

Get to the campsite.

I peer out from underneath the Jeep and see Skeeter's shed in the distance. This orients me.

But something is going down at the little brown shack. Skeeter's light is on. A silhouette of someone shifts outside the hut. They appear to be chatting with the old man—or whoever is inside—in an animated back-and-forth.

At first, the guest is nothing more than an amorphous shadow, but then the visitor shifts, creating a perfect silhouette.

Every ounce of me knows who it belongs to.

I can feel the blood on me. Glen's blood. I can smell it.

The silhouette's long, dark hair flows in shadow.

There's no doubt about it.

What if Skeeter is involved?

If this were some thriller TV show, the big reveal would be that Skeeter isn't the wise senpai of the story. He isn't here to aid the young hero, who he befriended over—*drugs.*

It all makes sense.

Clear as day.

They are in cahoots.

Skeeter's alone in the park most of the time. He doesn't fear the police, and he has nothing to lose by the sounds of it. Wife dead, and grandson gone.

The conversation seems to pick up. The volume of their cahooting grows louder than expected. Someone is clearly yelling now. One is disappointed in the other.

It sounds more like Skeeter.

This may be my only chance. The argument devolves into a shouting match.

They are both far enough away that if I make a break for it, I might slip past unseen.

But there's only one way to the site that I know of, and that will require getting closer to Skeeter's hut.

Which is why they're waiting here and not at the campsite.

I can still pull off a harrowing escape.

However, the possibility of confederates lying in wait is not comforting. I have to let hope drive.

Let's hope.

Hope's the gambler's drug. We need luck.

Luck is simply how fools rationalize the outcomes of their hopes.

I need to manifest this chance.

I envision it.

Me, the hero. Sliding into Glen's car and slamming my foot on the gas. Firing Glen's pistol into the shack. The Demon dives out of the way, while Skeeter leaps through the window, just in the nick of time, as I smash through the once-endearing brown shed. The collision sends splintering debris in every direction. Windshield wipers remove the last of the aftermath as I drive off into the freedom of the night.

Hope is there.

I can do this.

You can do this.

Hyperventilating absorbs every ounce of courage from the world around me. This would be a Medal of Honor run, as soldiers call it.

Count it down.

Three.

Two.

One.

I roll out the backside and pop to my feet. Each bounding stride pulses through me. I feel light. It's effortless. It's the Olympic 100-meter dash, and I'd like to see anyone try to keep up.

##:21

PYOW!

The now hauntingly familiar sound of a firearm echoes through the night with a reverberating scream, *"Hill! That way! The trail!"*

More shots ring out behind me.

I can hear the slugs whizz ever closer, colliding with stones and gravel near my feet. Each impact, a reminder of how fragile I am. How quickly this could all be over.

Each crack shatters the sanctity of the Wisconsin State Park.

FUCK!

Something moves the air right in front of my face.

That was too close for comfort.

There's solace in the idea that their aim can't be that good. One near miss out of however many.

I stretch my stride longer than I should. Longer than I have in years. Feet clip the ground a smidge lighter with every fall. A familiar high flowers as the balls of both feet attempt to manufacture as much distance and speed as possible.

It's a race, and only as I set foot on the dirt trail do I realize what had given me away.

Still soaking wet, my clothes slosh a slick, waterlogged sound announcing every move I make.

There won't be a second chaaaaaance...

Each footfall leaves a watery trail to pursue.

There'll be no hiding.

I have to get the gun.

Even then...

Was it loaded? Was there one in the chamber?

Do you even know what that fucking means?

I am so screwed.

Somehow, before one of the leaden pursuers can bite, I reach the fork toward the finish line.

Lungs labor through each breath. I regret those cigarettes now.

My sides burn.

I'm so close.

And just like that, the path deposits me at our glorious campsite. I skid across gravel and hard dirt, sliding down to my knees at the tent's entrance. Practically tearing it open, I leap headfirst inside.

There is Glen's bag. Just sitting there. It's the most beautiful thing I have ever seen.

Like a ravenous mountain lion, I rip it open. Clawing through the innards. Searching. Spilling its bowels across the floor with swelling urgency.

Footsteps crunch across the stones and sticks nearby. There's no telling how many sets.

They've slowed. More cautious.

It doesn't matter how many there are. My pulse slams blood throughout every last vein traversing my body.

I have to find this fucking gun.

Except, I can't. There's no cool metal anywhere.

Turn it upside down.

A familiar weight collides with a barrier.

The side pocket.

I tear that open and hear a haunting echo of The Demon's words in my head.

You see the hammer on the back of this here pistol. It generates a spark when it knocks against the firing pin.

I pull the slide back, which knocks the hammer into place. It has more resistance than I expect, and I fumble with the death-bringer. It bounces against the palms of my hands like a hot potato that I want—no, *need* to clutch tightly.

Then we require force from the action generated off that hammer clashing with the firing pin. Only then will you have the spark that ignites the propellent, and...

That strong feminine jaw and those green eyes peer through the opening of the tent, startling me backward.

čo

Instinct assumes command, and before I realize what's happened, a loud ringing *crack* explodes outward from my hands. The pistol's kick assaults my palms with a burly shock. Startled, I fall, tumbling onto my ass.

I try to fire off more rounds. The trigger frantically clicks, with no result. Empty, debilitating clicks that grease hope's razor-thin edge.

I fumble, trying to pull the hammer back again—it doesn't matter though. Hill's lifeless eyes stare through me. A third, cabernet-colored eye oozes viscera just askew from being perfectly nestled between her eyebrows. The weeping tears of wine hypnotize me, while the ringing in my ears encases everything in a sort of sensory deprivation.

Then, as if in slow motion, she collapses at my feet.

It's quiet.

##:22

Horror strikes.

Not because it has set in that I have just taken a life, but because a new face has already replaced Hill's in the tent's opening.

His dark eyes seethe with an icy rage foreign to this mortal world.

It makes me wish I'd used that round on myself.

The Demon's trigger clicks a hollow reflection of my own.

"You've got to be fucking kidding me! HOW? Twice in one God damned night?"

Malice tears through the ragged crags of those rich, midnight-teal icicles circling his pupils.

Another crossroads.

Sit.

Run.

The world oscillates in time with my heartbeat. Ebbs. Flows. Constricting. Expanding. All before my eyes.

A greater entity, from somewhere beyond, cups mismatched hands around us, tunneling existence from The Demon's eyes to mine. The psychedelics are making up for lost time.

Sitting still is *not* an option.

TRIP

I make the first move, launching myself up and forward. I'm going to bowl my way through him. I have to knock him over and never look back.

The Demon can't get out of the tent's opening fast enough. His slimy red lips pinch into a thin line. That's my target as I lower my shoulder and try to break through the blocker like a star fullback on the goal line. It's going to take all the panicked determination I can muster.

Open air comes as a genuine surprise, and the worlds of reality and mind sync.

The first step of freedom is terrifying.

The second step unfetters morbid panic as the lifeless corpse still lying warm beneath us ensnares my foot.

Stubbornly, I lurch forward, telling myself I will break free from the mass of torso and limbs.

Surging adrenaline tells me that's not to be. A hot and sweaty palm with clammy fingers strangles my ankle. It didn't need to be much, but their constrictor-like velocity is more than enough to topple me over.

The ground comes up fast, and my chin gets to be first in line to meet it. The entirety of my jaw absorbs the accompanying electric shock from impact.

I don't need to take inventory.

The collision forces me to bite down hard enough that I chip off half a front tooth.

The world spins with pain, metastasizing into a living nightmare.

All that euphoria in my veins amplifies the agony and terror of this moment.

Yet, everything is rendered inconsequential when I dare to peer over my shoulder and meet The Demon's glare. Frozen in this position I can see him clawing his way up my back like some sort of zombie from a horror film, gaunt and *hungry*.

He grabs a fistful of my hair. Using it like a dog's collar, he pulls the both of us to our feet. The pain is excruciating. Each individual hair hangs on for dear life.

Thoughts flicker through my mind of cartoon follicles wailing for help. Desperate to stay rooted on top of my head.

I want to laugh.

More so, I want to cry.

I want my mom.

I hate how vulnerable I am.

His eyes. They are—*fuck*.

Words are fleeting.

Trying to assign language is inconsequential.

Hate looms over me.

Pure. H A T E.

It's different from anything I have ever known. This loathing and detestation that burns with the frigid intensity of dried ice.

My bowels feel as if they are preparing to loosen.

I just want it all to end.

I just want to die...

Something hard and cold cracks across my face. The now familiar gravitational pull of the world escorts me downward, where darkness waits to receive me.

##:23

OKAY, THIS... IS... WEIRD...

Where am I?
   Why does everything look like it's underwater?

This whole place is just a dark void.
   Weightless, like a pool. Or...

A lake.

Of course, it's a fucking lake...

...
...
...

What was that?

—I—I saw—I saw...something?

Someone's over there.

I think?

It's so dark. But not black.
    Close though.

Like something I've seen on a beach...
    Maybe, a plant...
    Like, um, slimy, water grass...

Oh, thank Zeus and Allah and Jesus and Stan Lee and all the gods above!

Wait a fucking second...
    Why can't I talk?

I hear myself.

But only in my head.

I mean, okay—IF, and that's a B I G fucking if—I'm underwater, sure, makes sense...
    But I can breathe...

That does NOT make sense.

...
...
...

TRIP

Holy hell, that's—
  Well, fuck. I thought I was done with you.

So...I can't call out. But maybe she can hear my thoughts?

Trip! TRIP!
  Uhm... Mara?

                    Hello! HELLO?

Why's she just staring?
  With the cockiest fucking grin I've ever seen...

And why's she dressed like that?
  This place is getting to me.

              Maybe I AM guilty of appropriation?

                    Maybe—

...

...

...

Now who?

...

Why are you BOTH just staring?
  ANSWER ME!

                    w o a h.

How'd you get so close?

And how'd you move like that?
I can't move like that.

I can't move that fast.

CAN I move?

And what's with your head...
    That's definitely not a headdress...

Nope.

Real big nope.

Wait.

Trip...let go of him.
    what are you doing?

...

Jeez!
    Stop!

No!

...

oh. fuck. no.

...

TRIP

NO!
   STOP!
   PLEASE STOP!

...

LEAVE HIM ALONE!
   GET AWAY FROM HIM!

...

HAVEN'T YOU HAD YOUR FILL?

...

...

...

Oh. God.
   Why did I even try?

This has to be a dream.
   It HAS to be.

Just wake up.
   It's simple. Just wake up.

   Wake up...wake up...wake up...wake up...
      ...wake up...wake up...wake up...
         ...wake up...wake up...
            ...wake up.

   ...

##:24

W H E N I C O M E T O , I C A N A L R E A D Y S E N S E I H A V E N ' T H A D T H E F O R T U N E
of sobering up.

You're not that lucky.

No. I am not...

A flittering of images slowly meanders through mental fog.

A dream.

But, I can't reach it. I'm too slow, and the reverie moves too gracefully through my grasp.

Confused and aware of a simmering agitation, I take inventory of my person.

I haven't been shot, I don't think. It doesn't feel like I'm bleeding out.

Unfortunately, I'm not pain-free. Searing agony surges through my cheek in a headache-inducing thrum. Worsening with every minuscule motion.

In addition, each inhale of cool evening air sends a tiny convulsive shock through my chipped front tooth.

That'll happen when someone pistol-whips you, I guess.

There's no sign of The Demon. Things are fuzzy, but we're still at the campsite.

Glen's car is right there. Untouched. A taunting beacon of hope, despite the clock having expired just inches shy of the end zone.

TRIP

For the second time tonight—and in my life—I'm strapped to a friggin' chair.

Unfortunately, this time, my captor hasn't neglected my legs. Cinched tight with duct tape, there's nothing to do but accept this cheap folding chair as my prison.

Despite frantic internal pestering to remain calm, anger and panic flood in. My mind treads water, and lucidity is fleeting.

The panic creeps through as I struggle to orient myself to the present despite resurgent visuals. The powerful hallucinogen tightens around my brain. An organ now forbidden to serve its purpose, delves within itself.

I can *see* my fear, anxiety, and dismay. Like a swirling mass of colored smog, taking loose shapes of images meant to induce such emotions. All guided by an underlying current of euphoria.

It's not enough.

Until this point, that intoxicating presence served as a guiding light, buffeting the nefarious feelings that I allow to self-deprecate.

But now things are changing. Now the situation is dire. I have seen Death.

You pulled the trigger and invited Death into your life.

Tears drip down my cheeks.

You are forever a murderer...murdererr...muuurdererr...muuuurdererrrrr...

Depression, forever the opportunist, moves to inundate and sink my soul.

Now the tears flow like streams after a heavy rain. It's hardly a good cry.

An intense pressure immediately detonates an explosion of white-hot needles through my left eye. The awareness of the damage to it and the surrounding cheekbone threatens a deep, looming onslaught of grief yet to come.

Suddenly, sobriety presses down with an unfamiliar gravity. As if seeing its opportunity in my tears.

Legs aching, face pounding, clothes still sopping wet, I begin to feel the slightest bit normal. The waves of hallucinations steadily calm.

Every twinge of my eyelid radiates torturous pain through my face. The skin has grown tight. Is growing tighter, further blurring my vision.

Footsteps.

Baser human instincts settle in. The lizard brain knows we are prey. Some sort of fucked up hare caught in a trap.

The thought of gnawing off an arm and fleeing comes to mind. But I don't have that in me. Mostly because even the thought of biting into anything shoots a debilitating lightning bolt through my entire jawline.

All I can do is wait like a coward. Trembling, dreading what is coming.

Death.

A warmth floods my seat and spreads down beneath my thighs.

Some hero.

A mouse caught in a trap does the same, but they will still try to escape.

It was a release, a weight lifted.

Reminders of long-forgotten childhood nightmares would like to make themselves known now, and their skeletal remains wrack me deeply.

Every possibility of what comes next follows suit.

Torture seems likely.

I'm not James Bond.

If torture's involved, I will not handle it well.

It's going to be vengeful too.

It'll be for The Demon's sheer pleasure, which means I am, objectively, *FUCKED*.

##:25

THE RESONANCE OF HIS DEEP INHALE IS THE LONE SOUND overpowering all existence. Even the loud warble of cicadas in the trees seems to go silent.

He's approaching from behind me. Drawing nearer in a wide, arcing breadth, like a predator. His gait is almost a prowl as he comes into view.

Those dark globes now sit deeper in his skull. His skin appears more pale, clinging to cheekbones like only bone lay underneath.

"You." He chokes on air.

In that instant, he lost all menace as an otherworldly monster. In that gasp of air, I sense his humanity. He's restraining himself.

"You killed her. Then I...*had*...to kill *him. Because of you.*"

He's not crying, but he looks tormented.

I can't tell if it's fear or pity I feel toward him. But neither is my focus because I have enough wherewithal to pick up on the fact that he's killed someone else.

"*But, who?*" It just slips out.

##:26

He's disappeared from my sightline, but he's not far. I can hear him just behind me.

Then he saunters back into frame, and it's clear that he's abandoned his humanity once more. Only a bright red rage etches his sharp features.

But now—*now I know.*

I know there is an actual person in there who can feel, even if he is good at concealing it. The realization allows me to *feel* the fear drain from my body.

Artie sighs, "The old man. My old man. But his death—that's on you."

My mind clears slowly through the fog of exhaustion, pain, and euphoria and in an instant, it all makes sense. "Skeeter."

"Don't fuckin' call him that," he growls.

"Sorry. But, that's who, isn't it?"

Every piece of the puzzle falls into place.

"And you're the grandson who went off to college. That's why you picked this park, you already knew the lay of the land. Then you figure, *'Hey why not write a book under a pen name about all your drug-making exploits to further finance said exploits?'* Am I *warm?*"

Every word causes a searing pain through the side of my face, and the night air thrums electricity into my chipped tooth.

But I can't help myself. I *want* to tease him. I want to torture him mentally, prove he's not as clever and frightening as he thinks he is.

It's probably suicidal. But maybe that's what I want.

Just going to let him kill ya in your piss-covered pants.

Calm ebbs into my joints while watching him. My rationality feeds on his dwindling sanity.

"Quite the fucking detective, aren't you? That should have been your next book, might have actually turned out something worth reading for once. Too bad though. Absolute shame you'll never get that chance."

"Well, I mean, it wasn't hard. Honestly, it's kind of a disappointing story arc. Drug-addled teenager goes off to school, drops out, gets in over his head at the park he used to work at, and ends up killing his father. Oh, sorry. Not father, just the only person who could have ever loved you. Feels—*cliché*."

A smirk slides across my face, almost subconsciously. I can accept I'm losing my mind. I shouldn't get joy from egging him on.

But I do.

He slugs me with a quick jab to the opposite side of my busted cheek.

The pain says one thing to me loud and clear. That *busted* cheek is either a fractured orbital or the cheekbone itself. It's as if my skull is crackling open like an ice cube dropped into tepid water. Splitting on a jagged line toward my eye.

What if it pops my eye?

Not out of my skull like a pug, but similar to a balloon or a grape.

I still have some vision out of it, thankfully. So I chalk that up to the delirious waves of every drug and neurotransmitter coming together in a climactic vision.

"I *fucking* hate you, guy."

An unsettling slime fills my mouth. It exudes the taste of iron and it's *strong*. I need to spit.

"Why?" I spit out, along with the bloody slop.

A sense of dread creeps up my spine as those fucking eyes drill down into me.

"Why? *Because you've fucking fucked everything up.* You think you're the only one with dreams guy? Huh? I had dreams too. Beyond this shit heap of a park. But you. You went and fucked everything up. You killed—*probably* killed T. You killed my girl, and you made *me* kill my grandpa. Who, for some fucking reason, gave you *THIS!*" He holds up the yellow Ho-Chunk book.

Of course, he searched me.

"This was *MINE!* You don't deserve it."

His words are aggressive and simultaneously reminiscent of a petulant child.

"On top of *all* that, you are a disappointing as fuck writer."

I am in too much pain to respond, but I know he's just trying to hurt me. Because he's weak.

An overwhelming sadness mixed with relief wafts over me. Knowing that Skeeter hadn't been the mastermind behind this whole escapade is a weight off my shoulders.

"No." I hock another wad of bloody phlegm. "Why kill Skee—Clint?"

"Because he'd know where to tell cops to start looking when two campers show up missing, *obviously.*"

And here is the moment where I realize Artie is *literally*, certifiably, insane.

The greasy hair, the patchy goatee, the sallow face, and sunken eyes. Who knows how long Artie's been cooking drugs, but it's been too long, that's for sure.

The guy has probably rotted his brain on one too many occasions. He's paranoid. He's delusional. He seems to have mood swings ranging from depressed to violent and manic. He's no demon, just some kid who grew up lost, and fried all his marbles along the way. He's probably a sociopath currently losing the control he's worked so hard to cultivate.

Something overcomes me.

I think it's pity, and that pity overshadows most of the remaining fear I've been clinging to.

"What *the fuck* is wrong with you, man?"

##:27

He's still holding the book, ignoring my remark.

"I can't believe he gave this to *you*. This was *MINE*. Given to me by some old fucking Indian who thought I needed to know this place's *spiritual history*." The tone of his arrogant contempt would concern any HR rep from here to the furthest corners of the globe and back.

Flipping through the book, he stops near the very end. "The only story I ever really liked was the last one. Did you read it?"

I shake my head, but I don't think he's paying attention.

"Of course, you wouldn't have. You're probably too good to read out of order."

I assume his reply is a mocking assumption because he only has eyes for those yellowed pages.

"It's the best story though. It involves my favorite guy, *The Trickster*. He's kinda like Loki. He's supposed to be a spirit that oversees and protects the OG Indians, but he says fuck that, like, half the time and just messes with people. Turns himself into a lady to sleep with men, and then has them wake up next to a man or in one case a fox! Fucking metal. Whoever wrote that story definitely had a little too much of the old ayahuasca root. But, if you believe all this garbage, it's actually The Trickster who originally oversaw the protection of the Lake. Then some Feather-Head God decided to pull him up to oversee

Heaven or some shit. He had to watch as his brother, who's a fucking rabbit, I guess, gets murked by some green, panther-snake-thing that lives in the lake.

"But they're spirits, so ole rabbit-boy just has no body. But, Trickster, whose real name is too fuckin' hard to pronounce—*Wak-din-kow-ga, Wak-jelly-koala* or some shit like that—goes ahead and tricks ole God by giving Rabbit-brother his body and station to watch over Heaven or whatever. Then my boy the Trickster comes down here so he can spirit around and fuck with the panther-snake-thing. But by the time he gets back some fucker born from a fish already killed the damn thing. So apparently, they're both just, like, trapped here, bodiless, torturing each other for eternity. I mean, maybe ole *Wak-jelly* is providing a service against a monster. But I like to think he's also behind spooking little kids at night and fucking with the drunks who stray off into the woods alone."

The laugh that escapes him is animalistic and deeply unnerving.

"Gramps *hated* that story. He said it was just a myth. *Fucking moron.* They're all myths. At least this one's entertaining."

##:28

I WANT TO BELIEVE ARTIE HAS FORGOTTEN ALL ABOUT ME.

He has spent who knows how long manically destroying our campsite, chucking all our belongings into the trunk of Glen's car.

A lot of good it does, though.

Even with this precious time on the periphery of his attention, I can't seem to find a way to free myself from this stupid chair. Damn thing is constantly at risk of toppling over if I move too much.

"You know, no one comes to the park anymore."

It's an awkward and unsure statement, as if he can't tolerate the silence.

An unfortunate reminder, he has not forgotten my existence.

"And since Nan died, no one went to see *him* either, well except me. But no use for that anymore. I guess if anything, I've got an inheritance to execute."

He's chuckling. The guy is definitely transitioning toward fictional psychopath-level insanity.

"Now, we've got more pressing matters to attend." He slams the trunk shut with the last of Glen's and my possessions, punctuating the statement.

"One, what'd you do with T? Two, get Pa and Hill's bodies outta here, and three, some light torture, followed by a sweet dose of murder." He sounds like a kid sharing his three-day weekend plans.

But—

While he may be a piteous man-child, the way he speaks with glee about torture and murder is unsettling.

Panic returns, and it's paralyzing. My mind doesn't feel capable of focus. That is something that remains more of an ethereal concept floating around my skull. As if it has yet to finish solidifying back into the physical, cognitive processing organ I need it to be.

Fuck, you're losing it.

One man's crazy is just another's deity.

"Foot to the chest!" The shout is confusing, but revelation arrives less than a second later.

The sole of his boot flattens against my sternum, sending me toppling backward.

He leaves it pressed there, as I lay flat on my back. His weight fills the boot pressing on my ribs. Nerve endings alight exponentially as my lungs strain to breathe.

"So, out with it, what'd you do with T?" he growls gleefully, shucking his foot from my chest and returning his attention to the campsite.

"Mountain. Lion," I gasp.

"The fuck you say?" He looks back down as I lay helplessly amidst twigs and acorns.

"Mountain lion. It...It got him. Snapped his neck and tore him up."

It was horrible.

Oh, come on. We didn't even see it, and we've seen worse.

If I somehow make it out of this night alive, that moment will be a large part of my therapy going forward.

Well, that and the murders.

He peels off a trucker hat stolen from Glen's effects and begins cackling like a hyena. "Of course."

He has to catch his breath through fits of glee.

"Of all the," he's not even trying to contain himself, "of all the stupid fucking ways to go out, being eaten by a giant God damned cat—that makes sense for T. Well hopefully the damn thing ate the whole meal because I don't feel like trying to locate and clean up the scraps."

He saunters away, still chuckling to himself.

"Damn thing's probably ODed from all the booze in T's system!" The laughter re-intensifies as he doubles over, hands on his knees.

The cicadas sing their shrill buzzing songs as if backing up the lunatic's merriment.

Fireflies occasionally flash, and their presence reminds me we're not sealed in a vacuum. Yet, seclusion, isolation, and fear have already burrowed deep.

The amalgamating stenches of urine and body odor seep in through my nostrils. Slithering toward the back of my sinuses, the awful miasma forces out a gag. A retch follows shortly thereafter.

Disgusted with myself, I just allow the tears.

Humiliating.

Disappointing.

"Are you crying?"

I try to shake my tears away, but get the sense it makes me look like a pouty five-year-old.

"Christ. You are pathetic."

I feel pathetic.

Pathetic.

Artie struts like a prizefighter to retrieve the duct tape off the campground floor.

He'll probably use it to muzzle me.

Instead, he flourishes a flip-knife from his hip. Panic curls its way in.

He'll probably carve my face. Or dig at my gums, maybe my eyes. Shit, maybe even my fingernails.

I can see him sinking it into my abdomen, his hot breath sulfuric on my cheek.

He leans in close.

The knife slides in under my wrist.

The steel racks the nerve endings as it presses into the tape before—*freeing* me from my bonds.

His hands take advantage of my surprise and quickly snare my now-freed arm and pinches it against the tied-down arm.

Deftly, he releases the immobilized appendage and begins taping my two forearms together.

He's not all that strong. His grip is bony, but I expected more.

I guess that's what happens when you set the bar too high for your captor?

If you find yourself kidnapped or captured, just imagine the worst of the worst and hopefully, your captor disappoints with their cruelty standards.

Also, take two heavy doses of acid, with some ecstasy sprinkled in there, and that should do the trick.

He releases my ankles next.

Ushering me upward, I obey. But it's a struggle getting to my feet.

With my forearms bound together, it forces my shoulders and pecs inward. Everything feels squished and compressed.

"Alright, now I'm putting you to work. We got cleaning to do," he says, while awkwardly steadying me on my feet.

I notice one of the Jeeps from earlier now pulled up just to the side of Glen's sedan.

We're gonna dispose of the evidence.

Sure enough, "Alright, take down the tent on top of Hill. We're using it as a body bag."

With my range of motion so drastically restricted, I don't think I could get my elbows more than eight inches from my chest—let alone straighten my arms.

I have to finagle my hunched form at a forty-five degree angle to accomplish anything.

My mind forms an image of how this must look.

Dr. Frankenstein's assistant aiding his master as they collect the body parts for the future monster.

More like the bell tower of Notre Dame's kee—

Artie's quick to shove me aside and tear the tent down.

As he finishes, he shucks Hill's lifeless extremities into the collapsing tent like wet pants into the dryer. A subtle *thud* is all she is now. The noise of gravity pushing her deceased heels to the dirt. Her dead green eyes stare blankly through the mesh window.

In silence, we zip, roll, and carry the body bag to the Jeep.

I have the feet. Artie takes the head and leads the way, going backward. My wrists painfully cramp as I try to move slowly and gingerly, but Artie isn't on the same page.

I fumble her ankles, but think I've recovered—

Then one slips, and now I'm losing the other.

Her body slides down, and rather ungracefully, I make a last-ditch effort to regain my grip. But my feet are coming out from under me.

Vertigo slows time as I lose my footing.

My head collides with something soft and forgiving. I know exactly where my face is lying. My cheek caresses her chest, and I have an unsettling thought—*this is actually kind of nice.*

This is what happens when you've been away from the opposite sex for too long. You can even find solace in the female form of a corpse...

Foul.

Disgusting.

Nope.

I feel sick, again.

Lurching to my feet, I flounder and slip again—landing in the same spot.

This time, my stomach sloshes, and I have to hold back the searing bile at the back of my throat.

In a panic, I press down to get up and, unfortunately, my clumsy hands wrap around one of her breasts.

My first thought—*first fucking thought*—is that it feels *nice* in my hand.

Repugnant.

Embarrassing.

Okay, I get it. I know plenty of fucking words to talk shit on myself.

"If you're done feeling up my dead girlfriend, I'd appreciate if we could get a move on."

My cheeks flush hot, but the way he growls through his words sends a shiver between my shoulders.

With a major sense of urgency, I roll from the corpse to the ground and push myself up as quickly as my bindings allow.

Getting her the rest of the way to the Jeep is no problem.

My breath hitches in astonishment at how Artie drops her head into the trunk of the car as if she were nothing more than random rubbish.

Despite what she put me through, I lay her feet down gently. It seems the least I can do in reconciliation for the posthumous groping.

It's not like, you know, she tried to murder us.

But I murdered her. She'd be alive if it weren't for me.

To treat the corpse of someone who wanted to kill me with such—
Kindness...
Oh.

Before existentialism takes hold, the trip rushes in, unannounced, ready to swallow me once more.

##:29

SOMETHING SEEMS...*OFF*.

Almost like my insides are glowing with a gentle, white light. The hallucinations seem to have ceased, but I feel an eerie warmth forming a connection to everything around me.

The songs of the cicadas reverberate in my soul. Their rainfall of sound unleashes a storm of euphoria. The chorus of the night pitter-patters just beneath my skin.

Artie continues to toss items into the back of the jeep atop a corpse he'd felt I defiled.

I mean, you kinda did.

Isn't this worse, though?

He tosses each item with as much disregard for what lies at the base of the trunk as the items themselves.

Glen's cooler, still filled with a handful of drinks and sloshing water, lands with a *crunch*. It's an organic sound, the resonance of which physically shakes me.

I can hear his screams again.

Oh yes, the sweet muffled terror as life drains from him to another. Fangs crunch through bone.

In silence, the pair of us make quick work of the site. I imagine Glen and I would have made much slower progress, come morning.

The only trace left of my friend is the old red sedan. I know I'm not lucky enough to be handed the keys, but I am curious what he'll do with the vehicle.

"Now you climb in." He points to the brimming rear compartment of the Jeep.

I stutter intelligible sounds of reply.

"Look here, genius, I'm not letting you ride anywhere near me, especially smelling of piss. So hop on top of that pile of shit in the trunk and let's get moving. Don't forget, I still promised you some torture. That is, before I do the world a fuckin' favor and blast you between the eyes."

I chuckle. My mind has gone straight to the gutter. The psychedelics are not helping.

I don't believe Artie approves.

His knuckles swiftly connect with my diaphragm, confirming that hypothesis.

Foregoing the wind knocked from my chest, I struggle to climb atop the pile, doing my best to ignore the muffled noises from what lay beneath.

As I curl up like another dead bug in a trunk, he slams the door in my face, sending a treble of fear throughout my body.

The mixture of scents back here creates a sour aroma.

I really should have just stayed home and smoked weed all weekend while watching cartoons. But nooo, I had to "find myself" out in the fucking woods.

But you've found so much more than yourself.

##:30

THE SENSATION OF RIDING IN THE TRUNK, UNABLE TO SEE WHERE WE'RE going, presents an interesting dissonance.

The not knowing part—*anxiety*—the gentle rocking and rolling of the car across the uneven gravel surface—*soothing*. The two emotions in tandem feed the waves of my current euphoric affliction.

Which is fine by me. Sobriety didn't seem to offer much benefit.

What else is there but to relent and embrace this high?

Might as well enjoy what little life I may have left and escape the reality that seems hell-bent on premeditating my demise.

##:31

As the vehicle rolls to a stop, my heart sinks. Straining to see out the miniature, tinted back window I can just make out the dark silhouette of Skeeter's shed.

Artie exits the driver's side, and there's not much room to sit up. But as I do, the light of the shack turns on, and any hope that Artie had been fucking with me is gone.

He's the only figure moving around in the piercing illumination of the structure's yellow glow.

Artie swings the trunk open with violent execution. "Get out, *Disappointment*. We've got one more body to move."

I do as I'm told, somehow sticking the landing as I roll out onto my feet.

With an aggressive shove, he bullies me to the shed's threshold.

There he is.

Slumped against a table hardly big enough to be useful, and the aging wood of the wall is Skeeter. A dark, speckled, red blob coats the spot where his head would have been had he been sitting up.

I can keep it together, but I can't stop a tear or two from sliding down my cheek.

For the first time through all of this, I feel strength return to the tendrils of Depression.

Everything is pointless.

I can't imagine killing Skeeter. He was a good man by the sound of it.

Maybe if he were some horrible scumbag, but I'm sure he wasn't.

To kill a good man is one thing. To kill the man who took you in and fathered you is another.

Artie is without a doubt every bit the monster I took him for. Any sadness he held for Hill or Skeeter was either selfish or crocodile tears.

I hear Trip's voice, tender and clear as day as if she's sitting next to me.

Are you kidding me? Greasy Keanu up there probably cried like a baby. He's got some anger issues, which means he's emotional. If he hasn't wept yet, he will. And we can take advantage of that.

I wait for Cliff's reply, like it's not my own thoughts speaking for him. But nothing comes.

Yeah, Cliff's not available right now, sweet Galen. It's just you and me.

That last bit is lustful. It hangs on my ear like the breath of a wild lover.

My head involuntarily shakes, dismissing permeating thoughts like a dog would water from its coat.

Over my shoulder, Artie stands just beyond the shed's entrance, eyes locked on the corpse jammed into the corner.

Look at his eyes.

They do seem puffy and a bit red. But he looks pouty. Petulant?

No, something darker. He looks like the personification of a person unhinged.

An ominous ringtone fractures the tranquility of the darkness. I realize I'm startled only when my heels come back with a thud against the floor-boards beneath my feet.

"There you fucking are! Did you finish the batch? Good. Now get in the Jeep, drive out to the north site, burn down Clint's shed, and then get rid of the red sedan." He hangs up with hardly a second for his lackey to respond. "I said get moving, Fuck For Brains."

Did he though?

A smirk creeps its way across my lips. I'm aware of the levity this time. I make sure to '*get moving*' before Artie notices.

None of this quite feels real. Sobriety hasn't reclaimed me, but a sense of control may be within my grasp. A freeing weightlessness in my skull makes everything appear brighter.

"Hurry the fuck up and grab his fucking feet."

Artie elbows past me and hooks his arms underneath his grandfather's shoulders.

I feel blank. I feel like I've lost time. Maybe I'm losing myself to a blank slate, like resetting. Might be I'm in a trance. I hardly feel in control.

Once more, I'm hunched over, near ninety degrees, to grab a corpse by the calves.

Quickly, we lurch him up without losing balance.

Slowly, shuffling backward, I lead the procession. All the while, Clint's lifeless eyes stare at me from a half-cocked head resting against his grandson's chest. Those pale eyes are numbing, but the third eye marked with violent protrusions in the center of his forehead still weeps dark, entrancing tears.

With my focus drawn toward thoughts of third eyes, shimmering red tears, and ringing gunshots, I don't notice the threshold in time. My heel clips the raised lip, which practically bites down and rips me to the ground.

As gravity takes hold, my fingers dig into what they can.

Namely, the old man's sweatpants.

They're too loose, though. Hardly slowing my descent, they snag around his ankles. There's a brief second where I think I can stabilize myself, but Artie doesn't have a firm grip, and my final lunge tears the torso from his clutches.

With nothing behind me to break my fall, the impact is violent.

An instant later, the dead weight of the old man slams down across my chest and abdomen with enough force to once again extricate the wind from my lungs.

I'm getting real sick of lying on the ground wheezing next to corpses.

It's going to be another tough task to get back on my feet.

Then the cackle of a familiar hyena echoes across the old wooden panels. Looking up, I expect to see Artie losing his shit; instead what I see...is far more unexpected.

Old man Skeeter apparently lived life commando. What I find staring back at me is a sight reserved for early birds using the sauna at the health club. The most unsettling part, the old man's endowment, is larger than the one that built my alma mater's library. Its weight alone is noticeable on my chest.

"Holy shit gramps, would you look at that!" Artie cries hysterically.

I try to weasel my way out from under the dead man, but he's heavier than expected. Proving futile, I relent and grab the deceased park manager's flabby, bare ass and shove him off me with disgust and revulsion that assaults my pride.

But I'm free.

Artie's still laughing, and Clint's face down, his moon in full reflective glow of its counterpart in the sky.

I just want to make it back on my feet and get my bearings. Then a slap to the back of my head buckles my knees back to the dirt.

"Pull the man's pants up, have you no respect for the dead? The fuck's wrong with you, *Galen?*"

I dislike the way he says my name. To hear it spoken through his stained lips, unsolicited and with dictatorial force, pulls at electric spiderwebs down my back.

Alongside that sensation is something I have only felt flickers of tonight. Something I know I may be incapable of controlling.

Maybe you don't want to control it.

The heat welling up within me scorches every other feeling and emotion. It breathes a dangerous vitality into my lungs that I both want and *need.*

Life grows dull. The beast in my chest howls out a moment of raging sobriety as I get the man's pants well up over his ass.

The adrenaline powers me to my feet with ease. I bend down once more to hook the legs under my arms.

Hunched over, I look up at Artie with an awareness of the malice lurking behind my eyes. *"You going to help?"*

My lips spoke the words, but I didn't say them. There was venom behind them, and the look of shock on Artie's face sums it all up for me.

I wonder how much time remains before I lose control to this long-forgotten emotion. A fervent fire that plagued me in my youth. Unbridled and uncontrollable. Hypnotizing and clouding. The only emotion that devours all others in its wake, like a parasite, feeding off the strength of feebler emotions. Further catalyzing its power.

Rage.

##:32

THE RAGE, THE *BURNING* RAGE, COULD HARDLY BELONG TO ME. AND YET, it scorches through the dregs of the trip's euphoria.

Time doesn't seem to abide the natural law of things.

As we lay this second body in the trunk, Artie's features are indecipherable. This was once a person who loved, fed, and raised him. But he shows it as much reverence as he showed his *"girl."*

Despite my roiling hatred for Artie, I treat Clint with the kindness he'd briefly shown me in life.

The situation feels bleak as I nestle the man atop all the other belongings. The futility of it continues steaming my resentment.

I still don't have a phone. Artie has the only firearm. And to top it off, *he's fucking pissed.*

But then again...so are you.

"Get in."

"Fine."

"Ohhh, look who's getting a bit of an attitude." Artie pulls Glen's pistol from the back of his waistband. "Now, I imagine, you'll want to get back in the trunk," he says with the gun lazily pointed my way. The barrel is almost inviting.

End this fucking night.

No! Listen here. That gun is empty. We can get out of this. I know you don't REALLY want to die yet. Do you?

An icy laugh from inside my—*soul?*—contains the roaring inferno. The trunk will give me space to think.

So, I climb in as if this isn't the worst thing in the world. My fellow tenants and belongings bulge outward beneath my weight.

Despite Artie's fevered attempts to slam the trunk shut, it will not. I'll have to get out, and I can once more hear that cackle in my chest.

With frustration dousing his features, Artie relents. "Alright, you ride up front. But, any funny business, and I'll shoot—*to wound*," he growls with malicious vigor.

Strangely, I don't find it frightening.

Because the gun is empty.

His eyes look at me with a greasy stare matching his unkempt hair. "I'd much rather see you bleeding out at my side than lying there dead in an instant."

Fuck you.

I slowly climb into the passenger seat, surveying the space quickly. There's no forgotten screwdriver or pen in the door. Not even a loose ice scraper tucked under the passenger's seat.

So, along for the ride it is.

My still-damp clothes and the scarring images of four corpses should offer good company.

Well, three images and one set of sounds.

The sounds.

Teeth on bone and flesh.

The air feels chilly as Artie slams the door beside me.

Euphoria and dread coalesce, but it feels weaker and fleeting. The feeble fingers of a dying grip latch onto whatever piece of my reality they can.

The engine roars to life, snapping me back to the moment. Artie's jackrabbit start lurches the Jeep recklessly into the night.

##:33

"So, did you read it?"

"What?"

"My book you fuckin' disappointment." His dark eyes are piercing, but not unsettling like I remember.

Good. You get it. He's just an emotional child. You see that. He's gotten sad, angry, and now there's almost a sense of joy in discussing his book. He's more Looney Tune than he is Lucifer.

That dark and familiar voice is right.

How do I use this?

Telling him where I think he can go shove his book probably won't win me any favors.

Oh. I can handle this one.

"Well, I, I only just started it this morning, so I haven't gotten very far into it yet."

His eyes scan me, trying to detect the lie. "Well, that's unfortunate. I would have hoped you'd get to read a New York Times Bestseller before you died."

Hopefully, my face expresses fear, as the soft and vehement voice inside explores our options.

Idiot didn't bind our hands. We could crash this Jeep at least ten different ways. He's got you sitting up front, so we could just jump out the door when-ever we slow down.

Where's the gun, though?

It's empty, though.

Is it? Are you sure?

...no...

I try to scan the car for it, but I must look obvious, and I can't have Artie paying any extra attention my way.

An unexpected squeal of tired brake pads infiltrates the cab as headlights breach a corner, piercing through the early hours of the morning–or evening–darkness.

Artie eases to a halt alongside the oncoming metallic-grey Jeep. Through the darkness, I recognize the Asian guy who had been with Hill and T in the shed.

"Where is everyone?"

"Dead."

"Dead! What the fuck do you mean *dead?*"

"I mean, this fucking asshole shot Hill in the face, point blank, and let T get eaten by a God-Damned Mountain Lion."

Silence emanates from the other car. The night stills. The low melody of two engines idling side-by-side washes out the woods' natural concert of insects.

"A fucking Mountain Lion?"

Artie nods.

"Geez. What the hell happened after I left?"

"Too fucking much. I'm gonna take all this evidence back to the cabin, you burn down Clint's shed and find a way to get rid of Glen's car. It's the only fucking one. Lot 46."

Artie's partner looks nervous.

He's only doing this out of fear. He wants to run.

Coward. I bet he doesn't come back. Oh, loyalty...Such a fickle bitch these days.

That's it. The newcomer takes his orders like a beaten dog and moves on.

He *did* have the look of a coward. A look I have grown accustomed to seeing in the mirror.

"Think he'll come back?"

That knocks me off guard. Artie's dark eyes focus on me. Try to scare me. If it weren't for those eyes, I would probably swear blind that the question had come from inside my own head like all the others.

That's how he operates, through fear. If I had my guess, fear led T to be the alcoholic we saw. It led to Hill coping with sex, maybe a prisoner's infatuation. Then this last guy; he lives in fear of consequence alone. If anything, he's happy just to have distance between the two of them. He's not coming back.

"I don't know," I say, trying to sound broken.

"He will. My friends were all like dogs. Hill stuck around because I showed her love. T stuck around because I rescued him, and Win, well Win sticks around because of fear, a prime example of learned helplessness. It wasn't always that way. At one point he would have been the most reckless of the four of us. But that ain't the case anymore. Now, he's not much more than a coward."

Nailed it.

I just nod. More in agreement with my internal compatriot than with Artie.

"Maybe you're not so stupid after all. Tell me, how did you know to call my Gramps *Skeeter?*" The question seems oddly genuine. "Not many people ever took the time to talk to him, and he only said the Skeeter-thing whenever he was enjoying someone's company."

Bipolar freak.

"I uh, yeah. I mean, yes, I talked with him a bit. We actually smoked together. He was a cool old stoner." I try to stutter through it, giving Artie a sense of power and control.

My acting fills me with chills.

"He was alright. Bit of a pain in my ass over the years, always trying to be my dad, always being a hypocrite about drugs. Always thinking *he knew better than me.*"

There's a pause that I can't quite interpret.

"Well, he's dead now, so I guess it doesn't matter what he thought, does it?"

This feels less like a kidnapping and more like a road trip. Albeit, I've never been on a road trip while being poisoned with hallucinogens. Nor one where my arms are bound with duct tape.

The wordsmith in me might describe this interaction as motoring through

357

a dark void at impossible speeds. The shadowy abyssal colors of the woods whiz past, as if frantic to conceal themselves within the grim corners of a world that may offer sanctuary until darkness can reclaim the land from daylight's impending presence.

"Thanks to you that is. If it weren't for *you*, he'd still be alive. Hill would still be alive. She was my first. She was my only. I hoped to one day marry her and make her a true queen. But *you*, you ruined that." He's growling his words again.

What'd I say? Bipolar. Freak.

He's a peculiar see-saw of a man. Quickly moving from genuine human being with complex human emotions to this vindictive, animalistic predator. He's not exactly easy to gauge, or make sense of...

Oh. It makes sense. He's still debating whether or not to kill you. He's down two members of his tribe, so he may manipulate us with fear the same way he did the others.

"What? You've got nothing to *say?* You get my grandpa killed because you just had to go wandering off into the woods on drugs? Couldn't you have just stayed in the city? I mean for fuck's sake, now *I* have to find a new agent, and that's going to be a whole ordeal because I'm going to have to wait for him to be reported missing, then they'll have to search for him—*Wait. Who the fuck knows that you both are here?*"

He slams on the brakes, whipping me against my seatbelt as the contents of the trunk rocket forward, shaking the entire Jeep with the shifting weight as tires skid atop loose gravel.

"I don't know who Glen told. But I don't really have a lot of—*people* to talk to."

"Ah. A loner. How tragic," he says with a biting cackle.

Scanning me once more with that look of mistrust, Artie appears satisfied with what he sees. Possibly seeing something I want him to see.

Once more, the car pitches forward and the seatbelt locks me into place.

##:34

THE RIDE TURNS SILENT.

I thought Artie would crack on more than one occasion, but he refuses to say a word.

I presume he's toying with the idea of my death and how he can lord that over me.

There's also the possibility he's starting to realize he doesn't have control over me. That he failed to instill that fear.

Suddenly, the terrain changes and the Jeep dips down, traversing a steep trail that is hardly fit to be called a road.

At the bottom of the descent, Artie levels out and glides the big metal box toward a familiar oversized fire pit still aglow with a bed of coals. Not a single flame licks at the air for its energizing oxygen. Yet, the sheer size alone spreads an orange glow across the two buildings nestled amongst the immediate surroundings.

Artie hardly stops the car as he thrusts the shifter into park. It's a jarring halt, and I think we're still sliding a bit—that may be the drugs, though.

Without hesitation, he makes a beeline toward the main building.

There, he pulls what looks like a knife and a letter from between the slats.

I don't think I'll leave the car.

Artie has the keys with him, and anyone leaving daggers as messages is probably not someone I want to meet. So I'll enjoy the safety of a locked car for now.

Artie is unflinching as he twirls the unmistakable sight of a large blade. He's brooding over the note as he does so.

Probably deliberating where he's going to put that blade when he opens the car door.

It looks as if he's decided. Artie cranes his neck in every direction, looking like a dog who smells something in the air, desperately searching out the source of a scent.

He turns toward me. I do not like the face I'm seeing.

Artie looks...*concerned.*

##:35

"I know you're out there! Show yourself like a man, you fat piece of shit! Let's settle this."

Artie shreds the paper in his hands like confetti, before tossing the scraps aside with anger and disgust. Almost comically, they drift back toward him, fluttering to the dirt beneath his feet.

"Fine then! Keep on hiding. But, I know you're here, you over-bloated tiki!"

Incredibly confused, I sort of hope Artie has finally lost his mind. I know there's no way I'm that lucky. The fact he is just screaming into the night is promising, though. It's not even audible English. Just inarticulate screaming.

A temper tantrum.

Or he possesses the ability to echolocate.

"Show yourself, Butch!" His face is growing red, and a vein pulsates alongside his throat.

Unhinged.

Wild-eyed, his shouts continue. "I will fuck you up, Butch! Stop playing games and waddle your fat ass out here!"

Eerie silence fills the quiet between his wild shouts.

Without warning, the precarious reticence fractures beneath the malevolent melody of twigs snapping underfoot. All illusion of a quiet forest is gone.

Another sound creeps out from the shadows. A clicking of sorts.

T'ck. T'ck. T'ck. T'ck.

Each *T'ck* is louder than the last, until from behind the shed, the source appears. An oversized man in every sense of the word.

To say he's at least six-five might be short-changing him. And if my life depended on it, I'd put a fair wager on his weight being in excess of three-fifty. His face has a deep, olive complexion, predominantly concealed beneath a long, braided beard traversing his robust chest, hanging like a tail at navel height. On the flip side, an equally long and braided ponytail drapes over his shoulder, reaching down almost as far as his braided beard. The lengthy, thick rope of hair pulls away from one of the sharpest widow's peaks I've ever seen. It's almost cartoonish in its depth.

The *T'cks* are him clicking his tongue.

"Jesus, enough with the tongue already! I told you that the shipment was going to be on the road by the end of the weekend, didn't I?"

The closer the behemoth gets, the more intimidating he becomes.

I'm glad to still be in the car, as I notice his ears. Fighter ears—ruined by cauliflower scarring—and his nose appears to have been busted a time or three. Despite that, he's well-manicured in a shiny grey suit tailored to his exact measurements.

It makes a straightforward statement. This is not a large pudgy man. He's a pile of thickly layered bricks.

Pure muscle.

Like a whale.

A Killer Whale.

He moves with strength and control. Soldier-like. He is, as my father would have so eloquently put, a *brick shithouse.*

Adequate feelings of terror return.

Artie may be a sadist, but this Butch, he's a dangerous anomaly.

"That you did."

The behemoth's voice is raspy and deep. Exactly what I'd expect from someone of his stature.

"But, party drugs don't do us a lot of good during the week, do they?" His dull stare strikes me as capable of seeing beyond whatever he's looking at.

If I had to write him, I would pen something stupid, like, 'The man's thousand-yard stare gave the impression that he could see into your past. That he knew everything you'd ever done or said, and therefore trying to lie to him was an effort in futility.'

"What does it matter?" Artie exhales. "There's a party every day of the week in the city, and you all control every nightclub. So, it would seem to me that whenever I get the product to you, you can move it."

Artie has no fear of the giant. He speaks to the man as if he were nothing more than a patsy, a servant. As if he sat beneath Artie on some drug-pin totem pole. And even if the behemoth is, I can't help thinking only an idiot would slight him.

The man is constructed more like a comic book character than a real person. The sort of guy whose origin story begins with professional wrestling and whose powers include super strength on top of bulletproof skin.

"Right as always, Mr. Arthur. However, when I give you and your cronies a deadline, and then have the *generosity* to extend said deadline an additional month, I expect results. Now here we are. Two months past the deadline, and you tell me that you *still* need more time."

He pulls out a pistol that looks normal in his gargantuan hands, meaning that the thing is ginormous. Probably capable of taking down an elephant.

"WAIT! WAIT! WAIT! WAIT! WAIT! WAIT! It's just me now!"

The Goliath doesn't lower his weapon but appears curious. Like he might enjoy playing with his food.

"What?"

"*It's just me!*" Artie cries out. "T, Hill, they're both dead! Win's out doing some damage control, but it's just me here, and Win can't deliver the cook by himself, and neither can I."

The behemoth's hand remains steady.

"Butch!" Artie's pleading. He's desperate. "THEY'RE DEAD! Without me, your empire won't just stagnate, it will *crumble*. Your customers will look elsewhere if the product declines."

"That's a bit of a stretch Art. We've got any number of big-brained university kids who could use a generous scholarship to get out from under their debts, and all I need is whatever formulas you've got locked up in that shack of yours."

The giant's lips peel back, revealing a shit-eating grin of horrifyingly immaculate teeth. That kind of pristine ivory that ensnares the gaze of any onlooker because they're too square, too white, too perfect.

I can see the fight deflating from Artie.

"*Fuck*. Butch, is that how you treat your business partners?" he pleads, glistening with sweat tinged in the orange glow of the nearby coals.

"That's rich! You actually have to deliver on your promises to be considered a *partner*."

"Butch, we're making you something *completely* new! This is some shit that doesn't exist. Fuck man, when we're done you won't just have the only supply in the city, you'll have the only supply in the whole fucking *world*."

The behemoth takes a single elegant stride, positioning his towering size in Artie's face. He glares down at the visibly trembling man.

"You know, we've all had enough of your silver tongue. First, it was deadlines, then it was the book that still stands a chance of ruining this whole damned operation, and now it's the one-of-a-kind world-changing drug. Fuck all that. If you want me to believe anything that comes out that damned mouth of yours, you better show me some fucking results."

"I just need a *little* more time!"

"Always with the time."

Butch shakes his head and stares off into the distance beyond the trees. But then his head snaps toward me. Those lifeless eyes work me up and down, x-raying my past and future.

"So, who's the kid all banged up in the car? Doesn't really meet the diversity quota you been establishing here."

Artie stares at me with excited rage. "This fucking *kid* killed Hill and T! This fucking *kid* has created the worst goddamned night of my fucking life, Butch!" Artie practically bounces up and down as he passes the blame like an angry toddler.

Another stark difference between Artie and Butch, maturity and composure.

The gargantuan needn't say a word. His presence makes my bowels churn with each stride toward the car. I swear the Earth shakes beneath his footfalls.

It's Dr. Ian Malcolm all over again.

Holy fuck, he gets bigger the closer he gets.

Fear swiftly turns to exhaustion. The toll my nervous system has taken this evening has me nearing the point where I'll be relieved if the big man simply snaps my neck and discards me like a twig.

The high is evaporating too.

The comedown.

My brain's taxed to its limit. Like it just ran a decathlon.

It's impossible to say how much time's passed since Glen and I set out this morning, but it could have been days for all I know.

There isn't an ounce of fight left in me.

When he's close enough, the behemoth cocks his head as if to say, *get out of the fuckin' car.*

Probably best to get out of the car.

Before my feet set, he's on top of me. A dark shadow between me and the orange glow. Pinched between the behemoth and the Jeep, there's nowhere to go. I close my eyes on instinct, turning away, bracing for what I can only hope is a quick death.

His enormous meaty palm envelops the crown of my head with an uncomfortable, unwanted, and violating pressure.

Please, please, please, just do it quick.

"Open your eyes."

Fuck.

It won't be quick. I know it. It's another indisputable fact of nature. His giant paw pats me atop the head as if I were a faithful dog.

"I always hated that drunk, T. Good work. How'd you do it?"

I'm shaking. In the silence of waiting, I picture those gargantuan palms whipping my neck around hard enough that my final sight will be that of my own ass.

The exhalation of a caged breath unleashes a pack of nervous shakes.

"Uh, um, uh..." I stammer, hardly getting the next words out above a whisper, "*Mountain lion.*"

"*The fuck is a mountain lion? Shotgun? Pistol? Russian? Israeli? English?*"

I'd be in the same boat if he were speaking in tongues. I can't fathom what he's asking. He's—

Just slapped you across the face with his big steak of a hand.

He avoids my broken cheek, but I feel it. Oh, I fucking feel it.

The entire blow reverberates through bone and muscle. A lightning bolt surges down my face, through my torso, into my toes.

Somehow, I'm on my knees. Crying. An infant compared to this golem of a man. It takes everything I have to kneel there in a heap and not curl into the fetal position.

Though I'm reminded of its comfort earlier in the night.

"Now that I have your attention."

He squats down into a catcher's position, and still, he towers over me.

"You've got a broken orbital, doesn't take a doctor to diagnose that. And I can make it so you have two, or so that you never see again. Nod if you understand."

I do so as gingerly as I can. My face throbs indiscriminately. Cleaving my sense of self in the presence of the alpha male. Each pulse of blood through my veins threatens to shatter the cheekbone further and further.

"Now talk, and you know what I want to hear."

Talking hurts, but I know the alternative is worse.

"T was attacked by a mountain lion while chasing me through the woods." I can hear my voice shake as salty, hot tears stream down the non-broken side of my face. "I shot Hill in the face."

I shot someone in the face.

You sure did, sweetie.

It was self-defense, though.

Until this moment, the weight of that decision hadn't set in. That *I* did it.

I killed someone. I killed a woman.

Like gender matters. Get over it, you baby.

And it hadn't been difficult.

It had been instant.

One of the simplest things I've ever done, especially when considering the relative consequences.

I look up. The behemoth expects more.

When he grasps that I have nothing else to offer, his face twists, communicating an odd acceptance. Then the looming giant extends his hand, and I accept timidly.

##:36

BACK ON THE GROUND.

Smooth work there.

How he'd moved with such ferocious speed, I'll never understand.

I'm not sure I ever made it to my feet. I'm not even certain how I remained conscious, considering I can almost guarantee that this second slap ruptured my eye.

There's a fluid leaking from the swollen socket and it's not tears. Could be blood. But the sensation of his meaty paw connecting with my face is an inescapable haunt of pain.

"Stay down there, you little twerp."

With his finger in my face, I feel like an animal once more, disciplined for something done on instinct. But, much like a cowered mutt, I lay there fearing further injury. All while considering what life will be like with only one eye.

"Now as for you Art—"

He doesn't get to finish that sentence as he's cut off by the large echoing *CRACK* of a shotgun.

The look of surprise is unmistakable as the first shot strikes the brute below his shoulder, sending him spinning away like a top.

The next shot finishes him.

His momentum abruptly halts before briefly teetering. The last dregs of the shotgun's cacophonous blast vanish from reality as the giant drops face-first to the dirt in a motionless heap that indeed shakes the ground.

Artie practically glides across the surface of dirt and stones, a rancorous phantom. There, he looms for some time, leering into the back of the man's head. An embodiment of death, Artie appears to nourish himself on the sight of the behemoth lying motionless.

The giant's back heaves, and I can *hear* the sound of his oversized lungs filling with blood as he tries to roll onto his back.

"You...*fuck*..." the dying man wheezes. Any breath of air he manages is a success. "*Do...you...understand...*"

Blood is pouring onto the ground from his wounds, simultaneously flooding out the corners of his mouth. He'll drown before he ever bleeds out.

In the meantime, Artie seems to be the type of churlish child that takes a magnifying glass to an ant hill on a sunny day.

Before Butch can roll over, Artie slams a dark boot into the man's back with *cracking* force. A groan escapes the beast, eschewing finality. It's pretty clear the job is done. The monster of a man now lies motionless.

A shadowy harbinger of death lingers with glutinous desire.

Slowly, the malevolent head of Death pivots toward me. Cold eyes trace a path to a place only they can see. His sharp, scythe-like smirk reminds me—*I should be afraid.*

"What's one *more* body on a night like tonight?" he says before unloading the remaining shells into the dead man's back.

##:37

THE SOUND OF ROLLING TIRES LASSO ME BACK TO REALITY. I CAN'T SAY where I've been since the cataclysmic fall of Butch the Behemoth, but time has most certainly passed.

Above, darkness still clings to the heavens, but it's as if its grasp has become tenuous.

The blinding headlights of an approaching vehicle cause me to squint, sending a searing pain through the side of my face.

The door swings open, then shuts with disquieting ease, at odds with the harsh violence of the evening.

"Holy fuck! Is that—"

"Yes, Win."

"What the fuck? *What the fuck!* What did you do? *Artie!* We're so fucked. We're so *fucked!*"

"We're not *fucked*, and I don't need a parrot right now. It's just time for a...*reset*. We can have this place packed up by the end of the day, then we follow my backup plan. You do remember the *backup plan*, don't you?"

Win's breathing sounds like an asthmatic. He's not a large man, but he is broad-shouldered and barrel-chested, which both heave as he hyperventilates. "Yeah. Sure. But seriously what happened with T and Hill, this guy *killed* 'em?"

His eyes communicate a pain I don't rightfully understand. Win is the first human amongst the monsters I've met tonight.

Artie lets out a tart chuckle. "Yup. This *fucker*." A long malicious finger stabs the air in my direction. "I'm telling ya, he fucking shot Hill right between the eyes. *Right* in front of me, and somehow managed to let T get eaten by a God-damned mountain lion. Can you believe that?"

Win personifies anxiety as he visibly trembles.

For me, any traces of euphoria are fleeting. I think it's safe to say that I am finally, *finally,* coming down.

The dam has collapsed, and exhaustion, which has long since been seeping into every fiber of my muscles, begins its exponential mushrooming. Every tendon, ligament, and muscle stretches against a tightness that spreads the aches and pains. My joints are stiff, my eyes heavy, and my feet throb in a way I hadn't known since my high school cross-country days.

All I want is one of two things.

To lie down and sleep.

Or to blow my own brains out.

I'm not picky.

With impending death lurking behind the eyes of a malevolent lunatic, I imagine the sweet release of ending it myself.

I will not find mercy in these woods. That's the only guarantee at this point.

As thoughts of mortality continue, my mind drifts toward Cliff and Trip.

I miss the pair at this moment.

Oddly, it's mostly Trip.

Her form haunts my memory, and the lingering traces of her aura are intoxicating. A character with no earthly attachments, a wild card. The sort equally capable of premeditation and swift adaptation.

In essence, everything I am not.

While Win and Artie continue speaking, my mind journeys to the metamorphosis of a monster. True terror evolving from the ashes of losing the one and only.

For Artie, that was clearly Hill.

Was it?

It has to be.

I don't believe it. As he continues sliding into utter madness, I don't think it's the loss of Hill greasing the wheels.

In fact, I know it can't be.

Control.

That's what he's lost.

Control of Hill. Control of T. He's lost control of his entire operation, and now he's scrambling, grasping at whatever control he can dig those bony fingers into.

But what would that be for Trip?

The more I consider that the more I expect her voice to educate me.

Instead, it's crickets chirping upstairs. Still, the distraction is appreciated.

Not a single person on Earth has absolutely zero attachments. Well, maybe a Tibetan monk, but outside of them, everyone has some sort of bond. But when that bond is severed, a true demonic nature stirs.

So, what does a character like Trip lose?

Is it control? Innocence? An attachment.

I want to say a dog, but even the creature that loves unconditionally, despite all of humanity's flaws, feels wrong for her.

She's a sort of sociopath. Losing Fido probably wouldn't hurt her. In fact, having Fido would mean neglecting time and effort that she could spend on herself rather than her mangy mutt.

It's a seductive question, though. Most children don't want to be themselves. They want to fit in. They want to be normal.

Would that be the same for her?

What does losing her tether to normality mean?

A natural air of caution surrounds her. Never showing her true self, an instinctive wall guards her naturally cautious demeanor.

Still, a desire to fit in seems innate. It's animalistic. Fit in with the pack.

Yet there are always externalities.

A child who knew she was never normal. Would she lie to herself, though?

Would she have that last bastion of normalcy, only to see it torn away? Like a tooth on its last thread, and once it's out, there's no going back.

Freedom.

Yes, freedom.

Cage her like an animal, and she'll lash out like one.

"Aye, Disappointment, you with us?"

It appears Artie and Win have finished their pow-wow. An almost humorous dichotomy is present between the pair. Artie's, a mixture of anger and hate, while Win stares me down with some combination of remorse and confusion.

Despite those dissecting glances, I don't have it in me to fight gravity and rise from my seat in the dirt.

"See, if we end up needing a scapegoat, he'll be the perfect patsy. Our guy here is still probably tripping nut. I'm pretty sure T dosed him with the Lolly. When we turn him in for the murders of everyone tonight, they'll believe that poor, little, struggling author Galen Ramsey dropped acid and lost his mind. Killing a multitude of people, including innocent bystanders, and even his own friend and agent. Puts a nice bow on things don't you think, Galey?"

Artie's strides are purposeful as he saunters over to me. His shadow consumes me, and he places a dirty bootsole on my forehead. He gives my aching skull a forceful shove, putting me on my back with a thud.

"Win, I'm getting a cigarette and some shovels. You get the firewood and lighter fluid, we're going to need a lot of each."

Win appears more statue than man at the moment. He nods tacit agreement while Artie meanders off, disappearing into the distance, but his voice cuts through the night air. "Win!"

The poor guy startles.

"Get the body out of the shed too! We're burying all four!"

If I saw the guy walking down the street, I'd hardly expect such timid behavior. If anything, his aesthetic is more punk rock than—well, someone's bitch.

##:38

Win eventually does as Artie orders. The pain on his face reiterates that he might be the only human I've encountered in a night full of monsters. He takes no joy in maneuvering the corpse of my friend across the ground like he's nothing but a burden to be dealt with.

Like trash.

No. Trash usually gets more respect than that. You don't drag trash across the ground because it might tear open. Glen's body is less than trash. My friend. My agent. The one person who, from the get-go, had always been in my corner. Reduced to something given less care than trash.

Crying sounds like an acceptable option about now, but the mere thought of tears stings my eyes.

Probably just eye at this point.

As Win grows closer, there's an obvious suffering etched into his face, a sadness traces his lips, and fear dots his eyes.

You're not alone.

His haunted stare turns toward me, but I can't bear to make eye contact.

Just as I try to look away, I see it clearly. The shame he wears beneath his mask. The one he hides behind to protect himself from Artie's wrath. I can feel it. A life's worth of self-resentment for his part in this monstrous operation.

You read part of the first chapter.

It hits me. This is so far from what Win had signed on for. Originally, it had just been about making money, and I remember the book saying something about how they felt they could make a safer product. So, murder definitely had not been part of the deal.

He probably feels—in fact, I know he does—that we're both prisoners here.

Before now, he'd resigned to the isolation of being Artie's lone prisoner, but now there are two of us. And more importantly, there are only two cars.

And just one Artie.

Together, Win and I can do this.

Win hasn't done anything to wrong me. At least not murder or battery or assault. Hell, if he helps me, I'll be his strongest advocate.

It's time to get the wheel moving.

"It's Win, right?" My face hurts with each word, but the hope surging in my chest overwhelms the pain.

I can do this.

Hope, as it turns out, is a powerful pain reliever.

In return, Win steals a meek glance over his shoulder, gathering his composure. His eyes move back to me, then the ground. Wordless, he continues pulling Glen's body through the dirt.

I need him to see the light at the end of the tunnel. I need to bring him over to my side of this conflict. Though, to do that, I have to figure out a way to get him talking.

Then, *maybe* he'll realize he has a choice.

"I'm sorry about your friends."

I am, truly. Despite the borderline torture both exposed me to, I didn't wish for any of their deaths. And I certainly never wanted to be a murderer, but here I am.

"Thanks." It's dour, but a start.

"I really am sorry, man. I read the book, I know this isn't what you signed on for. *Right?* You just wanted to make some cash and ensure kids could party on safe drugs?"

He stares at me with honey-brown eyes.

I know that stare.

He's gauging me. He doesn't trust me.

No matter. I'm certain he's fighting that internal battle. Sitting on a precipice of deciding who he is going to be. A human. Or...

"That all feels so long ago. So many more people were alive back then." He gets lost in the canopy above.

Reveries clearly haunt him of days long since passed. Nights that make him shudder.

He doesn't look into the distance how I remember my grandfather on hospice doing, recollecting all the pleasant memories of a life enjoyed.

Win looks tormented. Like a soldier who made it home in body, but left pieces of his soul strewn across the battlefield. Only now is he finally coming to terms with the truth that there's no way he'll ever be whole again.

That's a place I can't let him stay. I need him in the present. If he sulks too long, he won't want to speak to me. But what can I say?

"I get it." Slowly, Win's eyes move to mine. "At least, I think I do. Today was just supposed to be about helping my writing and spending time with a friend. My *best* friend. Instead. Well...instead, I'm staring at his corpse and have literal blood on my hands. It seems like an eternity ago that I was laughing and enjoying a beer with my buddy Glen."

The G squad.

Now, I'm the one drifting toward reverie.

The G Squad. Galen, Glen, AND Gabi.

No more.

A pit opens up in my belly. Fatigue invites me down to the depths. Apathy wants to swaddle me in its embrace. There may be no point in fighting it.

"You never really forget the first time you see someone die. That haunting feeling isn't gonna go away. You'll just learn to live with it." His eyes dart every which way, except in my direction.

I don't think he's quite used to being this genuine.

"Ay! Get a move on it! We've got bodies to burn before sunrise!" Artie's voice slices through the sobering night air. Win drops his burden near the simmering coals. Glen's milky eyes are still open. Peering through me. Along with that horrid third eye that no longer weeps.

I can't look away.

TRIP

They call to me. To see what he's become. A lifeless heap with a head bored through.

And it's all my fault.

You've got to live. For the both of us, mate.

I can feel him pleading; an echo of the man who is no more.

##:39

ARTIE'S PRESENCE SNAPS BOTH WIN AND ME BACK INTO THE WORLD OF the living.

"Get it together, Win. *Here.*"

He hands him a cigarette and a vial of white powder. Win, without hesitation, opens the tube and pours out a small pile on the crook of his hand between his forefinger and thumb. With foreign confidence, he snorts up the substance, leaving his nostrils rimmed in white.

"*Woo!*" He reminds me of T.

Yet, his fingers move with greater deftness, finessing the cigarette to his mouth and lighting it in one fluid motion.

"Thanks, Art. Needed that." His voice shakes, but it's livelier than before.

"Hey, *you and me*, we're all we got now." He clasps a hand on Win's shoulder, and my stomach sinks.

Maybe Win won't be an ally.

"So don't fuck this up. Get the fucking firewood and the damn lighter fluid. Oh, and here's a fucking shovel you *twat*."

That last bit is directed at me. As was the shovel thrown in haste.

"We've got work to do. Actually, you know what? Fuck it. You two dig. I'll take care of the firewood. We're burning the midnight oil, as they say." Artie chuckles a maddening little sound to himself. "Make sure you dig deep enough that all four of these fucks, including Butch's fat ass, fit. Got it?"

He lumped Hill in with '*these fucks.*'

There isn't humanity in him, just rage-filled avarice. If I ever had any doubts about that fact, they just went up in smoke.

His loss had been *Control*, not any one individual. So, he copes with what is most likely cocaine. To the point that he's visibly jittery. A sociopath who's lost his last ounces of *Control*...

Do the math.

He said *four* bodies. There's no way we would find T's body.

Not that there's anything left.

Glen's here, the big fella, then both Hill and Clint are in the trunk.

So, I'm not going in the hole? But why? Oh yeah. They're going to pin it on me.

Good job, idiot.

Artie's already wandering toward the cabin. Meanwhile, Win's eyes are locked on the back of his greasy scalp with a vigor born of the substance in his flaring nostrils.

There's something else there, behind those eyes.

Those sad eyes.

I can't quite figure out what's going through Win's mind.

Then, in a flash, his cocaine-fueled tenacity consumes him. Win snatches up another shovel and begins to spear the dirt beneath our feet. There's no slowing him down as he heaves heap after heap next to the simmering coals of the once great fire.

"You too *murderer*. Don't expect Win to do all that diggin' hisself," Artie calls back without a second glance.

You do realize you've been handed a weapon? Murderer...

I'm in no shape to put up a fight.

I need the shovel as a lever just to pull myself to my feet. Everything hurts. Breathing is difficult, and I can barely see. My eye has to have swollen over by now. The tightening of the surrounding skin makes any movement seem like it's testing the limits of tension before bursting.

A disquieting thought, to say the least.

"Let's just dig, man."

Win continues to plunge his shovel into the soil with the fury of a man trying to avoid something else.

Thrusting the spade downward, I feel not only weak but like I'm about to dig my own grave.

Though, I know that's not likely. After all, I'm probably going to rot somewhere else. Under the headline, *CONVICTED MURDERER.*

At least Mom isn't alive to read it.

I push the dirt around like a despondent child. Repercussions don't really do anything for me anymore. My fate's already sealed.

My damp clothes oppressively weigh down my body like frosted, steel armor.

I'm fine letting my mind drift toward *The End,* once more.

Better to piss off Artie and force him to help dig a bigger hole than live out my days in prison for murders that I didn't commit.

Well, three you didn't commit.

A whirlpool of despair suctions me down to that place beneath the surface of guilt and panic.

The static returns.

I AM a murderer. I—shot a woman. I—shot her between the eyes. I—pulled the trigger.

I don't want to live with that on my conscience.

Yet, I deserve the repercussions of that decision.

Maybe prison wouldn't be so bad.

"Yo. He won't kill you."

I look up to see Win staring at me with concern in those bright brown eyes. "I know."

"If you know, then just dig."

The ground beneath me is hardly mangled. I don't even know how to dig a hole. Let alone with my forearms bound.

The old wooden handle of the rusty spade rolls between my palms. Nearby, my friend's body lay crumpled like a rag doll next to the giant fire pit. Then there are the bodies protruding from the trunk of the Jeep like a scene out of a Tarantino film.

A Jeep parked where it could be taken. Taken anywhere but here.

Just drive it off. Head West and never stop.

I wouldn't go home. There's nothing there for me. I don't even care to arrest these guys with a call to the police.

I just want my freedom. That and only that.

"Are you going to take it or not?"

I snap back to Win.

He's goading you into taking the Jeep?

My vision takes a second to focus on Win's outstretched arm.

Finally, things become clear.

In his hand is that vial of white powder. I hold up my arms to remind him I'm still taped up, and he quickly flourishes a knife, finally releasing me.

My chest can open up. I can breathe. I can roll my shoulders back.

Pops crackle down my sternum and spine with a few twists and turns.

I don't even mind the wax job my forearms receive as we rip the tape free.

"C'mon man, take the bump. The hole is gonna get dug, and it looks like you might need a little help from Ole Man *Yayo*. Or Artie will make ya do it with a whip to your back. Yes, he has a whip. No, he's not afraid to use it."

I stare at the vial long and hard for what could be an eternity.

Just as I start to feel a sense of normalcy, I get confronted with threats of whipping. Though, that's not why I will ultimately take that bump.

Commiserate with him. Do it.

I need Win on my side, whatever that takes.

Unfortunately for my brain, it appears that specific result demands the use of *more* illicit drugs.

I could use the pick-me-up if I'm being honest. My energy reserves are well beyond depleted.

As Win had done, I pour a little into the crook of my thumb and forefinger, and let out an audible, *"Woooo!"* as the cocaine burns on upward.

My nose might be broken...

I lick up the remnants, and almost instantly, my mouth goes numb with the bitter, chemical taste.

Together, both artificially renewed, Win and I plunge our spades into the Earth. Blemishing Mother Nature's face with a freshly unmarked grave.

##:40

EACH SHOVELFUL OF DIRT IS A MOUNTING KNOB OF SAND IN AN hourglass swelling imperceptibly. The hole's depth is the true marker of time.

We've made quite the dent. The accumulation of sweat around my bad eye—*which is putting it mildly*—stings relentlessly.

Thankfully, we've got enough cocaine to kill an elephant. Meaning my energy elevates to the point where I can endure the pain.

We're just working dogs with one simple objective.

Dig.

Win has already sweated through his shirt. Once discarded, the first thing anyone would notice is the patchwork of characters that emboss his chest. I've got no clue if they're Mandarin, Cantonese, Kanji, or what, but the language lines his ribs, arches around his upper chest like a long dangling necklace, and traces lines on his broad and bony shoulders.

I almost ask about them, but our entire endeavor has been silent and monotonous. Only pausing to numb our mouths or sting our nostrils.

In the background, Artie has moved from bonfire prep to pinballing between the cabin and shed with cans of gasoline.

They're going to start a forest fire.

They must be stopped.

TRIP

Jittery, exhausted, paranoid, drained of everything like the victim of a parasite, I think I now understand the phrase *'coked out.'*

Not exactly the person who should be playing hero.

But each bitter dose veils those detriments with invincibility. Like I could take on a hundred trained ninjas and walk away the victor—even with only the one good eye.

Holding a train of thought regarding what I should say to Win hardly appeals to the attention span. Focus is rare. At best, I can give my concentration to the next thrust of my shovel and where the dirt will end up.

##:41

We must be nearing the end of our sadistic project.

I say this because my mind's wheels are finally starting to spin. I think about why they are going to destroy the evidence, including the corpses, if the plan is to frame me.

There has to be something up their sleeves that will allow them to do so. Right?

What could possibly be going through Artie's head?

Probably terrifying dalliances.

Yet, I want to understand it. Him. I want to understand *him*.

No. I need to. And I mean, *need* to.

The task seems monumental. *I'm sure he wants to kill me*, a constant refrain.

Time's running out, and—that's it.

That's the plan.

This is all a setup to get me to dig my own grave.

Despite Artie's comments, I realize his lustful desire to end me will prevail and that the best fall guy he can have is a fall guy who can't contend his innocence or guilt.

A fall guy is only a worthwhile endeavor if they are incapable of undoing the lies. They're dangerous if left alive or reliable. So, if he's leaving you alive, you'd have to be discredited. Sounds like more work than putting a bullet in your head.

My brain feels like it's revving up now. Another idea comes to me in the flash of a single word.

Control.

That's why he enjoys writing. That's the author in him. Not just the author, but who he is in general.

Remember, he needs it.

He's lost individuals to control, so next up is the narrative. That is what he will take hold of. His entire purpose has become dictating his own reality.

Like earlier.

Despite killing Glen and his own grandfather, while also knowing that T's death was an accident, he still sees me as the enemy that started this all. I'm to blame in his eyes. There's no reason that Glen even had to die in the first place.

The narrative is always in his hands.

But why?

Was he always like this or had his mind warped over time? Had he become a monster, or was he born one?

All I know for certain; the man is delusional.

The only way to escape is to steal back some of that Control.

No, that would be too difficult. Better yet, force him to doubt how much Control he really has...

Now you're thinking.

##:42

"Hey Win?"

The skidding of metal on dirt is the only thing drowning out the deafening roar of cicadas.

"Keep digging. I seriously do not want to see him break out the...*motivation*." The word trickles out like the whisper of a superstitious child.

No, no, I guess I don't.

It's a half-assed effort, but I thrust the spade into the dirt, lift, and repeat.

We've dug down the distance of our waists, which in itself seems an impressive feat, but that's the only progress there is to speak of.

It might be the coke inflating my optimism, but I have a certain tingle in my lizard brain that urges me to recruit Win into an escape plan.

"Have you had to do this a lot? Digging...graves?"

His downtrodden gaze lifts from the work to reveal a glimmering sadness at the corners of his eyes.

"No."

It hangs there in the night. Cold but longing.

"But this isn't the first time we've had to get rid of bodies. It's just the first we've ever had to deal with one of our own."

His focus meanders toward the Jeeps. The pair of bodies are visible enough to induce visions of the living dead crawling out to feast on our mortal flesh.

"Well, one of *the group*."

"I'm sorry." It slipped out.

'I'm sorry?' Fuck no you're not.

Trip's voice has taken on a shrill and antagonizing criticism.

Or has it been her all along?

Did you really just apologize for killing someone who wanted to kill you, who actually tried? You're fucking pathetic. Look at me, I'm Galen, I'm such a pansy. I apologize for saving my own life. Fuck off, you little—

"Don't apologize. Hill was a cunt."

Well, that was harsh. No decorum in this one.

"Sorry, spent too much time in the wrong Welsh circles."

He heaves a long sigh that must have been brewing for some time.

"And I know I shouldn't speak ill of the dead."

A quick hand wipes the sweat from his brow.

"But, she had become such a horrid person. You know, one time, I saw her shut a gas station door in the face of an old granny using a walker? Just slammed it right in her face, and I don't mean let it close on her, or didn't know the lady was there. She donkey kicked the door back with full strength. Sent the old bird tumbling to the ground, and you know what? She fucking *laughed*. Laughed at the old lady, who struggled to get up from the ground. I mean I've seen her kick a *puppy*. Honestly, a fucking puppy. No rhyme. No reason."

Well, well, well.

The cicadas consume the silent lull between him and me.

"I'm glad she's dead." For the first time, Win's gaze leaves the Earth and moves to the heavens above. With just a whisper, he adds, "I don't have to watch her *devolve* anymore."

Even the hidden insect life seems to quiet, letting that last bit dawdle between us before vacating to the ether.

Neither of us is digging. I'm not with a captor. I'm with a fellow prisoner.

Now just get HIM to realize that.

Hope?

"What was she like before the, uh, *cuntiness*?"

What sort of...

Win laughs. A deep gut-busting sound that hunches him over. It could even be infectious—given different circumstances.

"*Cuntiness?*" He chokes down a breath. "That's a good one."

His forearm wipes away sweat once more.

"She was always a bit of a, as she put it, *See You Next Tuesday*. Hell, that was how she introduced herself the first time we met. But that's because she was tough. Raised amongst a family filled with marines and older brothers."

The memory seems to lighten not only Win's mood, but the fear we both breathe.

"I don't hear any digging!"

As if the night air has scolded us itself.

Win's not fazed, but I feel my feet leave the dirt on instinct. The spur of adrenaline hits as my weight slams the spade into the forest floor. Anxiety works me double time.

Damn sympathetic nervous system and cocaine have me antsy, and standing still tickles my lizard brain.

Win, however, continues to chuckle, still gazing through his past.

"I think that's why she ultimately was the one who would look out for the little guy. Man, I can hear her voice in my head saying, '*Why are you acting like a prisoner? You're supposed to make sure this kid keeps going. We break him the fuck outta here and then go get a fucking drink.*'

"I know it's strange, but she would have looked out for me, and hell, even you, back in the old days. When we started this. When we were a hodgepodge group. A rich Asian kid who lacked a home life, let alone any meaningful friendships, but possessed the resources to make whatever they needed *appear*, as if by *magic*."

He gestures flamboyantly.

"Then there was the misunderstood genius with a past so dark it'd make you jump out of your skin. Our tomboy, who wasn't afraid to tell it like it is. And lastly, the fearless take-charge leader. The one who would have been successful at whatever he put his mind toward. It's just a shame he chose an illegal drug operation over Fortune 500 CEO or Non-Profit Executive. Well, not that. He'd never do that...Artie did whatever it took to make something happen, which ultimately warped Hill."

There's a slight vibrato to his voice as if he's choking back several emotions in his throat. Ones both neglected and atrophied.

"She was so tough, man. She had a slew of older brothers. I'm pretty sure one of them is a professional hockey player, and another one is a strength coach for some NFL team. The rest were Marines. I mean she came from tough stock. Big dudes with bigger egos sort of family. So she was always the bullheaded one who took initiative. I think Artie knew that better than any of us. I think he used that against her. He manipulated her into believing she was untouchable. Unstoppable."

It's clear the tears are fighting their way past his defenses.

"You okay?"

A pause epitomizes the moment. A pause, where Win's making a decision. And with a deep breath, it seems he's made it.

"Yeah, thanks. I've wanted to get this off my chest for a while. Not exactly problems I can share with a therapist, ya know?"

I chuckle. "Yeah, I can't imagine they would support the illicit drugs or murder."

"No probably not."

That one, he had not found humorous. Win looks defeated. He takes a seat and whips out the vial. Speeding through the process, he motions for me to join him.

I do so gladly. Welcoming the rush of endorphins within my aching body as it teeters on the precipice of ruination.

Win looks at me, and we both have the same thought. We have too much energy, and we need to dig to expel it. So we climb back on our feet. Back to the monotony.

Plunge. Press. Lift. Toss. Repeat.

"Hill was the only one who knew my secret. Well, she was supposed to be."

A sniffle that may not be from the nose candy snaps me into processing what Win just said.

"I don't think Artie ever actually knew until she told him. But we slept together the very first night of college, Hill and I."

Another sigh.

"I didn't like it. But I was drunk and had thought, *why not?* She was butch enough. Plus, she came on *to me*, which I enjoyed. All because she saw me help some girl on those weird arm crutches move into the dorms.

"No one had been helping her. Not even the girl's mother. Who was too preoccupied with her cigarettes and the single dads who hadn't minded a break from their sons and daughters' move-ins."

He peers back through time, into that day.

"She was trying to navigate her crutches while pulling her stuff in a wagon, like one of those old, metal, red wagons. It was rusted on the sides and had wheels that wobbled across the shit pavement. Most of the kids, *and their parents*, stared with pity and annoyance.

"At first, I just talked to her, offering her a second to sit down on a picnic bench and rest. It was then that I asked her—Melody was her name. She passed away that year—But yeah, I pulled the wagon with her permission. She was cute. Like actually cute. Not, *cute for a disabled girl*. I think she would have really made something of herself because she was smart too. Some type of computer science."

His darting eyes communicate the trouble he's having staying on topic.

"Sorry. I digress.. Hill had seen all this. And it was her that opened the door for us into the building. Inside, we found her room, a handicap suite. Super spacious room. So, I made her wait there for a sec. When I came back with a laundry wagon and a wheelchair, Hill was still there chatting with her, Melody, and helped me transfer her to the wheelchair. The three of us then proceeded to load the wagon with the remaining stuff from her mother's car."

An almost paternal gaze tilts his lips upward.

"She could push the wagon from the chair. Well, I could push her, while she steered it."

Tears stream down his face now, dancing around that gentle micro-smile.

"Hill came up to me later that night as everyone got to know one another in our floor's common lounge. She'd whispered in my ear how attractive she thought that was. She wanted to reward my kindness. It wasn't something I was looking for. But I think her strength and forthrightness intrigued me. It hadn't hurt that she had a boyish haircut."

A sigh tinged with regret allows him to catch his breath.

"She didn't hit on me. She propositioned me. No eighteen-year-old girl should be propositioning a boy she just met. But, I let a shameful echo from the past manipulate me, convince me that I was...I don't know. Wrong...

"Then I'd be the son that my dad wanted. Resurgent thoughts reignited the urge to return to the closet. But Hill knew. She knew almost instantly. It was probably the look on my face when she got her pants off. I didn't mean to, but she wasn't dissuaded and tried anyway. I think it was a game for her."

Another sigh.

"That's not true. She...I think there was a challenge, sure. *Let's turn the gayboy*...I don't know. That upbringing of hers, man...She wasn't the type to accept her gender as a limitation. That probably doesn't make sense. But does any of this? I mean, afterward, we laughed and became close friends. She knew my secret. She knew my type, and we laughed about boys and hookups and dicks, and she was going to be my best friend..."

Win's lost in either the story or the stars above. I try to find the words to console him, but as I go to say something, I can see he's not done.

"Then, I don't know how much you read, but Artie talks about *their* first hookup. Almost like he was flaunting it. The timeline's a little off, and what he leaves out is that he convinced her to do Molly that night. But *He* never took any. He *preyed* on her. That's when this all began. It was never about *cleaner* drugs. It was always about manipulating. *Control*.

"He got Hill hooked. Then used her to lure me in. Whether or not he knew about the foundation of our friendship, he could tell we were close. But it wasn't just my trust fund that titillated Artie's avarice. If anything, he wanted to get to T. T was my roommate. A genius with an affinity for getting tanked, and..."

Pausing only briefly, his face twists as if he's just sucked a lemon.

"I don't know how long he had the plan in the works, but Artie knew he needed T's brain, Hill's fearlessness, and my pocketbook long before we ever got to cooking. We were the three amigos, and Artie wormed his way into that relationship like the snake he is. Maybe we were friends, at the beginning. But hindsight makes cynics of us all.

"I mean, Artie wasn't an idiot, ya know? But, he wasn't anything above average. In fact, he failed a class or two that first year, not because we were busy, but because he didn't understand the science. Thankfully for him, he understood how to manipulate people. He even—"

I don't think Win can finish that sentence. So we sit in silence, both propped against shovels like they were all that held us up.

I know he needs to finish this story. The ending is what will bond us.

Finally, he seems ready.

"He even. Uhm—"

Nope, he's going to cry. But somehow, sucking on that invisible lemon, he maintains composure.

"He played with my heartstrings, and he—he slept with me. I know now it was only to get in my wallet. He's no better than a fucking whore. I've replaced my trust fund five-fold since we started this, but I'll never forgive the way he manipulated my emotions."

This bombshell leaves me dumbstruck. What amazes me is that I don't see Artie being bi, queer, pan, you name it. He's so asexually sociopathic that he has no boundaries with anyone. Sex means nothing to him.

It's about power.

I agree. It's about power. It's about control. He'll do whatever he can to maintain that.

"He showed me an affection that only a sociopath can manage."

Called it.

"He manipulated Hill and made her co-dependent. He turned T from someone who would develop a drinking problem if no one helped him, to a full-blown alcoholic. He knew how to manipulate each one of us, and I feel so stupid in hindsight. But oh the heart wants what it wants, and I wanted to be loved, and I wanted my friends. I thought maybe just maybe it was real. But—"

He finally tilts his head back down to Earth.

"I should have left long ago. But, I'm—I'm," a new emotion dilates his eyes, "just so—*scared.*"

Tears continue to roll down his face in a gushing current.

The vigor of the coke is fading, and I know my opportunity to recruit Win's help is fast approaching.

The only problem?

I feel bad.

Now, *I* am the one manipulating this vulnerable man. This horrible moment that he's experiencing is because *I* want him to do something. But, my safety and his soul require him to see the light of day.

Right?

Not so different from Artie after all. Manipulation is rather easy. Once you get to know a person, and if we're not careful, we might learn this man's wonderful performance was only the lure concealing the hook.

"Sorry," Win chokes out. "We gotta get back to it."

TRIP

He's wiping at his face with his discarded, dirt-patterned shirt. The fabric leaves dusty brown streaks clinging to his face.

"Actually, fuck it. We've done enough."

Win is right.

Standing in a hole that *has to* be big enough for the menagerie of bodies the evening has collected, we brace for the next task.

Dragging the corpses to their ultimate resting place.

As we begin, I finally understand another term, '*deadweight.*'

##:43

MUCH LIKE THE REPETITION OF GRAVE DIGGING, THERE IS A LULLING monotony to corpse moving.

I desperately desire to respect the departed, but the cocaine brings objectivity to the situation. These unfortunate souls are dead and dragging them makes for easier work than respectfully carrying them.

It also prevents the leaking slurry of viscera and bodily fluids from spreading across us. The stench of which still hangs in the air and sullies the interior of the Jeep.

So, we drag. We drop. And we repeat.

The behemoth, we're saving for last.

We should have done him first. Not because we're exhausted, and moving the fucker is about the definition of backbreaking. But, when we roll his massive weight over the precipice, the sound that follows—of the thundering organic *crunch* of bones and cartilage beneath his weight—is *haunting*.

I have seen neither hide nor hair of Artie in a while. But that instinctual primal piece of my brain tells me he's lurking.

A predator lying in wait.

I know I can't run yet. The bodies implicate me as well. Letting them burn means one less weapon for Artie to use against me. My stomach turns with that thought.

But does any of it really matter?

As time trudges onward, I slip into a certainty that I won't survive to sunrise.

I look toward the fading night overhead with my lone good eye, while the other is a stinging hole in my head.

I can't say for certain what will haunt me most about this evening, should I survive it. But, if I do, I'm growing well aware that whatever time I have left on this rock will be marred in night terrors and afflictions requiring self-medication on par with some of the greatest writers in history.

Beneath me, rest the pale, limp bodies haphazardly crushed beneath the weight of the behemoth.

My vertebrae ricochet against the skin as a trickle of sweat drips a cold trail down to my ass.

The feeling of illness sweeps over me again.

I am crashing.

I have abused my body and mind with substances for who knows how long, and now I am in free fall, plunging hard and headfirst toward sobriety.

Staring into the empty face of a giant, of my only friend, of an old stoner who'd befriended me, and a young woman whose life I had stolen, I crash to my knees.

A hollow pang in my gut tells me what's coming.

The retch that projects up and out is violent in its velocity.

It drops me to my hands, and it's my turn to cry as hot bile drips down my chin and splashes across the limp carcasses below.

Silently, I relent to the tears.

The sight of these people. All gone before their time. Reduced to empty husks. All of which had teemed with life when the sun rose that morning...

Now they lay still. Tossed out to burn and rot where their families would never find them.

Not only that, they lay there disrespected in death, blanketed in my sick.

The sight breaks me.

What dignity do I have left? I have pissed myself, vomited, and nearly voided my bowels. There's no reason to sob.

So, of course, I cry harder. Snot runs from my nose. Streams of tears mingle with it, and I feel myself on the verge of struggling to breathe.

Oh, you child.

None of this was supposed to happen, and it's all my fault.

If I'd just written a better draft. If I'd just said no to camping. If I'd just faked sick or gotten too high to come, none of these bodies would be cold. They'd be living life.

I want to die.

I don't want control of my life anymore. I just want it to end.

Put me in the pit with them.

An unseen hand pulls me up from under my armpit with strength and care.

"Come on man. We've got to finish."

Win scans me with eyes that know hurt, that know sorrow.

"I feel your pain." His words catch me as the most sincere that I've ever heard in my life. Win looks around, searching the area, and in a low whisper says, "I'll get you out of here. But, I need you to trust me."

I just nod, too dumbstruck to fully process the granting of my one true wish.

He guides me toward the firewood, which we grab en masse. Despite the weight of it all, I gently place each log atop the bodies with care. It's the least I can do to ease my conscience, which seems leaden in my chest. Win does the same.

Don't trust him. This is all an elaborate act. Why would he help us? What reason do we have to trust him?

Eventually, the bodies are invisible under the bed of firewood. We've piled logs varying in size around three or four feet high. It will make a huge fire, and now it settles in, what we're about to do.

Win bends over to grab the lighter fluid, and I hear something jingle at his side. Sure enough, a pair of car keys with the big bright embossed letters—JEEP—catch a glimmer from the already burning coals. I look to Win, and I think he shoots me a wink.

It was quick, but I'm pretty sure it was there.

There's another bottle of lighter fluid, pretty much full. As I squirt it over the wood now concealing the deceased, I know in my gut that Win's going to get me out of here.

He tucks the keys away as quickly as he's revealed them.

Once both of us have emptied the bottles, Win ushers me backward. Making sure we're both a safe distance away.

He then whispers what I think is a prayer.

If it is, it isn't in English.

A final exhalation, he strikes a match, and flicks it into the heart of the soon-to-be pyre.

With an audible ingestion of oxygen, the fire immediately bursts outward from nothing. The eruption of lapping flames spreads rapidly, licking up each drop of lighter fluid.

In silence, we watch the flames consume, knowing what is being devoured beneath.

"Who told you that you could start the pyre without *me, N-gu-yen?*"

##:44

CH'CK-CH'CK...

My ears ring with the deafening blow of the shotgun shell.

"Well, there goes the whole family. Oh, and you've got a little something on your face there, pal."

I know what it is.

How many times can one man find himself coated in spewed brain matter in a single night?

Win's—*Nguyen's*—body has already hit the earth. His head, completely unrecognizable.

I want to retch.

I want to cry.

I want to die.

But my stomach is empty.

My eyes are dry.

And I'm not sure Death is coming to claim me.

Sure does seem like you've got a regular Trip on your hands. 'Cept yers grew old.

I think it's probably the shock, but I don't feel like I'm getting Cliff's voice right in my head. The accent feels forced. Like a poor impression. Maybe that's why I don't really understand what he means.

You are an idiot.

This ain't anything unique or abnormal.

See, humans like to believe in specialness. But they don't like to believe in monsters.

But monsters are special.

A true monster knows just how to dangle a carrot as a distraction.

They get ya looking the other way. Ignoring that same monster as they wield the stick from your blind spot.

Cuz of that they know how to play both sides.

Despite being wary of the stick, they can appear focused on that enticing carrot.

It'll appear that they won't even mind if the Reaper's own hands reach for their soul while their back is turned.

They will appear to want the carrot.

But that's when the monster's prey will be at its most vulnerable.

Now, if someone had stopped this man, then a lot more people would be alive.

'A lot more people would be alive,' echoes through my mind.

Most of this dissociative prattling is lost on me.

But I know how Cliff's story should end.

An older man taking the law into his hands to kill a wicked teenager. A young woman satiated by manipulation and blood.

To stop her isn't exactly heroic.

It's not villainous either.

It doesn't create a hero to revere.

In the end, he's depriving the world of some intelligent soul that *could* do good. But blood begetting blood is a tale as old as time. It's a choice of refusal that most of us couldn't—that most of us shouldn't—that most of us *wouldn't* ever make.

It'll be my ending though.

This feels monumental despite the given circumstances.

Judge, jury, and executioner. Heavy does weigh the crown. Better get it right then. Be an absolute shame to take the wrong life. Especially if that life was one that offers healing and sanctuary.

The voices in my head are an amalgamation, I realize. They are my voice. They are Trip's. And they are Cliff's.

The world around me returns to focus. Images of monsters and warriors swirl atop my consciousness like oil in water.

"Get up *Disappointment*." He uses his boot as his stick, toppling me from my knees onto my stomach.

When had I crumpled back to the ground?

I look up and finally feel a genuine sense of sobriety. There's no tickling feeling in the back of my mind, no euphoria, and no hope.

Artie's features greet me with harsher angles than before. His goatee, scruffy and lackluster. Hair greasy and spilling wildly from under a brown knock-off John Deer hat that reads, *Drink Beer*. His eyes are wild and blood-shot. From what, I can't say. But I have suspicions.

"Why didn't you tell me this batch was so good? *FUCK!*" He kicks the corpse of his fallen comrade. A *thud* disappears into the lingering veil of night as it permeates my skin.

The sound alone is a violent experience.

"Say hi to your bitch of a sister for me, will ya Nguyen-ey-boy!" He lashes at the corpse with a quick flurry of bone-breaking punts.

I have to look away.

Except, Nguyen's fallen body grips my gaze. Not out of shock or fear, but the regretful ache of prematurely forfeited hope.

On the ground, barely visible, spilling out of his pocket, are the car keys.

In death, Nguyen still might save me.

I have to remain calm.

The pump-action shotgun traces my movements as I carefully rise to my feet. Everything hurts and aches, but my body offers what adrenaline it can.

"I've never felt this good in my entire life! For all the stupidity that drunk made me put up with, T sure did know how to make fuckin' drugs!" Swollen blood vessels rim Artie's frigid and beady stare.

The message in his eyes is clear. *Acknowledge this statement and commis-erate with me.*

I refuse.

"Well, you're no fun." He wanders off in a huff.

This is my one and only chance. Each movement must be slow and silent. There can be no slipping up now.

Squatting down with as much deliberation as a human in my condition can muster, I feel my fingers inch toward the keys. They're so close.

Ch'ck-Ch'ck...

"What do you think you're doing?"

I'm caught.

I'm fucked.

I'm so fucked.

But at least this night will finally end.

"You've got to dig a hole for him! You can't just throw him on top for fuck's sake!"

I can hardly believe what I just heard.

Maybe I am still tripping?

Or maybe he's too fucked up?

Or is he fucking with me? Making my last seconds on this Earth a game...

Yet, a lingering opportunity whispers of hope and escaping these dark woods alive.

"Right. *Duh*, how, *um*, stupid of me."

I get back on my feet and walk over to one of the shovels.

A few feet away from the roaring pyre, I begin to dig. Nearby, Nguyen's lifeless corpse impossibly watches the repetitive act of grave digging through the tenebrous, cavernous gore that had once been his face.

A piece of the puzzle clicks into place.

The body at the beginning of DROPOUTS.

I understand why Nguyen wanted to help me.

So, I vow to Nguyen's parents, wherever they might be, that their children's deaths will not be in vain.

##:45

My thoughts are getting weird.

Paranoia forms a set of shackles mined from one's own thoughts, imprisoning the self deep within the mind. Its incarcerating influence is as easy to escape as the heart of the concrete beast that confines the worst of our kind.

I understand...*Nguyen.*

There's nowhere for me to go.

My arms hurt.

My back hurts.

My face hurts.

My brain hurts.

Meanwhile, *He* sits, legs dangling from the grey Jeep's trunk, drinking beers, railing lines of coke, and muttering to himself.

With my future veiled in the mystery of a whip, I retain a certainty that Artie might turn on me at any moment.

The same way he did Nguyen.

I can't risk a single misstep.

It would only take a lone loop of his emotional roller coaster for an impulse to dictate my time of death.

My chest tightens.

Hope of ever holding those keys dwindles rapidly.

Because they taunt me.

Laying there. Mere inches away.

And the cherry on top?

The torturous audio of a psychotic break narrates this endeavor.

No part of what Artie says to me, or the night air, makes a lick of sense. It's simply wild-eyed, lithium-needing gibberish.

The more I watch him, the further I sink into despair.

His madness is not born from grief or sadness but from the ashes of razed plans.

What does he have left to control?

His lackeys are all dead...

He'd have been hard-pressed to recruit anyone who could hear Nguyen's version of things.

So, he initiated a hard reset.

Maybe—

Maybe... I'm not the only one wearing shackles?

However, if metaphors are apt, then maybe he's no warden at all...

But a fellow inmate.

If both of us are prisoners within the subconscious penitentiary of paranoia, then the first one to take advantage of the other will control the yard.

##:46

WITH GREAT POWER...

I need Artie to assume as much power as possible.

I need him to be responsible for every action and decision.

Then he'll overwork himself.

Then I'll have my chance.

He'll slip up.

He'll get sloppy and focus on the wrong thing. I just have to think a bit further ahead than him.

We know he had plans to pack up this place with Nguyen.

We know that we have to fill in for Nguyen and be the new patsy.

We know Artie killed the Behemoth, who he seemed indebted to. Assumedly, he's burned a bridge, and can't show his face.

We know he needs the control of others.

Though he's not in his right mind. Something that can be either beneficial or detrimental to our cause.

If we can get the idea that he needs us burned into that thick skull of his, then there's a chance we can prolong this life just a tad longer.

We've gotta demonstrate we're more than a gravedigger.

It might mean that this nightmare continues for days...or months, but living is living.

Even a caged serpent is a threat to bite.

I lift Nguyen by his broad shoulders and drag.

The keys inch back into his pocket.

Despite that small victory, I hate the sight left in our wake. A slug's trail of blood.

At the hole, I take care to pull him down with ease. It's the least I can do for the only beacon of hope that shown through the fog of this nightmarish evening.

Of course, this is not an entirely altruistic gesture on behalf of the deceased.

I still need those keys, and if they fall out of his pocket, I'm as good as fucked—and not in the carnal way.

So, I play it safe, keeping his pocket tilted skyward, and never allowing the fob to slide out.

Concealed behind the mounds of dirt, confined within an unmarked grave, I make my move toward salvation.

This is our one and only shot.

My heart thumps as if rising toward my throat, reverberating back into all the nooks and crannies of my being.

Time slows, and my breathing hitches as my fingers strain, aching to reach our prize.

There, in the burnt-orange-tinged opening, I achieve a victory. The cold amalgamation of plastic and metal sends a shiver through me.

I manipulate my stance so it looks as if I'm tying my shoe.

In a move seeming too fluid for my own good, I snake the fob into my thigh pocket before patting my bootlaces as if commending them on a job well done.

Yet, as I rise and time greets me once more, I can't help but fear a shotgun looming overhead, waiting for the moment my head breaches the edge of this pit.

This may be my grave as well.

Let's take our chances.

The deed is done and there's nothing left to fear except the whims of a madman.

As casually as one can muster in this situation, I gather myself from the hole and turn toward the Jeeps.

As luck would have it, he's not paying attention. Those damned eyes fixed on the shotgun across his lap. I'm grateful it isn't threatening to make Swiss Galen.

Don't count hatchlings just yet.

And somehow I find a boldness deep inside to continue striding forward.

Forward is the only option.

The next thing on the list is to start the pyre.

I don't need to be told.

What if he thinks we're making a run for it?

We aren't. We move like a prisoner and all will go exactly as we desire.

Then we'll finally leave this place.

Yes.

However, I don't have the nerve to talk. So, I manage a glance that instinctually communicates my current objective of retrieving firewood.

He offers a nod in reply.

Trust. Many give it more easily than they should. Especially those who won't take accountability for their own actions.

##:47

THE WORLD APPEARS DIFFERENT NOW THAT THE FIRST PYRE HAS BEEN burning for...

Every dull ache and searing needle of pain impaling my face cools, if only slightly, a bit as I try to steal a second of rest.

I've earned it.

I'm drenched in sweat, and if it didn't feel as if I was regaining lucidity, I could almost convince myself that the twin blazes are ushering in the sun's coming arrival. Something that is still further off than I'd like.

So, I continue to enjoy this momentary reprieve.

It's not exactly like daylight equals safety anyhow.

Within the heart of the first pyre, fist-sized coals commiserate with one another, flickering against each breeze snaking through the valley.

Burning and sinking.

Above, thick plumes of smoke lift through the night with a weight and scent that feels permanent.

After all, if I survive this, I know the odor will be with me till death's door.

How is it the cons of survival haven't won out yet?

This acrid smell clings to everything. It trails from the smoke like the dense scent of city sewers following a heavy rain. It's earthy, with a stench that reminds me of burnt fat on the grill. Seasoned with the chemical scents of belongings and attire.

But something else lingers at the heart of that horrid aroma. Something that I can only describe as a tinge of humanity.

I can't explain it, but each sizzle and crack is haunting. Immobilizing sounds like those that frequent dark basement corners where the mind must serve the eyes and picture what lurks in the shadows.

Artie, on the other hand, seems to revel in each sizzling *POP!*

The sight of him sniffing at the air like a panting dog on a summer's day, enjoying the scents wafting on the breeze, is nauseating.

Except the fool lacks the dignity most canines have. Seeing him dangle his feet from the Jeep's trunk with that "shit-eating grin" on his face…

He's enjoying things falling back into place.

Everything's going to plan.

I have to agree. I mean, I do agree.

These are *my* thoughts, after all. A fact I must try not to lose sight of…

Despite the blending of voices portraying the numerous roles of dissonant thoughts.

Now, if I could just figure out which Jeep this fob belongs to.

My memory of loading the SUV and the return journey is hazy at best.

Was it the grey or blue?

Most likely the grey.

Let's see; Artie's sitting in the grey trunk. That should mean he has the fob to that one. I think he'd driven me back in the grey one.

Shit.

I'm far from certain.

Maybe we can distract him and find out.

Fuck that.

Distract him and take the right damn Jeep. Just get him into the shed or the house. He's given over to the drugs. Plus, shotguns are not made for distance, so that's all we need. Put enough distance between that thing and us; worst-case scenario, the spray nicks us in the ass. But hey, what's one more injury atop everything else?

"Hey, uh, Artie? We, uh, need lighter fluid."

Perfect amount of timid.

"Fucking, just toss a fire starter in there, and get a move on it. I got more work for ya." He's irritable.

But one thing is abundantly clear.

He still needs us.

"Yeah, uh, happily. But, I, um, don't have a fire starter."

"Mother fucker," he growls, hopping down from his perch before turning to open the stow compartment.

Somehow, I am unsurprised to see the contents are neither a spare tire nor roadside assistance tools.

In their place are packages of drugs neatly organized. Like in a TV show. Neatly packaged in Saran Wrap and duct tape.

But that isn't all.

There's a variety of different handguns, and several small, camouflage-design sacks that could be fanny packs.

I reach into my pocket while Artie's back is turned, feeling the key to freedom nestled inside. I dare to peek where the lock button is.

The right side. Unlock on the left.

Do I dare press a button and see which Jeep reacts?

Don't be fucking stupid.

Right. Patience.

"Fuck," Artie growls again. He's tossed several half-opened camo packs aside. Loose ammunition spills into the dirt.

He opens another pack. First aid supplies dribble out.

"Why the fuck don't we label shit?"

I don't dare answer.

Thankfully, the next pack appears to have camping supplies, or whatever similar category would contain fire starters.

Arson pack?

Like the degenerate he is, he lights three of the wispy tumbleweed-looking logs on the tip of his cigarette.

With a crazed look twinkling across his dark irises, the catalysts catch in his hand. He almost forlornly tosses them atop the unburnt wood.

Slowly, they spread and consume.

I don't know what prayer Nguyen had offered the others, but I wish I could say it for him now.

At least it wasn't us.

##:48

"ALRIGHT, THAT'S ENOUGH OF THAT. WE'VE GOT MORE DRUGS TO PACK."
An exclamation made unto himself as he finishes off another dutiful serving
of nose candy.

Using the barrel of the shotgun, Artie conducts me into the gasoline-
scented cabin where fumes play tricks on my mind.

I soldier on the best I can, hoping against all hope that there's some sort of
weapon lying around. Maybe the aforementioned whip...

But the fumes are making my head swim.

Think straight.

Ground yourself on something.

I wipe my hands across the front of my pants. The fob's presence soothes
me. There's reassurance that I have my out. I just need to stay alive long
enough to use it.

Unfortunately, the way things are going, I don't see an avenue to escape
from Artie's tight leash.

Without fail, he tells me where to stop, turn, and wait. And just like an
obedient hound, I do as he commands.

*Dogs are often quite loyal, but BREAKING them does not make them
loyal, only fragile and unpredictable.*

Even when broken and domesticated, a dog can bite the hand that feeds it, if backed into a corner.

Throughout the house, there are assortments of little bundles strewn about. We toss them in garbage bag after garbage bag, the only words between us being Artie's brusque orders.

'Grab that...Wait there...Set that outside the door...Don't say a *fuckin'* word...Move or I'll blow your fuckin' kneecaps off.'

Internally, I wait.

Watch.

Search.

The opening will come. It has to come. A tiny spot in time that will allow me to place enough distance between myself and that shotgun.

But he never puts the damn thing down.

Patience. He'll slip, and he'll regret it.

We clear most of the cabin and its tight spaces. The place almost feels new with how barren we leave things.

I think we're done when he prods my back with the gun's barrel, guiding me toward a door that probably leads us out back.

Is this it?

The Old Yeller moment.

Except, it isn't an exit.

Behind the door is nothing. A pitch-black closet with a dangling string.

Artie gives it a ferocious yank, igniting a single fluorescent bulb. The cold light illuminates a strange set of metallic doors at about knee height.

These are the type you'd expect to see in movies on an old farmhouse. The ones that lead down to a cellar or bunker. A pair of angled metal slabs, rust accumulating along their hinges.

It's like the room was built around them.

Even more peculiar is that they're angled as if the cellar wasn't directly underneath the cabin, but led away from the house.

Artie forcibly stabs at my back with the barrel of his weapon, so I grab the frigid, metal handles and fight each squeaking door open.

Beneath us, a set of cracked concrete stairs plunge into the Earth away from the house. A single light shines at the base of the stairs, only illuminating a concrete floor.

A proper dose of muzzle motivation gets me moving down the steps, which reveal an undergraduate chemistry lab. There are beakers and tubing everywhere. Atop each shiny tenebrous surface, multitudes of containers, vials, and flasks rest. Each is filled with mysteriously colored liquids and powders.

Whiteboards litter the walls, stained with different formulas and colors.

In one corner are several bails of packaged plastic vials. There has to be at least forty if not fifty bails, each the size of a football.

"Listen up, and listen to me *very* carefully," Artie enunciates with his signature growl.

Those deep eyes look more vacant than malevolent.

"We are moving *all* of this to the Jeeps. If you try *anything*, and I mean *anything*, I'll shoot you in the fuckin' back of your kneecaps and drag your wailing ass into the fire while you still breathe."

I want that to scare me.

But it doesn't.

There's no sense of impending doom. No terror. Despite Artie's villainous threats, I am un-intimidated.

Shit. That's a helluva good threat, though.

He doesn't know a thing about threats.

Hearing the voices in my head reminds me—I know darkness. I know despair, and I know hatred.

Whatever Artie thinks he is accomplishing with his words and actions can't rival the masochism I've inflicted on myself. I know so much worse.

I also know I have to live. I *have* to.

For the first time, I realize the unfamiliarity of that statement.

I nod a tacit agreement to my captor and retrieve an armful of the bails. As if I've done this same task a thousand times, I stride right up the stairs without another word.

Artie follows behind me, and whether or not he realizes, it's the first time he's not had the shotgun trained on me.

It takes us another four or five trips to move everything into the back of the blue Jeep.

After each trip, Artie appears more distracted with the pyres as they stretch for something high above the treetops. The twin raging infernos fling bits of their luminescence skyward, crackling as the ether of the heavens takes back the burning matter.

It's melodic, meditative almost. And I'm clearly not the only one who thinks so. Artie isn't following me past the threshold. His deep-set, bloodshot eyes, unfocused, stare at something beyond the flames.

I leave him to it.

He soon follows before I get more than a few steps inside.

Now someone else is the leader.

He's still got to think that he's in control.

I turn to him and ask what he wants next. He points lackadaisically at several whiteboards leaning up against the walls.

We each grab one and wordlessly carry them up the steps.

Then we go back down for the bigger boards. We have to carry these one at a time between the two of us.

With eyes locked on one another, I go up backward. All the while observing the man I'd seen murder his own friend, grandfather, and agent without a second's hesitation.

Bottomless shadows and spiderwebs of blood vessels consume his eyes.

His face looks like a wax replica.

It's the face of an addict.

He has so little control.

Not even the unpredictability of that makes him scary.

I bet he hardly even knows what to do next.

He makes it all up on the fly, hoping that we believe it's all part of a master plan.

Someone with a plan. Now that's actually frightening.

A plan. That's what we need.

As we head back toward the basement, a plan does begin to take shape. As if the blueprint already exists, and now I only have to execute it.

Artie is leading.

He's not stalking behind me anymore.

He's been lulled into a false sense of security. One where he clearly thinks I will obediently pad alongside his heels like a trained puppy dog.

We're at the top of the stairs, and the opportunity presents itself.

I don't enjoy taking risks, but I do like living. That in mind, if I am going to die, it might as well be on my feet, not my knees.

It's a simple cost-benefit analysis.

Artie begins down the stairs.

But I do not follow.

He stops over halfway down before turning to me. A bloodshot stare, stricken with panic, meets my gaze. He looks like a wild beast.

Perfect.

There's my cue to follow. He's motionless, waiting for me, trying to stare me down. Only when I am close enough, does he turn back around.

Still lulled.

This is the moment. He thinks I'm on the leash, but I've slipped my collar.

The shotgun dangles lazily at his side.

I have to seize this opportunity.

Now or never.

##:49

WITH AS MUCH FORCE AS I CAN MUSTER, A FIRM GRIP ON THE RAILING, and zero remorse, I deliver a ferocious punt square to Artie's groin.

His feet leave the steps, and he groans an echoing shock of pain.

It's difficult, but I refuse to linger and savor the sight.

The railing feels like it's about to rip from the wall beneath my spinning inertia. But my first foot finds purchase. Then the next. Somehow unhindered, I race upward.

His grunts and groans amplify and distort against the solid walls, making for a sweet accompaniment to the pounding drum of my heart.

Then comes the crescendo.

The sweetest sound of them all. The buzzing, snare-like rattle of a shotgun sliding across a concrete floor.

Don't hesitate.

I breach the closet and turn just in time to catch sight of Artie smashing into the floor.

Time's of the essence.

I slam the metallic doors and turn to run. The twin echoes of the metal slabs rebounding and settling reverberate into the halls ahead and the depths below.

I wish they were heavier.

But they add to the distance between me and that shotgun.

And that is all we need at the moment.

My legs stride on auto-pilot. I can almost feel the heat of the sun-drenched track beneath the balls of my feet again. It's nearly enough to mask the mosaic of shocks radiating through my cheek.

But who cares...

The pain's only going to get worse if I don't make it into one of those Jeeps.

The RIGHT Jeep.

The fires are visible from the main hall as their glutinous feast rages on. A putrid smog of burnt flesh seeps in through the entryway, but there's no hesitation in my legs as I burst headlong through it.

Even outside, the dark plumes form a tarp above the enclosure, confining the horrid scent.

The blue Jeep is first. Adrenaline throws the door open with enough force that it bounces back and clips my shirt as I hop into the driver's seat.

The starter is a fob.

Brake in, ignition pressed, and—*NOTHING!*

Panic and rage collide.

The walls are giving way.

In disbelief, I continue smashing the button frantically.

Surprise, surprise, not a single, fucking thing happens.

This is how a rat on a sinking ship feels. Incapable of anything beyond knowing imminent doom approaches.

Doom like torture?

My face burns. It's so swollen that I can't even tell where my eye is. Resisting the urge to look in the mirror, I realize how blurred my vision is.

I had yet to comprehend how quickly I adapted.

Not that it matters now.

I'm dead.

Fool.

I realize it too.

We piled bodies in the blue Jeep, which meant we drove here in the blue Jeep, which meant that Nguyen had driven the metallic grey Jeep, which meant that those were the keys in my pocket.

Anxiety almost prevents me from finding the door handle and getting out in time.

But it is—*just*—in time.

As soon as I get the door shut, the smack of the cabin's door violently swinging open startles me into dead silence.

The echo of the wood meeting siding is the only sound in the shadowed forest's entirety.

I take refuge behind the giant tires, but my heartbeat rages loud enough that I can't help but worry Artie will hear it.

The grey Jeep is so close.

It can't be over fifteen feet away. Twenty to the driver's door.

"Come out, come out, wherever you are *little Galen!*" Artie roars. It's a primal call, filled with anger. A predator.

And I, the prey.

He has to hear my heart rattling my ribcage.

He has to.

The damn thing's going to explode from my chest like a Xenomorph.

That would be a relief.

Each pulse sends more excruciating shocks across my broken face.

I want it all to be over.

But there's something more than that...

I want to live.

I want to see another day.

So keep going.

No matter what.

Pain is temporary.

So.

Calm.

The.

Fuck.

Down.

"Oh, when I find you, you're going to be in for it."

The shotgun cocks aggressively.

"First thing I'm going to do, is shoot off your kneecaps. Second, I'm going to break your other eye. And lastly, but certainly not least, I'm going to fulfill my promise to drag your ass to the fire pit and toss you in while you're still breathing."

He fires a shot into the towering smoke.

"The smoke inhalation will be what kills ya. *Suffocation*! But the pain! As all of your nerve endings fry to a crisp, that'll be satisfaction enough for me!"

The shotgun cocks once more.

Oh. He's good.

But, I'm better.

Artie's too angry.

I know he can't be thinking straight. He'll move on instinct. Like a predator. So, I just need to draw him away.

Peering around the Jeep, I see his back is to me. He's looking out into the heavy foliage of the forest.

He thinks we've run off.

Just like last time.

He does seem to be a creature of habit.

Meaning, he thinks other creatures go back to their same habits.

It would be great if he drove off looking for me. But if he comes near the cars, I might be in trouble.

And if he can somehow take the grey one, then I'll be up a creek sans paddle.

Oh. Wait.

I'd seen it done a thousand-and-one times in every TV show and movie ever.

Not bad for an idiot.

There are plenty of stones at my feet.

A nice, jagged one, about the size of a tennis ball, feels right in my hand.

Holding my breath, I find how it fits best in my palm and heave it in an arc over the Jeep, over Artie's head, and towards the barn.

There's no way he saw me.

From behind the tire, I can see his feet spin in the dirt as the stone hits dirt and bounds toward the shed.

Don't wait.

Caution lines my movements as I cover the ground between the two vehicles.

Keeping an eye—my only eye—on a *motionless* Artie.

He isn't racing off towards the barn as I'd hoped.

He's staring.

Leering.

"Oh little *Gayleeeee*...Are you trying to distract *meeeeee?!*"

My stomach drops and dunks me onto my knees, wedged just beside the driver-side tire.

How? How did he know?

"You're not the only one who watches too many movies! Trying to lure me away from..."

To hell with discretion, now or never.

Fervor and speed rip my body up and into the driver's seat.

"Oh, you fool! You can't hide in there! I have no problem busting a window to get to you!"

I look back and see that Artie's just strolling along.

Cocky bastard, ain't he?

Oh, he'll enjoy this.

With a smile dutifully owed to those lost tonight, I present Artie with the sharpest middle finger I've ever given.

I slam my thumb against the ignition.

The thunderous roar elicits an abrupt squawk of surprise from my throat.

Artie's face turns white. Then red with the taillights as I shift into Drive and gun the accelerator.

I'm sure I hear him scream something.

But who cares...

I'm off down the dirt and gravel trail. Practically flying.

##:50

There's no way I'm sober enough to be behind the wheel.

But what's a little DUI risk when the alternative is having your kneecaps blown off before subsequently being dragged into a roaring bonfire until your screams suffocate beneath burning oxygen?

With only the one functioning eye, navigating the thick forest terrain is as difficult a task as any.

I've got to be pushing the Jeep to unsafe speeds for the terrain.

Not that it matters.

My only concern is placing as much distance as possible between Artie and me. Much more important than the rules of the road.

The brights would help though. I get them on with a twist of a nob and for the first time, notice the digital speedometer. I'm crawling along at a brisk twenty-seven miles an hour. Nowhere near fast enough to outrun the set of round hi-beams that roar to life in my rearview mirror.

Stepping on the gas blurs the brightly illuminated forest further. This off-roading trail looks like it runs straight into a steep set of switchbacks winding up the hillside. It'd be a dangerous area to navigate under the best of conditions. Unfortunately, it appears to be the only avenue of escape from this terrifying compound.

Well, that oughta make it easy for him to catch up.

TRIP

As soon as I hit the first curve of the serpentine trail, I'm forced to decelerate.

Moving any faster than a crawl across the uneven, stone-infested surface might spell disaster.

My biggest worry is that if he gets close enough, he'll be able to catch me on foot. Or at the very least, get close enough to shoot out some windows.

He could ram us and send us over the edge.

That's what I'd do.

The switchbacks are frequent and harsh, but provide a reprieve from the hi-beam's invasive barrage. Darkness wraps around the vehicle with each. Then Artie turns, and the eruption of light fills the cab.

And the damned sympathetic nervous system sends sparks of anxiety through me each time.

The climb from the valley is nothing more than cat and mouse.

I think about trying to lose him on an access or rescue road that could be lying in secret, but that's just asking to be trapped like a rat.

The only option is forward.

Artie's driving like a bat out of hell, at least as much as one can, given the conditions. His headlights seem to grow closer and closer.

He's not taking the same care that I am.

I can see his headlights lurching at steep angles with each corner he takes. More than once, it almost looks as if his Jeep's about to roll.

I can't trust myself to push it any faster.

Feeling my own car tilt on its axis as we spiral uphill makes my stomach drop. I don't enjoy the prospect of rolling the big metallic cube down the hill.

If it didn't kill me, I am quite sure I know what will.

I clear the next switchback, and without warning the track gives way to a stretch of even dirt road that carries upward into the darkness. I can't be sure that there isn't another switchback ahead, but every instinct inside me says otherwise.

You're at the top, fucking gun it!

I floor it. The risk is worth it now.

A risk well worth the reward as the tire treads grip asphalt.

The road curves back and forth, but it's nothing compared to the trail I've just left behind. Not to mention, the stone guardrails and spacious lanes.

A quick glance into my rearview mirror sends a rush of optimism. The only sights are the first faint lights of the morning sun.

Optimism be damned, the oppressive glare from a pair of hi-beams shatters through the dwindling void. Artie's navigated the whole incline at greater speeds and hasn't managed to kill himself.

Damn.

Another curve up ahead means my focus drifts back to the road...

Watch out!

Swerving to avoid the thickly muscled buck meandering on the asphalt nearly kills me. The big boy has a set of antlers on him that would do plenty of damage, but his massive frame would undoubtedly total the SUV.

Crazy thing doesn't even flinch as I skirt around it. His head held high, and his chest puffed out, he has a proud nobility about him. As if he stands guard over the roadway.

Each *thud-ump* of heart-pumping adrenaline seems to be cracking the eggshell that was my orbital just a bit further.

I'm going to be free.

In an instant, the piercing headlights of the blue Jeep flare out from the dwindling shadows once more. The taste of freedom spurs me forward.

I've got to stretch the distance between us...

Holy fuck.

The squealing of rubber forcibly trying to stop, yet sliding across asphalt shatters through every other morning sound. It harmonizes with the deadly vibrato of thick metal crunching beneath the weight of something cumbersome and meaty.

Without thinking, my foot plants the break to the floorboard. The car's weight heaves into a fishtail, squealing rubber across pavement.

Once at a standstill, I flick my gaze to the rearview.

I can't look away from what I see.

There's smoke or steam rising from the engine, bathed in the flickering glow of a single dimming headlight.

It's difficult to make out, but something lay across the hood of the blue Jeep. I desperately desire to throw the shifter into Drive, and never look back.

Except, an unquenchable curiosity holds me prisoner.

Make sure he's dead. If not, well...

Well, it's worth investigating.

I can't help myself as I turn the wheel. It's almost like the car is on tracks. I hardly feel in control.

Inching closer, it's clear what that something on the hood of the car is.

The large buck.

Was hoping it was Artie.

Yeah. Me too.

Its crown of mangled points punctured through the windshield, carrying half the beast along with it. Motionless, the thing doesn't even have a death twitch left.

Before I second guess myself, I'm out of the SUV and timidly approaching the wreck.

Here I am walking toward the body of this man who's destroyed my entire world.

Is it just to see him dead?

Or are you trying to save him? Or maybe...finish the job?

Regardless, I listen to the compulsive itch in my arm to swing the cab's door open.

Inside, Artie's limp and unconscious form brings a smile to my throbbing skull.

Maybe he's dead.

The deer's antlers were long enough to have pierced through his lower abdomen and groin.

His chest heaves, and Artie's eyes slowly roll open.

I instantly recoil. Kicking aside crash debris as I do.

The sound snaps his vacant stare in my direction. Violence lurks behind those frozen eyes.

Time halts.

My feet feel like they're stuck to hot asphalt on a grueling summer day.

"No fucking way," breathlessly escapes my lips.

Artie grunts and screams, as his rage forces the antlers from his body with a long drawn-out *squeeeelccchhh.*

There's no stopping the bitter acidic retch that rips through my throat. The yellow-orange slime burns as it vaults across my tongue and coats Artie.

Frantic, he roars a guttural, hate-filled sound and frees himself from the beast's antlers.

It was that sound.

It's enough that just thinking about it rings my stomach like a saturated towel. Whatever bile could possibly remain within its confines expels out onto my rage-packed adversary.

You need to run.

My feet still feel cemented to the pavement.

MOVE! Your stupid fucking feet!

Just as I do, Artie dives through the open door. He crashes into my legs and sends us both tumbling into the ditch on the side of the road. I do my best to fend him off, but I can hardly see.

Dirt flies up into my lone eye.

Scrambling, I try to wrangle Artie down, but he's impossible to hold onto. The slippery swathes of blood and sick impede my every attempt.

Flustered, I lose focus and Artie takes advantage. Overpowering me, he claws his way atop my chest, his weight making it difficult to breathe.

I can just barely make out his features when I see his fist dart toward my face.

Miraculously, I evade it.

His punishment is the collision of his knuckles with the rocky pavement beneath us.

A mixture of acrid bile and iron wafts an assault that permeates across all the senses.

I try to shove him off, to escape, but I'm so weak. Everything hurts.

We continue to pitch and shove until my foot finds opportune leverage against the disfigured vehicle. Heaving with all my weight, I send the pair of us somersaulting through the ditch like two drunks engaged in a wrestling match.

We struggle until Artie manages to straddle my chest once more. Like a viper, his hand shoots out toward my throat.

As I struggle to breathe, I ram a knee into the small of his back. His body bolts upright and rigid long enough for me to buck him off. The action unfortunately sends his bloody groin sliding across my face, bringing with it another electrocuting wave of pain through my cheek.

I need distance.

I urge myself onto my feet, only to feel his bony fingers cinch around my ankle. It's like a bad horror film, the sight of his greasy and bloodied hair concealing a dark malevolent stare. Like a zombie, he tears my foot out from under me.

It's impossible to do anything but watch the ground grow closer.

I can't stop moving.

A desperate hand flails out and finds just enough of a purchase on the stone guardrail that I'm able to catch myself and pull away from his grip.

Instinctually, my leg rears back in a swift donkey-kick. Finding nothing but air, I scramble to regain my footing.

Before I even feel the pain of the blow, all the air is knocked from my chest. There's a grating explosion on the outside of my knee and...

I'm in mid-air.

Falling.

Backward.

Artie's face, looking paler than ever and covered in grime, looms overhead. Shrinking.

He'd used all the speed and vigor his broken body could muster, and slammed a shoulder into my side like some goon against the glass.

All I can do is flail as I wait for the ground to break me from behind.

My back hits hard, and any air left in my lungs explodes into the remaining threads of night. Then gravity takes over as I rag doll and cartwheel ass over tit down the hillside toward an inky abyss below.

##:51

YOU'VE LOST SO MUCH.
   I—I have...

Yessss...

   ...
   ...

I've lost so much...

   ...

What was that?

   Who's there?
   ...come out, you cowards!

TRIP

What...

Mom?
       Mom, is that you?

                              Mom...

                                        You're not supposed to be here.
                                           You can't be here.

no.
       Not again.

I can't watch this again.
       I can't!

Stop it!
       Stop showing me this!

Wasn't once enough?!

Oh, Mom.
       You don't deserve this.

                              To go through death twice.

                                           I'm so sorry.

                    ...

...
...

What now?
    Just leave me alone, whoever you are.

...
...
...

I said go away.
    Listen here, I said to STOP showing me this sh—

Gabi...
    No.
    No.

Please. Not you.

Please. Go away.
    I don't want to see this.
    I can't see this.

                        I never saw this.

                                    I can't watch...

Oh. God.

No. It can't have been like this.

TRIP

No. no. no. no. no. no.no.no.no.no....

She wouldn't have done that to herself.
Not Gabi.

She didn't.

There's so much blood.
Too much.

Why like this?!
Why?

You wouldn't!
You wouldn't do this!

I would know.

Someone would have told me...
Wouldn't they?

Maybe you did...
Maybe I missed the signs...

Maybe you left...
to spare me...

...
...
...

428

Don't make me see you like this.
   Please.

Not like this.
   Not. Like. This.

STOP!

This is wrong!
   This is vile!

A lie! A trick! A hallucination!
   Yes.

                              I'm hallucinating.

...
...
...

Glen?
   Oh Fucking, Jesus Christ!

                    How are you even moving?!

Right...
   This is a dream.
   A hallucination.

                    Yes. Keep reminding yourself.

                         Yes. A hallucination...

429

TRIP

...
...
...

What's that smell?
  Smoke? Smoke...

FUCK!

How is this even possible?

Is this my penance for not delivering you home?

            For immolating your remains to save my own skin?

...

What the fuck!
  What the fuck!
  What the fuck!
  What the fuck!
  What the fuck!

STOP!

This is too far!
  Too much!

            .   .   .

430

I can't—
> *I can't do this anymore.*

No more of this torture.
> *I can't take it.*

> > > *I can't.*
> > > *I can't.*
> > > *I can't.*
> > > *I c—*

> > > *What if you didn't have to?*

> > > *What if you didn't have to lose anyone ever again?*

> > > *What if you had a sanctuary?*
> > > *A place where you would be kept safe?*
> > > *Where you and your loved ones would be safe?*
> > > *Where you could heal beyond your wildest dreams?*
> > > *From pain. From injury. From heartache. From trauma.*
> > > *From a demon...*

...

Tell me.
> *Tell me how.*

##:52

Welcome back to the world of the living.

A world no longer steeped in the blackness of night. Primordial shades of blue enter the color spectrum overhead.

Everything's a bit foggy. Physically, mentally, perceptive reality—all of it. *It all hurts.*

On the ground, leaning against a thick tree trunk, I can hardly believe I'm alive.

It's enough though.

Enough to brandish that double-edged blade of hope. Its sheer edges capable of whittling down the excruciating pain emanating from my face.

Still, each movement to get on my feet sends sharp jolts along the fissures that web outward from my orbital. The exhaustive movements require shallow breaths that split not only my face but my sides.

You've definitely got some broken ribs. But those heal.

That sense of hope seems almost foolhardy as it slices deeper into my gut.

I think about climbing back up the hill to the Jeep.

I'd drive out of here with ease, and never look back.

Except, you're not at the base of the hill.

I don't even see a hill amidst the thick growth of woods. What I can see are the orange and yellow of flames flickering in the near distance.

Likely, the cabin. Where else would fire burn that bright at this hour?

How did I get so close?

There's nothing, and no one nearby, which can only mean one thing...

I've got a wicked concussion. Stupid concussion brain. Why would you take me back here? There's no way out. No cars. No...

Yes...

Maybe there is a way.

A memory lurches into the present as if it were waiting for this moment. Springing forth the same way Artie had during our first encounter...back in the shed...when he'd sat on—*an ATV.*

It's not just that image.

The memories of the world contorting at the behest of the psychedelics torment me in a flurry of reverie. Haunting sensations ring through my frame as if happening all over again.

The shot fired, my ears ringing, the blood dripping, the screams, the feeding—it spins out of order—the laughs, the campfires, the animals, the cold, the warmth, the water—lapping at my feet, cresting my head, flowing down my gullet.

It's all too much.

The flooding thoughts and sensations nearly knock me to my knees.

But I have to keep going.

I have to keep control.

There's only one thing worth focusing on.

The ATV.

##:53

EACH BUMBLING STEP SENDS ME DEEPER INTO THE CLOUD OF BURNT flesh lingering in the air.

I want it to make me feel sick. I want to be disgusted by it, but there's a part of me—a place deep inside that doesn't mind it. That almost revels in it, is nourished by it.

On auto-pilot, I feel my feet drawn toward the smell and the light, like a moth to a flame—or a Looney Tune to a pie on a windowsill.

Shaking from exhaustion, fear, hunger, and so many other things, there's not much I can do other than put one foot in front of the other and soldier on.

Each step brings pain.

Face—shocks.

Side—splits.

Legs—burn.

I can't even fathom how I'm enduring it all.

Foolish hope.

Or untapped strength?

It's more than adrenaline.

I understand that old turn of phrase, 'a man possessed.'

Despite all the pain and agony, I can almost picture myself striding forward. A dissociation. An out-of-body experience.

##:54

With daylight swiftly sweeping across the sky, the two structures come into view.

Just beyond, the discrete pyres have dimmed from roaring to simmering. And still, sickly black smoke wafts toward the dawning sky.

I'm optimistic, but not foolhardy.

I make my way as quietly and stealthily as I can, using the back side of the cabin as cover. It's easy to note there's no sign of the basement.

A pretty good trick indeed, but very discoverable if someone walks through the place.

How did they even build the cabin? Had they done it themselves?

Not likely.

Well, knowing Artie, whoever had, likely no longer walked amongst the living. Still, the feat is impressive.

I hate that I'm impressed.

The shed is *right* there, and I've got this lingering suspicion that Artie knows I'm here. He'll be lying in wait somewhere, like The Predator—invisible for now.

But each step closer to the shed remains unmolested.

This building is much older and had likely been here before the cabin. Although, its large wooden doors seem new.

I slip inside, half expecting Artie to be sat on the ATV again.

Except there's nothing.

Not even the fluorescent light dangling on a string sways as I gently close the doors.

There, in the spotlight of the minuscule fluorescence is salvation.

It finally, *finally*, FINALLY—feels like I have claimed control over the situation. Anything seems possible now, even the idea that it should be my turn to don The Predator's mantle.

Striding deeper into the shed, there's another sign that my luck is finally changing. It lay atop a wooden tool bench.

My breath catches in my throat, as if breathing may mean that the little red flip phone will somehow flee if it senses me.

With the all-too-satisfying flip of opening the little burner, I can see it's got two battery bars—and a signal.

I won't even need to ride off, I can call and wait for help.

Artie's probably dead anyhow.

Though, I really want no part of dealing with the police. I mean, there shouldn't be any evidence implicating me of anything.

Except lying on an adjacent bench are a handful of pistols. One of which might even be Glen's, but I don't know enough to tell which is which.

So, I guess that could be a problem.

Having watched enough murder TV, I'm sure police will discover GSR on my hands from the shot fired at Hill. Then the authorities will be able to match his gun to the bullet. And I'll be—

The bullet's not going to be found in the ashes. As far as fingerprints, well we're a mere strike of a match away from those not being here. Am I right?

Relief settles through me.

But it's short-lived. The distant sound of large rubber tires crackling across sticks and stones slinks in through the open shed door.

Artie's back.

Without hesitation, I dial 911.

"911, what's the nature of your emergency?" a woman asks calmly on the other line.

What's the emergency?

"Hello, is anyone there? Are you in danger? Do you need assistance?"

I quiet my voice to a whisper. Life and death creeps into each word.

While it hopefully sounds frantic, there's an ironic smirk creeping up the corners of my lips, knowing that for the first time tonight, it's just an act.

"Yes. Sorry. There's a man here. He tied me up and beat me. He's killed four people, and he's trying to kill me too."

"Ma'am, sit tight and please keep the phone on. We will track your location via GPS, are you...in the Forest at Devil's Lake State Recreation Area?"

I nod and speak a soft confirmation.

"Okay, ma'am. We will have help there immediately. We've notified local Sheriffs and the Department of Natural Resources." She pauses, and I laugh internally at the thought of being called ma'am.

"Send fire trucks." I toss the phone on the workbench, watching it spin and slide until it bumps against the line of handguns where it finally rests.

I consider taking a pistol but decide against it.

I want the ATV, which, as luck again provides, already has the keys trailing down from the ignition.

The gas engine roars to life and sputters thin wisps of smoke out the tailpipe. There's plenty of fuel left, and I laugh at how it all fades into the overpowering smell of the shed. It's sweet to the nose and an improvement on the smell of burning flesh that lay outside these four walls.

The growing sound of twigs and gravel rolling under rubber signals that Artie is pulling up now. But it doesn't sound like he's slowing down.

Without warning a familiar metallic crunch deadens the vehicle.

Peeking out through the doors, it's easy to see the grey Wrangler's grill wrapped around a large tree not far off.

I only now realize the fob has vanished from my pocket.

This is unexpected.

I watch, fixated on the site, unable to determine if these new events unravel any plans for a daring escape.

Artie stumbles from the car like a drunken sailor. Blood drips down his face, matting his greasy hair with a crimson tint. His entire shirt is soaked in blood.

It's amazing he's still alive.

My one good eye hones in on him, and he's clear in my vision.

A patient rage bubbles and boils inside me.

It may be contained, but it's malicious.

TRIP

Not all predators realize that sometimes they become the prey when another animal is threatened.

The soreness of my cheekbones somehow fades as my lips stretch ear-to-ear.

I want to hurt him for everything he's done to me.

With a malevolent calm, the doors move easily under my palms. I don't bother to look at Artie. I go back to the ATV, and right as I am about to straddle it, I notice an old pump-action shotgun sitting on a bail of logs.

Joy creeps its way up my spine.

The shotgun is actually lighter than I expected.

I feel strong.

The firearm rests comfortably atop the handlebars. With ease, I maneuver the all-terrain vehicle from the shed.

Outside the door, I let the engine idle.

There stands Artie.

Well, not *stands*.

He's wobbling and stumbling toward me. It's a pitiful sight.

He's ghostly pale and licking at his lips the same way a stranded Tom Hanks does.

The man I once thought of as an indestructible demon, reduced to nothing more than a raging drug addict with some anger management issues. And now—now he's been driven to this pathetic state.

He's hardly a monster. He certainly isn't terrifying.

He's sniveling and *pathetic*.

A real monster would not have acted on drugs and lack of inhibition.

A real monster is always in control. They're the game master, the referee, the director. They control every rule and every direction taken.

It's time for Artie to fear.

It's time that Artie gets a taste of his own medicine. I take a deep breath, and the pork-like smell of burning bodies feeds me.

The accompanying rage seethes throughout every appendage. It boils over and across muscles, through veins, and into my brain. Circulating and spreading, it reaches out for every nook of my being.

With it, the pain dwindles.

Vengeance is all I want.

Not so much for Glen, or Clint, or anyone other than myself.

438

It's entirely selfish, and I crave it.

Vengeance for the sake of vengeance.

The one who reduced me to cowardice and fear. Something that I solemnly vow never to feel again.

As he gets closer, it's clear his mind is slowly processing what's in front of him.

His anger flushes color back into his cheeks.

He's not in control of the situation or of himself.

I am.

And I lust for retribution.

Gently, the handle rolls under my grip, powering the ATV forward.

"You! You get back here! You're supposed to be dead! How the fuck did you even—"

I cut him off with a roar of the throttle as the ATV shifts gears, and I swing around the sinking fires.

A coughing fit befalls the dying man. Clutching at his knees, Artie nearly drops to the ground.

Somehow, he remains upright. A look of defeat morphs out of the anger in his eyes. Rage still colors his cheeks, but his eyes—are those of a dead man.

Those dark and demonizing pupils no longer ebb with malice. All that remains is fear.

"You're afraid."

His body sways then freezes.

His voice stutters as he tries to yell, "I, I f-fear n-n-nothing! You, you, you h—ear me! Nothing!"

He's running at me now, if it can be called that. One leg limps behind him, as he desperately clings to the wounds along his gut as if holding back his entrails.

The sight is enough to make me laugh. A cold, mirthless roar of delight.

Some predators play with their food.

I am one of those predators.

I floor the throttle and rush him with the ATV. Just as we are about to collide, I swerve right, away from the fires, clipping his hip forcefully with the butt of the shotgun. The impact sends him reeling head over heels into the dirt.

The frigid and sinister amusement of the act pounds another jovial screech from deep in my diaphragm. A dark sense of delight pours into the empty chasms left by the hallucinogens.

I hop down from the vehicle, still clutching the shotgun. It feels lighter still.

Each step circulates strength to where there had been none. Each footfall racks my once-aching body less and less. Pain is a long-forgotten childhood memory.

He looks up from the ground like a beaten dog, with eyes that comprehend his approaching end.

I have judged him.

I have determined his sentence.

And, I will be the one to execute it.

##:55

"*Heavy does weigh the crown,*" *I hiss in his ear.*

"That it does," I respond, excitement coursing through me.

"*So, you've come to a decision.*" *It's not a question, I already know his answer.*

"Clearly."

"*I offer you the same deal as those here long before you.*"

"A life given for health and sanctuary…" I hear myself respond to the hissing voice carried on the night air.

"What the fuck are you doing? You're fucking *insane!*" Artie's face is sniveling and contorted in fear, pitifully masked as rage.

Every iota of strength within me multiplies as the muscle fibers across my body tighten and swell. They hunger to be used and draw toward Artie like a compass for malice.

"I-I—I will fucking kill you, *Gay*-len."

"No, no you won't. You're broken. You're done."

"*Listen to the boy. I have waited a long time to strike an accord once more. Now, what was it you threatened us with earlier? Something about this barbaric weapon and kneecaps…*"

EPILOGUE

BARABOO, WISCONSIN
Devil's Lake State Park

TUESDAY
September (?)th

* * *

THE FALL COLORS HAD BEGUN TO STIR WITHIN THE PARK AND GALEN knew that the time was fast approaching to make his offering. Though, it wasn't the leaves that served to mark the calendar.

It was the reveries of *that* night...

Galen had wanted to pity the sniveling coward on the ground. Yet when the time to hold strong came, he allowed malevolent delights a crack through which to overwhelm him.

He wasn't prepared for what came next.

His mind *and* body needed protecting, as the last dregs of Galen continued to grapple with the repercussions of an acquiescence he hardly understood.

A man, much weaker, and more insignificant than a lone ant, incapable of defending himself, had his life in Galen's hands.

Vengeance was not a trait Galen had ever known. He knew Fear, Sadness, Pain, Grief, and Bitterness. Even Resentment and Loathing were not unfamiliar to him. But allowing himself to taste Vengeance's intoxicating nectar proved too much.

Manning his post in the present, Galen heard, before he saw, the first vehicle of the day approaching his station.

TRIP

There were only three scheduled reservations for the week. One was already a no-show.

He liked his odds of banishing these memories before the weekend. Otherwise, they'd grow more vivid. More tactile.

Despite being unable to feel the weight of deadly metal in his hands, he had glimpsed familiar bite marks on the nail and cuticle of the finger that squeezed the trigger not once, but twice.

One for each kneecap.

He saw the shock of greasy black hair cinched between his knuckles. However, he never felt the strain or struggle as those predictable shrieks and cries of cowardice protested the sentence to be carried out.

The lone good eye in his head observed the sight of Artie's writhing contortions and spasms, but he did not have the presence to savor the surging strength that radiated within the fibers of every muscle as he tossed Artie like an insignificant plaything to the fire's edge.

And yet, a brief sensation of heat lingered on his weather-worn skin all these years later.

The puttering of an engine, as old as he, announced the final approach of his newest arrival.

The sound formed a twisting tunnel to the past that sat him back atop the ATV. A brief and subconscious hesitation burned away as his hand seized and gunned the throttle. The machine had roared into the dawn like a King of Beasts.

But now, no sensations coursed through his body. Not yet.

And still, he was *there*. And he dove from the ATV at the last second.

His eye fixated on Artie as the powerful four-wheeler's grill smashed into the man's face and torso.

Neither the sound of metal on flesh nor the screams that accompanied it have begun to haunt him. But they will. Soon.

Laughter, however, chorused through the early morning glow. The reverence of *that* moment overpowered Artie's exhausting wails as they slowly fizzled into mortal fits of suffocation.

What came next was the waiting game. Which he had gotten rather good at since that day.

A dull maroon hatchback pulled up to the side of his shack, and before the driver could roll down their window, Galen glimpsed his reflection.

A reminder of where he stands in time.

A smirk twisted the now-familiar salt and pepper mustache that tickled his upper lip, and crinkled the obsidian leather eyepatch concealing the mangled eye he'd chosen to lose.

The sun glinted off the visitor's hood, and Galen was drawn back to the brightness of *that* morning.

A stunning vestige of the past that shone magnificently amidst the roaring inferno from the cabin and shed.

Yet, like most images from *that* experience, his consciousness uploaded them with the speed of dial-up. It was more motivating that way. The slow incremental torment.

But he could always recall the bright colors baking a warm and timid blue into the sky that morning.

"Good day sir, how can I assist ya?"

A young man sat in the driver's seat of the hatchback and handed over his paperwork.

Galen cared little to make sure everything was in order, and quickly offered it back to the owner. With his usual spiel for newcomers and a wave, he ushered the young man off toward the campsites.

As the automobile drove off in a flash of red beneath a familiar blue sky, Galen slid back to the images of flickering sirens infiltrating his peace amongst the flames.

Several police officers had managed to descend the path into the valley, along with an accompanying fleet of Forest Fire utility vehicles. An off-road ambulance appeared on their heels.

Of the gathered collection of officials, none took notice of Galen sitting on the periphery, watching it all burn.

A sense of satisfaction ebbed into dormant consciousness, the savory enjoyment of surviving to the very end.

Mankind is like that. Loss doesn't stop them, it merely teaches them the realities of mortality.

It was only as the cabin's fire began petering out that an EMT noticed Galen. He'd been a sight to see with his fractured orbital and clothes covered in blood, sweat, and dirt.

A sheriff, stood nearby, drew his service weapon with a fearful gasp.

But the EMT waved him off. "Sir, can you hear me?" they'd called out.

Affirmation came in the form of a nod.

"Good. Now what happened here? Where's the woman who called?"

Sitting there had allotted sufficient time to rehearse a tale.

But the fact that they thought he had been a woman was intriguing.

Now he understands why.

But back then, he had performed with a tremble in his vocal cords.

The events of the evening shocked the EMT into grave, placid reverence. Very few details were spared. Though, certain incriminating anecdotes *were* omitted.

No one ever doubted his story. After all, the only other witnesses to the night's events had all departed for the halls of the dead.

Still in awe, the EMT uttered a sympathetic, "Alright sir. I'm going to get you an IV and we're going to get you some fluids. The ride to the hospital will be slow and bumpy at first, but we'll get you there as fast as we can. However, you should be prepared to hear that it is very likely you will lose your eye."

The news wasn't disturbing.

Their agreement could have prevented such a thing...if he'd so desired.

He hadn't, though. That was where he hid his heart now.

In the back of the off-road service vehicle, the EMT pulled a charting document from a binder nestled within a floor-level compartment.

"Last thing sir. What is your name and date of birth?"

"*Ma—Mu—Mmm—*" The collapsing *CRASH* of the log cabin's failing integrity interrupted them briefly. "*My name is Galen. My name is Galen Ramsey-Cantrip.*"

If he'd given the other name, would it have been wrong?

He didn't think so.

After all, she was still there. Accompanying his heart wherever he went. And he only had to work one day a year to hold his end of the bargain. Thus, protecting both himself and *It* from the torturous images of that fateful trip.

.

Afterword

Thank you for reading *TRIP*. This was nearly my first novel.

Now, it's either my second or fifth, depending on how I look at my four-part serial novel...

Any who, as the tale goes, *the year was 2019...*

I began scribbling down story ideas like crazy. Once I'd amassed over twenty prompts, I told myself it was time to turn one of these daydreams into a full-fledged manuscript.

Well, in order to write this *Afterword,* I tracked down the notebook with these infamous ideas. Of them all, I couldn't tell you what drew me to number ten on that list. But I know when I dove into this idea; it took me for a ride that was far more tumultuous than I ever expected.

> A STRUGGLING AUTHOR GOES ON AN LSD TRIP TO FIND A WAY TO FINISH HIS BOOK. BUT INADVERTENTLY STUMBLES ON SOMETHING HE SHOULDN'T. HILARITY ENSUES AS HIS TRIP PROGRESSES AND HE MUST SURVIVE THE THREATENING AFFAIR ACROSS WAVES OF HALLUCINATION AND EUPHORIA.

Afterword

As I got into the throes of my first draft, COVID hit, and I doubled down on finishing this crazy ode to psychedelics and horror.

This was not my first attempt to delve into a feature-length novel, but it was the first time that I accomplished writing "The End."

(Which did not make it to this final version, thankfully.)

Only after finishing that first draft did I realize I had no knowledge on how to publish.

So, I did what I thought would be easiest. I edited and researched the worlds of Literary Agencies and Publishing Houses. Sure, there were delusions of grandeur there, as I trekked the traditional publishing route, but I thought it would be a lot simpler than it was...

The next two years were anything but simple.

I created a digital presence and made friends with several individuals who would later become critique partners. Despite overwhelming support, I faced rejection after rejection.

So, I took a page from Stephen King and nailed each rejection to my wall. As they mounted, I resolved to shell out the cash for an online querying class hosted by the owner of a fairly prominent Literary Agency. They even went as far as to praise my work and give me feedback that included wanting to see the manuscript.

They rejected *TRIP* as well.

I was ready to throw in the towel. But not without one last shot.

So, I hired a developmental editor, found more beta readers, and began the process over again.

Sometime thereafter, the rejection letters ballooned to 69, and *TRIP* went into the drawer.

It was then that I tried my hand at serialized writing for the next two years. As I finished up that labor of love, i.e. the *Season of The Monster* saga, the itch to dust *TRIP* off and return to Devil's Lake hit pretty hard.

It helped that my folks regularly pestered me with the question, "So when is *TRIP* coming?" I say 'pestered' lovingly.

After all, my mother had received the first ever printed copy for eyes other than mine. Dad got the second.

Since they last laid eyes on it, *TRIP*'s changed a lot.

Part of the inspiration for this change was Daniel Kraus' *Whalefall*. The way he captured the moments of his protagonist's journey through the PSI gauge on his respirator was ingenious. I wanted this novel to have a similar feeling. That each chapter of the story would capture a particular moment in time, and as time becomes less important, the moments add up.

A few other changes happened as I played with the perspective and tense. But I think the most dramatic changes appear on paper. The story's chapters have been reformatted to look entirely different, and read at a much quicker pace. Thanks for the inspiration Mr. Kraus.

I then did something that I hadn't done with a single volume of the *Season of The Monster* saga... I hired an editor.

Stephanie, you did a fantastic job with my baby.

Then I got bold. I hired a cover designer. I love my designs for the SOTM series, but I wanted something more professional this time around.

Paramita, I'm grateful I gave you the reins, nothing I designed was half as good.

All that said, I believe *TRIP* is still, very much, that same story. I'm proud of all the work that went into this novel, and I hope that you all have been able to find the "Easter Eggs" I've hidden throughout the prose.

For example. Did you notice in the prologue Artie mentions,

"I did enjoy his use of hiding meaning in the character's names..."

Well, let's just say that's a trait I made sure was active in the historical fiction author's conscious. I'll give you a little tip too, if you're curious and want to do some research.

Look up the meaning of the first name, "Mara." Specifically, pay attention to the Latin and Hebrew usages. And for those of you who enjoy extra home-work, check out the story of The Buddha and Mara.

* * *

In the end, *TRIP* may not be my *FIRST* novel, but it is the first that I was able to publish as owner of Dark Journeys Press! It certainly won't be the last.

That said, I am thrilled with how this story turned out, and I hope you enjoyed it as well!

Afterword

Thank you for taking a chance on Galen's chaotic and psychedelic adventure! And of course, for supporting me.

Journey Safely Into The Darkness, My Friends.

AJ Humphreys
December 27th, 2024

Acknowledgments

This is the hardest piece of writing this book. When I look back on the YEARS it's taken me to get *TRIP* published, the list of names grows and grows.

So, I'll do my best to be succinct.

First and foremost, I want to thank my editor, Stephanie Huddle. You took on this project with excitement and completed it through some rough times. I appreciate you more than words can state. But let me say this, yours and Savannah Fischer's warm reception and generous support at the *Glorious* screening in Chicago, not only earned you both a friend for life, but lit a fire in me to believe in myself. Thank you for continuing to do exactly that throughout the editing process.

Oh, and Savannah, Master of Penguins, your fervent, borderline-crack-head-level enthusiasm for the indie author community has become a pillar as far as I'm concerned. Appreciate you, lady.

Next up is Paramita Bhattacharji. {creativeparamita.com} You were the quintessential professional throughout this process. You kept me focused, asking all the right questions that not only helped you, but moved me past procrastinating the answers to those questions myself. After almost thirty emails back and forth, you had successfully taken one of your designs and tailored it perfectly for this story. I think people will agree with me. Great work Paramita!

While those two got *TRIP* across the finish line, there were countless others who read the alpha and beta versions of this story, and without their positivity and constructive feedback, I may have quit on this novel years ago.

So, thank you Jen Sequel and Zack Lester for being the beta eyes on Galen's psychedelic adventure. Jen you especially were such a motivator in my life. Thank you for continuing to ask about this project. It may have taken me almost two years since you last read *TRIP*, but it's here now.

Before them, however, were the alphas. Those who saw the draft after my first round of edits. They had a lot more to say, but they made my life so much less stressful though their encouraging faith in me. In particular, I want to thank and acknowledge Esmee Lo, and Kevin Nepomuceno. The pair of you are so knowledgeable and enthusiastically optimistic that I know I wouldn't be here without the pair of you.

Now, I'd be remiss if I didn't include Emily Yau on this list. Emily was my developmental editor back in 2022. Though I didn't address those edits in earnest until 2024; they were the perfect kick in the ass. They gave me a direction to move in, and even though I didn't implement everything you suggested, you definitely sped things up, which was probably most important.

If you've read the SOTM books' "Acknowledgments," you might recognize the next person I need to thank. Roland Gnadt aka VVolfgxng. Roland, throughout the past three years, you've been one of my best friends, and I love watching you chase your dreams of making music. Good luck in Nashville, maybe save your boy a seat at the Grammy's?

Funny enough, I have to acknowledge one of mine and Roland's coworkers at the restaurant we all work at. Author Maya Gouliard, thank you so much for continuing to share your own journey as an indie author (*The Chroma Series: Waterweaver; Terraweaver*). I love talking about the process with you, and our conversations somehow always keep me grounded when things aren't going the way I planned. (Thank you Mayars!)

Now, I *know* I wouldn't have had the success I did last year without my friends Angelica and Dennis Magdato. You two made some things possible for me in 2024 that wouldn't have been so, if not for you opening up your home to me. I'm indebted and eternally grateful for the pair of you. Oh and Indie too!

There are three groups that I need to thank for all the wisdom and support they've shown me this past year, as Galen's tale finally morphed into its ultimate form. Andrew Van Wey's Ghoulish Gains, Books of Horror, and Gage Greenwood's Chaos Scribes. If these groups were physical places, I'd be at one of them 24/7.

Lastly, and certainly not least of all, thank you to my family. My brother,

Grant, I love you, man, and I am so incredibly proud of you. I wish I showed it more.

TJ, my cousin, I'm so happy we've gotten closer these last few years, and I am truly impressed with how mature you've grown. I appreciate all the hours spent chatting on the golf course.

And finally, Mom & Dad. I know I've been...*difficult*...for lack of a better word, over these last few years, and yet, you've continued to support me through it all. Dark Journeys Press wouldn't exist without your guidance and support. Not only that, but *TRIP* wouldn't exist without your pestering encouragement. You kept asking when I'd get back to it. Well, here it is. I hope you enjoyed.

And to anyone I forgot, know it wasn't on purpose. My squirrel brain has been distracted since the soldiers of Birddom attacked...

* * *

P.S.

To My Best Buddys in the Whole Wide World, Commandant Zig-Zag, The Floof King, My Goober Boi, Mr. Kobers, everything I do is to keep you in finery. If only you could read.

About the Author

AJ Humphreys is an emerging author of spooky thrillers, mysteries, and dreadful tales. The small-town serialized four-volume supernatural mystery saga, *Season of The Monster* served as his debut within the publishing world.

A member of the Horror Writers' Association, AJ is also the founder, owner, and chief operating officer of Dark Journeys Press.

When AJ isn't writing, he can often be found outdoors, possibly walking eighteen holes with his parents, brother, or cousin.

Otherwise, it's almost a sure bet he will have his best buddy, Kobe The Husky, at his side. Together, they both enjoy hiking, and swimming. AJ operates as an amateur landscape and wildlife photographer, which fits in well with the pair's thirst for outdoor adventuring.

Subscribe to *The Authors' Journey* Newsletter at **_linktr.ee/aj_humphreys_** and stay in the loop on new releases, merch drops, photography, and some awesome interviews with Indie Horror Authors featuring giveaways!

AJ currently lives in Urbana, IL, working as a server part-time to support his dream of writing full-time.

* * *

amazon.com/author/ajhumphreyswrites

bookbub.com/profile/aj-humphreys

goodreads.com/ajhumphreys

facebook.com/AJHumphreysAuthor

instagram.com/ajhumphreyswrites

threads.net/@ajhumphreyswrites

tiktok.com/@aj_humphreys

youtube.com/@ajhumphreyswrites

Also by AJ Humphreys

SEASON OF THE MONSTER

(Pt. I)

SPRING

(Pt.II)

SUMMER

(Pt.III)

FALL

(Pt.IV)

WINTER

* * *

FEATURED IN

CRUMPLED: Stories from the Horror Archives

(Wicked Ouija Press)

* * *

COMING SOON

COMMUNE

Untitled "Irrational Fears" Anthology

(Wicked Ouija Press)

SEASON OF THE MONSTER: THE COMPLETE NOVEL

www.ingramcontent.com/pod-product-compliance
Lightning Source LLC
Chambersburg PA
CBHW060811120726

47909CB00006B/1879